Copyright © 2012 Ross Husband

Not for sale in the United States of America

First published 2013 in The United Kingdom
by GlenRoss Editions, Norfolk, England IP21 4YG.

ISBN: 978-1-48279-072-6

Also available as a Kindle ebook
ISBN 978-1-84396-268-7

Pre-press production
www.ebookversions.com

Ross Husband has asserted the moral right to be identified as the author of this work under the terms of the 1988 Copyright & Patents Act.

This book is sold subject to the condition that it shall not, by way of trade or otherwise, be lent, resold, hired out or otherwise circulated without the copyright holder's prior consent in any form of binding or cover than that in which it is published and without a similar condition, including this condition, being imposed on the subsequent purchaser. With stated exceptions, the characters appearing in this work are fictitious. Any resemblance to real persons, living or dead, or any descendants thereof is purely coincidental.

All rights are reserved to the author and publisher. Reproduction in any form currently known or yet to be invented, or the use of any extract is only permitted with the written approval of the author. Violation of these terms may result in civil or criminal prosecution.

'The Master Engraver' is officially authorised
and approved by The Administrator of the Conan Doyle Copyrights
and Director of the EU Trademarks

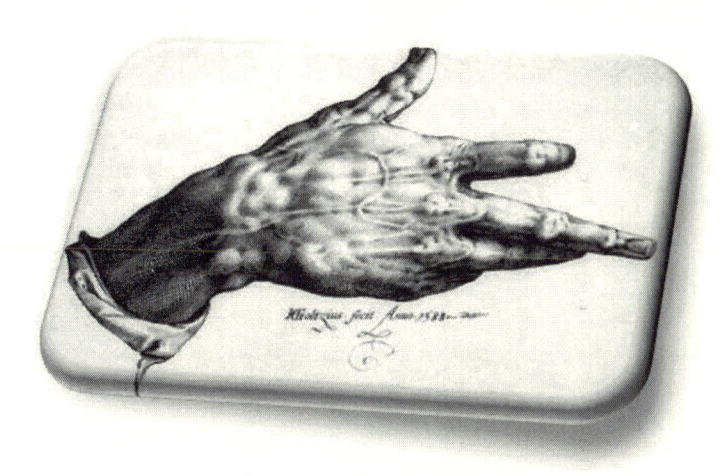

Cover illustration:

Self-portrait – Hendrik Goltzius's
Right Hand, 1588 – Pen and brown ink;
9 x 12 5/8 in. (23 x 32.2 cm)
*Teylers Museum, Haarlem –
courtesy of Wikimedia Commons*

Philosopher John Gray,
on Sherlock Holmes:

"An exemplar of logic who lives by guesswork, a man who stands apart from other human beings but who is moved by a sense of human decency...

"Holmes embodies the modern romance of reason ~ a myth we no longer believe in, but find it hard to live without."

(Kind permission of English Philosopher John N Gray, BA, M.Phil, D.Phil)

"It is easy to accept that a piece of paper that costs a few pence to produce is worth five, ten, twenty or fifty pounds...

"Gaining and maintaining public confidence in the currency is a key role of the Bank of England and one which is essential to the proper functioning of the economy"

The Bank of England Museum – 2012

SHERLOCK HOLMES

&

THE MASTER ENGRAVER

is for my late father, H Robertson Husband, one of the wisest men I ever knew who, fifty years ago, first introduced me to the beautifully logical world of Sherlock Holmes. He also showed me how simple it is to make a tolerable low-powered microscope to facilitate my childhood attempts at forensic investigation. I have it still.

CONTENTS

ONE	THE MASTER ENGRAVER'S DILEMMA	1
TWO	*'ANGRAECUM SESQUIPEDALE'*	23
THREE	MR. NATHAN MADGWICK	49
FOUR	A NIGHT IN BEDLAM	63
FIVE	A DEN OF THIEVES	75
SIX	THE GAME'S AFOOT	91
SEVEN	THE MIST THINS	129
EIGHT	THE CHAIN IS BROKEN	145
NINE	THE FIRST PROOF	185
TEN	A NEW ALLIANCE	217
ELEVEN	ASA BORMANSTEIN	231
TWELVE	THE CHIEF CASHIER'S DILEMMA	259
THIRTEEN	THE SMELL OF MONEY	271
FOURTEEN	JUDAS SILVER	281
FIFTEEN	THE VILLAINS ARE TAKEN	313
SIXTEEN	A CALL TO ARMS	331
SEVENTEEN	A RAT TRAP IN BELGRAVIA	347
EIGHTEEN	JUSTICE IS SERVED ON A PLATE	371

SHERLOCK HOLMES & THE
MURDERS ON THE SQUARE:
SAMPLE CHAPTERS   407
AUTHOR'S NOTE & ESSAY   437
ACKNOWLEDGEMENTS   447
ABOUT THE AUTHOR   448

CHAPTER ONE

THE MASTER ENGRAVER'S DILEMMA

It was an unseasonably mild, late November afternoon in 1889 when I concluded my final house-call of the day at a private patient's house in Marylebone. The gleaming mahogany doors closed softly behind me and as I descended the imposing granite steps I reflected that having a wealthy hypochondriac patient or two was no bad thing for a retired army surgeon with a new wife to support, and setting up in a small but promising private practice.

It being only three in the afternoon, and with no other matter pressing, I chose on impulse to visit my old roommate, Sherlock Holmes in nearby Baker Street, having seen him but once or twice since my marriage.

To be candid, despite my blissfully happy new married estate, I still hankered for that dangerous frisson of excitement and cerebral stimulation that invariably ignited within me when in happy proximity to Holmes' remarkable mind and its uncannily logical workings.

As I reached for the door-handle at 221B, I hesitated; momentarily it seemed to me for just the briefest of instants that all might be as before, just as it had been for several most lively years; that the door to my old room would yet be ajar, could still be open to me, and Holmes might hail his willing amanuensis from within a dense cloud of pungent tobacco smoke as he wrestled with whatever devilish puzzle or villainy he was in train of addressing; or was I merely indulging emotion in the absence of rationality?

Wishing to surprise my friend I ascended as silently as one may on a stair which I well know to creak loudly on five of the seventeen treads; I had long memorised their sequence and how to avoid them. Soundlessly I turned the doorknob and entered the silent parlour.

Frequently, our rooms at 221B Baker Street had been redolent of some aroma; most typically it would be strong shag tobacco, or perhaps cigar smoke; on occasion pungent chemicals might pervade the air – formaldehyde, spirits of alcohol and once even, the distinctive and heart-stopping lethal almond perfume of prussic acid. I had become accustomed to such miasmas.

Nonetheless it was with a degree of revulsion that I was assailed by the overwhelming, sweet coppery reek of decaying blood that afternoon. The source was evidently the open carboy, half-full of the stuff, upon his work-bench.

Holmes was seated at his desk in a great cloud of tobacco smoke with his back toward me, head down, pipe in hand and all but inundated by a great litter of crumpled news-sheets and journals. The room remained still and quiet – he had not detected my stealthy arrival.

I paused, and was about to say something light-hearted as, for example "A caller to see you Mr Holmes" when he abruptly set down his pipe. Without turning he murmured "Do come in Watson and please, for heaven's sake, stop tiptoeing round like a thief in the night!"

He spun round, and my bewilderment mixed with deep vexation must have shown, for my friend burst out laughing uproariously. "Oh Watson, to see your face; what a glorious study in frustration!"

"But how on earth could you have known it was I?" Disappointment seized me; "Oh, obviously, you merely observed me arrive, from the window."

"I have been seated at my desk since noon."

"Then you simply heard the street-door close."

"I overheard no such thing."

"Then assuredly you did not hear the stair, for I avoided those steps which screech an alarm."

"That is perfectly true. I see that matrimony and your practice have been keeping you rather more exercised than you had anticipated." I was accustomed to these abrupt changes of subject as Holmes' mercurial mind leapt ephemerally from one thread of thought to another. "As it happens Holmes, you are perfectly correct; how does that bear upon the matter?" My friend smiled.

"It is simply that for some weeks before you abandoned me and upped-sticks for Kensington, you had repeatedly vowed to send those favourite old ox-blood leather town shoes to be re-soled on account of the abominable squeak from the right.

"It has since abated somewhat, and no doubt the autumn dampness has further quieted it; however, the all-but inaudible, peculiarly high, still near-perfect A-flat, occasioned when you lift your right heel in climbing the stair is perfectly distinctive to a student of the violin, particularly one who explores the higher registers of which the instrument is capable. And thus you betrayed your arrival most individually and musically.

"I merely surmised, therefore, that you have not yet found the time among your other busy professional and private affairs to have them sent for repair. Other than that treacherous heel, your ascent might have been quite silent.

"But enough of this inconsequential nonsense; tediously, events have of late become somewhat slow and I find myself applying my brain to the most trivial of puzzles. Now how are you old friend? This is truly the most capital of surprises!" I sat in my old chair once again.

"As no doubt you detect, Holmes, life treats me very decently by and large; my patient-list grows almost weekly; indeed, I imagine that by the coming spring I shall likely have to refrain from accommodating further new patients – that or perhaps seek a junior partner.

"But all in all, I count myself a fortunate man, and providentially rather more in funds than when first we took these rooms all those years ago. And yet..."

"I tailed off wistfully and paused. Holmes looked up from perusing his papers and fixed me keenly; "And yet *what*, Watson?"

"And yet this, Holmes; I recall how very *alive* I felt this summer past when we were up in the Highlands investigating the Ballantyne Castle murders. True, it was a grim and bloody business and, granted, I took another gunshot wound but truly, tell me this Holmes — what other London medical doctor of the ordinary has enjoyed the privilege of assisting Europe's only consulting detective in his work?"

My companion chuckled. "Should you imagine that I have been continuously engaged in unravelling chilling mysteries, I regret you are in error! There is little currently to challenge me. See here..." and he rummaged impatiently through the more sensational pages of the news-sheets;

> **'ENTIRE SIDE OF GREEN BACON STOLEN UNDER MYSTERIOUS CIRCUMSTANCES!'**

"And here, look further" — I read the item he had indicated with a rap of his pipe stem:

> **'BAFFLED POLICE HUNT FRAUDULENT SALESMAN'**

"Was there ever any other variety of either species, Watson?

"Am I to scour the capital for a stolen ham, no doubt by now consumed and much enjoyed, or shall I perhaps turn my wits to hunting down some mendacious vendor of patent nostrums and quack remedies?"

I had, on occasion, observed my friend in this condition of irritable *ennui* before. I turned the pages of the newspaper he had passed me.

My eye settled upon a short news item; "Now what of this Holmes"? I read aloud:

> **'SCOTLAND YARD SQUAD MYSTIFIED BY NORTH LONDON BURGLARIES'**
>
> *Detectives are puzzling over two burglaries in a wealthy suburb of North London. On the same evening, a person or persons unknown appear expertly to have picked the locks of two substantial houses in the same area of Harrow and its environs, searched both residences thoroughly, owned respectively by a Mr Perkins and a Mr Bacon, but left with no theft*

occasioned, despite the presence of various valuable items openly displayed. Both unusual events were reported the following morning, in the absence of the occupiers, by a house-keeper and maid, respectively. The highly-reputed Inspector Lestrade of Scotland Yard commented: 'The criminals were evidently disturbed in the course of their burglary and were forced to flee empty-handed. However, we have a good description of a man seen acting suspiciously in the area – medium or tall build, dark hair and possibly with a moustache. We are confident of an arrest in the near future.'

"Now surely that odd account might carry hidden promise? A burglar who troubles to break in, is confronted with numerous valuables, yet leaves quite without gain – not so much as a snatched snuff box – and twice on the same night?"

Holmes snorted. "Come, Watson; you are quite right to note it as an oddity, and I intend to look into it further; but you know well my methods – those were not burglaries as Lestrade believes; entry was effected not with a stout jemmy – the common burglar's favoured and speediest tool – the locks were proficiently picked, valuable items were prominently displayed, yet none was taken.

"And if the 'burglars' were disturbed, then who disturbed them? It does not accord with the facts and I am afraid it will not serve.

"The account does not mention anyone reporting unusual sights or sounds; unsurprisingly, I suspect Lestrade is, as usual, on the wrong scent, for these were clearly searches, and whatever was being sought was not discovered." After a short, thoughtful pause he said "Nonetheless, it is an intriguing account that may promise something of the *outré*; I have already made a small enquiry of friend Lestrade. It will be diverting to discover the identities of the two house-owners, for assuredly they share something in common.

"But as to his over-weaning assertion: "*...we have a good description of a man seen in the area – medium or tall build, dark hair and possibly with a moustache... We are confident of an arrest in the near future...*'

"What arrant nonsense! Why, that perfectly describes you, old friend, along with ten thousand others! I wish him luck in his fruitless hunt!"

"But, hey-ho, no matter; I shall bide my time and without doubt some curiosity of at least moderate interest will come my way." After this mildly entertaining interlude we spoke of other matters; I promised that I would attempt to locate an old research paper from my student days that might assist his malodorous investigations into the properties of haemoglobin. And so, on the comradeliest of terms, we parted, having agreed to meet again before the festive season. I left him moodily tuning his treasured Stradivarius, seated amid the wrecked remains of a week's newspapers...

December passed briskly enough in a great surge of sufferers of common colds and influenza but by the start of the festive season my practice became quieter...

* * *

...It was a bitter Christmas Eve morning; I had set off to deliver the promised treatise on the life-cycle and properties of haemoglobin and move in for a few days with Sherlock Holmes at Baker Street.

My sweet wife, Mary, had made little objection as she planned to leave that day to spend several days visiting old friends in Cambridge. I was delighted by the unexpected opportunity to spend a little time in our old rooms, back in company with my clever and unusual friend.

Upon my arrival at Baker Street Mrs Hudson served soft-boiled eggs, tea and toast accompanied by her excellent quince jam, following which Holmes and I were companionably, but separately occupied; I reviewing the notes I had made throughout the Ballantyne Castle affair, and he engrossed in his obscure experiment at his work-bench which appeared to involve several vials of congealed blood, not a few vicious digs with a bodkin into his own fingers, and numerous gobbets of brown modelling clay which, temporarily affixed, precariously supported various components. There were many noxious-smelling chemicals which, from time to time, he introduced with pipettes into the labyrinth of chemical glassware; occasionally I heard a vesta being struck, and the soft pop of a Bunsen flame igniting.

Outside, the harbingers of Christmas had started swirling like dervishes, thick and white past our windows, while down in the street, breath plumed from horses and scurrying passers-by alike; a small gang of scruffy urchins bickered and jostled good-naturedly for the warmest places around the hot-chestnut seller's glowing brazier.

Already the snow was settling sufficiently to induce that curious consequence of quieting everyday street sounds; the wheels of passing hansoms below made no more than a low gentle rumbling; horseshoes on snow-covered cobbles became soft thudding noises; human footfall on fresh snow was an all but inaudible chorus of soft creaking sounds.

Now perhaps it is a matter of age, or of our preferred styles of life, but neither of us has ever made particular observance of the festive season, which in any event, either through cause or by effect, seems usually to result in something of a marked lull in the number of occasions when clients come to seek out Sherlock Holmes' singular talents, which respite often caused him to become indolent and low.

And so it was with no small measure of surprise, approaching noon, that I observed him yawn, stretch expansively and turn from his bench with a most uncharacteristically sanguine look upon his face and startle me by exclaiming merrily "Now, Watson, do we cry 'Humbug!' and play a pair of wretched skinflint Scrooges, skulking in our rooms on Christmas Eve, or shall we venture out for a splendid lunch?

"It so happens that the contents of this flask will require a good four hours to complete its reaction, which I believe will afford us ample time to eat at leisure – which would be your choice, Simpson's Divan or Rules?" I signified my preference for the latter.

And so it was that shortly after, our driver deposited us, slipping and sliding in Maiden Lane at the door of that most august of old English eating houses in Covent Garden. As one might suppose of a Christmas Eve lunch service, almost every place was taken.

As the head waiter seated us at a discreet table for two at the far right-hand corner of the Glass House I noted that most of our dining companions appeared to be prosperous well-heeled city types, bankers, stock-brokers and the like; conversations, loud or murmured, punctuated with raucous gales of mirth or forceful assertions, more or less sober, were of government bonds and the stock exchange, the economy and the state of the Empire, investments and commodities and the stability of the pound.

My companion appeared to be gazing abstractedly at some faraway point and I sensed that he was in that rare, expansive frame of mind when his inclination was most likely to expound, and so indeed it proved.

"It occurs to me, Watson, that this calling I have adopted, as Europe's only private consulting detective, confronts me with something of a conundrum."

"How is that, Holmes?"

"Simply, it is this; my life is wholly dedicated to the detection, pursuit and bringing to book of criminals, the logical result of which – were I to be entirely successful – would be the elimination of major crime. I speak of course, of those wicked clever men, quite devoid of moral principle – of that higher confederacy of criminal ingenuity that so challenges the greater intellect and thereby defeats the plodders of the regular force.

"Yet without the continued industriousness of our criminal brethren my very *raison d'être* would be extinguished like a snuffed candle. And thus it is that I am compelled to feed upon that very malignity that I seek to quell; the machinations of the superior criminal mind are my preferred meat and drink; but should I perfect my self-created science and frustrate their every effort I should surely starve. On which apt subject, my dear fellow, I do believe our lunch is here."

We enjoyed the hearty meal in companionable quiet; I broke our silence: "I have noted you scouring the news-sheets. I presume therefore, you have no prospect of a case at present?"

Holmes smiled and steepled his fingers beneath his chin; "You are correct, of course, Watson. And yet criminals do not cease their unremitting criminality simply because the rest of the city at the festive season shivers or starves, carols or carouses." With a mischievous smile he added "Indeed, was I so inclined and of that disposition, I would choose this precise time of the year to perpetrate a crime of the very greatest audacity!"

As Holmes finished speaking I observed Burridge, the elderly maitre d'hotel approaching our table bearing a card upon a silver salver. "I do beg your pardon Mr Holmes, but there is a gentleman of quality waiting on you in the lobby. Most perturbed he is too. It appears that your landlady advised him you were dining with us; I have told him you are in company, but he will not be put off. He insists he must see you this day, indeed this very instant, on a matter of the highest importance."

Holmes studied the card briefly and appeared oddly satisfied, almost as if he recognised the identity of this quite unanticipated visitor, perhaps even had expected him.

"Aha Watson! It seems that merely to speak of the Devil brings him unbidden to our table! As I had very much hoped, the trio is complete - a case, unless I am very much mistaken. Pray show Mr Petch over directly." I knew not to what trio he referred.

Burridge ushered in a tall, silver-haired, wiry and distinguished-looking gentleman – possibly exhibiting Morfans syndrome – who was enjoying, I would guess, the middle years of his seventh decade; he appeared to me to be in extremely rude health, and also in a state of some considerable agitation. His attire was perfectly sober, but unmistakably of substantial cost and quality.

He peered from Holmes to me and back again through extraordinarily thick, gold-rimmed eyeglasses. In some confusion he asked querulously "Mr Sherlock Holmes?"

"I am he, Mr Petch" said my colleague genially; "The season's greetings to you. This is my friend, confidant and close associate, Doctor John Watson. Perhaps you wish to remove your great-coat, draw that chair to the table and tell me how I may be of service. But you appear to be somewhat agitated; will you perhaps take a calming glass? I anticipated most keenly that I might hear from you."

Our visitor appeared puzzled by Holmes last statement, as was I; the moment passed. "The same to you, gentlemen, both, and I will take a small whisky with a little water Mr Holmes; perhaps it will settle my shattered nerves. I trust you will forgive my interrupting your lunch, but the matter is of the greatest exigency and, to be blunt, I am afraid I pressed your landlady into revealing your whereabouts."

Holmes gestured encouragingly for him to continue, and while the waiter poured out a liberal measure of whisky with a dash of carbonated water from the gasogene for our unexpected guest, he started to pour out his story.

"Perhaps it would be as well if I begin by telling you a little of myself, and then shall I describe the dreadful events that have befallen our business, Mr Holmes?"

My colleague glanced up from our visitor's calling card.

"That would be most helpful, as at present I can glean little more than that you are right-handed, and when you are not cultivating exotic flowers in your heated glass-house, you are an accomplished master engraver of printing plates for the production of banknotes and other valuable securities for The Bank of England; I much look forward to hearing of the matter you have come to bring to my attention. Your concern must be pressing indeed to warrant an unannounced visit, in such bitter weather, and at this season."

Our distinguished elderly visitor stared wide-eyed at my colleague in bewilderment.

"Good Heavens Mr Holmes! That is either a baffling marvel of deduction, or a rather tasteless charlatan's parlour trick. How and when did you learn these things? Be so good as to enlighten me."

Holmes smiled briefly with manifest satisfaction. I waited for his inevitable summation, based as far as I could determine, solely upon the briefest of introductions, upon our unexpected visitor's appearance and attire, and a simple calling-card. He replied "My dear Mr Petch, I have known them from the moment you presented yourself at our table. As to how I know them, it is my business to know such things. But let me set your mind at rest – you are a walking autobiography Sir! I note from your calling-card that your firm is the well-known and respected London printer of currency and bonds, though it does not advert as much in so many words; that you are a senior partner is likewise similarly evident.

"That you are a master engraver required a little more application.

"Your gold spectacles are evidently costly and new, and of an unusually strong prescription – clearly, therefore, you require to work at unusually close range to your task. Given the senior years you have attained, I assume that they are not your first pair of eyeglasses; therefore a man who renews his spectacles from time to time, unless through loss or misfortune, may likely be compensating for progressively deteriorating eyesight, in your case hyperopia and possibly strabismus, caused by many years of intense and concentrated fine detail work, at extremely close distances.

"In addition, I observe a faint circular impress around your right eye, which could result from nothing other than the sustained use of a jeweller's loupe for several hours a day.

"Add to that the most distinctive callus on the pad of your right thumb, running length-wise, and its cross-wise partner on the outer edge of the first digit precisely between the first and second joints, then nothing save an engraver's burin used habitually in your right hand serves to provide a satisfactory answer. Hendrik Goltzius' self-portrait of his own right hand admirably illustrates the general effect. And with foreknowledge of your firm's particular line of business, the matter resolves itself with ease."

"And my heated glass-house?" Holmes pointed down. "A man who unwittingly walks around with a tiny orchid-bud lodged in his trouser cuff in the depths of winter could surely have acquired it only in his tropical glass-house."

The cadaverous master engraver glanced down, retrieved the minute bloom and smiled briefly, the only occasion since he had entered the salon, then studied his right hand as if for the first time; he looked up.

"Startling Mr Holmes; indeed astonishing. It appears that you have a mystical knack of being able to observe a man, shake his hand, and after the briefest conversation, divine his occupation, his history and his station in life; truly that is most extraordinary." For the briefest instant, a look of exasperation clouded Holmes' aquiline face. Somewhat coolly he replied "Sir, I do believe that is the first occasion I have heard my precise science of observation, analysis and deduction described as 'a mystical knack'. I hope it may be the last.

"But should you have appetite for further magic and mystery, I shall tell you that you have very recently handled game poultry." Petch's eyes narrowed sceptically. "Then you will have spoken with the maitre d'hotel who surely informed you of the brace which my wife required me to collect, and which now rests in his custody on the counter in the lobby!" For answer Holmes smiled thinly, reached out a bony white hand and delicately plucked a tiny, red-gold iridescent feather from Petch's cuff, held it high over the table and released it theatrically to float gently to the table-cloth – "*Phasianus colchicus* I rather fancy – the common pheasant." The elderly engraver peered closely at it; he nodded and smiled ruefully, conceding equally the unqualified accuracy and absolute authority of Holmes' remarkable faculties.

"I see from that rather arresting demonstration, Mr Holmes that the high recommendation I was given is well merited; you are accurate in every particular.

"I pray that when I lay our difficulty before you, you may be able to shine some light on what appears to me to be the very darkest of situations? There is all at hazard here – indeed, most likely the very stability of the entire economy of the British Empire!"

My colleague's cold grey eyes glittered as he absorbed this grave statement and I could see that he was now as concentrated upon Mr Henry Petch as is a gun-dog upon a falling bird. I saw upon the instant that the case was entirely to his heart.

With a trembling hand, our client set down his glass upon the table and said "Mr Holmes, I will be direct. I presume I may speak candidly and in absolute confidence?"

"If you do not speak candidly, I will be unable to assist you. And unless you have come to confess your own criminality, my confidence is assured." Petch took a long breath, like a man steeling himself for a terrible ordeal. Wary of the city-types all around he lowered his voice to an almost inaudible whisper.

"Mr Holmes, the new printing plates for The Bank of England have been stolen!

"To compound the disaster, a considerable supply of the unique security paper upon which they were to be impressed is also taken! A robbery has occurred yet there is no sign of forced entry! At this very moment, as we speak, some villain has all material and requirements to print as much money as the paper will allow, which could easily amount to more than a tenth part of all the sterling now in lawful circulation!

"If it becomes public knowledge, as surely it must, that an immense quantity of unauthorised but apparently authentic money has been insinuated into general circulation, you may imagine the profound effect upon the world's trust in the British pound! Its value will plunge in days; it will become suspect in any form of business or commerce, anywhere in England or the Empire! There may well be a run on The Bank of England!"

He took a deep, shuddering breath, and proceeded to wring his bony hands in the most extraordinary agitation. "What am I to tell the Chief Cashier and the Governor Mr Holmes?

"The implications are dreadful; nay, I do not overstate the case – ruinous!" He sat with his head in his hands, rocking to and fro, all self-possession now lost. Holmes gestured for the waiter to replenish our visitor's glass.

"Please do not exercise yourself so, Mr Petch – all may yet not be lost. From your brief account of the circumstances I am happy to declare instantly that I shall be pleased to act on your behalf in this matter, although to be perfectly candid, I doubt if there exists another agency in all of Europe that might be able to assist you in such dire circumstances.

"You have done wisely to consult me. Have you also consulted the police?"

"I have not, Mr Holmes; I judged the matter to be far too sensitive to become a matter for uninformed public discussion. I thought it preferable first to present you with the problem."

"Then you have been doubly wise." He glanced circumspectly at the diners on the adjacent table, who were beginning to show an understandable but unwelcome curiosity in our highly-agitated visitor. Holmes glanced meaningfully around and very quietly said "I suggest that we retire to a more private place where we can talk freely; please finish your whisky and soda Mr Petch, perhaps lodge your game with the kitchen porter for safe-keeping, and follow on to Baker Street directly, when I assure you I shall devote my entire attention to the matter.

"I cannot at this early stage warrant a successful outcome, but I will assure you of my most strenuous efforts to retrieve your plates and paper, and apprehend the criminals behind the theft."

I have observed many of Holmes' prospective clients, both haughty and downcast. I have seen them fearful, importunate, and distraught, even begging, but seldom have I seen a man as completely and abjectly grateful at Holmes' words as was Mr Petch at that instant.

His relief was quite palpable. He grasped Holmes' hand and pumped it vigorously. "Thank you, thank you, a thousand times, thank you Mr Holmes. I have no doubt that you are very likely the only man in England who may succour us!

"I pray that you are right – perhaps all may yet not be lost."

Upon this hopeful note Holmes and I returned to Baker Street to await Mr Petch. Upon our arrival, the ever-maternal Mrs Hudson served us an afternoon tea of toasted cheese and chutney.

* * *

CHAPTER TWO

'ANGRAECUM SESQUIPEDALE'

Once more before the fire at 221B, Holmes dabbed the last crumbs from his lips, drained his teacup, then stretched cat-like, eyes half closed, and gazed contentedly up at the ceiling. The coals in the grate settled, occasioning a shower of crackling sparks and a welcome, jolly blaze. We lit cigars, eagerly awaited Mr Henry Petch, and companionably pursued our own private trains of thought in silence, wherever they might lead us.

The Hampson ticked quietly and soothingly; in the distance I heard the faint strains of a familiar Christmas carol being sung most sweetly and harmoniously by children at some front door further along Baker Street.

My gaze wandered idly around the strange and – some would say – eccentric environment in which we two singletons had co-existed for some years since first we met. My eye chanced upon Holmes work-bench, where he had constructed his incomprehensible and madly jumbled array of tubes, condensers and glass retorts, many containing their evil-looking, vile-smelling, perhaps even deadly poisonous, liquids; I then took in the bullet-pocked outline of the letters 'VR' patriotically emblazoned by him with his revolver in the plaster chimney-breast; surely target practice with a firearm is not to be encouraged in the confines of a London parlour!

From here my eye wandered to my unusual friend's 'in-tray', the stack of correspondence yet to be attended to, skewered to the mantelshelf with a vicious seaman's clasp-knife.

To its right hung the shabby old Persian slipper, in whose toe he stored his tobacco, alongside which rested several malodorous old dottles from the day's pipes, which he habitually dried overnight and used for his first smoke of the following morning; on a faded tapestry-covered footstool to the right of the fireplace lay his beloved Stradivarius violin, partially covered with a chaotic and precariously piled stack of sheet music, though in truth, he rarely needed to consult it for his playing, preferring instead to improvise according to his mood.

I next took in his desk, the faded scarred green leather top of which was all but obscured by an anarchic jumble of books, a stack of blank telegraph forms, cigar and cigarette ash, several live loose revolver rounds, numerous news-sheets and scientific documents, unexplained oddities like a razor-sharp Balinese Ratmaja kris, and a fine Limoges porcelain salver covered with small lumps of assorted soils and clays.

In pride of place rested one of his most treasured possessions; the walnut-cased, matched pair of deadly accurate, exquisitely engraved Manton duelling pistols which, along with a single Louis d'Or gold coin, he had desired as his sole remuneration for his services to Admiral Lord Robert Cameron. One of these fine weapons had long ago been used by a previous Lord of the Realm in the drunken and reckless taking of his own life; and the other, or perhaps the same, had been used by Holmes to shoot down his descendant in cold blood decades after.

Finally, my gaze alighted on the letter from Lady Mary Cameron of Ballantyne Castle, the missive that had drawn us into that chilling adventure. I almost fancied that the mere memory of those few days in the Highlands had started the wound I sustained in the course of our investigation, to throb a little.

But these vicissitudes seemed of small consequence when compared with the infinite privilege of witnessing at first hand the great consulting detective's prodigious intellect at work. I smiled to myself and settled back in my chair.

All in all, I reflected, it was well worth a little clutter, an occasional foul atmosphere, and the odd peppering with a fine sporting gun. And despite these many tribulations, I was looking forward with the keenest anticipation to Mr Petch's imminent arrival and the start of yet another puzzling, perhaps even perilous, case. I checked my watch, then glanced across at the sheaf of blank telegraph forms Holmes habitually kept on his desk. I debated wiring Mary to propose she stay in Cambridge long enough to allow me to assist Holmes and record the case to its conclusion when my deliberations were interrupted;

"A capital notion, Watson! There is still time for Billy to run to the telegraph office."

"What the Devil Holmes! I did not speak!"

"Perhaps not aloud, I grant you, but your chain of thought and your resulting conclusion was as clear to me as had you spoken it."

With mock severity I replied "May a man have no private thoughts in your company Holmes?" though in truth, I knew it occasionally amused him to exercise his extraordinary deductive talents for sheer devilment. My companion chuckled.

"Forgive me Watson. It is merely that when I observe a sequence of events, you know it is for me no more than second nature to arrange my observations into a coherent sequence or whole, and then deduce its most likely meaning. But perhaps I irritate you?"

I smiled. "Not in the least part; but I do confess to being deeply mystified as to the reasoning behind your suddenly agreeing heartily with a man's unspoken sentiments. Pray continue."

"The matter is surely simplicity itself, a fact you will no doubt churlishly disparage when I list my separate observations. My comment appears startling merely because I omit to tell you of the first six, and state only the seventh."

"Come Holmes, you know full well in what high regard I hold your powers of observation and deduction; I would not be such a scrub as to decry your reasoning."

"Very well then; you sat back perfectly contentedly with your cigar when suddenly your eye fixed disapprovingly upon my bench over yonder. To the uninitiated, it looks indeed chaotic and untidy, but in fact it is a most precisely ordered experiment, and is greatly assisting me in refining my own unique test for identifying the minutest of haemoglobin traces; from there your gaze wandered to my ballistic embellishment on the chimney breast, when you frowned severely, pursed your lips, shook your head and even let out a tiny 'Tut!' of reproof.

"Thereafter, in short order, and with varying degrees of disapproving frowns and grimaces, you dealt with my filing system, my tobacco pouch, my violin and the precarious pile of music, the matters I have in train on my desk, whereupon your gaze finally came to rest for some moments upon the letter from Ballantyne Castle, there propped behind the mantel-clock.

"At this you displayed a gamut of emotions, by turns thoughtful, then you briefly screwed your eyes tight shut, as if you were suffering a twinge of pain; a tiny tremor passed over you, instinctively your hand went unbidden to nurse your lately wounded shoulder, but then you leaned back in your chair with a beatific smile, and a contented sigh of satisfaction at the prospect of a new adventure; finally, you confirmed your line of thought by checking your watch and glancing across at the telegraph forms there on my desk."

"Yet still I fail to comprehend your assertion."

"It is somewhat obvious, is it not?

"Clearly you deeply disapprove of many aspects of life here at 221B – the clutter, the untidiness, the apparent disorganisation, and the infrequent though very real perils we occasionally encounter, but having considered the matter in the round, all in all you undoubtedly concluded that you would not change one jot or tittle for the world – and hence, you still yearn for more of the same! And so you are quite as delighted as I at the prospect of a case, and you are now considering wiring Mrs Watson to suggest she extend her visit for a few more days – hence I say, a capital notion!" I smiled. "Had I observed myself in a mirror, I believe I could have reached the same conclusion with ease Holmes." He raised an admonitory finger.

I relented. "As always Holmes you are correct in every detail, and I shall wire Mary today. Perhaps, also, I shall remember to avert my face when next I require private thought!"

He gazed wistfully up at the Scottish letter and sighed.

"Would that such devilish puzzles as that would present themselves with rather greater frequency than of late; I have no doubt you will eventually write it up in your customary lively manner. But meanwhile the tides of human wickedness are flooding this great capital, and yet, without a case, I am as Canute against them; and so I like you, am singularly grateful for the timeliest appearance of Mr Petch with his unprecedented dilemma which..."

He was interrupted by a rap on the parlour door; "Come!" he called; the door opened to reveal Mrs Hudson disapprovingly proffering a calling card.

"It's that Mr Petch again Mr Holmes. This time he says he has an appointment to see you." Holmes raised his hand in a placatory gesture. "Quite correct Mrs Hudson; please be so kind as to show him up directly.

"Watson, be a good fellow and throw another shovel of coals upon the fire. The night is fast cooling and I am sure our visitor will welcome a respite from this bitter evening chill."

Mr Petch, still visibly most agitated, stepped into the parlour. Holmes smiled benevolently at him; "Please draw that chair to the fire Mr Petch, and compose yourself if you will.

"It is my invariable experience that an emotional and disturbed state of mind, brought about by harrowing occurrences, is entirely detrimental to a clear account of its origins."

Mr Henry Petch drew a long slow breath, exhaled through pursed lips and appeared to regain something of his earlier self-control.

"Of course Mr Holmes, but I believe I should first wish to address the matter of your fee. We are by no means a poor company, and I myself am not without substantial means, but I have no experience of the costs of consultancy work such as yours." Holmes scrawled swiftly upon the reverse of a calling card and passed it to Mr Petch. "I have only one scale of fees Mr Petch which I rarely vary, save on very singular occasions when I may waive it." Petch peered at the card. "That seems eminently satisfactory Mr Holmes; indeed, for the speedy and discreet return of the plates and paper I would willingly pay several times as much.

"Very well, I shall commence; my story started some seven days back, the 17th of December, when I had at long last completed one of the finest pieces of work in my entire life's career – after three months of the most arduous and concentrated effort and many revisions, the new steel plates for the next issue of ten pound notes for The Bank of England were finally finished.

"Though I say it myself Mr Holmes, and I do not wish to play my own toast-master, they were an oeuvre d'art, my zenith and magnum opus, and I doubt I shall ever surpass them in skill, elegance and beauty or fine complexity of detail, even should I live to be one hundred.

"After being examined, approved and much admired by my two partners, they were wrapped in chamois leather and placed within the safe, where all master plates are stored. It is a most elaborate and advanced safe, incorporating the very latest devices offering the ultimate in security.

"As we would be closing the offices, workshops and printing room the following day around noon for two weeks ~ our annual Christmas closure you understand, for the purposes of maintenance and repairs ~ I resolved to proof the plates upon my return from the Christmas festivities.

"We were fully aware that this year's holiday would be somewhat busier than usual, because not only was there important routine maintenance to be performed upon much of the machinery within the printing room; in addition there would be the small team of workmen selected by Mr Perkins, applying pitch and bitumen to the flat roofs over the buildings, white-washing the walls and repairing and repainting the window-frames."

"I trust I do not weary you with these details gentlemen, but they may perhaps be germane to the events I will shortly narrate for you. Any elision of these facts would be to present you with a less than complete account."

"Not in the slightest part, Mr Petch; I find your detailed description thus far most informative." Drily he added "I will, however, be grateful if you reserve the more convoluted elaborations and florid ornamentations for your engraving, where they serve their proper purpose." I smiled to myself; my colleague was famously intolerant of prolixity.

"Ah... just so, Mr Holmes, just so. To resume then, at 4 o'clock on the afternoon of the 17th, when the last of the employees had left, Mr Perkins, Mr Bacon and I set off on a methodical round of the premises, so as to ensure their absolute security with our own eyes – a particular practice we have maintained for many years, despite the fact that we have both a day and a night watchman.

"And they are...?" Holmes interjected.

"Ah yes, Jacob Gunton and Jeremiah Shadwell – exceptionally sound fellows; late of The Royal Irish Fusiliers, sergeant-major and private respectively, both invalided out of India, men of quite irreproachable character, outstanding references vouchsafed by their commanding officer." Holmes made a note in pencil on his shirt-cuff. "Thank you; please continue."

"When we arrived at the plate vault I confess I succumbed to an overwhelming desire to view my finished work a final time before I would see it once again two weeks hence to produce the first glorious, pristine proofs. I unlocked the vault with its special key, and enjoyed a few quiet moments in self-indulgent appreciation of the elegance and sheer exuberance of the scrollwork, the regimented exactitude of the stippling and cross-hatching, and the truly sublime and noble appearance I had contrived to impart to the figure of Lady Britannia.

"After restoring the plates carefully in the safe, I re-locked it, a fact most positively confirmed by my watching partners – I myself instituted the affirmative procedure whereby I say *'It is locked'* whereupon Mr Bacon will say *'I see it locked'* and Mr Perkins confirms all with *'I know it locked'.*

"By this simple means we all may be assured that all master plates are safely under lock and key. We then checked and secured the paper-store, which somewhat resembles a large steel, close-barred cage of the sort still to be seen in Newgate or Millbank military prison, with its own unique key, performing the same ritual; you will understand that complete security for the special Henri Portal water-marked banknote paper is every bit as necessary as that for the plates that will eventually print upon it. I collected my document case from my office, and the three of us departed the premises, whereupon the watchman of the day, Sergeant Gunton, made all secure behind us. The time now would have been around half after the hour of four. I arrived at my house in Richmond, by hansom, somewhat before six, whereupon my wife and I sat down to dine.

"After dinner I read by the fire while my wife played the pianoforte until perhaps a half after ten, when we retired to bed."

Holmes nodded somewhat impatiently.

"Events now turn very much for the worse. The following day, Wednesday the 18th, I arrived at the offices at my customary time of half after eight o'clock. Along with my two partners and the regular staff, the only other employees on the site were the watchman of the day, Jacob Gunton, our engineer, Samuel Hollum, and Orman's Roofing who had started upon their maintenance and decorating work.

"Mr Hollum left a little after noon having completed some important work on the proofing press. I checked the plate vault a final time and then we three partners made our customary tour of the premises, before bidding Gunton a festive farewell.

"I arrived home at about two o'clock, and the remainder of the afternoon was one of agreeable, quiet domesticity. My wife spent much of it in the kitchen with the new maid, in preparation of Christmas fare, flowers and the like, while I was occupied in my heated orchid house, where my greatest passion, second only to the love of guiding a razor-sharp burin through mirror-polished metal, is the cultivation of the exotic taxonomy *Orchidaceae*, most particularly, the magnificent but tender Madagascar species

Angraecum Sesquipedale – they are beautiful but very demanding.

"At 4pm it was becoming dark, and my wife called me in to take tea. I secured the orchid-house and returned to the house. The evening passed pleasantly enough.

"About midnight, we were awakened by suspicious noises from the lane at the bottom of the garden – the glasshouse end – shortly followed by the sound of breaking glass.

"Collecting a poker downstairs in the drawing-room, I made my way with all haste to investigate. Upon reaching the glasshouse I heard loutish laughter and the sound of running footsteps receding into the distance; upon examining the glasshouse I discovered no fewer than seven large and three small panes shattered; further, the picket fence had been torn down and several specimen shrubs torn up by their roots."

Holmes furrowed his brow quizzically.

"What wicked iniquity is that, Mr Holmes? What manner of Goth takes joy in wantonly destroying a man's simple, harmless enjoyment for no reason?"

After a moment's thought Holmes responded.

"You may well be correct Mr Petch; it may be nothing more than a random act of cruel hooliganism. On the other hand, you will perhaps own it's a rather curious business when someone troubles to pick their way along a dark country lane at midnight in the freezing depths of winter, solely with the intent of wrecking your glasshouse and destroying your garden? To what end I wonder? But please continue. There are already several aspects of your account which greatly arouse my interest."

"By the time I conclude my tale Mr Holmes, I warrant you there will be a great many more. Much of that bitter night was occupied in nailing old blankets over the shattered panes to protect the tender plants from the frost – I should be sorely aggrieved to lose any of my specimens so unkindly and so senselessly.

"Having stoked up the small boiler which heats the water pipes in the orchid house, I retired feeling not a little angry and perturbed.

"The following morning I resolved to go into town early and locate, with all possible haste, a workman or two who might effect speedy repairs before the weather turned even colder. My hopes, however, were not high, as this was now last Thursday the 19th, just four days before Christmas Eve, and indeed, my fears were realised; I could find no man open for trade and also agreeable to visit Richmond so close to the festive season.

"I returned home quite disconsolate, so you may imagine my complete amazement, Mr Holmes, when upon my arrival as dusk fell I discovered all had been repaired, the fence sturdily fixed, the shrubs replanted, as if the vandalism had never occurred! It was as if I dreamed the whole affair!"

Throughout our client's precise, even pedantic, narrative Holmes had been reclining, eyes half-closed, as was his habit when his interest was intensely aroused. Now he opened his eyes.

"My wife informed me that we had enjoyed the most fortuitous of good luck; shortly after my quitting the house, it seems two respectably-dressed tradesmen had arrived at our door. My wife learned from them that they had happened by chance to be passing along the lane shortly after my departure that morning, observed the damage, and offered to repair it at an exceptionally keen price, that self-same day! What astonishing good fortune is that, Mr Holmes?"

At this last disclosure my colleague sat bolt upright, eyes wide and shining, and exclaimed "That is indeed most suggestive. I have remarked it! Did your wife mention any other visitors to the house in your absence?"

"None that was received, Mr Holmes; she did however say that a smartly attired, well-educated and most distraught lady had knocked on the door seeking help for her husband who had apparently taken a turn for the worse in the street. As our local doctor lives just a few doors away my wife sent Dulcie indoors for a glass of water for the gentleman, while she ran to summon Doctor Bentinck.

"Providentially, it seems that when she returned with the Doctor some fifteen minutes later, the afflicted gentleman was quite recovered and he and his wife were able to go on their way unaided..."

"Hum" said Holmes thoughtfully. "Tell me when your new maid first took up her duties?" The old engraver pondered a moment. "It was the last week in November Mr Holmes. Her letter of application for the post in response to our numerous advertisements in the newspapers, accompanied by a most outstanding reference, decided my wife upon the instant. She was insistent, indeed adamant upon engaging her, and certainly her work is perfectly satisfactory."

"And the reference was furnished by...?"

"Let me recollect now; it was... ah yes, it was the Baroness Amanti, a lady of Italian extraction I believe, now resident in France."

Holmes scrawled a further swift note on his cuff. "Then now let us move directly to the matter of the missing plates. Please start by telling me when and how you first discovered that they had vanished."

"It happened in this way, Mr Holmes. Today morning I rose at my customary hour which is around six o'clock. Having made a pot of tea and examined my orchids, finding all as well as might be hoped under the trying circumstances visited upon me, I returned to the house where I determined to complete once and for all, a particularly complex design for some extremely high-value bearer-bonds I had started upon, now sadly fallen behind but still faithfully promised to no less august personages than the partners of the Swiss bank of Lombard Odier, upon our factory re-opening less than two weeks hence.

"Searching my document case I discovered to my great exasperation that I had neglected to bring home a folder containing some of the preliminary sketches, dimensions, textual matter and so on, so necessitating a return visit to our printing works.

"However, it happened my wife required me to collect a last-minute order of pheasant from the poulterer, so it was a matter of no great moment as I could accomplish both tasks with one excursion; our business premises are in Fleet Street and the poulterer is hard by in Leadenhall Market.

"I retrieved my keys from the bureau in my study, and walked to the local railway station, where I engaged a hansom, arriving at our premises in Fleet Street shortly after the day-watchman had started, around nine o'clock. He had nothing of consequence to report beyond the routine comings and goings of Mr Hollum the engineer, and the builders who had completed their work and departed upon the evening of the 21st. I made my way to my office where I retrieved the desired sketches and papers.

"About to depart, I was seized once more with the strong desire to enjoy one final glimpse of my plates, and so unlocked the safe. You may imagine if you will, Mr Holmes, my utter horror and shock at discovering that they were gone, taken, yet I and my partners had confirmed them safely under lock and key only days before!

"You may perhaps speculate as to my agitated state of mind! Curiously, two of my burins had also been removed from my bench!

"Now in a most fearful panic I investigated the remainder of our premises, including the stores, where I discovered that a large quantity of the unique watermarked Portals paper upon which the new notes were destined to be printed, was also gone! If the two stolen items, paper and plates, are proficiently brought together upon a suitable printing press, the consequences will be catastrophic.

"I have calculated, Mr Holmes, that the quantity of stolen paper – twenty-five boxes each of five thousand sheets – will be sufficient to create well over two millions in currency – two hundred and fifty thousand ten-pound notes – a huge increase in the present currency supply in circulation in Great Britain, constituted apparently of *bona fide*, but quite unauthorised money! With additional paper, the hardened steel plates themselves could generate many times more.

"The Bank Charter Act of 1844 requires all notes issued to be backed by gold reserves held by the Bank; this will not be the case if a vast quantity of credible but fraudulent money is known to be in circulation; inflation would be the inevitable consequence.

Confidence in our British pound will vanish like a puff of smoke when word spreads!" Again he buried his face in his hands and returned to rocking in a state of pitiable misery.

Holmes closed his eyes in thought for a moment.

Our client mopped his brow with a large silk square and struggled to regain his earlier composure. "My apologies Mr Holmes; of course I am entirely at your disposal. You may ask me anything if it can help to avert this calamity."

"Very well; you say you have keys to all the principal locks on the premises?" Petch nodded. "And you carry these upon your person at all times?" Again Petch nodded.

"I do Mr Holmes, upon my watch chain, except when at home, where I place them in my bureau" and he produced a bunch of most unusually complicated keys at the end of a heavy gold Albert chain. Holmes extended a sinewy white hand; "May I?"

Our client detached his watch and chain from his waistcoat buttonhole, removed the strange keys and passed them to Holmes.

"Now Mr Petch, please be good enough to describe the function of each of these keys; this, for example?"

"That first is merely the key to my domestic front door; the next two are respectively the garden back-door and my orchid-house. The small steel key winds my watch and then, in succession, you see the key to the pedestrian door through the main gates to the delivery yard, the next opens the main door to the offices and printing works; then you will observe my private office key, next the special key to the paper store, and finally you now hold in your hand the compound key that releases the four locks of the plate safe.

"Since lunchtime, it occurred to me that an indication of the layout of our premises might be of value to you; while finishing my whisky I took the liberty of preparing this sketch, that you may be aware of the locations of the various offices, departments, and of the plate vault itself. It is correct in its general arrangement, but I regret I did not have sufficient time to create it to true scale."

"My dear Mr Petch, you are the epitome of a model client! This appears to be extremely precise; I see you mark here the main gate, the watchmen's hut; this, the main entrance and... Ah, here I observe your office marked and the safe indicated within, and off here the print room and paper store. Admirable, quite admirable; now, let us back to the keys."

Holmes carefully separated the last four keys and at strikingly close range, at the very tip of his nose, almost as if he were sniffing them, he examined each most minutely and then again at some considerable length through his powerful lens.

"These are indeed most unusual keys – certainly not the variety which one might ordinarily take to a commonplace high-street locksmith to have copies made. The four that particularly interest me are these – to your office, to the paper store, the print room and to the plate vault. The safe is clearly a Chubb diagonal-bolt model is it not?"

"You are correct Mr Holmes, as are you in the matter of commissioning duplicate keys. No reputable locksmith would even consider making copies without solid proof of ownership of the safe – at the very least the certificate issued only to the legitimate and registered purchaser. In practice, a requirement for another key is customarily addressed directly to the manufacturer, thus eliminating the risk of additional keys being made and dishonestly retained by a villainous locksmith, without one's knowledge.

"And we were assured at the time of the purchase that a criminal locksmith – even a skilled one – would apparently experience considerable, in all probability insurmountable, difficulty in creating working duplicate keys."

Somewhat cryptically Holmes replied "That may be so Mr Petch, but in my experience, there is very little in this world that one man can devise, that another cannot discover. Who else possesses a full set of keys?"

"Only four sets exist, Mr Holmes; you hold one in your hand this minute; a complete set is carried by each of my two partners – again on their watch-chains – and there is a final set shared by the two watchmen.

"As the one always hands over duty to the other upon the nightly and morning change, he likewise hands the keys to his incoming colleague. Do I make myself clear?"

"Perfectly; I shall return to the matter of the keys presently. Meanwhile, tell me why it was necessary to create a further set of plates; are they perhaps of a new design, or a new denomination?"

Petch grimaced despondently; "No they are not, and that is what makes the situation so very alarming. Were they so, the matter would resolve itself with great facility. We would simply put out a general notice that there is to be no new design or denomination of note, and thus, at a stroke, eliminate all possibility of financial reward for the perpetrators."

"No Mr Holmes, it is the most unhappy of all possible situations; the plates are a direct replacement set for the current issue of £10 note; the present plates are showing significant signs of wear, and thus are producing inferior impressions, which makes them considerably simpler to counterfeit.

"The new plates do you see, will create, in every respect except one, vast quantities of £10 bank-notes, quite perfect in appearance and almost indistinguishable from those presently in lawful circulation throughout the world, except to an expert!"

Holmes made no response, but instead stepped to his bench where at some length, with his back to us, he performed some intricate and arcane operations with the keys, whose objective I was quite unable to comprehend. Returning after some considerable time, he wiped the keys on a rag, handed them back to Mr Petch and said "Tell me more of this one singular characteristic in which any notes produced may not be quite perfect? The engraved plates are complete and finished, are they not?"

"Indeed they are, the most perfect I ever created as I have stated, and I pray I may now never see in my billfold or be handed a resulting impression from them!

"However, what they will lack, and what they must incorporate, for unqualified perfection, is a proper cipher and a run of allocated serial numbers of the correct sequence. That progression the criminals are most unlikely to guess; such numbers are applied in a second over-printing and in confidence I may inform you that the basic secret formula for those letters and numbers rests on the distinction between odd and even-numbered years.

"Merely as an example, let us take the numbering on this London £5 note." His gnarled finger traced over the components of the serial number.

"In even years the Bank generally uses the first half of the month, and in odd numbered years, the second half." He indicated the relevant characters. And here, Mr Holmes is a perfectly genuine London £10 note, essentially identical to that embodied in the new, stolen plates, bearing this cipher and in this example, the serial number 41512, as you can see from the impress; however this complex but consistent formula the thieves are most unlikely to fathom.

"You will note, too, gentlemen, that the top, right and left edges of this particular note are not cleanly cut – or guillotined as we say – but exhibit the Portal's manufactured deckled, or ragged edge of the paper; only the lower edge is sharply cut.

"This is on account of the notes being printed in pairs – two-up as we term it; the twin of this note will have been impressed immediately below on the same sheet, and after the cutting process between the two, will exhibit a sharp upper edge, with the right, left and lower edges remaining deckled and uncut. This effect, too, the villains will achieve with consummate ease as they are now in possession of the correct paper. They lack only a simple guillotine.

"My greatest fear, however, is that any sequence of letters and numbers of apparently plausible appearance, correctly placed and overprinted, will not deter the criminal underworld from eagerly purchasing the notes at a discounted value and selling them on down a chain of ever-more petty criminals, until they start insidiously to flood the market.

"You will appreciate, Mr Holmes that large-scale forgeries of currency are rarely uttered – or circulated – by the forger himself – rather, he passes that perilous risk on to lesser villains. Within my own lifetime, the penalty for circulating forged currency was hanging or transportation – this heinous crime quite rightly being regarded as high treason. However, I digress.

"Such lesser criminals will purchase counterfeit currency in exchange for, perhaps a forty percent amount of the face value; conceivably more if the forgeries are of an exceptionally high standard.

"These, as you now know, will be little short of perfection. Every £10 note in circulation, legitimate or fraudulent, will become suspect until checked by the bank.

"And what man, having been paid £10 for his services, will take the note to the bank to be verified, knowing full well that should the note be a forgery, it will instantly be confiscated and he will lose all, with no hope of recompense whatever?

"No, gentlemen, he will of a certainty retain it and pass it on in turn as settlement of his own obligations.

"That, Mr Holmes, in a very small nutshell is our very considerable dilemma. Time is now of the essence; somewhere a printing press may be running even as we speak.

"Clearly we cannot withdraw all the legal notes now in circulation, but unless you can use your powers to assist us in tracing the whereabouts of the stolen plates and paper before a deluge of counterfeit money makes its malign appearance we must, I fear, prepare ourselves for a national crisis of the very gravest proportion!"

CHAPTER THREE

MR NATHAN MADGWICK

The parlour at 221B Baker Street fell silent. I was shocked by these startling revelations and their grim implications; Petch returned to rocking distractedly, his hands clenched tight until the bony knuckles showed white, while Holmes had reclined back in his chair, looking for the entire world as if he had fallen asleep, though I knew different.

I could almost hear that remarkable brain of his whirring like Babbage's analytical engine running through numerous permutations of possibilities, most of which would of a certainty not appear worthy even of scant consideration by run-of-the-mill Yarders like Lestrade and Gregson.

But then again, Holmes was no run-of-the-mill Yarder.

Mr Henry Petch evidently mistook this apparent lethargy for disinterest, or perhaps a resignation to failure. "Good Heavens Mr Holmes! I beg your pardon but is this your response to the looming disaster that faces us? Is the matter too opaque or too complex for resolution, for assuredly if you accept defeat, then so must we all! Do you see no hope whatever?" Holmes remained silent throughout this little diatribe, smiled, and then opened his eyes slowly and lazily.

"Defeat, Mr Petch? Defeat? Never in life my dear Sir; as to a resolution, some aspects of the conundrum are even now becoming apparent to me.

"Indeed, I suspect I may already have the *how* of the problem, and to within a day, I believe I may know the *when* of it.

"But even with the corroboration of my suspicions, a Sisyphean task still remains – that of locating the identity and whereabouts of the perpetrators, the stolen plates and paper before they can combine to full effect and thus achieve their nefarious objective."

Once again our volatile client had returned to wringing his hands, now not in agitation but in gratitude. "My dear Sir, how could I have doubted you? Please forgive me! You will perhaps understand that a burden of this gravity rests heavy on an old man's shoulders; but already I feel the weight lifting! May I make as bold as to enquire as to your direction of enquiry from here on in?"

"You may Mr Petch, or at least such that directly involve you and your staff; I shall require to interview the watchmen, to which end I would propose to visit your works somewhat before nine, when I assume I shall be present at the changeover? Thereafter I shall examine the premises."

"That is correct Mr Holmes; I shall send word ahead so that you may be expected and conducted around. What more may I do to assist?"

"I also wish to speak with Mr Perkins and Mr Bacon as urgently as it may be arranged."

"Oh dear, Mr Holmes; that presents considerable difficulties." Holmes frowned.

"Why is that?"

"Because both, you see, left for long-planned visits to foreign parts after we closed the premises – Mr Bacon for Ireland, somewhere near Belfast as I recall, and Mr Perkins is, I believe, visiting his daughter in France. I regret I have no address for either, and they will not be returning until the New Year."

"They are still absent then? Does that not strike you as strange Mr Petch, that this theft should occur precisely at the time that your partners are both abroad and unreachable?"

"A most curious concurrence – the more regrettable in that it may severely impede my enquiries. I assume, therefore, that neither is yet aware of the theft? No matter, it cannot be helped at present. On another point, did your wife by chance obtain a calling card from the two workmen who repaired your orchid-house?"

"She did, Mr Holmes, and I believe I have it…" he rummaged through his pocket-book and produced a grubby scrap of pasteboard "…here."

He handed it to Holmes who examined it in a perfunctory fashion, then passed it to me. "What do you make of that Watson?"

I studied it closely and read:

> **NATHAN MADGWICK**
> 'Small Building Works, Brick-Laying,
> Glazing, Plumbing & General Repairs'
> ESTIMATES BY ARRANGEMENT
> 98 Clerkenwell Road, London E.

"I see nothing particularly out of the ordinary here, Holmes; it appears on the face of things to be a very run-of-the-mill workman's calling card. Or do I overlook something?"

I knew of a certainty I must have missed some point of significance, else Holmes would not have sought my comments.

"In that it is a perfectly ordinary tradesman's card you are quite correct, Watson. But consider the time of year, and the vast geography of London. Does it not strike you as being somewhat implausible that a Clerkenwell builder should happen to be passing along a remote Richmond lane some miles distant, with no work in prospect, and approaching Christmas, with all the necessary materials ready and at hand, and the very morning following the vandalism of the glass-house? Oddly, the Clerkenwell Road is considerably closer to Mr Petch's premises at Fleet Street than it is to the leafy lanes of Richmond.

"That certainly strikes me as rather irregular, that or an astonishing coincidence – and you know well how much I mistrust coincidences; they are somewhat rarer than most people suppose. The matter will without doubt bear considerably closer enquiry."

He returned his attention to our client. "Now I am sure you will understand, Mr Petch that my consultations are based upon, if you will, my own exacting science of what you might term reverse reasoning.

"That is to say, I am presented with a problematic circumstance, perhaps a theft, a disappearance, a murder even; it is my craft to deduce backwards, eliminating in due order of time and circumstance all those explanations which will not serve, until at last I arrive inescapably at the only one, no matter how improbable, which will.

"You may view this as the reconstruction, through observation and deduction, of events now passed. At the outset there are a great many suspect individuals who may fall within my purview, some rather more plausible than others."

Petch sat forward in his chair. "Am I then to understand, Mr Holmes that you have already formed a view as to the party or parties involved in this dreadful business?" Holmes laughed, but entirely without humour.

"Consider, if you will, Mr Petch, the cast of players you have already furnished; we have the watchmen

Gunton and Shadwell, the engineer Hollum and the rest of your staff, the walk-on characters of the glazier Madgwick and his unidentified assistant, your maid, your wife, countless unknown others who may have general or particular knowledge of your work, not to mention the illustrious Messrs Perkins, Bacon and Petch themselves. Can you name one, or a union of several of these, who would not stand to profit from the illicit possession of authentic Bank of England printing plates and paper to match?

"At the very least, I do not doubt that they could instantly, and with exceeding ease, be sold on for a very sizeable sum of money to any number of eager bidders from the shadowy under-world of criminals, both at home and conceivably, even abroad, with no requirement whatsoever even to become involved in the actual process of the printing itself!"

Petch stared, horror-struck. "But my wife, the watchmen, myself and my partners? Sir, I do believe you overreach your mark! I will not hear of any complicity on their part or mine! Why, it was *I* who came to seek *your* assistance!"

"That is explicitly my point, Mr Petch, and in the tediously banal case of the Billingsgate poisonings, it was the cherubic-faced architect of the murders himself who sought my help after he had administered arsenic to his wife when she had become profoundly suspicious of his clandestine, murderous activities – he sought to divert police attention away from himself by very publicly enlisting the services of Sherlock Holmes. It was a naive attempt to create a distraction, a most imprudent and transparent subterfuge. It availed him naught; I was not deceived, and he was duly hanged for his pains, regardless.

"And desperate criminals have resorted to more deceitful courses than merely retaining a consulting detective or the police in their attempts to construct for themselves an alibi.

"I recall the case of one Feodor Herzog – the first violin of the Württemberg Symphony Orchestra who brutally garrotted two fellow musicians with an E string, having baselessly supposed his unfortunate and innocent victims – a cellist and the timpanist – to be engaged in improper relationships with his wife, then a prima-ballerina on tour with the Bolshoi; upon sensing police enquiries pointing alarmingly in his own direction, one night he applied a like ligature deliberately and viciously to his own gullet resulting in a most spectacular, but not life threatening, wound; this in order to divert suspicion to some other quarter. His allegation that he had unaccountably been attacked by the same unknown strangler who had murdered his wife's supposed lovers was not believed.

"In point of fact, he was cuckolded by the orchestra conductor, a notorious Russian lothario who walks free to this day, while Herzog languishes in jail.

"In short, Mr Petch, it is not without precedent for conniving individuals to report their own crimes, destroy their own property, or even harm themselves in an attempt to appear as injured or blameless parties. Do you now perhaps begin to take my meaning?"

Throughout this somewhat ruthless monologue, Henry Petch sat silent, eyes downcast; he appeared to me to be staring again at his curiously evolved, sinewy right hand. Holmes continued: "I tell you these things Mr Petch simply that you may have an understanding of my commission at this early stage; I must commence with a canvas large enough to accommodate all the subjects, and use a broad brush. The fine detail, I anticipate, will be concluded in due course.

"As to the players in this dark tableau, there are many reasons why one of them might have turned for the bad – greed, envy, pressing debt. Too, it is conceivable that a man may be complicit in a crime perhaps, for example, through imprudent talk, or falling victim to a blackmailer.

"Now let us consider the circumstances Mr Petch. The safe was neither removed nor was the lock picked; explosives such as Nobel's Blasting Powder were not employed, yet still the plates are missing. You assert that to copy the keys is a virtual impossibility, and that there are only four sets on the face of this earth, three held by you and your partners and a further by the watchmen.

"Yet it remains an incontestable fact that the safe has been violated. How else, except with a functioning key? And who else could have knowledge of the plates' existence or location? If I eliminate all those hypotheses which are impossible, then that which remains, however unbelievable, must be the truth. The believable truth is that a key was used in this theft.

"Where, pray, would you start your search?"

Petch remained silent.

"But the blameless may rest easy — it is only the guilty that need fear my attentions.

"Now as you stated, Mr Petch, delay is a luxury we can ill afford; therefore it is essential that I visit your house and speak with Mrs Petch. To our certain knowledge, she is the only one who observed the two workmen is she not?"

"Correct Mr Holmes, she and of course, Dulcie, the maid; she will visit our house at four o'clock tomorrow, to assist my wife for the evening; then she will not return to her regular duties until Boxing Day morning, but you will be welcome to interview her if it will assist."

"I shall, and it will; by-the-by, do you by chance recall where in France the titled lady who furnished the maid's reference resides?" Petch pursed his lips and furrowed his brow in thought. "Yes, I have it now; a small village called Obânes St-Amarin. I recall from her letter that it is in the south-west of the country, I believe not very distant from the coastal town of La

Rochelle." Holmes jotted a further note. "Now in conclusion, Mr Petch, be so good as to describe candidly your partners, in particular their general character, any foibles or eccentricities, their private interests and fallibilities. Please be entirely honest and direct in all respects."

"Very well Mr Holmes. We three are much of an age and many think, of an appearance – indeed, on occasion we have been taken for brothers –but otherwise we are quite disparate in character.

"Mr Perkins I would characterise as a model of sobriety, perhaps a little gloomy, discreet, utterly trustworthy and quite indispensable in the business. He controls all expenditure and contracts for the partnership – we may always rely upon him to select the keenest quotations.

"A confirmed bachelor, he lives quietly in Harrow and is, I understand, deeply involved in fund-raising with his local Parish. On occasion he appears to struggle with something of a moral conflict between earning a very satisfactory income from the business of manufacturing money for those who already have ample, while working assiduously to raise desperately-needed funds for those who have none.

"Mr Bacon is cut from an altogether different bolt of cloth; his work is by-and-large diligent and satisfactory unless he is tardy in his time-keeping – an occasional failing he regrettably exhibits, particularly after playing late at cards and a little too much, ah, refreshment at The Bagatelle Club, something of which he is perhaps rather too fond.

"He is by nature rather more flamboyant and garrulous than I or Mr Perkins, and thus the task of gaining fresh business, new clients and commissions falls within his remit. He, too, eschews the institution of matrimony, but I believe he enjoys the company of several of London's, ah, livelier female socialites.

"As to myself, I imagine you already know all there is worth knowing." Holmes concluded his scribbling and looked up intently at our client. "I believe I do, Mr Petch. Now there is little more that need concern you.

"I shall visit your business premises, and I shall also explore Clerkenwell. Perhaps it would be as well, so as to forestall idle gossip and rumour, if I were to assume another guise for these enquiries – I suggest a surveyor examining your premises with a view to further refurbishments and security enhancements?

"In that way I shall be able to access all areas without exciting undue speculation – I suspect that gossip of Sherlock Holmes investigating the premises of Perkins, Bacon & Petch would serve only to fuel unnecessary speculation, which would be exceedingly unhelpful, both to my enquiries and undoubtedly to your relationship with The Bank of England."

"An excellent idea Mr Holmes; I shall send word ahead and make it so. Under what identity shall you attend?" Holmes pondered briefly. "A solid name, an

English name, one unlikely to excite comment." He glanced across at me with a flicker of amusement. "Would you object, Doctor, if I were to borrow your *persona* and become Mr John Watson, Surveyor, for the day?" I laughed. "Not in the least Holmes. Then I shall be your assistant, Mr..." my eye happened upon a brewer's dray passing in the street below "...Whitbread?" And so it was that the newly-incarnated John Watson, Surveyor, along with his assistant, Mr Whitbread, prepared to survey the Fleet Street engraving and printing works of Perkins, Baker & Petch, and then to seek out Mr Nathan Madgwick. Holmes returned his attention to our client. "Mr Petch, I will cautiously add that there is yet reason to be optimistic. Still, we must plan for the worst while hoping for the best. In passing, I would strongly urge you to double, at least, the number of occasions when the watchmen tour the premises, and replace all your locks as soon as practicable. I have a great deal to accomplish, and so I bid you goodnight; I shall contact you when I have news." The audience was at an end; Holmes clearly had learned all that he needed to commence his hunt. Mr Petch departed, seemingly with rather greater fortitude than when we first had encountered him at lunch. As the door closed Holmes sprang from his chair, rubbing his hands in glee. Brandishing Petch's calling card he cried: "What a splendid conundrum, Watson, and what a perfectly splendid Christmas gift has been delivered to us! I would rather sink my teeth into this tough little nut than the tenderest Christmas goose in all London! I sense it is grown from greed, coated in cupidity and liberally dipped in deceit. Noel, Noel and thrice Noel!

"But to the business at hand Watson; no matter in how high a regard I hold both your company and your invaluable assistance in these matters, I doubt much that your new domestic estate would be improved if you did not immediately telegraph Mrs Watson and inform her that you may, perhaps, be occupied here for some days longer."

* * *

Chapter Four

A Night in Bedlam

Sleep came hard to me that night, and when finally Morpheus grudgingly admitted me to his salon of somnolence, he served me not with that sweet nocturnal interlude of rest and blessed oblivion, but instead, with a night-long pageant of nightmarish and bizarre tableaux.

No doubt the day's surfeit of overly-rich food, sweetmeats, strong cheese and wine took its due toll, and so it was that my first night back at 221B was broken by the most troubling of images, occasioned – I realised the next morning – unquestionably by the disturbing revelations of the elderly master engraver.

Mr Freud, I am led to believe, proposes the notion that dreams may be the brain's subconscious attempt to bring order and understanding to the tangled chaos of matters which the conscious, analytical mind is unable to comprehend.

Eventually, a strange form of sleep overtook me...

...I stood in night so black I might have been a blind man. The air was suffocatingly humid, tropical and heady with the thick, cloying scent of exotic flowers. Steadily the temperature was rising – the ground beneath my feet was becoming hellishly hot at a fearful rate!

Cautiously I felt down through the gloom to investigate the cause – and cried out aloud in mingled pain and shock; nursing my seared fingers, I realised I was standing over a serpentine maze of giant gurgling metal pipes as fiercely hot as Dante's inferno! To my horror I felt my scorched right hand blistering and tightening into a malformed sinewy claw, although, curiously, I no longer felt pain.

Warily I stepped forward, feeling before my face with my good left hand. The footing beneath me became blessedly cooler.

Something large fluttered past me so close I felt the touch of its wings; suddenly I was engulfed in a swarm of huge soft, furry insects – giant moths or butterflies I calmly decided; not so alarming – indeed, perfectly reasonable; after all I was apparently in some tropical jungle...

Just when the swarm seemed never-ending, abruptly it passed by. I felt my way on through the humid heat, along a seemingly endless path bordered with what felt refreshingly like cool damp foliage; thousands of leaves seethed around me as if trying to identify this alien intruder in their private, exotic and rarefied domain. My investigation was halted abruptly when I encountered a smooth hard wall; I explored it cautiously and found it, perhaps, to be cold glass – so I was not after all in a jungle, but mayhap in the palm house at Kew or some-such? Much reassured I resolved to continue my journeying.

Abruptly and shockingly, and with an enormous report, the glass wall shattered inward, cascading razor sharp daggers all around me but I, strangely, remained quite unscathed.

Peering through the resultant jagged hole I was confronted by a cheery, ruddy-cheeked workman; grey dawn light and a bitter cold wind assaulted me, pungent with the distinctive odours of his trade – paint, burnt paraffin, putty and linseed oil.

All around me the tender seductive flowers shrivelled, drooped and died in face of the icy blast. The workman grinned demonically;

"If you'll just step aside through here Sir – mind the glass – I'll get on and fix this lot up in short order."

That seemed to me to be an eminently sensible proposal and so I unquestioningly complied. Passing by his tall moustachioed companion, whose features I was not quite able to discern in the gloom, I observed that outside, dawn was breaking and it had started to snow exceptionally heavily – gigantic flakes drifted down all around me. I reached out and caught one, but no sooner had I seized it than it turned to paper – a ten-pound banknote. Wonderingly I caught several more and all at my touch transformed into real money, so I gleefully pocketed as many as I could. This seemed to me quite splendid sport.

I had just determined to track this unusual torrent of incessant money to its source, when a smartly dressed lady, evidently much distressed, accosted me. I noted that I now found myself to be outside the doorway of a large fashionable villa on a smart suburban street.

"Doctor Watson, please will you help my husband? He is suddenly overtaken by the most dreadful turn! I fear he may not last out the hour!" Not in the least bit mystified by this perfect stranger knowing me by name, I rushed instinctively to oblige.

A pretty young woman in smart maid's attire brought a glass of water for the gentleman who, to my great relief, speedily recovered. I waved a cheery farewell to the grateful couple as they continued upon their journey.

When I turned to thank the maid, unaccountably she had vanished. Thinking little or nothing of this, I - quite naturally - continued to follow the wondrous, never-ending, blizzard of money; whenever the fancy took me, I reached out and further augmented my fast-growing wealth - indeed, my pockets were soon stuffed to overflowing, and still the great magical ice-crystals fell thick and fast around me. If only Holmes could be with me upon this grand adventure, we could both garner our fortunes with little more application than is required to pick cherries from the tree! I trudged steadily on, and soon noted that I was approaching close to Baker Street.

Turning a corner, I encountered some young rascals engaged in the age-old game of snowballs; one mischievous lad launched his projectile at me.

Deftly I caught the ball of ice crystals in my bare hands, whereupon it instantly metamorphosed into a great cloud of crisp ten-pound notes that fluttered to the ground around me.

Chuckling, I walked on, followed by the gleeful cries of children and adults alike as they harvested the magical currency that seemed to materialise only when I touched the snow.

Stepping around a group of uncouth labourers engaged in stirring a vast cauldron of boiling pitch, I was halted in my tracks by a news-vendor's bill:

> **'OFFICIAL—
> BANK OF ENGLAND
> GOES BROKE!'**

Dumbfounded at such a startling event, I handed the customary few coppers to the vendor, that I might learn more of this astonishing news.

"When was you born Sir? Everyone knows The London Times is a tenner a copy! 'As bin for ages!"

Wonderingly I handed over a £10 note, a mere fraction of my crisp new-found affluence, to the news-vendor which he added to a huge and fast-growing mountain of notes piled high behind his stand.

As I scanned the front page, a tall, skeletal, well-dressed silver-haired gentleman wearing monstrously thick gold-rimmed eyeglasses, whom I somehow felt I had met previously, also purchased a newspaper. "Sorry Sir, it's twenty pounds a copy now. Best buy one nippy 'cos it'll be thirty in a few minutes." The vendor pointed at me; "Mebbe that gent there will let you have a quick gander at his for a fiver."

I decided to depart this scene of lunacy and headed for the familiar, comforting sanctuary of my old lodgings at 221B, Baker Street.

The door opened unbidden at my approach. Mrs Hudson gravely offered me several huge bundles of crisp new ten-pound banknotes on a silver tray and said: "Mr Holmes gave me this Doctor but I've got so much already, perhaps you would like some?"

"That is most considerate of you Mrs Hudson but I, like you, have more than sufficient of my own." I reached out and captured a handful of snowflakes. "And here is ample money to cover Mr Holmes' rent for some years ahead" and I mounted the stairs. As I approached the door to the parlour, I became aware of a metrical hammering noise issuing from within, the most astonishingly raucous musical performance, and a Babel of voices in animated discussion.

Tentatively I opened the parlour door and peered within; I was greeted by a most curious sight. Holmes was seated before the fire, furiously playing his violin, a manic grin on his face, fingers mere blurs as they flew over the strings. He was accompanied by a cellist and a timpanist, who beat his kettle-drums fit to bring down the walls of Jericho, all conducted at an insane tempo by a rakish-looking conductor of eastern European aspect with extravagantly pomaded moustache and sleekly oiled hair.

I noted with detached professional interest that all but Holmes, of this odd musical troupe appeared to have fresh ligature wounds on their necks, although this did not appear to inhibit their extraordinarily spirited performance. A prima-ballerina pirouetted at possessed speed to the frenzied rendering – a favourite of mine by Boccherini, but rather comically played in at least four-four time.

Across the room, a vast printing press was thundering away. Again and again the gleaming engraved steel plates hammered down on an endless supply of sheets of crisp white paper, while an equally incessant stream of money poured out of the maw of the great mechanical beast. The whole operation was being supervised by three tall, thin elderly, silver-haired gentlemen who appeared to be marking time, each referring to a heavy gold watch on a gold Albert chain, festooned with intricate keys; they were accompanied by a dark moustachioed man, who was presently engaged in counting out money into the waiting hand of the maid I had earlier encountered, while upon the settee an elegant and elderly lady poured forth a voluble stream of rapid Italian.

A gang of tar-daubed labourers was busily occupied in stacking ten-pound notes in neat, regimented bundles.

Holmes paused at my entry, smiled oddly, then set to fiddling with renewed vigour. As the whole assembly appeared to be quite immersed in their revels, I decided my wisest course would be to make my way home and discuss these interesting matters with Mary.

I descended to the street, hailed a cab and was not in the least bit surprised to see that it was driven by the same cheery glazier who I had previously encountered repairing the tropical glass-house.

I paid the cabbie his very modest twenty pounds fare, tipped him a further ten, and entered the house to find my wife sobbing her heart out. "John, the butcher has presented his account for the Christmas goose and it is eighty pounds! Where ever shall we find the money?" I smiled cheerfully. "Never fear my dear" - I reached into my pocket and passed her a generous handful of... rapidly-melting snow...

While I make no claim to be an expert on the inner workings of the human mind, I am cognisant of the commonplace that the imaginings of our dreams are oft-times more readily understood upon waking, when critical reason once again assumes direction of that most baffling of organs, the human brain... Waking early, I spent the dogwatch hours considering - even jotting down in lengthy, but rather more ordered, detail – my recall of the events of my dream.

Now, reviewing my notes it seems to me that I had not so much spent my night in bed, but rather, in Bedlam.

As a medical man of some considerable training and experience, I do not particularly hold Mr Freud's theories in any special or credulous regard. They do not to me, upon rigorous scrutiny, appear to be particularly scientific in their origination.

And so I do not necessarily suppose that unconscious dreaming thoughts provide the key to unlock the secrets of one's waking dilemmas, and yet I was oddly and most forcefully persuaded that somewhere in that lunatic nocturnal adventure, I had glimpsed deep into the heart of this dark mystery.

Was there, concealed within that insane play in which I had taken the passive observer's part, a compass that might point to the culprits? Reader, how profoundly I yearned to possess Holmes' unique analytical abilities; to be able to exercise that mysterious skill which only he can bring to bear in such problematical situations – the gift of sorting the players into their proper places – the prime suspects, their accomplices, the unwitting assistants and lowly hired hands quite ignorant of the far greater and more sinister enterprise into which they had been gulled. At the conclusion of my lengthy but quite ineffectual deliberations I was really none the wiser, save for the fact that I was struck by one most disquieting notion; every player in my nocturnal escapade could readily be accounted for within Mr Petch's narrative, with a single notable exception.

Who was the tall shadowy man I glimpsed behind the glazier? I was convinced he was one and the same, apparently heavily moustachioed, as the man who appeared to be directing the printing of the currency at the lunatic revelry of my dreams in Baker Street. I could make no more of the troubling matter and resolved to keep my thoughts private until such time as matters became clearer.

* * *

Christmas day passed quite uneventfully. I spent much of the time reading before the fire; at two o'clock Mrs Hudson served a very decent lunch of goose and plum pudding, which I consumed with relish. Holmes, by contrast, was in a high fever of activity; he spent the morning issuing a flurry of telegraph messages, drafting and then despatching letters by hansom, and throughout all, paid scant attention to my various comments and questions, and even less to our meal, much to Mrs Hudson's evident frustration.

Only later that Christmas Day evening, after he had consumed three pipes of Barkers' strongest Twist in complete silence, and a lengthy telegram and two hand-written notes had been delivered, did his mood mellow. The contents of the telegram appeared to cause him some small perplexity, while the two notes plainly improved his spirits considerably.

"Forgive me Watson; I don't doubt I have been a somewhat churlish companion at Christmas, but now matters are resolving themselves by the hour!"

"I am heartily pleased to hear it. What news?"

"Well, for one thing I suspect I now know who is *not* the perpetrator of the crime, and second, it is not only London's sole consulting detective who was at a loose-end over the festive season!"

"To whom can you be referring Holmes?"

"I refer to a pair of our city's most accomplished criminals. They exist at the polar extremes of their mischievous trade, and I have crossed swords with both in years past. But they have their uses.

"So do not be in the least bit surprised if, in the morning, there are one or two rather unsavoury types at work here. But be most circumspect in what you say in their hearing – they are both exceedingly proficient criminals and will only be present in, what shall I say, a technical capacity. They need know no more of our commission."

* * *

Chapter Five

A Den of Thieves

The following morning I again awakened early, and upon entering the parlour, was greeted by a strange sight, and two even stranger visitors. I could discern upon the instant, from Holmes' lively demeanour, that he had made significant progress in his enquiries.

The workbench had been moved and quite cleared of the, presumably concluded, chemical experiment, now replaced by a rank of Bunsens, a gas-ring, retort stands and other small equipment whose application I could not immediately determine. Holmes desk, for the first time in my recall, was wholly cleared of any papers or articles of any kind. The room smelled faintly of hot wax.

"There you are Watson, timely as ever! There is hot coffee on the table. But first some introductions; gentlemen, this is my estimable friend and advisor Doctor John Watson, who works closely with me from time to time. Should either of you sustain hurt during our work, I advise you to stay close by him, for he is a very fine physician and surgeon.

"Watson, these gentlemen are what you might rather loosely term 'professional associates.'" I nodded in the direction of the two gentlemen, the one – small, scruffy and unkempt – occupied at the chemical bench, the other, tall, richly and expensively attired, lounging languidly by the fire.

Holmes indicated the occupant of the fire-side chair. "Watson, let me first present Herr Otto-Dietmar von Huntziger, who takes great interest in fine jewellery, old masters, bullion and precious stones – sadly, other people's. I recall we were last professionally engaged over the matter of the stolen Hartz sapphires. Apart from his unparalleled expertise, I especially commend him for the fact that in no case in which I suspected his involvement, was violence ever employed; but too, I never have been quite able to secure evidence conclusive enough to bring him to trial… yet."

Von Huntziger snapped out of his chair like a jack-in-the-box, clicked his heels for all the world like a Prussian cavalry officer on full-dress parade, and bowed stiffly. He was a tall, lean, athletic and handsome man, I would guess between fifty-five and sixty years with dark piercing eyes, heavy moustache, rather self-consciously cultivated and cultured, but still carrying that aura of late youth that departs so many, so early. Expensively – almost foppishly dressed, – rather dandyish, he cut a fine figure if you like that sort of thing.

With only the very faintest of accents – high Austrian I thought I detected – he replied with a grin; "I give you good morning Doctor Watson." And we shook hands. The robber-aristocrat addressed Holmes.

"Come now, Mr Holmes, those little adventures are surely history for us now. Certainly you came close enough in the Hartz caper to warm my back, but you have to own there was never any proof of my involvement. You and I have lunged and parried on several occasions in the past, and I admit that never have I had a greater care than when I sensed you had your eye upon me.

"But that is all in the past. We must accept that in our few little duels, we both wear our Schlager-scars with honour, with a worthy draw for both combatants. And anyway, as you well know, I am now retired in my modest house in London, where I occupy my days cataloguing my small collections and live a very quiet life."

"Pah!" cried Holmes. "Balderdash and piffle! Flatulent nonsense!

"For your amusement Watson, von Huntziger's 'modest house' happens to be a rather elegant Belgravia mansion built over four floors, with more bars and locks than could be employed in a moderately-sized private Swiss Bank, and the most charitable view you might take of his 'collections' is that he is their curator on behalf of others, all of whom have rather stronger title to them than he!

"And, my dear von Huntziger, retired you may be, but I am in my prime; have a care that I may not have lost all interest in the Hartz sapphires – perhaps I shall revisit the matter in due course."

"The pleasure would be mine Mr Holmes; I confess to missing our little matches, though not, of course, when you come too close to scoring a point! But today we are colleagues, are we not?"

Holmes turned to me and remarked drily "You might well be advised to count your fingers Watson – the gifted Herr von Huntziger may have removed one without your even being aware."

And the oddly likeable von Huntziger grinned carelessly once more – apparently a confident man with nothing to fear from Holmes, or at least not imminently. However, I have learned from long experience that where Sherlock Holmes is concerned, it is usually prudent not to start the process of chicken-counting, until after the eggs are hatched – on occasion, well after...

Holmes, too, smiled amiably with no apparent malice. "Now Watson, let me present our other partner in crime: yonder sits Mr Elias Pollitt, expert locksmith and self-proclaimed 'consultant on security', once thought to be the finest crib-cracker in London... by strange coincidence, also now retired! However, I am quite satisfied that he is again on the straight and narrow path."

"The *second* finest until I retired..." interjected von Huntziger good-naturedly. I smiled at this criminal, yet highly professional rivalry between two men so clearly from utterly different backgrounds and education, yet each according the other his due rank in the pecking order of their own villainous but ordered hierarchy.

A small, ferret-like, shabbily-dressed character with crooked, badly stained teeth turned from the workbench and awkwardly knuckled his forehead to me. "Pleased to meet yer I'm sure Doctor, an' I truly was only ever an innocent suspeck, God's truth." He giggled "Heugh heugh heugh."

And so with I little the wiser, he returned to his task, and with a soft roar of gas, ignited a whole cluster of hissing Bunsens directed at the base of some sort of blackened, smoking ceramic vessel. The sharp tang of hot metallic fumes, smoking white and acrid, soon started to taint the air. Holmes opened the window to clear the room.

While Pollitt continued with his work, Holmes, I and the elegant fop-doodle, von Huntziger, gathered around the fire; I observed that Holmes was keeping an unusually keen eye on every move the little man made at the workbench, having so arranged it that all was plainly visible.

"Perhaps, von Huntziger, you would be good enough to commence by summarising our earlier discussion, for the benefit of Doctor Watson?"

"Gladly Mr Holmes, but I would still give a handsome sum to know the location and contents of this safe that so urgently occupies your attention!"

At this unabashed impudence, Holmes shot him an icy stare. Von Huntziger raised his hands in mock apology. "No, of course I speak in jest! From the items Mr Holmes showed me, Doctor, we are talking of a very superior Chubb safe, diagonal-bolt model, although I am sure I merely confirmed what I suspect Mr Holmes knew already.

"As to the matter of illicitly purloining the contents, there are really only four feasible methods, one being markedly more practical than the others, a view with which Mr Pollitt agrees. Least practical in my opinion would be the use of explosives; not only would they occasion a significant report, and therefore would almost certainly raise an alarm; there would also be considerable risk of damaging the contents of the safe – it is extremely difficult to judge the size and placement of explosive charges precisely such that the locks are released or destroyed, without jamming the mechanism or damaging that which is stored within.

"A second possibility is the removal of the entire safe that it may be taken to a remote place to be dismantled and opened at leisure. However, the removal of a safe like this would involve large excavation works to free it from its secure fixings. This would also entail considerable noise and would necessitate the use of extremely large and bulky mechanical equipment to lift and transport it. Again, a swift hue and cry would be the almost inevitable consequence."

Although von Huntziger's lecture was absorbing, I nonetheless found it a bizarre experience to be observing Europe's most renowned consulting detective seated companionably with one of Europe's most proficient and prolific thieves, and I a respectable medical man, calmly discussing matters of high criminality in his consulting room while a locksmith and master safe-cracker worked industriously alongside, for all the world as if we were merely debating the preferred approach to repairing a broken cartwheel or freeing a stuck sash-window. Von Huntziger blithely continued:

"A third method which may appear to be attractive to the foolish, would be to attempt to pick the lock – a procedure with which I am sure you are probably quite familiar Mr Holmes, and indeed many lesser commercial locks can be defeated by this means." Holmes chose neither to confirm nor deny von Huntziger's speculation.

At this juncture Pollitt looked up from his work and snorted derisively. "As you see gentlemen, Pollitt agrees with me on this point. These Chubb high-security safes incorporate a mechanism designed to disable the entire system after one failed try at picking the lock; at this point any further attempts are quite futile, and the safe can now only be returned to normal operation by use of a special key which would be held by the registered owner.

"The need to employ this special key would immediately alert him to the fact that an illicit attempt had been made.

"By far the safest and simplest method is, therefore, with a working key, either one held by a legitimate key-holder or, greatly more challenging, to manufacture a perfect replica.

"The former route presents the not insignificant problem of purloining a key and returning it without being detected, or of co-opting, how do you say it – an inside man? This is not unusual in large robberies.

"The second, though more involved and complex, has the great advantage that the safe may be opened and closed at such an opportune time, and on such an occasion, that detection may be delayed for some hours or even days, thus much facilitating a safe and undetected escape.

"I may add, Doctor Watson, that Mr Pollitt and I are entirely in accord with this analysis – our expert credentials you have already heard from Mr Holmes." This last was delivered without the smallest hint of irony.

Throughout this extraordinary dissertation, which in any other circumstance would surely be tantamount to conspiracy to burglary, I observed that Pollitt had ceased working with his massed burners, and was now engrossed in many intricate operations involving the use of exceedingly fine and thin files and a small metal vice which he had clamped to the bench, confirming my belated but growing suspicion that Holmes was in train of somehow manufacturing duplicate keys!

At this point in our somewhat improbable convocation, the long-suffering Mrs Hudson entered bearing a tray piled with meat and cheese sandwiches, along with a glass of wine for von Huntziger and small beer for Pollitt, showing no particular sign of disapproval beyond a sniff in the shabby little locksmith's direction, before sweeping out of the room in a rustle of bombazine.

A further hour or two passed, during which time Holmes and I took turns at watching Pollitt closely. In Holmes' case, clearly to ensure that only one of each key was made, whereas my interest lay rather in marvelling at the precision, speed and dexterity of the man – a true craftsman at work.

Eventually Pollitt clambered down from the laboratory stool and approached Holmes deferentially. "'ere you are Mr 'olmes" and he dropped four complex, gleaming zinc metal keys into my colleague's outstretched hand.

I remained silent as Holmes scrutinised them minutely through his lens from every angle.

Von Huntziger strolled over and peered down at the newly-formed keys. "May I look please?" Holmes passed him his lens. Von Huntziger examined them closely and smiled. "They are fine, very fine, indeed quite perfect. I believe I have never seen better."

Holmes nodded languidly. "Now Mr Pollitt, what assurance do I have that these would open a lock, assuming of course, that there are locks to match?"

Obsequiously, the diminutive Pollitt replied through a mouthful of meat sandwich "Well Mr 'olmes, Sir, there ain't no guarantees in this kind of what you might call private consultin' work, but my guess is that if ~ only *if* there was a safe to match o'course, just supposin...'" again his snigger "heugh heugh ~ these will likely work first time out, sweet as a nut.

"They're as perfick as anyone could make from what you give me. An' there ain't many as could do what I just done, even if I does say it meself. But if, an' I'm only sayin' *if*, it don't work first-orf, 'ere's a little dodge."

With some curiosity I studied the crooked little scoundrel as he fawningly discoursed with my clever, elegantly-attired colleague and I reflected that there is, strangely, about some free-born Britons a cringing and innate baseness, a quite needless and uncalled for lick-spittle awe of rank, wealth or education which appears not to exist even in the most despotic tyrannies in Europe, yet is principally and almost exclusively to be found thriving among the English working classes. Perhaps, I reflected, it affirmed for them some comforting value which anchored them securely at their allotted station in life, cheerfully above their lesser brethren ~ the hucksters, itinerant tinkers and drink-sodden brawlers, yet reassuringly beneath their acknowledged betters, the men of learning, letters and position. In such a way, I supposed, were their lives ordered.

I watched Pollitt select one of the simpler keys – my guess would be the one to Petch's office – and take it to the bench where he smoked it in a sooty candle flame. He returned with the smut-blackened key and a small selection of wafer-thin files.

"Now Mr 'olmes Sir, if it don't work first orf, you smokes it so, and tries again. You takes the key out ever so gently and see where the lamp-black has gone bright on the bit – them's the parts you 'as to file away."

He walked over to the parlour door, inserted the key in the lock and attempted to turn it, with no result of course, but that was clearly not his point. Returning he indicated those areas on the blade, now showing bright, which had conflicted with the levers of the lock mechanism.

"Nah Mr 'olmes, supposin' just in case you ever *did* find a lock to match this key, heugh heugh, I'd better throw in these files, compliment'ry o'course."

Holmes nodded curtly, looked up, and addressed our two visitors, his face now a stern pale mask, cold and deadly serious.

"Now listen gentlemen both, and listen very closely; I believe our work here is complete.

"You, Pollitt, will leave here everything you brought with you; you will take nothing away. Not even your recall of the last two day's events. You have never visited Baker Street. The fee buys all. The same strictures bind you also von Huntziger.

"Any loose talk whatsoever – believe me, I *will* hear of it – and you will discover to your very great discomfort, just how fast and how far Sherlock Holmes can reach out. Is that well understood?"

Both divined instantly that the good-natured badinage between consummate detective and wily master criminals had now quite evaporated, and that Holmes was in deadly earnest. I myself would dread to cross him, and I am his close friend and confidant. I shuddered to think what anguish he could cast across these two rogues' lives should they ever be minded to turn their hand against him. "Very well, gentlemen; if that is clearly understood, here is your payment as agreed."

In a flat, chilling tone he added "I am satisfied with the results of our short association. Have a care that you keep matters that way" and he passed over two envelopes, both of which vanished in a blink, one into a grimy inner pocket, the other, considerably thicker, slipped deep inside a rich velveteen jacket.

"Oh, one more thing, Pollitt; who in London, other than you, might be unscrupulous or skilled enough to perform the work you have accomplished, and to this standard, with no awkward questions being asked?" A crafty look passed over the ferrety little locksmith's face – clearly he perceived an opportunity to extort more money. He scratched his head, feigning great perplexity. "Well, I can't say as I rightly knows Mr 'olmes, and my memory ain't what it was. I ain't a peach you know. An' then again it'd take some time but I could make some enquiries I s'ppose..."

My friend rolled his eyes heavenwards at this shameless attempt to fleece him. Patently it beggared belief that a reformed criminal locksmith and safe-cracker would not have such information readily at his fingertips; but Holmes indulged him. "Very well; you have until ten tomorrow to regain your memory Pollitt. I'm sure this will speed your recovery."

He handed over a further white note which vanished in the blink of an eye. "Ten o'clock mark you and no later. If I am not present, hand a clearly-written message to the boy in the hall, or to Mrs Hudson."

Knuckling his forehead furiously, the diminutive Pollitt fled as if Holmes had let slip all the hounds of hell to chase him home. Von Huntziger, however, paused at the door and turned in a leisurely fashion.

"It has been a pleasure to be of service, and a privilege to renew our acquaintance Mr Holmes, but I doubt we will ever have reason to meet again, so I will say my final *adieu.*"

Holmes looked up from the keys he had been examining and smiled cryptically. "Mayhap, von Huntziger, mayhap, but who knows how the future will turn? For my part I shall merely bid you *Auf Wiedersehn.*"

After the door closed behind the aristocratic rogue, I turned to my colleague. "Good Heavens above Holmes! As far as I can determine, you have spent an entire day or more illicitly conspiring with two of the country's blackest villains to forge the keys that will open the vault that guards the printing plates for The Bank of England!"

He threw his head back and laughed aloud.

"Guilty as charged m'Lud! Send me down!" he intoned in a sepulchral voice and held out his hands, wrists together. More seriously he continued "I grant you it was indeed a dubious and motley meeting that you joined with, my dear Watson, but I have high hopes that it will prove part, at least, of my reconstructive theory. You have wired Mrs Watson I trust? I can manage without my Boswell, but my lieutenant is quite indispensable."

Now I am well aware of Holmes' views on the estate of marriage which, though not precisely misogynistic, are at the very least, deeply sceptical.

I am certain he felt that intimate involvement with a woman would distract him from that total self-absorption he regarded as critical to the science of precise and minute observation, relentless machine-like analysis, and cold, logical deduction which he so much prized, and so had made of it his own superlative domain. Nonetheless, I was pleased that he still valued my assistance in these affairs. "I have Holmes, and as matters turn, Mary is delighted to spend a little more time with her friends."

"Capital! I had hoped as much! Then let us prepare for tomorrow."

And so I settled down to watch, intrigued, as Sherlock Holmes prepared for the following day.

From a drawer in his desk he retrieved a shallow wooden tray, heavy with ordered slugs of printers' type in compartments, together with a crumpled lead tube of black printer's ink, a demi-quarto sized slab of plate glass and an India-rubber roller, a small closely grooved hardwood block, tweezers, a few slips of ivory paste-board and a hand-press that was little larger than the single-impression embossing devices favoured by lawyers to place seals upon legal documents.

Having selected the characters he required, and arranged them right-to-left in the rack, he inked the roller upon the slab of glass and applied it to the type. I watched in silence. An hour or so later, after a few attempts, he smiled at the results of his work – a half a dozen calling cards in black on ivory that soberly proclaimed:

Mr. John Watson M.R.I.C.S.
CHARTERED SURVEYOR
Caversham Heights, Reading

After carefully setting them out to dry before the fire, he assembled in a battered attaché case such items as might ordinarily be carried by a surveyor – a leather-cased retractable fabric measure and boxwood yardstick, a small compass, yellow legal pad and pencils, his small ivory slide-rule, and a miniature brass sextant and theodolite which customarily sat atop his desk. Finally, he swiftly scrawled two telegraph messages to destinations in France and Ireland respectively and despatched the boy downstairs clutching the forms and a half-crown, to the telegraph office.

Thus prepared to his complete satisfaction and being mindful of the unaccustomed but nonetheless eagerly anticipated early start the following day, we each retired early to our rooms.

* * *

CHAPTER SIX

THE GAME'S AFOOT!

A few minutes before nine o'clock next morning, Mr John Watson, Surveyor, inconspicuously attired in sober gray suit, worn black fustian overcoat and freshly brushed billycock hat, with his assistant Mr Whitbread, alighted from a hansom in Fleet Street at the massive iron gates of Perkins, Baker & Petch. The watchman attended our ring almost upon the instant; a steel shutter slid open and Holmes announced us. The door in the large iron gate swung wide to admit us.

We were greeted by a smartly uniformed gentleman, clearly tanned from many years spent overseas, and around sixty years of age, unmistakeably of military comportment, and lacking his right arm below the elbow.

"Good morning and compliments of the season Sah! Mr Watson I collect; and you will be Mr Whitbread. Mr Petch told me to expect you, Sah!" Wryly I noted that though I significantly out-ranked the sergeant, I did not merit the honorific.

Holmes proffered his new calling card. "Indeed, and you would be?"

"Sergeant Jacob Gunton Sah, late of Her Majesty's Royal Irish Fusiliers, at your service Sah! Of course in my day it was The Princess Victoria's 89th Regiment of

Foot. Mr Petch said as I was to give you all assistance necessary in your work here, Sah!"

"This is all well Gunton, but you may simply address me as Mr Watson."

"Very good Mr Watson, Sah!"

I nodded sympathetically at Gunton's gleaming steel hook. "I see you paid dearly in your service to your country Gunton." I added "...as did I at Kandahar." The old soldier stiffened, and then laughed easily. "It's not so bad Mr Whitbread Sah, lots of the lads came off worse than me Sah; six-pounder at Meerut gave me this little memento, compliments of the Rani of Jhansi. Wouldn't have minded so much except that it was one of our own – treacherous damned Sepoys had pinched one of our artillery pieces, hid it up in a nullah and then used it on us, the ungrateful beggars, 'scusing my language Sah!"

Wonderingly he added "And me getting safe and sound all through the Crimea without so much as a hair on my head being touched too! He returned his attention to Holmes. "Now Mr Watson, how may I best be of help?"

"As you will know, we are here to survey the premises with a particular view to further refurbishments and recommending improvements in security; we shall require access throughout the buildings. Describe first, if you will, the general procedures upon admissions, deliveries, contractors and the like."

Gunton deliberated. "As you might suppose, in our line of trade, nobody gets in unless I knows them by sight – or Private Shadwell, Jeremiah, if he's on duty – or if they has an appointment in the book; definitely no casual salesmen or the like. Jemmy will be here to relieve me shortly, and then I shall go onto night duty for the coming week.

"Tell me Sergeant, what nature of fellow is your Jeremiah Shadwell?" The tanned old sergeant ruminatively scratched a red-veined nose with his gleaming hook and grinned.

"Well Sir, he's a sound enough lad but if I tell you he's twice as large as your biggest bare-knuckle booth boxer, and half as quick-witted, you'll maybe take my meaning. 'Biddable' was how Captain Oakes described him; but just as long as he smokes you're an officer and a gentleman he'll do anything you order.

"He was the best gun-layer in the regiment but he was pensioned off after a musket ball creased his noddle something wicked and took his right eye and half of his wits with it – 'liable to be unpredictable in action' was what the surgeon said. 'An' I was always telling the great daft sod to keep his head down, too; but 'e could never resist standing up to see the fall of the shot.

"Never mind – he still couldn't shoot a musket worth a tinker's cuss even with both eyes but 'e could lay an artillery piece so prettily 'e could take a cocoa-nut off a palm-tree at three hundred yards. But don't you mind 'im Mr Watson; if he takes a fancy to you, he'll be as devoted as a guard dog." I smiled to myself, for I had encountered a fair number of that staunch species of privates and non-commissioned officers who would doggedly offer their loyalty to an officer they felt to be above the usual cut; their judgement was rarely wrong.

"Very good Gunton; now I understand that you have performed the day duties for the week past? That I may have an idea of the general procedure for comings and goings; tell me what you have observed this week gone, for example. I would like you please to exert yourself and try to remember everything, no matter how small."

"No need whatever for exertion Mr Watson. Every visit, departure, delivery and collection is written down in the day-book, along with the time, together with any other observations or unusual happenings. The partners are most particular in that respect." He reached within the watchman's hut and retrieved a battered foolscap-sized register with the week's callers listed in some detail and handed it to Holmes, who scrutinised it at length.

"Ah yes, I see here that Wednesday was the day you closed the factory. Now what else do we have..? I see Hollum arrives at eight, now followed by employees Miss Hodgson, George Smee, then Edward and Sam Porter, and one Peter Hope, all by half past the hour, as are the partners. And here, at nine o'clock listed as visitors, we see a Mr Orman accompanied by three others. They would be...?"

"Orman's Building Contractors Sah. Laying pitch on the roof and general decorating Sah. And between you and me, I'm powerful glad they've finally packed up their wagon and finished; you can see them signed out here at five o'clock on the twenty-first; the smoke from all that black boiling pitch was something terrible. What with the banging and sawing and the bloody fumes, you couldn't even take contentment in a pipe of shag, it was that bad – an' considerable worse than the rotten-egg stink of musket smoke! It made you cough something really dreadful, didn't it just?"

Holmes nodded understandingly.

"I observe that Thursday was singularly quiet by comparison... the builders turn up for their work, Mr Hollum makes a brief appearance to collect his tool-bag at ten o'clock... and departs at twelve. And here at two in the afternoon I note a delivery from Portals Paper Mill, thirty boxes."

"That is correct Sah; all safely delivered to the paper-store. No doubt you shall see it in due course."

"Indeed; now I note here that apart from the roofers' visits, little or nothing occurs from Saturday the 21st – when the builders finally attended to finish off and depart with their tools and wagon – and nothing more?"

"Everything was quiet – the street was quite empty – not as much as a single wassailer Mr Watson. And if it hadn't been for the jolly old organ grinder who'd set up outside the gates that Saturday, a penny'd win a pound I'd have turned up my toes with world-weariness! Champion tunes too, like 'Kitty Dear' and 'Meeting of the Waters'. Why, the old gent even played 'The British Grenadiers' especially loud for me whenever I made a quick walk around the site!"

Holmes smiled indulgently. "How very thoughtful of him; I'm sure that was a most welcome diversion on a cold winter's day; no doubt much the more so knowing that all the while your fellows were tucked up in their homes by the fire or in a cosy ale-house?

"I see that on Christmas Eve, Mr Petch visited."

"Quite so Mr Watson, and a tedious quiet time I was having of it too, so it was a welcome surprise when Mr Petch turned up unexpectedly, carrying three fat pheasants, one of which he gifted to me which I thought pretty handsome of him; it seems he had left some drawings or such-like he needed to take home with him but he plainly found them because he emerged carrying a burlap bag about an hour later.

"Mind you, he did seem most troubled, not quite himself at all. Prob'ly not my place to mention it Sah, but I thought he appeared to be a bit jumpy-like, nervous and rather fretful. Not hisself at all, oh no Mr Watson Sah, not at all hisself." Holmes appeared to take little heed of this information.

The old soldier chuckled. "But enough of my gripings; shall I be opening up the building for you now Sah?"

Before Holmes could respond there was a soft knock on the wicket gate and a deep, quiet voice spoke; "Mornin' Sarge - Jeremiah sir." Gunton opened the gate to admit a colossus of a man wearing a black eye-patch, at least six and a half feet tall, whose weight was perhaps two-fold that of Holmes.

The giant warily eyed Holmes and me with evident suspicion. Holmes considered him with wry amusement.

"Ah, good morning to you Private Shadwell; I can well see why you are a watchman at Perkins, Bacon & Petch.

The massive Cyclops ignored Holmes' comment and turned to Sergeant Gunton. "Who's this Sarge?" he asked, clearly unsettled by our irregular disruption to his familiar, uncomplicated routine. "Easy Jeremiah, you mind your manners now; this here is Mr Watson - he's visiting us at the particular request of Mr Petch, and this is his assistant Mr Whitbread. Mr Watson is *a surveyor*" - Shadwell looked uncomprehendingly at Sergeant Gunton - "That means he's just like an officer, Jeremiah, and Mr Whitbread is an officer too, so mind you do whatever they asks of you, just like it was an order." Comprehension dawned on the simple giant's face.

"Very good Sarge, just as you says - whatever they asks it is." After the keys were handed over and Gunton had departed, Holmes swiftly consulted the plan of the buildings furnished by Henry Petch, then addressed the giant. "Very well Private Shadwell, I shall require a ladder to be placed against the wall over there, so I may first inspect the roofs. Then you may open the building including the internal doors so we can make all necessary measurements. These are most important so we shall require complete peace and quiet, with no interruptions whatsoever."

The giant, obediently trotted off and returned shortly with a heavy ladder over twenty feet in length, which the man-handled into place as if it were a child's toy.

When Shadwell was safely ensconced out of sight in his watchman's hut, Holmes and I scaled the ladder and stepped onto the gleaming black expanse of the newly-tarred roof. With the sketched plan in one hand, he carefully paced out certain dimensions, until he had narrowed his area of investigation down to two areas, apparently no different to my untutored eye, to any other.

He strode around with long, slow steps, looking for all the world like some giant exotic species of spindly black insect; on four occasions he lay flat and examined the surface minutely with his lens, at the conclusion of which he let out a soft grunt of satisfaction.

We descended the ladder, whereupon he proceeded to examine the windows closely, occasionally sliding the blade of his pocket-knife between frame and window – all appeared solid. Eventually we entered the building. To our right ran a long corridor leading off which, on the left, was a short corridor and beyond that, doors accessing two rooms. The interior was aged and utilitarian, dingy green and white, and smelled pungently of metal, oil, ink and paper.

We stepped into the smaller corridor to the printing room door, which was now open. Using one of his new keys, Holmes locked it, tried the door, then unlocked it and entered. We threaded our way between three large, silent presses. Holmes strode to the far end of the room, where stood a steel-barred cage the full height of the room, filled with boxes and stacks of paper.

He stood in deep thought for some minutes before this massively armoured steel cathedral, stacked high with some of the most precious paper in the land. He scrutinised the ages-worn, stained stone floor around the cage minutely, and the massive fixings of the heavy steel cage both to the floor and ceiling. It appeared to me to be inviolable. Holmes used his second new key and proved it was not so.

Some minutes later, with an air of quiet satisfaction, he emerged from the printing room and slipped a folded blank sheet of watermarked paper into his briefcase. Exiting the smaller corridor we turned to our left and entered what I assumed to be Henry Petch's office. The room was simply but tastefully furnished with a fine old Oriental carpet on the highly-polished wood floor; the oak-panelled walls displayed an assortment of framed, coloured engravings of orchids, along with proof copies of various security documents and bank-notes. The centre of the large room was dominated by a wide twin-pedestal, brown leather-topped partner's desk.

To its right against the wall stood a massive oaken work-bench, illuminated by a substantial frosted-glass, heavily barred window and three gas globes; on the bench sat a long rack containing a row of much-worn, gleaming steel burins; I counted thirty slots but twenty-eight burins; there were two empty places. Needle-sharp, hair-thin curls of steel and copper glittered here and there across the work-top.

But what seized Holmes' entire attention was the huge, gleaming green enamelled, steel and brass Chubb safe embedded deep in the wall at the far right-hand corner of the room.

We stood before it in silent deliberation for some time; it was about the height of a tall man, and sufficiently wide to admit the two of us abreast; so this was the impregnable fortress that safeguarded the modest yet priceless slabs of elaborately incised base metal that had the power to raise, or to ruin, an entire economy..?

Returning to the oak workbench Holmes opened his attaché case; carefully he set out the wafer-thin rat-tailed files, a stub of candle and a box of vestas. Before the safe once more he retrieved a long, slim gleaming key from his waistcoat pocket. With all the extreme delicacy of an entomologist pinning some matchless specimen to a card, I watched him gently slide the key deep into the lock's inner mechanism. Imperceptibly slowly, holding his breath, he turned it.

Throughout the ensuing interminable seconds I was gratified to hear four soft metallic clicks. Exhaling slowly Holmes grasped the heavy steel release lever.

He gently turned it anticlockwise and we were rewarded by the sound of well-oiled bolts retracting effortlessly into their keeps. The heavy door soundlessly swung open on its massive forged hinges to reveal steel shelves stacked with neat leather packets of differing sizes – before us lay the plates to print almost limitless supplies of many of the world's major currencies, and the means to create bearer-bonds of infinite value.

Any one of them might be used to devastate a nation as mercilessly as would the mightiest army. Satisfied, he made to close the safe, when he paused in thought, smiled, and placed his new calling card within the vault, then relocked it and packed his attaché case along with the duplicate safe key and the unneeded candle and files. His hypothesis appeared to be taking substance…

'...there is very little in this world that one man can devise, that another cannot discover...'

After a detailed but apparently unrewarding examination of the remaining rooms and offices, yielding little fresh intelligence, we returned to the gatehouse where we were greeted by a newly-amenable Shadwell, plainly now much-impressed by Holmes' enhanced stature as a senior officer. With a childishly solemn face he saluted crisply. "All in order Mr Watson Sir? Any further orders?" Holmes nodded benevolently at the simple giant's zeal to please. He eyed the burly private's huge shoulders, brawny arms and fists like hams. "No Shadwell, you have performed your duty well today, but I may perhaps have need of your unusual attributes in the future." The ex-soldier flushed at this unexpected praise. "I'm your man Mr Watson Sir; anything you need Sir, you just ask Private Shadwell Sir."

Our next port of call was at number 98, Clerkenwell Road, where we speedily located the premises and house of Mr Nathan Madgwick, builder. In keeping with his trade, Madgwick's modest house, yard and workshop appeared to be in trim repair, contrasting with the adjacent buildings which, once genteel, had now assumed an air of faded neglect.

The door opened at Holmes' knock to reveal a short, homely woman in a pinafore with three curious young children clutching at her skirts. "Mrs Madgwick I presume – I am sorry to inconvenience you but I am so rarely in London, and I would much like to discuss a small business matter with your husband. He has been highly recommended to me by an acquaintance", and he handed her his new card.

"Might I have a brief word?" Mrs Madgwick, somewhat flustered, curtsied and darted into the small, tidy parlour taking her clutch of wide-eyed infants with her. Several moments later, after a whispered conversation within, which we were unable to overhear, Mr Nathan Madgwick appeared; of early-middle years and moderate height, a little on the corpulent side and with an open, amiably rosy countenance, he was respectably dressed in what I took to be his Sunday best – rusty black suit, fresh white collar and tie.

With a slight air of puzzlement he said "Mr Watson I believe? Sarah informs me you have a business matter you wish to discuss. Gentlemen, will you step inside and take a small noggin to celebrate the season? We can be comfortable by the fire in the parlour."

A moment later, Holmes and I were seated before a small cheery fire in the neat cosy room, affecting to enjoy an execrably poor glass of Madeira while Mrs Madgwick shooed her inquisitive brood from the room. "Now then, gentlemen, how may I be of service? I understand I have been recommended, Mr Watson – may I enquire by whom?"

"To be candid Mr Madgwick, the works I wish to discuss are not for me, but for a good friend of mine who is casting around for a reliable workman who might refurbish his orangery.

"Quite by coincidence a business associate happened to mention to me that you had performed similar excellent work for him and at a very keen price as well."

Madgwick smiled. "I like to think that is a trademark of all our work Mr Watson. Who, pray, was it recommended my services to you?"

"Ah yes - a Mr Henry Petch of Richmond; I am sure you will recall him. I understand you and your partner did excellent work on Mr Petch's orchid house?" The builder's rosy face instantly clouded over. "Am I in some sort of trouble gentlemen?"

"Why ever should you suppose that, Mr Madgwick?" said Holmes.

His Adam's apple bobbed nervously. "Well, I knew right from the start there was something a bit peculiar about that job Mr Watson. But the fact was, what with three little ones and Christmas on the way, and being short of work, I badly needed the money."

And then his account poured forth, as so often happened when Holmes artfully revealed a trifle of what he knew. Madgwick continued "However, as you appear to know something of the matter already, I may as well tell you the whole outlandish story. It was earlier in December I was visited by a very smart gentleman, a Mr Asa Bormanstein - he sounded English but I thought he had a very faint accent,

German maybe - anyway, he said he knew where there was some profitable work to be done, glazing and the like, but it couldn't be done except on the 19th of December – not a day before and not a day after.

"I thought this a rather odd business but he assured me it was just his way of doing things, and the pay would be generous, very generous indeed, and as I said Mr Watson, I needed the money.

"I was to have so many panes of glass of such-and-such dimensions ready-cut for very early on Thursday morning, about five o'clock, and he would call for me."

Holmes listened closely, and made the occasional note on his legal pad. "This certainly was a most unusual commission. Can you describe Mr Bormanstein for me?" Madgwick considered awhile.

"I would say he was well set-up, perhaps of middle or late-middle years, army-style moustache, smart and athletically-built, strong-looking, well-dressed, maybe a tad taller than average. And there was one other thing – I had the distinct feeling he might have been a military man at one time; just from the way he carried himself you understand, as if he were rather more accustomed to giving orders, than asking favours."

"Thank you. Your description is indeed precise to a point - I feel almost as if I have already encountered the gentleman myself. Please continue with your most interesting account Mr Madgwick."

"Very well; I had old Noah fed, watered, harnessed and in the shafts, and the wagon all loaded in the yard by five o'clock as instructed. Mr Bormanstein had told me it would be a tolerable fair ride to the customer so I threw in the nose-bag as well.

"Now imagine my complete astonishment when he arrives, attired in common working man's clothes and carrying a bag of tools and a shovel, which he held was on account that he would assist with the work, but did not require any imbursement for his time. Now how strange is that?" Holmes made no immediate reply, except to smile briefly as if satisfied with an expected outcome. "A most unusual tale Mr Madgwick; please do continue.

"There's not much worth the telling for some considerable while now; we set off and for the entire journey it was like travelling with the Sphinx. I tried to draw him on the client, where we were headed, the nature of the works, but all he replied was 'all in good time' or 'you'll see by and by' and such-like. We left London by the Chiswick High Road and shortly after, we passed over the bridge at Kew.

"This cheered me considerably, as the folk who live thereabouts are in the main a well-heeled lot, but when we went straight past the Royal Botanic Gardens I realised we must be headed for Richmond, and indeed, so it proved to be.

"And now, something very funny occurred; he told me to pull over on a smart suburban street and wait, where he sat in perfect silence, watching a large villa a short ways along the road most intently. I will confess I was starting to feel a mite uneasy about this whole outlandish business, but as I said, I much needed the money, and so held my peace.

"We waited for perhaps half an hour in silence, when at a little past nine o'clock, the front door of the villa that so occupied his attention opened, and out stepped a tall, elderly, bespectacled man, very well dressed and distinguished-looking; he set off at a brisk pace in the direction of the railway station and as he passed us on the far side of the road I noticed that the poor fellow seemed rather agitated, muttering and frowning and shaking his head.

"For some reason this appeared to suit my strange companion very well, for as soon as the old gentleman vanished around the corner, Mr Bormanstein directed me to drive to the small lane at the rear of the villa, and wait there while he confirmed the arrangements with the owner of the residence.

"With that he sprang down and walked over to the front door, where I observed him in conversation with the lady of the house; I directed old Noah around to the back as instructed. There, from the seat on the wagon, I could see a large, most ornate hot-house with all manner of strange flowers within, but there appeared to be numerous missing or broken panes, and I perceived what looked like old sheets and blankets fixed over them. I also noticed that the white garden palings were broken down, and several shrubs seemed to have been uprooted and left on the lawn."

Holmes nodded in satisfaction.

"Anyway, a little time after this my odd companion emerged from the rear door of the villa and summoned me over to the hot-house. He required me to replace all the broken panes, while he would repair the palings and gate, and replant the shrubs; this we did and the work was completed comfortably by two o'clock, when Mrs Petch came over to inspect all, and most happy with our work she seemed too. At this point she said to us something much like 'Excellent gentlemen, my husband will be quite delighted; I believe, Mr Bormanstein, the sum we agreed upon was seven pounds five shillings was it not?'"

"Well gentlemen, you might well imagine, that set me right back on my heels; my materials amounted to more than five pounds on their own, let alone my time, extra feed for Noah and all the travelling!

"I was about to protest when Bormanstein gave me a very dark hard look; I don't mind telling you Mr Watson, I was chilled by his expression at that moment; he did not appear to me to be a man to cross lightly.

"When we mounted the wagon, I was yet again much startled when he very cheerfully passed me ten pounds, which was more than enough for my trouble.

"I made to remonstrate with him but he appeared to take this as dissatisfaction, and upon the instant pressed another tenner on me. You can be sure that with that, I piped down pretty smartly, and privately blessed him for a gentleman! So, strange affair or not, that day's work meant that the missus got the brooch she had set her heart on, and the little ones got their rocking-horse after all, with enough over for a fat goose, a fine ham, and this excellent wine we're enjoying."

Holmes took a polite but minute sip of the abominable brew, pondered, and then raised a quizzical eyebrow. "I wish to be wholly clear on this point Mr Madgwick – you say that this Mr Bormanstein paid almost three times the disbursement he had received from Mrs Petch?"

"That is so Mr Watson."

"Remarkably generous do you not think?" The rotund builder shifted uneasily in his chair but made no reply. Holmes smiled lightly. "Well, no matter; all things considered it was a pleasant Christmas surprise for you and your family, and I wish you joy of it" and with this he made to rise. "Did Mr Bormanstein give you his card, by any chance?"

"No Mr Watson; he said he had neglected to bring them with him, but he did refer to interests east of the City near the docks – somewhere around Rotherhithe and The Isle of Dogs, I recollect. However, I understood that you came to speak to me about some work for your friend?"

"Ah yes, of course; if you will kindly give me your calling card I shall be sure to pass it to my friend, along with a hearty recommendation - on that you may depend; I expect you will hear from him in due course."

And so with thanks and further earnest assurances, we departed the house of Mr Nathan Madgwick, builder, of Clerkenwell Road, and presently, hailed a cab for the lengthy drive to Richmond — as cabmen call it, a clock-and-a-half. Consequently we had some little time to ponder...

* * *

From the look of quiet satisfaction on his pale, lean countenance, I felt that Holmes was content, pleased even, with what he had learned thus far; indeed, I sensed that the facts we had gathered fitted most satisfactorily to support whatever theory he was pursuing with that remarkable intellect he possessed. For me, however, this welter of diverse new intelligence served for the most part, only to further confuse the mystery. I recalled the exigent question Holmes had put to Petch after listing the players in the puzzle: *'Can you name one, or a union of several, who would not stand to profit from the illicit possession of authentic Bank of England printing plates and paper to match?'* And in truth this, too, was my quandary.

That a key, or keys, had been used in the perpetration of the theft seemed eminently clear, which undeniably tended towards the notion that one or more of the partners were involved, or either or both of the watchmen.

I could give little credence to the involvement of Petch, appearing as he did to have no conceivable motive to jeopardise his own comfortable station, his reputation, that of his business and its, no doubt, lucrative association with The Bank. But what of the two curiously, coincidentally missing and unreachable partners? And did they indeed, even leave the country at all? I recollected that Perkins was said to feel some ambivalence about his prosperity, and ardently laboured to raise a very substantial sum for his mission work... and Bacon certainly seemed to live a lavish, perhaps costly, social life; might he, through indebtedness or some indiscreet liaison with an inappropriate partner, have made himself vulnerable to coercion or blackmail?

As we passed by The Ritz Hotel, I considered what we had learned of the two watchmen, the hook-handed Gunton and the simple Jeremiah Shadwell. While I could not immediately envision any possible motive they might harbour, beyond simple avarice and opportunism, the inescapable fact remained that while they probably lacked the wit or the resources to effect such a crime, between the two of them they surely had unfettered access to the entire premises, both day and night – and more sinisterly I suddenly realised, ever since the complete factory closure for Christmas; they certainly did not lack for opportunity.

But if they were not themselves directly responsible, surely one of them would have had to be complicit to facilitate so audacious a theft? I recalled von Huntziger's unsettling words:

'*...or of co-opting, how do you say it – an inside man? This is not unusual in large robberies...*'

Then, too, had appeared this curious, chameleon-like character Mr Asa Bormanstein; a smartly-dressed gentleman one day, a mean labourer the next; and possibly with a slight German inflection – von Huntziger? Or might he perhaps be the shadowy, moustachioed and unaccountable figure I had briefly glimpsed during my troubled night in Bedlam?

But then, as a professional man, trained to the exacting disciplines of medicine and surgery, I could scarcely venture such a fanciful and wholly irrational trope to Holmes, who functions in every respect by means of the application of rigorous observation, scientific deduction and adamantine logic.

I put the thought once more from my mind.

Diffidently I ventured: "Holmes, I suspect you have learned much, and yet to me you have clarified very little!" My companion smiled insouciantly. "Oh, I would not say that; on the contrary my dear Watson, I believe we have clarified a very great deal.

"A few exemplars for you – I have certainly established the day, and most likely the time of the robbery to within a few hours; too, I am almost certain of the criminals' modus operandi; and incidentally, I am perfectly assured in my mind that Mr Nathan Madgwick, though a decent man, is sadly the gullible and unwitting dupe of a villain infinitely more cunning than he."

Presently we arrived at Richmond; all was as one might expect of a man of Mr Petch's station; a fine big Georgian sandstone villa in large lawned grounds, set back from the road and a good distance from its neighbours. Mrs Petch appeared to be a pleasant woman, moderately educated and refined, but in her answers to Holmes' questions, she was as woolly as her husband was pedantic.

It was evident that Petch had wisely not apprised her of the facts of the theft, and so we confined ourselves to hearing her account of the interval when her husband was absent on his fruitless search for a glazier. Holmes indulged her enthusiastic and lengthy account of her short encounter with Madgwick and his generous sponsor, and their apparently matchless work, and also of her unexpected caller – the lady whose husband had taken a turn in the street, all of which corresponded precisely with Petch's account of events.

But her protracted portrayal – indeed, it was a positive paean – of the virtues of their new maid, proved quite extraordinary in its fervour; if Mrs Petch was to be believed, this paragon of domestic service ironed, cleaned and cooked to utter perfection, and served tea as if to the noble Highness herself! I began to wonder if Mrs Petch had some private and undisclosed reason for being so singularly determined to bring

Dulcie Hobbs into her household, or she may have been of that aspiring type of only tolerable education and moderate breeding, who seek to augment their social standing by appointing domestic staff referred by persons of noble title.

Only too frequently chided by my wife for the several shortcomings of our present clumsy maid, I wryly thought if only to quiet my own household, enjoy my breakfast toast somewhat less than incinerated, and have my boots correctly cleaned, I reflected that I too would immediately employ this paragon of domesticity! Mrs Petch rang a small brass bell and shortly after, Dulcie Hobbs entered the drawing room.

She was a moderately attractive dark-haired woman of around five and twenty years and of short, slim stature, tidily presented and well-spoken in the self-conscious manner of the self-taught. Holmes smiled briefly and blandly at her. "Please be seated Miss Hobbs. I wish to ask you a few simple questions in connection with the damage to Mr Petch's orchid-house."

A look of alarm passed over her face. Holmes raised a hand to calm her. "Do not agitate yourself Miss Hobbs; I merely want to know a little of your past history with the Baroness Amanti, and what you observed of the two workmen who repaired the damage. I assure you that you are under no suspicion whatever in the matter of the vandalism to the hothouse."

Under Holmes' gentle but persistent prompting she recited at some length the story of her past career, her time in service with the Baroness, first at her grand house on the Sussex Downs, and later for a short while at Milady's estate at Obânes St-Amarin in France where she received Barons and Dukes at her mistress' *soirées*, directed the house in style, and even accompanied Milady Amanti as her lady-in-waiting in her *barouche* to the monthly ball.

In support of her story, she produced the letter of reference from her purse and handed it to my colleague.

Holmes nodded, apparently impressed, while Mrs Petch beamed with pride at her new household addition. Abruptly Holmes murmured in a low tone *"Madame Amanti – quel âge a-t-elle? Elle vieillit?"* Madame Amanti – what age is she, is she old? – At which the maid appeared puzzled, flustered and blushed deeply. I was about to offer an attempt at interpretation when I realised that Holmes must have had sound reasons for his odd interjection.

With a small dismissive gesture he moved smoothly on; *"Ca ne fait rien"* – It matters not; "tell me Miss Hobbs, what you recall of the two men who repaired the damage..." He checked his notepad "...Mr Bernstein and Mr Sedgwick, I believe?"

"I only saw them from afar and, begging your pardon, I think it's *Bormanstein*, Sir."

"Ah, of course I see that now – I really should make my notes in a clearer hand." It occurred to me that it was most out of character for Holmes, renowned for his encyclopaedic memory for detail, to mis-remember so important and recently-learned a name. Hobbs proceeded to describe Madgwick reasonably accurately, and Bormanstein exactly as Madgwick had portrayed him to us.

"And this was the first time you have ever seen these men, Miss Hobbs? You have not encountered either of them previously?" A small hesitation – then "No Sir, I never seen neither of them in me life." I put the momentary lapse in grammar down to the strain of being quizzed by a man as daunting as Sherlock Holmes must surely appear to one of her station. After a swift examination of the ground-floor rooms of the elegant villa, when Holmes paid particular attention to Petch's study and bureau, and to the soil in the flower-border immediately beneath the study-window, we departed Richmond.

It was not until we had progressed well along the Cromwell Road into London that Holmes broke our silence. "Well Watson, what have we learned from that little encounter, do you suppose?"

"In my estimation, very little that is new, save that both Mrs Petch and her maid seem to confirm everything Mr Petch has so far related."

"Then you do not think it odd that Dulcie Hobbs managed the Baroness Amanti's French household to perfection, yet does not comprehend the simplest phrase of schoolboy French? And does it not further strike you as strange that when I – apparently in error – referred to Mr *Bernstein* and Mr *Sedgwick*, she – without thinking – swiftly corrected me only in regard of Bormanstein's name, a man she claimed a second earlier never to have met, nor even seen, before the day he and Madgwick visited?

"I am certain she knows Bormanstein, but not Madgwick; her unease was signalled by the momentary grammatical lapse into her normal uneducated idiom. Trust me, Watson, that young lady is deeply involved in this affair – perhaps well over her head."

I smiled; I should know by now that when Holmes says or does something quite inexplicable, it is never without good point, and always calculated to confirm some suspicion he harbours. "But you have been deeply suspicious about that young lady for some time, Holmes. I confess I am somewhat puzzled." We alighted at 221B.

As we climbed the stair at Baker Street a playful grin flashed across my friend's gaunt face. "Of course you are puzzled dear fellow, and you have every right so to be! Because mischievously I have saved the most comical until last – an interesting little poser you may wish to ponder; an acquaintance of mine, Louis Lépine

– the Deputy Prefect of police in the district of Fontainebleau – a most admirable fellow, replied to one of my telegraphic enquiries and intriguingly, his first-rate intelligence indicates that the last recorded member of the Amanti family – a frail old bachelor of over eighty, one Giuseppe Carlo Amanti – died of syphilis in 1878 in total penury in Naples with no issue, and rather curiously furthermore, it would appear there is no such place as Obânes St-Amarin to be found near La Rochelle or, indeed, very likely anywhere else in all of *la belle* France!" We entered the parlour and took our usual seats.

"Now what light may we shed on *that* curious report, Watson?" And with this he applied a vesta to a cigarette, leaned back in the most contented manner and smiled through a swirling cloud of fragrant smoke.

I have sometimes considered that Holmes' personal passion for ever seeing society as a moral and intellectual battleground between good and evil, crime and punishment might perhaps, on occasion, obscure a simpler, more direct and less sinister explanation.

Now it may be my natural inclination to gallantry towards the distaff side, or perhaps my lack of that acuity which he possesses in such abundance, but in this matter I thought I could offer a more straightforward, logical and rather more charitable solution to this small domestic conundrum.

"Even were you correct, may it not be possible, Holmes, that here we are presented merely with an over-ambitious young lady who, to further her humble station in life, has deceitfully presented a reference from a supposed titled sponsor – reprehensible I agree, but not precisely actionable – and at least she appears to offer her employers the high standards of service they have been led to believe she acquired in her prior, perhaps fictional employment; Mrs Petch without reservation seems perfectly satisfied. Does that not serve as well or better than your more cynical, and menacing explanation? Should you not, perhaps let sleeping dogs lie when all parties seem content? I cannot in any event see how this woman can be central to the case in the slightest."

"Nobility to the fore, as ever Watson, but should you wish to pursue your interest in my little mysteries, I fear you must hone the harder, more sceptical aspect of your analysis." He stood and started to pace. "She certainly is a sleeping dog, and she certainly is lying. However, my own discreet research with The Yard informs me that the genteel lady's maid, Dulcie Hobbs, is also well-known to them as Maggie Betts, sometime petty thief, pick-pocket, and barmaid at the Anchor Inn in Rotherhithe – I doubt we would enjoy its hospitality – prior to which she was Betty Belle, a dancer in an inconsequential vaudeville act of doubtful taste which performed under the unlikely name of 'The Bow Belles'.

"She is rather more than a sleeping dog, Watson; I believe she is a viper in the bosom of the Petch household; a willing, paid instrument deliberately insinuated there by the organiser, the mastermind if you will, of this entire crime – and as such, I suspect she is our key link in the chain that will lead us to the very principal of the criminal gang!"

This revelation, allied to my own purblindness, left me speechless for some moments. I briefly recalled my thoughts when attempting to bring order to my chaotic dream of Christmas night...

...How I yearned to possess Holmes' unique and mysterious analytical abilities; to be able to exercise that arcane skill only he can bring to bear in such problematical situations – the gift of sorting the players into their proper places – the prime suspects, their accomplices, unwitting assistants and lowly hired hands quite ignorant of the far greater and more sinister enterprise into which they had been gulled...

He continued "And that, my dear Watson, is why even now I have this rather ignoble young lady under continuous watch at her place of work in Richmond and at her room in Chiswick High Road, by two of the keener-eyed of my 'irregulars'. They will report to me her comings and goings, and more importantly, who she visits, and who visits her, and thus shall we draw her patron into our web."

Throughout this animated discourse Holmes continued to pace distractedly up and down the length of the worn old Turkey carpet, hands thrust deep in his pockets, angular jaw sunk on his chest. Abruptly he spun on his heel and fixed me with an intent stare, a fierce light gleaming in his cold eyes.

Quietly and slowly he said "Watson, understand that this crime was no mere speculative theft, perpetrated on impulse by a single man, overcome by a moment of weakness or greed. Indeed, I consider that the breath-taking scale, evident planning, organisation and sheer audacity of this business signals quite clearly that we face not a mere gang of opportunist thieves but a veritable nexus of organised criminality, presided over by a most dangerous, gifted and cunning adversary. I advise you now of these matters not to alarm you, Watson, but to counsel you that as the most valued and stalwart aide a man might ever hope to join with, and also in consideration of your new matrimonial estate, this business will likely lead us into considerable danger – perhaps even into mortal peril.

"That is an occasional risk which I, as a singleton, am happy to take; you, dear friend, might perhaps be advised to observe and record matters from a more distant and detached position. Your situation is now such that I would not wish you to be utterly careless of your own safety."

He paused, perhaps to let the implications of this chilling statement become clear.

It seemed to me that he could be referencing only one man – the self-same he had once described as *the single most dangerous man in London.* Holmes had previously told me he been moved to research this shadowy individual after he conceived the notion that numerous of the crimes he encountered were perhaps not necessarily the spontaneous and disconnected efforts of casual criminals, but rather, the interlinked and highly orchestrated manoeuvrings of a vast and subtle criminal network.

"You refer, I presume, to Professor Moriarty, Holmes?"

"A logical guess, Watson, and I confess that that too was my first instinct the moment I began to grasp the sheer dimension of the criminal talents that have been so precisely coordinated and deployed in the execution of this impudent crime.

"However, I am persuaded that he is not the direct instigator of this business; I have received a further telegram from M. Louis Lépine – and his invariably trustworthy intelligence is that he currently has Moriarty under the closest observation in a small *pension* in a seamy outskirt of Fontainebleau, where he appears to be recruiting relatively low-level felons for a planned jewel robbery in central Paris.

"His mail and telegraphs are all intercepted, his visitors noted, and the most capable Lépine assures me that had any reference to our present case surfaced he would have been aware of it immediately.

Nonetheless, Watson, your instincts are fundamentally sound; and Moriarty certainly is more than adequately blessed by genes, nature and nurture to be the architect of a crime on this scale."

"I am well aware, Holmes, that you have taken rather more than a passing interest in this evil man and his gang; it appears to me that you rate him as your equal on the dark side?"

"I do, Watson. He is well-born and of excellent education, gifted with an unparalleled facility for mathematics, and once had contemplated what seemed to all to be assured – a most brilliant academic career lying before him. But he became a most ignoble blot on his family's escutcheon – the man soon revealed an inbred disposition of a most devilish sort. A cruel strain of amoral criminality ran in his veins, and it became ever more dangerous, thanks to his remarkable intellect.

"He is in my estimation, the complete Machiavelli of crime – the evil overlord of a criminal hegemony that controls much that is wicked, and almost all of that insidious villainy that passes undetected with impunity in this great metropolis. I must reluctantly concede that he is nothing less than a criminal prodigy, and undoubtedly a genius in his field.

"Even so, I would one day still much relish to go right to the very brink of the abyss if necessary against such a gifted criminal as Moriarty; my continuing existence is Watson, make no doubt of it, a considerable inconvenience to the dark endeavours of Professor Moriarty..."

(Only a few short years later would I realise how chillingly prescient were his words *to the very brink of the abyss,* that day.)

Holmes concluded "...but in view of his virtual incarceration under Lépine's vigilant eye, I am confident that while he probably had oversight of a crime of this scale, and certainly has the means to fund such an enterprise, it is more likely to have been implemented by one of his anonymous and shadowy inner circle of strong-arm lieutenants recruited expressly for their low cunning, utter mercilessness and bizarrely perverted loyalty.

"Be good enough to pass my index of criminal biographies." I retrieved the appropriate binder from the collection in which Holmes retained that information which would aid him in his cases; he flipped through the pages and found what he sought.

"Here we are Watson; you may choose any of these charming folk. Our quarry might – I only say *might* – be any or none of them; it is a list of my own compiling of those I suspect of having been associated with Professor Moriarty since I began to take a close interest in his affairs." He commenced to read aloud:

"Henry Witham, undertaker to the gentry, of Shoe Lane, thought, but never proved, illicitly to have

disposed of the bodies of Doctor Daniel Rawlins and The Reverend Erasmus Dawkins.

"Sebastian Moran, Eton and Oxford, Colonel late of the First Bangalore Pioneers, lives in Conduit Street, plays cards at the Tankerville and Bagatelle Card Clubs – a crack shot, thought to be Moriarty's hired assassin and the executioner of Mrs Stewart of Lauder two years ago.

"Sir Aston Cunninghame, Harrow and Cambridge, of Lambourne, moderately successful racehorse owner, high-society socialite and confidence trickster, thought to be a fund-raiser for Moriarty's crime syndicate.

"Obadiah Jenkins of Turnham Green, pawnbroker and London assayer, thought to handle stolen goods for Moriarty, especially gold, gems and securities.

"Edward Palmer, printer of Turnham Green, suspected of being behind the great land-sale fraud in Arizona; he produced and sold to the gullible, certificates giving them all title to the same tract of quite useless land which he neglected to mention was several hundred miles from water.

"Benjamin Wilkes of Gerard Street, noted watch and clock-maker, rumoured to have masterminded the platinum robbery at Albion & Co of Hatton Garden.

"And here we have William Jarman, a respectable metal fabricator and steel-worker by day, and by night a cat-burglar and safe-cracker.

"Finally, I list the most unsavoury of all, *Lieutenant-Colonel Roland Chatsworth, retired* – cashiered actually – and also that most squalid and despicable of miscreants – *a thief of other peoples' secrets and a blackmailer.*

"As I say, Watson, you may take your pick! I am convinced that all these men work for or with Moriarty, and all pay tithes to him." Villainous as they sounded, it seemed to me that his list of miscreants did not seem so promising; with Moriarty apparently under such close surveillance, I could envision few of these confederates who might have masterminded the theft of the plates of The Bank of England. I looked dubiously at Holmes. "I agree they sound a most unsavoury lot, but I cannot see that an undertaker, an ex-Indian army big-game hunter or a Lambourne racehorse owner is especially qualified for the commission of this crime, less still a cashiered Colonel who exists by blackmail; but perhaps the dealer in stolen securities, the cat-burglar or the watch and clock maker-turned precious metal robber..?"

"I have an early notion Watson, but at this stage it is, perhaps, founded upon a coincidence and I have told you how deeply I mistrust them! Coincidence is very often a feeble vindication for two strikingly similar data for which everyman is unable to perceive an explanation" and he resumed his pacing. I had listened attentively to Holmes' discourse, the lengthiest I had yet heard him deliver of the sinister

Professor Moriarty and his gang; and from his precisely chosen words I realised with a thrill of fearful exhilaration, tempered with that caution natural to any recently-married man, that should we pursue this investigation full-course we might well face mortal hazard once again.

And yet at that instant I already knew that I would without hesitation join with my friend to the end of this adventure, for better or worse, wherever it might finish.

* * *

Chapter Seven

THE MIST THINS

Unsurprisingly, after talking well into the night, I slept somewhat later than usual next morning; I clearly longer than Holmes, which I observed from his evident early departure and the cold remains of a meagre breakfast – occasioned no doubt by that unfeasibly feverish state in which he habitually existed when scenting the spoor of his quarry – the exact opposite of the dismal, self-pitying, condition of lethargy and ennui that invariably overtook him when he lacked the stimulus of a case to kindle his excitement and mental powers.

Having breakfasted, and awaiting his return, I was in train of stripping and cleaning my long unused service revolver when Holmes burst into the parlour in a state of some excitement. He eyed my revolver.

"So despite my counsel, you have decided to run this business to the end Watson?" I turned and laughed; "I might pretend that old habits die hard – that I am merely following old army instincts and maintaining my weapon – but could you ever have doubted that I will offer whatever support I may?

"You will allow that an army Surgeon-Major, even one invalided out of the service, if equipped with a commandingly heavy-calibre revolver, and with the experience to use it to good effect may at some desperate point in the game, be able to tilt the balance somewhat in our favour?"

He looked quietly thoughtful for a moment. "With or without your revolver Watson, there is no other man I would rather have at my side in a tight pinch. If you are, indeed, prepared to throw in your lot with me on this adventure, then it is certainly wise that you have that heavy gun loaded and in good order; but your eternally dependable steely nerve will serve equally well for me, my friend."

This comment pleased me to the highest degree. He joined me at the table and dropped the customary bundle of the morning's newspapers between us. "Now Watson, the talented but unlovable Isaiah Pollitt did duly deliver a note detailing the only two locksmiths in London he considers capable of forging keys suited to the task. It is my belief that one of them most likely made the keys used in the robbery. I propose today to establish which one – I trust you are free to join me?"

We travelled first to an address in Tavistock Street, to the premises of *J MacFadzean – Locksmith*. Mr John MacFadzean was without doubt an accomplished and respectable locksmith – with a busy, tidy well-equipped establishment, indeed he showed every outward indication of a skilled and honest man about his lawful occasions.

He smiled and greeted us. "Good day gentlemen; how may I be of assistance?" Holmes released the latch on his attaché case. "Mr MacFadzean? I require keys to be made from these – could you oblige me?" and he opened the case to reveal two perfectly flat slabs of hardened brown modeller's clay, each bearing a row of impressions. Abruptly the man's smile vanished, and his eyes hardened with suspicion. Coldly he replied "I could, Sir, but I will not. I am sure you are perfectly well aware that these impressions are of keys to some of the highest security locks ever devised. Whatever it is that they safeguard, it is clearly of huge value. I would respectfully suggest, *Sir* that if you were indeed the legitimate owner of these safes, you would well know to approach the makers, who will be happy to supply additional keys upon the appropriate proof of ownership. And you are not the first to approach me with impressions of these self-same keys..." His voice took on an edge of scorn "... a Mr Bormanstein – perhaps one of your associates? I refused him also" and he turned away. Holmes closed the attaché case; "I owe you an apology Mr MacFadzean – I have been less than candid; the matter is, you see, of some considerable delicacy." He placed his own calling card upon the counter. "I am investigating an extremely serious crime."

Comprehension dawned on the locksmith's honest face as he studied Holmes' personal card. With a broad smile he said "Now I understand Mr Holmes; in that case I shall repeat my earlier question, how may I be of assistance gentlemen?"

"I have reason to believe that keys made from impressions very similar to these were used in a most audacious theft – I suspect they were made with common glazier's putty, by a Mr Bormanstein. I believe him to be both dangerous and determined, and I am most anxious to apprehend him. Be good enough to tell me all that you recall of his visit, Mr MacFadzean."

The locksmith nodded sombrely. "I'll be glad to help Mr Holmes – I knew from the moment he set foot in my workshop that there was something seriously amiss. It was late on Thursday, the 19th of December – a most perturbing episode – I was visited by a rather unsettling gentleman of extremely sinister appearance. He was dressed in smart business attire, perhaps fifty-five or sixty, slim but muscular and athletic, somewhat above average height, a pale complexion with a heavy moustache, something of the military trim to it.

"He carried an expensive leather attaché case. At variance with his outwardly respectable appearance was the odd fact that he appeared to have what looked much like fresh garden soil under his fingernails, one of which had a smear of something, perhaps putty, upon it. I thought this rather strange for a man of affairs.

"His eyes were most striking in appearance, smouldering under a heavy beetling brow, cold and unforgiving – deep-set, giving an entire appearance of great menace.

"He required me very speedily to make an additional set of keys for his premises, including the one to his Chubb safe. The cost, he claimed, was of no consequence; the work was to be done solely by me in complete privacy, in the shortest possible time – and certainly by or before the 21st day of the month, and with absolute discretion.

"Somewhat taken aback by such a suspicious commission, I enquired his name and the nature of the premises for which the keys were to be made, and if I might see the originals from which I would have to work; he replied that his name was Bormanstein and that the keys were for one of his warehouses out near the London docks. He could not provide the original keys, as he claimed they were all in constant use for twenty-four hours of every day. Instead he showed me a set of impressions taken in putty.

"You may imagine, gentlemen, that upon hearing this suspicious tale I resolved to have nothing to do with the affair, and terminated the conversation. He left with a veiled threat to the effect that I should forget him and his request, less mischief befall me."

Holmes completed writing a note and frowned darkly. From long acquaintance I knew well that his demeanour, like a sharply shaken kaleidoscope, could change in an instant; a thunderous frown might pass over his countenance in a moment, to be replaced instantly by his customary saturnine inscrutability; on this occasion, however, a radiant smile illuminated his sharp features – and vanished in a second; those unfamiliar with his unusual character mistook it for disdain. I knew, however, something lively had lightened his mood. "I am greatly obliged to you Mr MacFadzean; your account has been both concise and precise, and your description of this Bormanstein character, quite invaluable."

Outside on the pavement Holmes commented happily "If the likes of friend Lestrade and his colleagues were even half as observant as that young man they might well improve their performance. The mist thins, and my web draws ever-tighter."

"Clearly Holmes, this ugly-sounding Bormanstein character did not possess an authentic set of keys, but how on earth do you suppose he managed to search Petch's house and locate his keys without being detected?"

"Because he did not, Watson – another performed that small service for him. Let us walk for a while – I have been certain from the events described at our first encounter with Mr Petch that whoever surfaced in this affair would *not* have a set of authentic keys. But I suspected they would have something very nearly as good, in the hands of a locksmith possessing the appropriate skills You might call to mind the examination to which I subjected Petch's Keys."

I recollected the evening in some detail; I had been particularly struck by the odd manner in which Holmes had scrutinised the keys at inordinate length, extraordinarily closely, practically at the very tip of his nose.

"You see, Watson, my suspicions were deeply aroused by the apparently meaningless and random destruction of the hot-house, the predictable panicked departure of Mr Petch, and the curiously coincidental arrival of two workmen coincidentally 'passing by', miraculously equipped with all tools and supplies necessary to effect immediate repairs, and at a price which cannot conceivably have been in the slightest part profitable.

"I examined Petch's keys and found something strange that had no natural place in association with their ordinary usage."

"I saw nothing out of the ordinary, yet my eyes are perfectly sharp."

"Indeed they are Watson, and yet I discovered the minutest traces of glazier's putty, confirmed by its distinctive odour."

"Good Heavens Holmes! How on earth did you find them?"

"I found them precisely because I was looking for them."

From all the foregoing I started to see some pieces in the puzzle falling into place, but if my few deductions were correct, of a certainty Holmes would have most of the jigsaw assembled already – perhaps much of it from an early stage in this case.

"And what of the next locksmith?"

"Aha! He, Watson, our next port of call - one Aloysius Hawes by name; with the first locksmith certainly eliminated, it seems more than likely that we shall now meet the man who made the keys for Bormanstein! However, we will need to be rather more devious with this fellow. I shall take a small gamble – let us see if it pays a dividend."

We located Hawes' shabby premises in a squalid alley in Shoreditch; my instant impression was that he was certainly the type of dog to make the keys used in the robbery - a more impious, pernicious and degenerate-looking scoundrel I have not observed in some time.

We entered the slatternly place, whereupon, somewhat out of character, Holmes appeared to become nervous. "Mr Hawes?" he enquired tentatively; "My name is Henry Bormanstein. I am led to believe that you are skilled at your trade... and, I hope, discreet?" I noted Hawes' weaselly eyes signalled instant recognition of the name. "My business is of the utmost importance, Mr Hawes, and an honest answer to my questions may very well make my fortune and yours into the bargain."

"Mr Bormanstein, you say?"

"You have heard the name before?"

"I might have, I might not. What exactly is your business with me, Mr Bormanstein?" Holmes fretted and appeared to be unsure of his next step. Hesitantly he said "I must now take you into my confidence Mr

Hawes. My father, Mr Günther Bormanstein has two sons – I, and my brother, Asa Bormanstein." Again I noted a clear sign of recognition in the locksmith's eyes. "Our father is an eccentric old man, bitter, aged and sick, and soon to meet his maker; he holds no particular affection for either of us. Likewise, there is no great fraternal bond between my brother and I."

Hawes appeared perplexed; "And how does all this involve me Mr Bormanstein?"

"This, Mr Hawes; over his lifetime my father accumulated a vast fortune in the South-African diamond business. Concealed in the family home – which is huge and rambling with many hidden passages and secret doors – there are two cunningly concealed vaults which contain a king's ransom in cut diamonds, and stocks in gold and diamond mining concerns. Only he knows where they are, for he designed the house. His will takes a strange and spiteful form; he gave both of us one hour, separately, with the keys to the vaults, to find the treasure – the first to find it was to win all."

I was quite dumbfounded by this fantastic fairy-tale, although I could see that Hawes was entirely gripped by it. Holmes continued his extraordinary fiction; "My brother, Asa, spent his allotted hour searching – greedily, and fruitlessly I trust.

"In view of the number of concealed compartments, trap-doors, passages and secret rooms throughout the house, I used my hour more wisely, Mr Hawes, in making my own arrangements that I may return at a time of my own choosing and search at leisure; it could take weeks to comb the place thoroughly. I will pay a tenth-part of the fortune to whoever assists me in finding it.

"Your next words may well make you richer than you ever thought possible Mr Hawes, or with a lie, you will never see me again, and you will continue making keys for shillings until the day you die in Shoreditch. On the other hand..."

I wondered where on earth this curious masquerade might possibly be leading. Hawes cleared his throat apprehensively. "And your question, Mr Bormanstein?" For answer, Holmes opened his attaché case to reveal his clay impressions. "Now think most carefully before you answer Mr Hawes; your future prosperity may depend upon it.

"Have you seen these keys before, and if so, did you manufacture a like set for my brother?"

Hawes peered at the slabs of clay; in swift succession I observed his crafty countenance signal recognition, suspicion and indecision but perhaps in the greatest degree of all, avarice.

He looked up at Holmes. "A tenth-part you say?"

"I believe I made myself perfectly clear on that point Mr Hawes."

"Then your brother hasn't found the treasure yet, else you would not be here now" Hawes retorted craftily.

"You may beat about the bush as much as you wish Mr Hawes, but I would remind you there are many other competent locksmiths in London."

"Very well Mr Bormanstein. Your brother did visit me on..." he paused in thought "... the 19th it would have been. He required me to make a set of keys from impressions taken in glazier's putty; he said they were for his warehouse somewhere on The Isle of Dogs, and they had to be completed for the morning of the 21st."

"You obliged him?" In a bitter voice Hawes replied "I did Mr Bormanstein, but he never told me about the diamonds – all he paid me was four pounds and fifteen shillings."

"Damn and blast my luck!" cried Holmes in apparent despair. "Then he has likely beaten me to the prize!" A thought seemed suddenly to strike him. "That I may be quite certain it was my brother who approached you, please describe him for me, for he is quite distinctive in appearance – short and rotund, rosy face, always smiling, clean-shaven and some years younger than I?"

Hawes appeared confused. "Then your brother has an accomplice, for the man who visited me was taller and older than you, perhaps fifty-five years of age, lean, strong and muscular-looking, and he was very severe of countenance – a heavy military-style moustache, bushy eyebrows and black, glowering eyes. To be candid gentlemen, he rather gave me the shivers."

"Did this accomplice collect the keys, or did you deliver them? Did he leave his address?"

"No Mr Bormanstein, he collected them in person."

Holmes locked his attaché case. "Thank you Mr Hawes. I shall visit my brother; if he has not yet located the safes, I will return, you shall make me a like set of keys, and I will search the mouldering pile from top to bottom. You may yet become a wealthy man..."

Back at 221B I pondered Hawes' all too-coincidental description: '*...perhaps fifty-five years of age, lean, strong and muscular-looking, and he was very severe of countenance – a heavy military-style moustache, bushy eyebrows and black, glowering eyes...*' I had heard something like it elsewhere, and recently too. I hunted through the jumbled stack of old newspapers nearest Holmes' desk, where he had been seated the day I paid my unannounced visit in November; for once I was thankful that he was a compulsive, if untidy magpie for all data and news that might one day be usefully indexed in his numerous reference binders. I could not find it. Holmes looked at me with a knowing smile.

"The item from The Telegraph you seek, concerning the two burglaries in Harrow, now sits folded beneath the Mantons atop my desk where I placed it. I did indeed question Lestrade and learned that the houses were owned by the absent partners, Messrs Perkins and Baker. That is why I was not so very surprised – indeed

I was expecting the timely interruption of our Christmas luncheon by Mr Henry Petch.

"The expert search was, of course, for the vault keys at the houses of the absent Messrs Perkins and Baker as I have now established but how, I wonder, did our moustachioed friend know that they were partners and key-holders at Bacons Perkin & Petch, that there were new plates and paper stored at Fleet Street, where they resided, that they all possessed keys, or even that two partners would be travelling abroad leaving their houses largely vacant?

"However, praise where it is due, your instinct is sharpening wonderfully Watson – the moustachioed character described by Lestrade in that news item is indeed, I make no doubt of it, our man!"

At this I smiled with quiet satisfaction, replaced the cylinder in my revolver, spun it twice and looked up at my colleague. "From long experience, Holmes, I am convinced you already know considerably more than you have revealed. Certain strands of this dark affair are becoming clear to me, but I suspect you may already be in train of weaving them into a snare. Might now not be an opportune point to tell me all that you already know?" Holmes gestured expansively toward the easy-chairs before the fire. "Now is indeed as good a time as any to enjoy a cigarette while I explain the circumstances as I now see them, though my analysis is, as yet, sorely incomplete.

"At the outset, we must assume that our moustachioed desperado – let us call him Bormanstein, for want of proven identity, somehow came by extraordinarily detailed intelligence about the partners, the plates, the watermarked paper, and the firm's closure over the festive season and more. There may be even more than one ring-leader.

"I urgently await more data from the estimable Monsieur Lépine, but from his reply to one of my earlier telegraphic enquiries, and another from the equally competent Detective Inspector O'Connor in Belfast, I have established beyond doubt that the two absent partners are indeed where they claimed they would be.

"Bormanstein first breaks in to the houses of the two absent partners in his opening foray for the keys – to no avail; they are abroad and evidently carrying their keys with them. Thus he is compelled to gain access to the sole remaining partner's keys. Through his intelligence he somehow knows of Petch's passion, indeed his near-obsession, with his hot-house filled with tender *Angraecum Sesquipedale* specimens and determines that therein lies a near-certain gambit to draw Petch out of the house in the depths of winter.

"Thus, the vandalism to the glass-house; thus Petch's predictable and fretful departure next morning to find workmen; and thus the extraordinarily propitious and remarkably timed arrival of the ingenuous but genial Mr Madgwick, accompanied by his scheming sponsor

Asa Bormanstein, an alias almost certainly — moments after Petch has departed, and undertaking to repair the damage at an unfeasibly low price, the which payment he cheerfully trebled to placate the outraged Madgwick!

"But for what the scheming Mr Bormanstein cunningly gained, he would readily have paid a minor Nabob's ransom; in the event however, for a mere twenty pounds and a little light gardening, he won a perfect set of impressions to the keys to the vaults of Perkins, Bacon & Petch, engravers and printers to The Bank of England, in much the same manner as did I at my workbench using modelling clay!" Holmes frowned darkly for a long moment, and then laughed drily.

"And yet twenty pounds seems a paltry enough price for a licence to print money, does it not Watson?" Despite this explanation, there were still, for me some puzzles yet unexplained.

Holmes resumed his agitated pacing, and continued on his discourse with much the same passion as a lawyer summarising the case for the prosecution, bent on driving home his damning points of evidence. "There are now perhaps two more players to whom I would particularly direct your attention. The maid, Dulcie Hobbs, was planted like a malign weed in a flower garden. Her primary task was to locate where Petch habitually kept his keys, and her second task was to cooperate with the two stooges who knocked upon the door with their cock-and-bull story about the husband being taken ill in the street.

"And thus, when the solicitous Mrs Petch went to seek the Doctor, Hobbs performed her final, vital, treacherous task of passing the keys swiftly out to Mr Bormanstein, probably through the study window, below which I noted two clear footprints of a man standing for some minutes, and then restore them to their rightful place before Mrs Petch's return.

"The other players in the cast I commend to your attention are the gang of roofers who evidently were upon the premises right up to December 21st, but more of that in due course. For now I await news from Wiggins and Smith who, between them, have both Hobbs' place of work and her room under continuous observation, reporting all visitors and meetings she may have, for that is now our best – in all probability the only chain connecting us to Bormanstein."

With this Holmes abruptly sat down at his desk and resumed work in silence on yet another of his interminable monographs, this one I recall upon the arcane matter of forensic methods and classification for the invisible impressions left by our fingers upon suitably receptive surfaces. I, meanwhile, sat and pondered these revelations.

* * *

CHAPTER EIGHT

THE CHAIN IS BROKEN

For perhaps two hours — for it was now past three o'clock in the afternoon – Holmes worked at his desk in silence, broken only by the scratching of his pen and the occasional exclamation of "Ha!" or perhaps "Hmm..." while meanwhile I recorded such notes as I could to create a usable record of our case, as best I understood matters. Outside, the thin snow had turned to sleet and coursed bleakly down the window panes.

Abruptly, the peace and calm of our rooms was rudely shattered by a frantic tugging at the downstairs bell followed by the most frenzied hammering at the street door. "Good Lord Holmes! Now this is surely a matter of the most desperate urgency!"

Holmes leaped to his feet, his brow furrowed in concern. "I am quite certain of it Watson – hear how those boots take the stair three at a time!"

I stepped to the parlour door but even before I could grasp the handle, it burst open to admit a much-distressed, panting, and grubby Wiggins, commander-in-chief of the band of street urchins Holmes affectionately regarded as his 'Baker Street Irregulars'. Wild-eyed, he struggled to speak but was manifestly too short of breath, or too exhausted to articulate a single intelligible word for some moments; the poorly dressed urchin was clearly chilled to the bone from his long night's vigil and his ride clinging probably to the back of a cab and, I judged, also near to collapse.

Holmes gestured urgently for me to minister to the lad; I guided him gently to a seat before the fire and placed a plaid travelling rug around his shoulders as my colleague shouted down for some hot broth and a warm cordial for the shivering urchin. Presently the boy's teeth stopped chattering, the blue tinge left his lips, and after greedily gulping the broth and cordial, he blurted out his report.

"Mr 'Olmes, somefink dreadful's 'appened at the 'ouse in Chiswick! It must 'ave, 'cos there's coppers arrived, an' that Mr Lestrade as well!" ~ His voice lowered in awe ~ "an' amb'lance too!"

Holmes frowned, clearly concerned..

"Slowly, Wiggins, tell me exactly what has happened and what you saw – oh Watson, call down to the boy to have a hansom waiting! We shall be departing in moments!"

With a more kindly look he returned his attention to the boy. "Now Wiggins..?"

"Well this was the way of it Mr 'Olmes. At midnight I took over from Squinty Smith, who 'ad nothing to report 'cept that the lady come 'ome at seven o'clock and 'adn't come out of the 'ouse since then. I found myself a cosy little crib out of the rain an' sleet in a shed in garden of the empty 'ouse opposite – an' there was some old sacks to stay warm under. So I settles down wiv' a perfick view of the front door an' waits, but nothing much 'appens for a time – unless you count an old geezer coming out and throwing cinders on the path – 'til around ten in the evening, when a cab rolls up outside.

"Out steps a tall toff carryin' a bag, wiv a big bruiser an' I 'ears the toff tell the cabbie to wait. They vanishes into the 'ouse an' dashes out about an hour later pretty sharpish on account of the sleet an' rain comin' down like cats an' dogs, an' then orf they goes towards Kew and Richmond in the cab at a rare old clip. Oh, an' I fink the toff 'ad a key to the door Mr 'Olmes."

At this, Holmes' cold grey eyes narrowed menacingly – he smacked a clenched fist into his palm. "This is our man Watson, I don't doubt it!" he cried. "Can you describe him for me Wiggins?"

"Sorry Mr 'Olmes but I only glimpsed 'im for a second an' anyway he was wearing an Ulster wiv the collar up an' a big muffler. But 'e was tall an' thin an' might 'ave 'ad a 'tache."

"Did you by any chance note the cabbie's number Wiggins?" The boy rolled his eyes heavenward in scorn. "Wot do you fink I am Mr 'Olmes – one of them slow-witted bleedin' plodders from the Yard? O' course I did – 1107 is your man!" Holmes made a note and nodded in quiet satisfaction. "Very good – continue Wiggins."

"Well, nuffink much 'appens till about ten o'clock this morning, when suddenly I hears a lady scream from the alley-way down the side of the 'ouse, an' what a dreadful scream it was Mr 'Olmes, it fair made yer blood run cold! I run over the High Road and down the side-alley and there's the landlady, white as a sheet and fit to faint, staring into the basement through the window. I says 'Missus, what's the matter?' an' she chases me away before I could get a peek, but I think she must've seen somefink bad through the big window.

"She runs inside and I goes back to my crib to watch what occurs. Next thing, the bobbies and Mr Lestrade's there, an' then the amb'lance rattles up, so I grabbed on a growler quick as I could, but after that I had to jump off an' run most of the way from Marylebone."

Holmes patted the boy's shoulder, with a satisfied air. "Excellent work Wiggins; you have done well—here is your reward and a little extra besides" and he handed the lad a half-sovereign "and here's another for Squinty Smith." The poor ragged wretch's eyes became as large as saucers at this munificence. "Blimey, thanks Mr 'Olmes. Most 'andsome of you, most very 'andsome indeed!" He tied them inside a filthy kerchief and pocketed it. Holmes nodded. "Now be off with you and go back to your fellows."

The grimy little lad scurried from the room with his new-won wealth and clattered down the stair. Holmes turned and fixed me with glittering eyes. "Now Watson, are you with me, for assuredly the game is well and truly afoot!" He donned his Ulster and selected a stout, lead-weighted Penang Lawyer. I smiled "Could you doubt it Holmes?" I speedily dropped a half-a-dozen cartridges in my pocket, retrieved my revolver from the table, and we departed.

For much of the journey, my companion remained quite taciturn, his chin sunk low on his chest, his eyes closed in deep thought. I left him to his reverie.

As we passed Hammersmith he spoke at last. "I fear this does not bode well Watson; I have a dreadful presentiment about what we may discover. Let us hope that the scene has not been disturbed for while my role is not to compensate for the inadequacies of the official police, there are invariably those subtle signs which, even if missed by the police or dismissed as irrelevant, are the vital traces which may combine to bring about a successful resolution. Until a thorough scientific observation has been made, their movement, or worse complete removal, can only lead the way to uncertainty and confusion."

Presently we alighted in a thin, chill sleet at number 64 Chiswick High Road, a handsome, wide brick-built terraced property arranged over three floors. Two constables stood stamping their feet against the cold on the still-icy cinder-strewn path, talking in subdued voices at the front door while a small crowd of curious onlookers waited in the hope of seeing whatever morbid object might emerge from the house; the ambulance with doors open, quite vacant, remained with its attendants at the kerb-side. Holmes grunted in satisfaction. "That is well Watson. It would appear that whatever poor soul that requires medical attention is still within." At this moment, Inspector Lestrade emerged from the house. He started and appeared taken aback to see Sherlock Holmes.

"Well well Mr Holmes, and you too Doctor Watson; and what brings you here? There'll be no need of either of your services today – there's no mystery for you to unravel in a simple suicide Mr Holmes, for that is certainly what we have here, and unless you can revive a stone-cold corpse, Doctor, no patient for you to attend either." Proudly he declaimed "I have even discovered charred fragments of a suicide note in the hearth. You'll see them arranged in their correct order on the table where I placed them."

Holmes' brow was thunderously dark. "In which part of the house has this business occurred Lestrade, may I enquire?" The Scotland Yard detective pointed through the open front door; "Straight ahead and down a few steps – there's a sort of semi-basement that used to be a store-room by the look of it. A young woman by the name of Dulcie Hobbs rents it, or perhaps I should say, used to rent it, for she'll surely not be paying next week's."

At this news, which chillingly confirmed the terrible truth of Wiggins' report, Holmes' lean face turned pale with anger. Lestrade stared curiously at my companion. "May I enquire what your business is here in Chiswick Mr Holmes? How does it come to be that we were alerted by the landlady no more than a few hours ago, and yet you and the Doctor mysteriously appear shortly after – or will you have me to believe you were merely passing by and stopped out of sheer curiosity?"

My colleague pursed his lips and considered briefly. "No Lestrade, you are too shrewd by far to be deceived by such an improbable feint. The fact of the matter is that I am slightly acquainted with the young lady's employer, for whom I am looking into a small problem – a trivial matter and certainly beneath your attention. Would you object if I were to look inside, purely from a professional standpoint you understand?"

The little detective shrugged and replied easily "By all means Mr Holmes; I have no objection whatever but I much doubt you will find anything here to excite your unusual interests. Once I have filed my report, and the coroner has examined the body, the case will be closed. Now if you will excuse me, I have some routine arrangements to make with the constables here. I shall join you in ten or so minutes."

"That is very good of you Inspector, and I am sure you are right in all respects; oh, by the by, has anything been moved or disturbed? I do find the scene of any unusual incidence to be so much more instructive at the first viewing if all remains untouched since its occurrence."

"Beyond the obvious of entering with the landlady's key – the door was locked from the inside – checking the body for signs of life and performing a short search, there's not much in there beyond a bed, a table on a rug and two chairs, a small stationery box containing some paper and envelopes and a wardrobe – all is just as it was." Holmes nodded with satisfaction. "I am sure we shall find things just as you describe; however, it occurs to me that if the door was locked from the inside, would the key not most likely remain turned in the lock, so preventing the landlady's key from being used?"

"Not so Mr Holmes; there you are in error. When we entered we discovered the key lying on the inner passage floor, no doubt inadvertently dropped by Miss Hobbs after locking up. You will find it upon the table where I have placed it."

"Ah well, perhaps it is of no great consequence; come Watson, let us briefly examine the scene and see what we may learn." We entered into a large airy entrance hall with a highly polished wood floor. To our left were ballustraded stairs to the upper floors, while straight ahead of us were three steps down to the room where these troubling events had taken place. As I had learned to do in such circumstances, I followed in Holmes' wake, attempting where possible to follow his path unerringly that I might not risk contaminating or obliterating some faint sign or clue evident to him, but too subtle for my eyes or for my modest deductive talents to comprehend.

At the foot of the three steps Holmes examined the floorboards carefully, and ran his fingertips lightly over the smooth polished timber, muttering all the while under his breath as was invariably his habit when examining a scene of crime. Next he minutely scrutinised the brass lock-plate through his lens, then slowly pushed the door wide.

We entered into a short, gloomy inner hallway where the key had been discovered on the floor; to the left was a tiny dingy bathroom and on the right a small dimly-lit kitchen.

Ahead was a panelled and glazed half-open door to the main room, large and plain, sparsely furnished, scrupulously clean and tidy, but all in all, rather ordinary – ordinary, that is, but for a single object quite unspeakably out of place...

It was the body of Dulcie Hobbs – hanging by the neck on a rope suspended from one of the iron beams which spanned the room beneath the pitched roof.

Grotesquely, the body was slowly rotating, no doubt as a consequence of Lestrade's recent attentions. Immediately beneath the appalling entity were an overturned chair and a shallow stationery box, evidently the components of the improvised gallows platform, kicked away at the final dreadful moment.

As we entered the room the body so happened to be facing away from us; I stood transfixed in horror as it slowly completed its ghastly silent pirouette like some grotesque puppet on a string, until for a few hideous seconds it stared straight towards us, before just as slowly turning away again.

Now there are quite singular differences between the physical trauma resulting from a judicial hanging, in which the victim drops a precisely calculated distance through a trapdoor, carefully computed according to body-weight, thus effecting virtually instantaneous death through massive dislocation of the upper vertebrae and severance of the spinal cord - and self-murder by hanging, whereby the suicide excruciatingly strangles to death by slow agonising degrees - typically perhaps ten or fifteen ghastly minutes may pass before death finally occurs.

The *post-mortem* differences between the two instances are so marked as to be immediately recognisable; in the former case, the cadaver will typically exhibit a substantially normal visage, a slight elongation of the neck, with the accompanying unnatural lack of upper vertebrae rigidity that follows such a severe dislocation.

By marked contrast, a suicide by strangulation exhibits a countenance distorted in agony, darkly suffused with blood, eyes bulging wide, and a swollen tongue protruding to an extreme degree, resulting from a long, slow and painful throttling.

It was certainly the latter which confronted us that gloomy winter afternoon, and as a medical man having viewed examples of both types of cadavers *post-mortem*, I had no doubt in my mind that this was a suicide by strangling.

I doubted that there was much more to be learned in this sad room beyond that which Lestrade had already gleaned, except perhaps for the unfortunate woman's motive.

"Good God Holmes – whatever the woman's past sins and errors, what manner of desperate circumstances could possibly have driven her to take her own life in such horrid a way?"

Holmes made no reply, but gestured for me to remain at the doorway; slowly, almost balletically, he walked the perimeter of the room minutely examining the three large casement windows, the small fireplace, the wardrobe and its meagre contents; on a brass hook upon the wall hung an overcoat, which Holmes felt with his fingertips; next he explored the heavy mahogany table, the key thereupon at some length with his lens, the few papers lying there, and then with his back to me, the mean little bed. I was amazed that he yet appeared to pay little or no regard to the most grotesque occupant of the room – still almost imperceptibly moving as if reluctant to relinquish the last signs of life.

"Surely Holmes there is little more to be learned here except..." Like an owl, without moving his torso, he rotated his head almost half around in an instant and placed one finger to his lips. Gravely he said "You could not be further from the truth Watson; there is *everything* to be learned here!" Meticulously he examined the rest of the room, particularly the wood floor between the door and the table, until finally he went to gaze up at the now, mercifully, immobile body.

After minutely scrutinising the hands and the feet – where he took particular notice of the soles of the shoes – he positioned a chair close to the awful object and stepped up, from which elevated viewpoint – he being over six feet in height – made the closest and most microscopic examination with his lens of the face and neck, paying particular regard to the gaping mouth and distended tongue, or so it seemed to me. Using his Penang Lawyer, he appeared to take approximate measurements of the body and the rope, and the gap between the feet and the wooden floor.

Frowning, he leapt down and darted directly to a far dark corner of the room where he examined closely a red woollen scarf apparently discarded on the floor and hitherto unnoticed by me. With a single sharp ejaculation "Aha!" he straightened and then, with no heed for his attire, kneeled among the cold ashes in the small fireplace and proceeded to rake through them minutely with his bony fingers, winnowing out fragments of ash and other charred detritus which appeared much to interest him, then laid them carefully within his folded white kerchief.

Finally, he peered up the chimney flue, then turned and beckoned me to join him at the table where

Lestrade had arranged some small scraps alongside the key from the entrance hall floor. "What do you make of that Watson?" He passed me his lens and I scrutinised the scorched fragments as arranged by Lestrade, some almost illegible. With some difficulty I made out:

```
I HAVE    HAD      ENOUGH
A HUN     CHASES M
END       MY LIFE  NOW
DULC      OBBS
```

"Good Lord above Holmes! It certainly looks like a suicide note does it not? I can decipher most of it but what of this 'A HUN CHASES M' – surely that 'M' must have been 'ME'!" Or might it perhaps have been... MORIARTY?" And then it struck me! " 'A HUN' – Bormanstein? Or von Huntziger – surely it must be one of the pair Holmes? And 'DULC' 'OBBS' is without a doubt the remains of her signature!"

He snorted with derision; "My considered view is that the fragments – a small selection only from those available – there are more in the grate, reference neither of your 'Huns'.

"I quite agree that when these selected scraps are organised thus they perhaps appear to be the last tragic words of a desperate suicide, but consider Watson what, commonly, is the intended purpose of a suicide's note?

"Surely you would agree it is intended to announce to an uncaring world the troubled reasoning behind your sad decision to quit this life in total anguish – a last defiant, angry or despairing statement before taking the desperate, final step into eternal oblivion?" I nodded my assent.

"If so, then pray tell me why someone would trouble to write such an anguished note, only to destroy it before committing to the final act?" I was unable to answer. "And what of this Watson?"

He passed me one of the papers from the table; it appeared to be a short letter from the dead woman to one Molly Hobbs, resident in Brightlingsea. "Read it aloud if you will Watson." The script was not lengthy:

Chiswick, London W

My Dearest Moll,
How much I look forward to seeing you next week dear sister! I have obtained six whole days of leave from my employers, so meet me at the railway station at eleven o'clock on Saturday next and we shall go for gin and water at The Queen's Arms! What a grand time of it we shall have! Be sure to dress up for the most elegant swells! Afterwards we shall have the finest jellied eels and mash with plenty of liquor!

And as a particular delight I shall treat us both to pretty new bonnets at Hopgoods the milliners, as I expect to be in funds by then to the sum of one hundred pounds! Can you

imagine my dearest Sis - I believe I have never seen so large a sum of money in my life!
   Your loving sister
   Dulce

PS: My best duty to Mum

Holmes raised his eyebrows and fixed me with an inquisitorial look. "Construe, if you please, Watson."

"I surmise that notwithstanding its cheery tenor, and the optimistic anticipation of somehow coming into a large sum of funds, this unsent letter clearly proves that within hours of writing it some devastating news arrived, or some event must have occurred after she wrote this Holmes, and before she could post it; something so terrifying that she felt compelled to take her own life?"

There was a silence for some moments. Holmes looked up from picking through the scraps of detritus he had gathered in his kerchief.

"Masterly my dear Watson! Quite brilliant; you surpass yourself to the very highest degree." I basked momentarily in this unaccustomed praise, which helped to take a little of the sting out of some of his more acerbic comments upon my earnest endeavours to record his cases. My pleasure was to be short-lived. After a brief pause, he resumed.

"Indeed, I do believe that had you not so excelled in the medical profession, I declare that you might well have enjoyed a career at the Yard as lamentably undistinguished as that of the blundering Lestrade!

"No, do not look so downcast old friend, but exactly like the meticulous though unimaginative Lestrade outside, even now planning to write a confident report of a suicide you and he, as have I, have seen everything necessary to deduce what truly occurred in this room sometime between ten last night and, most likely, eleven o'clock at the latest, yet you have both signally failed at the last hurdle – that critical final leap of simple scientific deduction. You, like he, have committed that most cardinal of sins by shaping the significance of the evidence to fit with the apparently obvious end-result, now hanging there before us. However, that she died on a gibbet of her own devising beggars belief, and flies in the face of all the evidence and all reason!

"With a few words I might easily set Lestrade upon the right trail, but as yet I dare not, because such intelligence would alert him to our quarry, and hence directly to this most sensitive investigation."

I protested "But surely Holmes, the fragments of the suicide note, the cheery letter so soon rescinded by her decision to end her life, the door being locked from within, there is no sign of forced entry, this must..."

Holmes raised his hand to still my remonstrance. "Swiftly now, Watson, we have little time, for Lestrade will certainly return shortly. Allow me to present you with proof positive that this is no suicide, but a cold-blooded execution!

"Estimate for me if you will the height of the wretched young lady yonder."

"Quite short – perhaps around five feet and an inch or perhaps two inches at most?"

"Just so – I estimate five feet plus two inches. Now approximate the distance between the soles of her shoes and the floor below."

"I judge it to be a shade over three feet three inches."

"Excellent; I would guess about the same. Now assess the height from the beam to the floor."

I glanced up. "A shade under eleven feet I imagine?" He nodded. "And the length of the rope?"

"I should say two and a half feet?"

"Splendid Watson! You appear to have an assured eye for dimension. Quickly now; the overturned chair and stationery box we may assume to have been the step which she ascended, then put her head in the noose, and finally kicked over the improvised gallows platform – you would agree? Yes?

"Then do me the goodness of placing the box upon the upright chair, and the whole beneath the feet." In a low murmur he added "*Res ipsa loquitur.*"

Even as I complied, my entire being reeled in horrified disbelief.

It was manifestly and shockingly plain that the woman, had she climbed upon the makeshift gallows platform, could never have put her head in the noose unaided; the mathematics lacked a full eighteen inches!

No more could she have tied the rope to the beam, for there was no sign of a set of steps in the rooms. As Holmes had told me so many times:

"When you have eliminated the impossible then whatever remains, however improbable, must be the truth." Yet the inevitable, the only remaining alternative was surely too appalling to contemplate... she could only have been forcibly lifted up by other hands and hanged, murdered – by the late-night visitors? I looked at holmes, aghast.

"I see you now perceive the problem inherent in your suicide theory, Watson. You see for yourself the diminutive stature of the woman. To commit self-murder she would have to reach up for the noose and by main strength, lift herself up, at which point her feet would be perhaps one and a half feet off the gallows platform. Having hanged herself, are we to believe that the chair and stationery box then obligingly fell over?" I acknowledged the irrefutable logic of his words.

"Now work swiftly if you please Watson. Do me the service of copying these fragments and phrases here upon the table into your pocket book, along with these which Lestrade inexplicably missed in the fire-grate, that we may leave the evidence as we found it for the police, though I doubt much they will derive any benefit from it. Oh, observe here this slightly charred length of slim wooden dowel; he sniffed one end of it. "Gum Arabic I believe" then made no further comment.

"Now Watson, before we quit this dismal scene, you might perhaps perceive some small significance in the lengths of charred and knotted twine in the grate, the odd circumstance of the key being found on the floor in the entrance hall, the red woollen scarf incongruously and carelessly thrown in that dark corner, so far from both the door, the coat-hook and the wardrobe, further the new position of the table on the rug, and finally the faint cindery footmarks on the table-top. I believe that is all that we may remark here; small details to be sure, but together, they speak to me as eloquently of what occurred here last night just as surely as I had in my hand a detailed, confession from the killers, lacking only their signatures!

"And now let us step outside and speak with the landlady, for it was she who first discovered and reported the crime."

We encountered the lady in question, a small, neat, fidgety middle-aged woman with greying hair drawn back in a severe bun, pacing nervously up and down the entrance hall, restlessly twisting and untwisting her pinafore ties. Holmes greeted her with a disarming smile.

"I imagine you would be the landlady of this fine establishment Mrs...?"

"Mrs Rose Smith sir and you are...?"

"Ah yes, I am Sherlock Holmes madam and this is my associate, Doctor John Watson." At this her eyes widened in amazement. "The same Sherlock Holmes whose thrilling adventures I read in The Strand Magazine? My goodness, I shall love to see the look on my Bert's face when I tell him I have met the great Sherlock Holmes!"

I swear that she made as if to curtsey. Holmes flashed a tiny, impatient smile. "You are very kind madam; as you may know, I have some small experience in these doleful matters. I am present today with the full approval of the very able Inspector Lestrade outside. Please be good enough to tell me how you came to discover the sad circumstances we now find?"

"Well it was this way Mr Holmes. About ten this morning I took some scraps out for the cat, Mr Dickens, as I do each day. I feed him in the little side alleyway on account of him being so nervous and it's always quiet along there. One side of it is bounded by a plain brick wall and the other is the side of this house, and Miss Hobbs' rooms; there are no curtains in her window, as passers-by can't see in anyway.

"As I returned to the back door I glanced in ~ Miss Hobbs often gives me a cheery wave but at first she seemed not to be at home. Something made me stop and look closer; I thought I saw something moving, high up. It was quite gloomy within so I approached the window and peered more closely.

"You may imagine my fright Mr Holmes, when I realised it was a pair of legs!

"I could not see the upper part of the body on account of it being too high up and out of my view, but it was obviously Miss Hobbs.

"I believe I may have screamed, because a pinched little street urchin appeared from nowhere, to ask me what was wrong, but I chased him off as I thought this not a fit sight for a child. Then I sent my daughter Margaret to the station to alert the police. I durstn't enter her rooms. And that's all I can say."

"That is very helpful Mrs Smith. Tell me if you will, did you speak with Miss Hobbs when she arrived home last night? How did she appear to you?"

"Oh, I always have a little chat with her, for she is my only tenant at present, although I have rooms for five; she was in the very best of spirits Mr Holmes, most cheerful as she had obtained permission for a few days of holiday leave from her employers. She told me of her plans to visit her sister in Brightlingsea shortly, and she was most excited and much anticipating it. Then she bid me goodnight, entered her rooms and locked her door. I always tell my young ladies to leave the key turned in the lock for safety" At this, Holmes shot me a meaningful look.

"Very wise; two final questions, if I may impose a little longer Mrs Smith; when did Miss Hobbs first contract to rent the rooms?"

"It was only last month in November, Mr Holmes, but it was not she who rented them; it was her guardian on her behalf, a Mr Bormanstein; very plainly he doted on her – said she was the apple of his eye. Very handsomely he paid me two months' rent in advance. He said that the rooms were most conveniently placed for his ward's new position in Richmond. He required keys for both for himself and his ward."

Holmes nodded, as if this rather startling information came as no great surprise to him. "I am sure that in your line of business Mrs Smith, you have cultivated a sharp eye for a face, and I expect you are pretty handy at assessing the character of a prospective tenant; tell me, what manner of a man was Mr Bormanstein?"

"Oh, he was very much a proper gentleman Mr Holmes, no doubt about it. He was of middle-age, tall and muscular with a moustache, polite and very smartly dressed – a businessman I should imagine. Apart from maybe a slight foreign accent, very faint you understand, I noticed his eyes were rather strange; when he fixed you, you almost felt as if you dared not look away." This of course, matched precisely the description supplied to Holmes by the honest locksmith, MacFadzean, and the shadier Hawes.

"Thank you; and finally, can you recall when the ashes were first strewed upon the front path?"

With an air of puzzlement the landlady replied "Indeed I can Mr Holmes. Miss Hobbs mentioned as she came in last night that the wet sleet and snow on the path was again freezing hard and was becoming wickedly treacherous under-foot, so when Albert – that's my husband – came back at nine o'clock from the Dog and Rose, he immediately scattered some cinders. That's why I placed that old cocoanut matting at the door and you can be sure that I made Mr Lestrade clean his shoes very thoroughly. I'm most particular about the hall floor – I polished it only this morning." Holmes nodded with evident satisfaction. "Indeed, and it does you great credit. Did you observe anything else out of the ordinary – any visitors for example?"

"There was only one Mr Holmes – well, two really; about ten o'clock I heard the front door open and as Bert was already home I thought perhaps Miss Hobbs was going out; I peered down the stairs but it was only Mr Bormanstein and another gentleman visiting Miss Hobbs so I thought no more of it." Holmes frowned; "Did you greet Mr Bormanstein – was he aware that you saw him arrive? And would you recognise the other gentleman if you saw him again? It may be important."

"No I did not call down Mr Holmes, and I am certain he did not see me." Holmes appeared extremely relieved at this news. "As to Mr Bormanstein's companion, I would certainly recognise him again – he was a very large, heavily-built man and he had a most pronounced squint. I then went quietly back to my room."

"Thank you Mrs Smith. You have been most helpful; I believe I need not detain you any longer – I bid you good afternoon."

Outside the house once again, we encountered Lestrade together with the ambulance men crunching back over the cinder-strewn path, bearing a stretcher and a funereal black sheet. "Ah, there you are again Mr Holmes; I suppose you have seen everything? I'm sure you agree with me that this is no more than a sad but nonetheless rather straightforward business?"

Holmes made a noise something between a snort and a chuckle. "Indeed Inspector, certainly I have seen everything. And like you, I also am now quite confident of the circumstances surrounding the unfortunate young woman's death."

At this, Lestrade paused thoughtfully, and his eyes narrowed cynically as he asked "Do you then propose a different explanation Mr Holmes – if so I would be much fascinated to hear what fanciful alternative you might propose to explain away the simple fact of a solitary young woman discovered quite alone, hanged, in her own locked rooms, key within and no signs of intrusion, with the obvious remains of a suicide note not ten feet away from her dead body? I will own that on occasion your eccentric theories have been of minor assistance to the force, but perhaps in this open and shut case might you not be conjuring up imaginary ghosts where none exist."

My colleague shrugged almost imperceptibly and smiled genially at the Inspector. "Perhaps you are right Lestrade, perhaps you are right. Well, I'm sure you have your report to complete so I shall bid you good day." We turned to leave and were almost at the pavement when Holmes spun and called back.

"Oh, Lestrade, you might perhaps with some small advantage take note of a few instructive items in the young woman's room, or so they seem to my fanciful mind.

"I would commend to your particular attention the burnt twine, the charred stick, some additional paper fragments in the grate, and the red scarf rather oddly thrown in the far dark corner which mayhap you overlooked; further, the stature of the unfortunate lady concerned and particularly the condition of her mouth; too, the positioning of the table and the state of her shoes, most of which I am sure you have already noted. They may have some small relevance. However, I expect you will work your way and I shall work mine.

"Incidentally, have you noticed how these wet cinders adhere to the soles of your boots Lestrade? Most annoying would you not agree?" Puzzled, Lestrade smirked back from the doorstep and said witheringly:

"You know Mr Holmes, if only you would learn simply to see what's before your eyes, you might one day have the makings of a tolerable detective." A thin, smile flickered briefly over Holmes' pale gaunt face. Drily he replied "Indeed Lestrade. And perhaps, one day, so too, might you."

With this he turned and strode to the kerbside, leaving the baffled Inspector standing at the front door. I whistled a passing hansom and we were soon well on our way back into the metropolis.

As on our outward journey, Holmes remained stubbornly taciturn and deep in contemplation, dismissing all my comments with a peremptory grunt or an impatient hand-gesture, until we were once again seated before the fire at 221B Baker Street.

Silence reigned for some few minutes, when abruptly Holmes cried "It's broken, Watson! The chain is broken!" I looked up at him quizzically. "Don't you see, the Hobbs woman was our only link in the chain to Bormanstein? Mark my words Watson; this villain's game is indeed deep!

"Intimidation is the glue that holds his evil enterprise together, and now we can be sure that he will not shrink even from cold-blooded murder if someone like the foolish and greedy Dulcie Hobbs is rash enough to meddle in his affairs.

"But that you may understand the perils of the dark and dangerous labyrinth we have entered, you must be fully aware of the events which I am certain occurred in Chiswick late last night." I gestured encouragingly for him to continue, for while I had followed some of his deductions, I was by no means entirely clear about some of his more obscure leaps of logic.

I recalled Holmes' words to Petch: *'...it is my craft to deduce backwards, eliminating in due order of time and circumstance, all those explanations which will not serve, until at last I arrive inescapably at the only one, no matter how improbable, which will. You may view this as the scrupulous reconstruction, through observation and deduction, of times and events now passed.'*

However, it seemed I would have to be patient a little longer...

"But first things first Watson, it is essential that I solve a small but vital conundrum. Be so good as to hand me the page of fragments from your pocket-book." I tore out the requisite leaf and passed it to him, whereupon he took it to his desk and proceeded to snip the page into small pieces, which he spread upon a blank sheet of writing paper. Once again silence reigned in the cosy parlour for perhaps an hour or more, while Holmes was deeply engrossed in positioning and repositioning the scraps of paper, punctuating his deliberations with small grunts of exasperation, and occasionally of approval.

* * *

At length he sighed contentedly, leaned back in his chair, skeletal white fingers laced behind his head and gazed up at the ceiling with a small smile of satisfaction. I waited expectantly for the revelations that were without doubt imminent.

"You know Watson, in all the years I have spent plumbing the infinite depths of man's iniquity to man, I have never ceased to marvel at the unfailing and predictable superficiality of his intellectual processes, which failing leads inevitably to incompetent observation, unscientific or even non-existent deduction, and ultimately to a flawed conclusion!

"Such, my dear Watson, is the charge I would lay at the door of the industrious, well-intentioned but sadly, somewhat inept Lestrade.

"Consider, he receives a report that a young woman has hanged herself in her rooms in Chiswick; from this point on he is more or less settled on his conclusions. Upon his arrival he finds the door locked from within, a solitary young woman hanging from a beam, no apparent signs of entry – already his case is almost proven. And yet it is the most capital of mistakes to form a conclusion without the benefit of the available evidence.

"Now further imagine his exquisite satisfaction when he retrieves a few charred scraps of paper from among many hidden in the cold ashes, and without thought or hesitation he triumphantly arranges them to form a fragmentary suicide note which tidily but quite erroneously confirms the circumstances he believes he perceives. *Et voila* - his case is complete!

"In short, he chooses selectively from the available facts to support the conclusion he sees – the surest way to err in any scientific observation.

"I, by contrast, observe, analyse and then deduce from all the evidence without bias, that it may freely tell its tale. And if that tale is incontrovertibly and unambiguously one of murder and not of suicide, even though at apparent variance with the perceived circumstances, why, then it must be the truth.

"The evidence therefore defines the crime, and not *vice versa*."

I winced ruefully at Holmes' excoriating appraisal of Lestrade's ability, and by inference, mine too, for initially I also had reached the same conclusion as the Scotland Yarder.

"Let me now relate you to within a whisker, precisely what occurred in Chiswick, Watson. At around ten o'clock, Bormanstein or whatever his real name, arrived by hansom along with his rather muscular wall-eyed support. Bormanstein tells the cabbie to wait, as they know their brutal business will not be over-long in completing.

"They walked up the newly cinder-strewn path and entered using the keys Bormanstein has already procured for himself from Mrs Smith. Note the weather now - rain and sleet.

"They crossed the hall to Dulcie Hobbs' door, leaving faint damp footprints of cinder ash upon the floor – which Mrs Smith scrupulously cleaned the following morning but she did not polish the steps down to Hobbs' rooms, thus the prints which I discovered outside her door, and inside her room.

"Bormanstein stealthily attempted to enter using his key but is defeated by Hobbs' key being already in the lock, but he is prepared for this eventuality. Taking from his pocket a slim wooden dowel – the same I found charred in the fire-grate, he applied a bead of glutinous gum Arabic to its tip, inserted it in the lock and, engaging the end of the other key, carefully and silently rotated it until it could be pushed out of the lock, whereupon it fell softly onto the small mat below; this is where Lestrade later found it. Lestrade missed the distinctive traces of gum Arabic left on its tip and on the escutcheon-plate.

"Bormanstein unlocked the door, entered silently, and then relocked it with his own key from the inside for he has desperate and exceedingly private business at hand. He found her lying on, but not in the bed, most likely dozing or asleep; he confronted Hobbs with the blackmail demand that she had sent him."

My bewilderment must have showed, for this was the first I had heard of such a note.

Exasperatedly Holmes cried "The fragments in the fireplace Watson! They were no more a suicide note than they were a laundry list or a sonnet by Shakespeare!

"It is my certain conviction that they were the charred remains of a blackmail demand. Step over here and see if you think I have solved the rest of our word puzzle." I peered over Holmes' shoulder and examined the fragmentary words he had assembled upon his desktop though what I saw seemed even less illuminating than Lestrade's presumed suicide note:

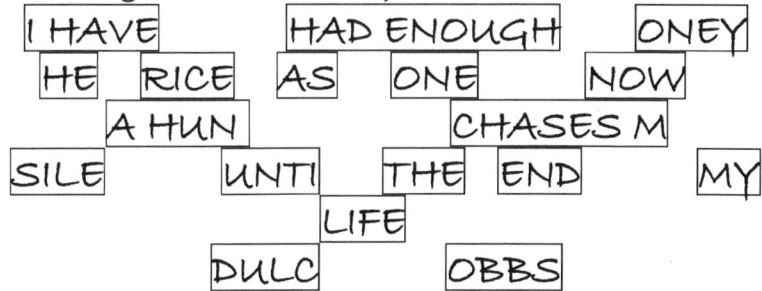

```
I HAVE    HAD ENOUGH    ONEY
HE  RICE  AS  ONE       NOW
    A HUN      CHASES M
SILE    UNTI  THE  END      MY
            LIFE
      DULC        OBBS
```

I noted that Holmes had re-ordered the fragments retrieved by Lestrade, and inserted several further pieces, although why he had placed the whole in this particular sequence was still a mystery to me. Holmes chuckled at my evident confusion. "Consider the first three fragments Watson, and tell me what they might originally have said."

"Well, 'ONEY' could only be 'HONEY' or 'BONEY' or... 'MONEY'? But who would say 'I have had *enough honey*, or stranger still, *enough money*? And what is this reference to 'RICE'? The other fragments I can make nothing of." Holmes reached for a soft lead pencil and boldly scrawled in some additional characters between the fragments.

"No doubt some minor parts were entirely consumed, but I believe this represents the spirit of the original note when it was written." I re-examined the page with his additions...

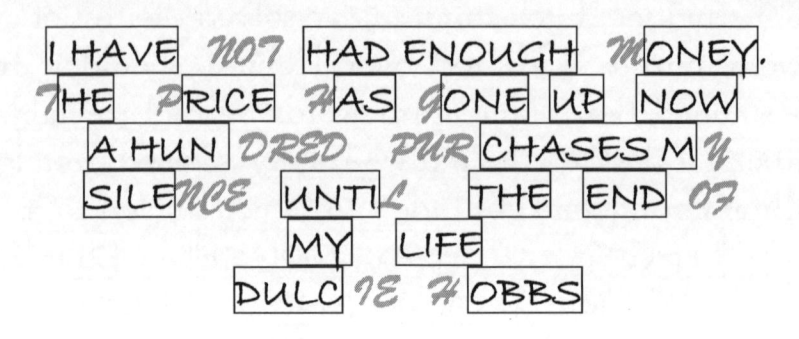

I HAVE NOT HAD ENOUGH MONEY.
THE PRICE HAS GONE UP NOW
A HUNDRED PURCHASES MY
SILENCE UNTIL THE END OF
MY LIFE
DULCIE HOBBS

"I suggest, Watson, that this reconstruction, or something very close to it, explains events rather more logically than Lestrade's presumed suicide theory. It explains the nonsense of writing a suicide note, then promptly incinerating it, which appears to strike Lestrade as not in the least bit strange. It further clarifies the odd notion that someone should write in such cheerful and optimistic vein to their sister one day, send their affectionate respects to their mother and then take their own life the very next evening! It also explains the oblique reference to her anticipating imminent funds to the tune of £100. Which finally provides a most compelling motive for Bormanstein's need to silence her.

"The ambitious but imprudent woman thought to sell her silence for an additional £100, but Bormanstein guaranteed it for the trivial cost of a length of hempen rope! It was a most reckless and foolish move on Hobbs' part to threaten such a dangerous man, for her job was already done, she had become expendable, and he would certainly not tolerate a mere foot-soldier jeopardising his entire elaborate operation in which he has already invested significant time and resources and doubtless, not inconsiderable financial disbursement.

"He would also be perfectly aware that blackmailers are rarely satisfied by a single payment; inevitably, further and larger ones would follow the first successful demand.

"And thus he sought to conceal her callous execution with the subterfuge of an elaborately staged suicide, which illusion Lestrade immediately accepted, but it does not serve; it does not serve in the least part at all!

"And in passing Watson, you might pause to consider just how many criminals we have traced, even seized, in some manner of close association with the female of the species.

"And the best proof of this may be had at Scotland Yard any day, where if you ask whichever officer of the establishment how they take most villains, he will tell you - *at the houses of the women*. And thus we draw closer."

I listened enthralled but chilled, as Holmes revealed the cold, inexorable steps of logic that underpinned his deductions and the more he spoke, the more credible became his explanation, and the more ludicrously improbable appeared Lestrade's (and my own!) hasty conclusion.

He continued. "From this point, events moved rapidly. Perhaps Hobbs pleaded for her life; if so it was surely to no avail. Her time on earth was already as good as ended; Bormanstein is decided upon his plan of action – for he has come prepared with a hangman's rope, and twine to secure her hands and wrists.

"One of them, probably the wall-eyed bruiser, seized Hobbs. To prevent her screaming they cast around for something with which to gag her. They espied her still damp overcoat and scarf hanging neatly and logically to dry on a hook by the wardrobe. The red woollen scarf was swiftly stuffed in her mouth – hence the red wool fibres I discovered upon her lips, tongue, and deep within her throat.

"While one of them secured her wrists and ankles with strong twine to thwart her struggles – this the cause of the chafing which I noted but which was missed by Lestrade – the other moved the heavy mahogany table from the rug to a position under the beam. Climbing thereon, and leaving several cinder-smudged footprints, he was then able to reach up to the beam and tie on the prepared gallows noose.

"The table was then replaced, but not precisely as it was – hence the four deep impressions which I observed now revealed in the thick carpet – not by itself conclusive, but nonetheless suggestive.

"The terrified woman now had mere minutes to live, and she must surely have comprehended the awful means of her end, for she would have observed these measured preparations being made for her heartless, coolly-calculated and cold-blooded elimination."

It may be because such gruesome matters are his routine stock-in-trade, or perhaps because he has become inured through years of plumbing the limitless depths of human evil, or perhaps his mathematically logical mind precludes any personal or emotional response to the shocking findings of his own deductions, but regardless, Holmes delivered his chilling narrative as clinically and dispassionately as if he were reading aloud a passage from a learned paper on some aspect of forensic science.

"And now there is little more to tell, Watson. They callously lifted the gagged and bound woman up, inserted her head in the noose, and then they stood back and waited.

"Indeed so composed were they that one of the pair enjoyed a small cigar while they waited for her agonised death throes to subside – I discovered a stub and three separate and distinctive ashes from an unusual cigar of Indian manufacture on the hearthstone. The cigar I find noteworthy for its country of origin.

"At length Hobbs' agonised death-throes turned to spasmodic twitches, then finally she expired – it is time to dress the stage, but it was also now that fatal blunders were committed. Our foe was cunning, but not astute enough to deceive me. The scarf was extracted from the dead woman's mouth, but instead of being replaced upon the hook, for some inexplicable reason – perhaps of haste or guilty concealment – it was carelessly thrown into a dark corner, illogically far from the door and the wardrobe, and quite at variance with the extreme tidiness of the rest of the room and the orderly neatness of the wardrobe.

"An upturned chair and the tumbled stationery box were placed beneath the victim's feet, but no-one troubled to check that the two combined would have been tall enough for her feasibly to have committed suicide unaided. Finally, the bindings were removed from the body and thrown with the gum-Arabic dipped dowel into the still glowing embers of the cooling fire, along with the now redundant blackmail note, where they started to smoulder; satisfied with their work Bormanstein and his thug left the room and headed for the outer door.

"Unnoticed by them the fire was even then dying fast and they would have done better had they applied a match to the note, for now the rain and sleet outside intensifies – you may recall I peered up the flue? As I expected, it follows a straight vertical path and there lacks a cowl on the chimney pot, which allows heavy rain to fall straight onto the fire. And thus the increasingly rain-spattered paper charred, but only slowly, leaving legible fragments; the twine merely scorched, the sleet and rain became heavier still and the fire was finally extinguished. Bormanstein had not, as he confidently supposed, destroyed the last piece of evidence linking him to Hobbs.

"Instead, sufficient fragments remained to bamboozle the official authorities – rarely a challenging task I suggest – but certainly enough for us to deduce and, I venture, prove a somewhat more credible state of affairs. As they quit the rooms, they encountered a final dilemma.

"In order to simulate a convincing suicide, the door must clearly appear to have been locked from the inside. They could not use Hobbs' key upon leaving as this would leave the room secured but with no sign of a key within. Nor could they lock the door from within and depart the scene by another exit. Thus they left Hobbs' key where it lay upon the mat, and the door was secured from the outside with Bormanstein's duplicate.

"They then departed around eleven o'clock in the waiting hansom, exactly as reported by young Wiggins. Our task now is to discover their final destination."

"Bravo Holmes! I declare you have quite amazed me! My estimation of your abilities is doubtless of little importance to you, but I would own that this is unquestionably one of the most skilful examples of your craft I have observed in some time!" He permitted himself a small smile of pride; to my surprise he seemed indeed pleased at my appraisal, but in truth, I know he is never more content than when delivering one of his bravura displays of deduction to an admiring audience.

"It is not of itself a remarkable, singular or even great ability, Watson, but perhaps I may claim for myself, it is a unique talent. My eyes observe – as do yours; my brain freely deduces, and then my usually faithful cranial partner dependably presents me with the only feasible conclusion.

"It is the way I am made. It functions with the same logic as does a common sieve. Throw all the facts, obvious and subtle, within and agitate; the most evident, and eagerly seized upon by the slowest dullard, remain within the sieve, but the small particulates of understanding – missed by most – drift through the fine mesh of observation. For me, it is among those carelessly overlooked motes that may be found the answers.

"And now Watson, there is little more constructive that we may achieve today. I have dispatched the boy in buttons with a note to see if we can discover the identity of the cabbie who conveyed our villains to and from the murder scene, for he may be our last link in the chain to Bormanstein, – but for now we await his return. I expect Mrs Hudson will bring us some supper shortly; meanwhile old friend, do me the kindness of handing me my violin."

Later I retired to my room, to the soaring strains of a Haydn violin concerto...

*   *   *

Chapter Nine

THE FIRST PROOF

I arose early next morning, quite unable to remain longer abed after a horrid, restive night spent plagued with hideous visions of the agonised and livid countenance of the murdered woman in Chiswick.

In the parlour Mrs Hudson had already made up a cheery, blazing fire and was laying a sizeable breakfast out upon the starched linen. From beneath the silver covers issued the savoury aroma of kedgeree and crisp bacon, and the fragrance of fresh coffee and hot toast filled the cosy room, lifting my low spirits but little.

After a few minutes Holmes entered the room, fresh from his toilet. "Aha! Another early bird ~ my ever-dependable Watson! I feel that if we are to resume the hunt for our early worm, we should fortify ourselves ~ I very much hope for a lively and industrious day ahead.

"But come, my dear fellow, you seem somewhat low this morning. For what reason?" He heaped kedgeree generously upon his plate and poured coffee for us both.

I shrugged apologetically. "Oh, you will probably think this pretty poor stuff Holmes, but I spent a most disagreeable night of dreams, in which that poor foolish woman's awful discoloured face was slowly rotating back and forth, her bulging eyes seemingly appealing to me for justice and vengeance; I imagine that with my medical training and my warm times in Afghanistan, you suppose me to be quite hardened to such sights; I realised this morning however, just how very deeply I was affected by the awful events that occurred in that room of horrors.

"You, by contrast, appear to be utterly unaffected by such appalling proceedings, and coldly related the whole horrifying account as if you were describing a lunch with your brother at The Diogenes Club. I suppose I may simply conclude that I am a weaker man made of ordinary flesh, blood and emotion, though sometimes I wonder if you are not become something strangely other – a cool and calculating machine, quite indifferent to human tragedy, taking pleasure solely in your cerebral struggle with the forces of evil."

At my words Holmes became still, a fork of kedgeree halfway to his mouth.

He set it slowly back to his plate, a sombre and deeply thoughtful look upon his angular features.

Abruptly he assumed an altogether more kindly and benevolent aspect and he reached across the small dining table to lay a strong, sinewy hand on my shoulder. "You gravely misapprehend both yourself and, I fear, me also old friend. You are by no means the weaker man, and by a country mile too! As my only, my chosen, companion on our strange adventures you consistently demonstrate the most valuable and admirable of qualities. It is simply that they somewhat differ from mine, yet they are quite indispensable and perfectly compatible.

"I rate your bravery, dependability, loyalty and steadfastness as being of the very highest order; indeed no man could want for higher. As to your sensitivity to the suffering of individuals, it is utterly commendable, it is the hallmark of your innate decent nature and compassion ~ all those fine qualities which have led you to the most caring of professions ~ that of medicine."

He paused. A mischievous twinkle danced in his eyes. "Why, Watson, even your modest attempts at chronicling our investigations together have come on quite splendidly ~ some are even pretty stylish, and indeed I believe one day the adventures of Sherlock Holmes and Doctor Watson may become classic chronicles of criminal investigation which will be studied and enjoyed for a hundred years and perhaps more!

"Your words will likely outlive us both."

At this flattering but wholly improbable and ludicrous notion I laughed aloud; but still I realised that my friend, with his light-hearted but deeply sincere words, had lifted my low spirits quite immeasurably.

Much cheered, I helped myself to a breakfast of Olympian proportions, and attacked it with a will, while Holmes looked on with an air of benign amusement.

"Now that's more the old trencherman I know, but still I leave one of your points unattended; you observed, I believe, that I *appear to be utterly unaffected by such appalling proceedings.*

"Your comment is important, and worthy of some punctilious debate; inasmuch as I may *appear* to be unaffected, you are quite correct in your observation, but to believe that I am indifferent to individual human torment would be to err gravely indeed.

"If I seem detached and dispassionate in the matter of the foolish young woman's terrible end it is, do you see, Watson, *because I must be!*

"Were I to sublimate even the least fraction of my concentration into emotional concern for an incidental victim of Bormanstein's evil plan, I would surely start to erode any small advantage I may possess. Remember, he has now demonstrated that he will exterminate his enemies mercilessly and without compunction, and thus it is no longer a mere game that is afoot – it is a veritable battle that has been joined! Comparisons may be odious, yet I, perhaps like our own noble Lord Wellington, may not pause even for the briefest of moments in the heat of battle merely to grieve over a single tragic death or even a thousand, and thereby risk losing my initiative!

"And while Old Nosey may publicly have declared his men to be 'the scum of the earth', inwardly he cared most deeply for their welfare, and they in turn, willingly fought and died for love of him.

"Only when the battle of Waterloo was finally won at the cost of incalculable pain, suffering and loss of human life, and the ambitious Boney vanquished for good, did the great man allow his true feelings free reign.

"I believe I quote him more or less aright when he surveyed the battlefield and the awful results of the bloody clash between two military titans; sorrowfully he commented *'Next to a battle lost, the saddest thing is a battle won.'*

"You see, Watson, *his* butcher's bill surpassed many thousands and mine is yet but one. And so I would beg you to reserve your judgement of me until the day we survey our own final battlefield."

Never before had I heard my famously private and guarded friend speak so candidly of his innermost emotions, and I was much touched and affected to be the confidant of these unusually intimate revelations.

Then, almost as if he were embarrassed by his own candour, he abruptly turned the conversation in a more business-like direction.

"Now, today I have great expectations, having last night instructed the boy Billy to visit the cabstand in Marylebone and enquire the identity of the cabman who carried our killers to Chiswick last night, and rather more importantly, where they later alighted. I would expect the fellow to appear at any moment."

At that instant we heard the distinctive sound of a hansom rumbling to a halt below our window.

"Hulloa!" he cried, peering down into the street below. "Yes, I do believe that is he as we speak. But hold! No I speak too soon, for the cabman is still atop, whipping up and departing!"

Footsteps pounded raggedly up the stairs and the door crashed violently open to admit not a London cabman, but another, now-familiar figure. He looked pinched and haggard, and appeared to me to be even gaunter than when we first met him, if such were possible.

For the second time in as many days we had received a caller close to collapse. He stood swaying in the doorway, one hand clawing weakly at his thin heaving chest, gasping hoarsely like a landed fish, eyes wide with panic, and stared clear through us with a hysterical, glassy look. His clothes were shamefully awry, his toilet sorely neglected for he had not shaved nor combed his hair since rising, and he lacked a spat on his unlaced left boot.

Had I not known him for who he was, and recognised the evident quality of his attire, I would surely have taken him for some unfortunate, bewildered and be-whiskered tramp, clad in discarded clothes benevolently donated to him by some charitable gentleman. It was Mr Henry Petch.

My duty as a physician was immediately evident; he required the most urgent assistance. Even as I made to aid him, he sagged to his knees, and would have collapsed quite completely had I not grasped his arms and hauled him upright. I helped him gently into the easy-chair before the fire while Holmes arranged the old plaid travelling rug around his shoulders.

After several inhalations of Spirits of Hartshorn his breathing moderated somewhat, though still he remained unable to speak coherently. Weakly he struggled within his private pocket and laboriously retrieved an envelope which he dropped upon the table beside him, weakly indicating for Holmes to open it, before collapsing back in the chair.

While my colleague examined the envelope I poured a stiff whisky and water for our client. Once Mr Petch was over the worst of his hysteria I returned my attention to Sherlock Holmes.

With his powerful lens he scrutinised every inch of the outside of the envelope. "Delivered by hand I see, your name but no address, a man's thumbprint faintly impressed in..." he sniffed the mark "...black printer's ink I declare." With this observation his countenance clouded. The still near-speechless Petch flapped his claw-like right hand, urgently gesturing for Holmes to explore within the envelope. Lifting the flap, Holmes removed two items. The first was a sheet of writing paper folded in half, from within which he slowly and delicately withdrew the second item. I realised I was holding my breath; and as it emerged I recognised it upon the instant.

It was a perfect example of a pristine, uncirculated Bank of England £10 note. Undoubtedly this was the first earnest of the villains' criminal intent. Holmes examined it carefully, and sniffed it deeply.

At the sight of the note, held carefully aloft between the tip of Holmes' forefinger and thumb, Petch recoiled even deeper into his chair. The room became as still as a tomb.

Holmes seated himself beside this trembling nervous-wreck of a man that had once been the ardent seeker of beauty, the aesthete, the enthusiastic botanist and accomplished master engraver we had first encountered in the convivial Christmas-Eve setting of Rules' Restaurant; he had degenerated beyond all recognition.

Holmes addressed him softly but firmly. "Mr Petch, I understand your extreme distress, but I beg that you will compose yourself. This, I make no doubt, is a proof from the missing plates is it not? When did you receive it?"

Petch nodded bitterly. "Last night; they have prostituted my art Mr Holmes; they have taken my finest work, a thing of virtue and beauty and corrupted it into a gambler's plaque for Mammon, a plaything for Gog and Magog, a vile instrument of criminality to gratify their untrammelled avarice and depraved greed!"

Petch stared as one hypnotised at the banknote, almost as if it possessed some force for evil of its own deep within its flimsy form. "Before me is my worst nightmare made incarnate; if they can produce one they can produce one quarter of a million! We shall all be ruined!

"We must surely now alert the Bank Mr Holmes without further delay, before we are drowned in this base, vile counterfeit money!"

Holmes smiled sceptically. "You may be right my dear Mr Petch, but let us hold that course in abeyance for a moment, and turn our attention to the banknote itself, and more particularly, to the message that accompanies it. To my eye the banknote appears to be quite the proper thing, and I imagine it would pass in exchange almost anywhere, which allowing your undoubted artistry, is only to be expected; I shall require to retain this for a period." Abruptly he again sniffed it all over.

"But the letter is for me of rather greater interest:
'*As you value your life consult no-one. Await my instructions.*'

"Does that not strike you as somewhat curious Watson?" Here, at last, was one of those rare but infinitely agreeable occasions when I felt passably confident that my own modest deductive method coincided precisely with that of Holmes. I apprehended my colleague's meaning and made so bold as to address my answer both to Holmes and to Mr Petch.

"You must own that Holmes has the right of it, Mr Petch. If the thieves' intent were simply to print counterfeit money for their own gain, what need have they of sending you the first proof? They already have all the means to hand. This proof merely serves to demonstrate that they have co-opted a competent printer into the gang. So why trouble to alert you – why raise an alarm so early in the game? No Mr Petch, if I read my colleague aright" – I glanced at Holmes – "there is a deeper motive here, hence '*Await my instructions.*' I would hazard a guess that there is some matter they wish to negotiate or discuss, now that they hold the advantage."

I glanced tentatively at Holmes and was gratified to see him smiling, in full accord. "Doctor Watson is quite accurate in his analysis Mr Petch – indeed there is little more that I can add except perhaps to advise you that in view of circumstances I anticipate shortly, I see no reason whatever why this matter need yet be broadcast beyond these walls.

"I have some modest hopes that we shall recover your plates, paper, and any notes already printed in advance of their circulation, within..." he paused, closed his eyes and appeared to perform some brief mental calculation "...let us say a matter of a very few days.

"I rather fancy these villains have a particular reason of their own for informing you that they can and have printed successfully, and I very much expect we may not have long to wait before we hear from them again..."

He looked thoughtful, and then concluded with a somewhat enigmatic smile "...unless, that is, they hear from Sherlock Holmes first..."

At this, Petch looked up sharply, a small glimmer of hope shining in his exhausted, rheumy eyes. "So soon Mr Holmes! You have made progress then?"

"My justice takes a swift transport Mr Petch, but I will not be pressed further; I have a preference to be the bearer of fact, rather than the purveyor of speculation. For now, I await quite essential information, which I believe will dramatically advance our patriotic crusade. These matters you may with confidence leave in our hands.

"But with the arrival of this ill-omened note, there is a more urgent matter which I fear may involve us all. We have debated the meaning of the second sentence. The first is no less significant – you note that you are cautioned: *'As you value your life consult no-one.'*

"Watson, do me the kindness of stepping over to the window and see if the ill-looking ruffian I observed earlier is still loafing in the doorway opposite... No! Do not disturb the curtain!"

I peered warily through the narrow gap between the gauzes, and sure enough there he was, a vicious-looking, beetle-browed mountain of a brute idling directly opposite, casting occasional shifty glances up at our window. I turned and nodded grimly at Holmes, confirming his suspicion.

He addressed our client once more. "I do not wish to alarm you unduly Mr Petch, but we are, even as I speak under surveillance; it is not unreasonable to suppose that the bruiser standing watch over the road is reporting back to his principal, and will certainly carry news of your visit here today. Thus are we all under grave threat in this business.

"These are risks to which the good Doctor and I are accustomed, but I fear you also now must look to your own close protection, for these villains will stop at nothing. Do you possess a personal firearm?"

The elderly gentleman looked up at Holmes with a curious air of something between defiance and resolve.

"I do indeed Mr Holmes; as a younger man, a significant part of my responsibilities was the conveyance of securities of particularly substantial face-value around London, and I routinely travelled with a fully loaded six-barrelled revolver in my pocket. I believe I can readily lay my hands upon my old 20-bore Beattie Pepperbox; like me, it may be somewhat vintage in years, but I believe together we may still offer a formidable deterrent!"

"That is well Mr Petch" said Holmes. "Hereon I would strongly urge you keep it loaded and about you at all times."

Privately I had reservations at the notion of this volatile septuagenarian engraver, aesthete and orchid-grower, already in a state of considerable emotional distress, loose upon the streets of London and heavily armed with an ancient, lethal six-barrelled large-calibre revolver! However my colleague seemed satisfied enough with the arrangement, and I put the thought from my mind.

Holmes delicately cleared his throat and addressed Petch once more. "One final matter Mr Petch; when did you last speak with your maid?"

"I recall the occasion well; it was the day before yesterday. She bade me farewell at around six o'clock, for my wife had granted her several days free so that she might meet with her sister – I do not expect her to return for a week."

Sombrely Holmes replied "I regret I have bad news Mr Petch; Dulcie Hobbs will not return in a week, or a month, or even in a year for you see, she was discovered hanged in her locked rooms in Chiswick early yesterday morning."

"Good Heavens! There must be some dreadful mistake; she left our house in the highest of good humours, so pleased was she at the prospect of seeing her sister and mother! Why on earth would she then go to her home and commit suicide?"

"I did not say she committed suicide Mr Petch."

Our visitor looked puzzled, frowning. "But you said..."

"I said she was discovered hanged."

The elderly engraver's eyes widened in horrified comprehension, as he digested the awful meaning of Holmes' words.

Succinctly and clinically my colleague related the events which had occurred at Chiswick High Road, and his certain conclusions, though delicately excising the more appalling details of the scene. After showing the shocked old man the scorched, reconstructed note he concluded: "It is important that you retain this news privately to yourself Mr Petch, for you see, Inspector Lestrade of the yard, while a decent enough fellow, is of the firm conviction that this was a suicide – I have little doubt that you and he will be in some communication shortly. However, for the coming days it is essential that he retain his erroneous conclusions, for if he is alerted to the true facts he will likely launch a clumsy murder hunt with all the inevitable vulgar tantarah that will ensue.

"The name of Perkins Bacon & Petch will be blazoned across every penny-dreadful news-sheet in London and the City – the result will be that our quarry will instantly go to earth who knows where, concealing with him that which we must at any cost retrieve – the plates and the paper. Therefore I urge you to remain entirely circumspect for the present, and certainly until I lay my hands upon the criminals responsible.

"And now I advise you to return to the comparative safety of your home and await my wire.

"You shall leave discreetly, and in disguise – I observe we are not so very different in stature, you and I. The boy downstairs will summon a hansom to the door so you may mount unseen; however, I suggest you cover your face with your muffler and don my old town-coat and this deerstalker; in the event that our watchful friend over yonder should glimpse you, he will most likely believe it is I departing.

"Should he follow it will because he will want to learn where *I* go and whether you may have told me anything which might threaten their plans."

And thus it was that around noon, a somewhat calmer Mr Henry Petch departed Baker Street. Holmes stepped to the window, peered cautiously down into the street and chortled "Most entertaining Watson! Come see! The apparent sight of Sherlock Holmes jumping nimbly into a cab has put yonder Neanderthal ruffian into a perfect lather of bewilderment! Should he follow or should he stay?

"He is quite irresolute in the matter. Aha! He hails another cab and... Yes, now he intends to pursue with all speed! Let us trust he takes pleasure in his fruitless chase to Richmond, for that leaves the coast clear for us to depart unobserved."

I looked up at Holmes quizzically. "We are leaving? Where then, do we journey?"

He laughed lightly. "To be quite candid, I have not the faintest notion! But the sooner the blackguard yonder departs, the sooner may we make our plan. Our destination will depend entirely on what we learn from the cabman I have summoned, for only he knows where his murderous fares finally alighted after completing their wicked mission. He should be here..." For the second time that morning we heard a cab rumble to a halt in the street below. "...momentarily I do believe."

There followed shortly the sound of the heavy street door slamming shut, then cumbersome footsteps slowly mounted the stairs, pausing twice in their ponderous ascent. The parlour door opened to reveal quite the stoutest, baldest, widest, most corpulent, muscular, strongest and jolliest-looking fellow I believe I ever clapped eyes upon.

That this preternaturally large gentleman could even pass between the door-jambs was to me a physical wonder, let alone the notion that he might be spry enough to vault atop a cab.

Shrewd dark eyes peered out from his spherical phizog like two plump currants in a glossy suet pudding. He beamed at us amiably which disconcertingly but rather comically caused his eyes to vanish momentarily into his melon-like face. Holmes addressed him genially. "Mr Solomon Warburg I believe?"

The mighty Mr Warburg turned towards my colleague expectantly. "Ah, then you will be the renowned Mr Sherlock Holmes; I have here the note which your page delivered to the cab-stand earlier, though for the life of me I cannot see how attending here may be to my advantage, unless you wish me, in particular, to convey you gentlemen to some destination of your choice – if so I believe I may justly claim that few cabmen know the streets of London better than I!"

Holmes produced his leather pocket-book which he carefully positioned upon the dining table just beyond reach of the cabman's giant, scarred, crab-like hands, whereupon the latter's eyes reappeared upon the instant.

"I'm sure your knowledge of this great metropolis is quite unequalled Mr Warburg, and indeed it is that particular competence which may today enrich you a little. You will find that I am not ungenerous in such matters.

"The fact is that I wish urgently to locate an old friend of ours from many years ago. Regrettably I have mislaid his details. Now my colleague, the good Doctor Watson here, happened by chance to be hurrying along the Chiswick High Road the night before last, in the direction of Shepherd's Bush, and he swears he believes he glimpsed our friend alight from your hansom around ten o'clock in the evening and enter a large house on the High Road, while you appeared to remain at the kerb; lacking the time to stop and enquire he smartly made a note of your number.

"Now I am wagering on your memory being as sound as your knowledge of London's Streets, in which case..." and Holmes meaningfully slid the wallet to within an inch of the huge meaty hand. "Do you perchance recall the fare in question; if so I would be much gratified to learn where he hailed you and where he finally alighted, and thus I may be able to locate his place of residence?"

Warburg furrowed his brow in thought for a space. "That would be the tall gentleman, moustachioed, in company with a rather muscular, squint-eyed and very much overly-weighty man," (which struck me as droll uttered by Warburg, provoking comical private thoughts of pots and kettles) "...and he hailed me on the Embankment. From there we journeyed to the High Road in Chiswick, where he instructed me to wait at the kerb-side. He was carrying a small, bulging canvas bag. Nothing of significance occurred for almost an hour, except for a skinny street urchin who stopped briefly to pet the old nag. In due course my fares reappeared and directed me to proceed with all haste to an address in Richmond, where he delivered a letter or some such to a large, handsome villa. I also noted his bag now appeared to be empty."

Holmes nodded eagerly "And from there, Mr Warburg? At what address did you eventually drop our friend? Tell me exactly what you observed, with no embellishment or conjecture if you please."

"Well Mr Holmes, it wasn't precisely what you'd call an address as such. We drove for some while until we arrived south of the river at Greenwich Marsh right by the reach on the peninsula. They set down by the footpath that leads off to the right to Manor Way, which is where I expected them to go, towards East

Greenwich or maybe Over Brickfield; but no, not a bit of it.

"Now here's the oddest thing; they alighted and climbed down the stone steps at the pier to a rotten old wooden jetty on the East bank of Blackwall Reach, where they clambered into a brand-new skiff and brisk as you like rowed away into the sleet and rain and the dark, and then they vanished from my sight, to go I saw not where."

At this Holmes appeared somewhat vexed. Tapping a bony white finger meaningfully on his wallet he said "Oh dear Mr Warburg, I had hoped you might have been rather more helpful; I had anticipated you might have an address, or at the very least, a more limited locale. This is indeed most unfortunate. Think man, think! Is there nothing more you can recall, no matter how trivial it may appear to you? It really is a matter of considerable urgency that I contact my old friend."

Without taking his intelligent beady eyes off Holmes' thick wallet for a moment, Warburg said carefully "From what I recall Mr Holmes, I do believe you required me to relate exactly that which actually occurred, *with no embellishment or conjecture*,' by which I understood you to mean, that which I myself saw until the moment the pair of them vanished from my sight. This I have related most accurately."

Then with a smile: "If, however, you are prepared to reward me for my paltry efforts at your own craft, which I know to be the observation of events and the deduction of their causes or likely outcome, well then..." he let the notion hang, charged with promise but clearly lacking a satisfactory financial transaction for its completion. Holmes smiled at this cheery impertinence, slid a ten-pound note from his pocket book and placed it before the cabman.

"*Touché* Mr Warburg; perhaps this may encourage your deductive capacity?"

"Well Mr Holmes, as a younger – and considerably lighter – man it so happens I used to skull that stretch of the Blackwall Reach; at that time of night it flows north, then becomes Bugsby's Reach and turns south. Once the tide turns it runs pretty fast thereabouts. This means that if you propose to cross the water, you may not row directly over because the fast-running northerly current will defeat your best efforts; you must start your journey further upstream from your intended destination, and so effect your crossing slant-wise. Your, ahem, 'friend's' very muscular companion was a powerful hand at the skulls and clearly calculated not to run due North with the current, but to cross the Reach over to the far bank. If I am right in this, then at the point they disappeared from my view, I deduce their course could only have headed them for Saunders Ness landing-stage at Cubitt Town which is on the south-eastern tip of The Isle of Dogs, just south of the Millwall Docks. They could not land anywhere else, for either side there are deep mud-flats for some distance, where only barges may anchor. I could with ease have delivered them directly to Cubitt Town by a less circuitous route; I therefore conclude that whatever their business, they were most anxious that even a lowly cabman such as I should not have recollection of their final destination." He grinned roguishly and quoted from the Old Testament: *"Consider this, and be thankful for the wisdom of your most humble Solomon for telling it."*

Holmes beamed with evident approval and slid the bank-note beneath Warburg' waiting fingers.

"Admirable work Mr Warburg; I commend you for it. Clearly you possess uncommonly sharp eyes but also the all too-uncommon wit to understand what they observe! Now I am intimately familiar with the majority of this great Capital of ours, but I confess this Cubitt Town is somewhat unknown to me. What manner of place is it?"

"If you have the stomach for it then I will tell you Mr Holmes. It exists on the proceeds of manufacturing cement, bitumen, asphalt and shipbuilding. It is nowadays a noisome, Ungodly, mean and squalid place, much frequented by scoundrelly rogues, footpads and ne'er-do-wells.

"The airs from the black marsh are sickly and evil, and most of the denizens worse. It is a perilous place where disease, drunkenness and paucity abound, while honest men are ground down until they are become little more than ill-made, weary, scraggy nubs of their former manhood, blear-eyed and tallow-complexioned.

"In Cubitt Town there are no sunlit uplands, only dark alleys and darker creeks. The fetid dwellings are become unwholesome tumble-down rookeries, squeezed cheek by jowl with open cess-pools and dank crumbling warehouses, where I doubt not that fierce and wicked men pursue their nefarious trades.

"Poxed whores and shell-and-pea shysters ply their shabby trades, while innocent babes cry plaintively for food in their cold cribs. That, Mr Holmes, in answer to your question, is what manner of place is Cubitt Town, and in this I do not speak the least slander of it.

"To be candid, and I do not wish to affront, I am astonished that a 'friend' of two gentlemen of evident quality such as yourselves would, by choice, visit so mean a place... unless the man you seek were a detective like yourself – or mayhap... a villain?"

Holmes scrutinised our visitor shrewdly with renewed interest.

"You are an astute and clever man Mr Warburg; I trust I may also count discretion among your several evident qualities? However, I choose not to answer your unspoken question except to confirm that yes, you are perfectly correct; the man I seek is certainly one of those two!"

Warburg smiled knowingly. "Then I shall not cause further offence by venturing my own personal opinion as to which I believe him to be Mr Holmes." He fell silent, and for a man apparently so articulate he appeared to be at a loss as to how to proceed. Somewhat diffidently he cleared his throat and continued:

"I would not wish to presume Mr Holmes, but I have ardently followed Doctor Watson's accounts of your cases with the keenest interest and have, since reading the first relation, hankered once more after directing such modest capabilities as I may possess to assisting in the solution of such puzzles.

"Indeed, throughout most of the Doctor's early accounts, I believe I stayed almost apace with your own astute conclusions. I once had thought to pursue a living in the merchant banking business; however, I became aware that my name and Semite heredity might militate against me in certain circles.

"I very quickly realised that analysing the past and predicting the future values of currencies and securities was not so very different from the analysis of subtle facts and the causes of puzzling circumstances, and thus I tried my hand as a private investigator, with some success as matters turned out.

"You see, for a few years, Mr Holmes, we shared much the same profession, or as I prefer to view it, a precise and scientific calling, although I am sure you would not have been aware of my lowly endeavours; I was by a long measure further down the professional ladder, but I followed your activities on your lofty top rung with the greatest admiration.

"Sadly certain, shall I say, adverse circumstances contrived to cast a dark eclipse over my little enterprise and made it all but impossible for me to continue with my promising vocation. Nonetheless, would you take it improperly if I were to state that my humble services could be at your future disposal?

"I can assure you that for the purposes of close and stealthy observation there is nothing more unremarkable, nothing more commonplace and of a certainty, nothing more unmemorable than a growler and its driver engaged in his lawful business, whether waiting outside a railway station, a villa or an hotel in Mayfair for an hour or even two; or following discreetly behind a like vehicle, it may pass ubiquitously throughout London.

"One may go anywhere, observe and record everything, and yet remain quite unremarked. Should you judge such small service to be of value Mr Holmes, you may summon me generally within the hour by means of a note delivered by your page to the stand; otherwise, I am to be found most evenings at the Wig & Pen in Fleet Street where I room.

"I also have, somewhat unusually, discreet dark-shades fitted in my vehicle that may be drawn at the fare's private determination, which small provision has on many occasions proved quite invaluable to certain distinguished clients who, for their own reasons, desire privacy and discretion.

"In conclusion, I would add the minor but perhaps useful credential that despite my rather uncommon stature, in a rumble I am still well more than a match for most big fellows, or even two – in my younger days, not so very long ago, I was the Shoreditch heavyweight boxing champion for four years running.

"My elder son, Joshua – a shipwright at Green's Dockyard – now holds that title also and the younger, Samuel, the light-heavyweight.

"When the Devil presses, we may perhaps be of use..." Holmes made no immediate reply to this perfectly unexpected and rather startling petition; presently he responded.

"I believe it may be possible that I shall call upon your unusual services before very long Mr Warburg."

The improbably large cabman solemnly nodded his acknowledgement. "May I now assume our business here is concluded? In that case I shall say thank you and bid you good day gentlemen, both." With this he discreetly pocketed his imbursement, made a remarkably graceful bow for a man of his immense bulk and after squeezing through the doorway, quietly closed the door behind him.

Holmes looked animatedly at me, his eyes alive with a look of fierce exultation. "I do believe Watson that the remarkable Mr Warburg has just repaired the break in our chain to Bormanstein, and in all probability, with a rather stronger link than that which our quarry so cruelly severed!

"Within the cranium of the observant, articulate and unfeasibly large Solomon Warburg I declare there resides more acute perception, imagination and deductive competence than might be exhibited by a half-a-dozen commonplace Yarders in a month!

"I fear his talents are sadly wasted in his present profession, but for all that, I believe he may be an exceedingly handy gentleman to know. Now be a good chap and hand down my cuttings index marked 'R to T' – I do believe I have heard of this unusual Mr Warburg prior to his appearance here today...

"...In connection with, was it Strathmore...? Strathspey... Strathdown...? No, I have it now! If I recollect aright it was The Strathcarron Diamond Theft! The year of '82 if my memory serves?"

I ran my finger down the clippings pasted under 'S'. "*Saratoga Conspiracy Foiled... Seamere Green Abductions... Last Minute Reprieve for Strachan...* Ah, I have it now Holmes! – it is from the St James Gazette, dated the 7th of May."

I read the item aloud:

Strathcarron Diamond Theft: Private Investigator Freed by Scotland Yard!

The legendary Strathcarron Diamonds, property of the titled Streatley family for four generations, have vanished under mysterious circumstances. In an official statement issued today, Scotland Yard stated:

"Following the apparent theft of the famous diamonds, and their substitution with paste replicas, a private investigator, Mr Solomon Warburg was arrested on suspicion of theft. Warburg claims he was commissioned by Lord Streatley's private secretary, Sir Martin Russell at a private, unfortunately unwitnessed, meeting at the family seat in Berkshire with the responsibility of personally conveying the diamonds securely to the family's summer residence in Nice and delivering them in person to Lady Joan Streatley. Warburg signed a receipt for the stones, the which receipt he later passed to the yard in his own defence.

Lord Robertson Streatley was to have followed on a week later. When Warburg arrived in Nice and presented the stones to Lady Streatley, she instantly declared them to be high-quality paste replicas, a fact swiftly verified by the internationally renowned jewellers Chaudière Et Fils. Warburg subsequently claimed in his defence that the stones were the self-same that had been handed to him by Sir Martin, after which he insisted they were upon his person day and night for five days of travelling, until in Nice he *passed them into the possession of their owner; Warburg averred therefore that he must deliberately and maliciously have been given the paste replicas by the private secretary for nefarious reasons of his own. Since then, it transpires that Sir Martin has subsequently disappeared without trace along with the family's 22 year-old French governess. In the absence of conclusive evidence, Solomon Warburg has been released without charge, although with such a grave matter remaining unresolved, his prospects of continuing his promising career as a hitherto sought-after private investigator in matters demanding integrity and discretion might, to some, appear to be under a dark cloud and his future career somewhat in jeopardy. Under the strange and puzzling circumstances the insurers, Lloyds of London, have declined to comment as to whether compensation will be made for the loss.*

Inspector Gregson added that the whereabouts of Sir Martin, the inexplicably missing French governess, and the real diamonds is a mystery to this day. The case remains open.

"Good Lord, then it would appear to me from this account Holmes that Mr Solomon Warburg, the poor fellow, was hoodwinked by the good-for-nothing of a private secretary into signing a receipt for counterfeit stones, after which the self-same and not-so noble Sir Martin made off with the real gems, and the French governess for a little added lustre!"

Holmes chuckled. "I believe you have the perfect right of it Watson; and with our rotund acquaintance's reputation thus publicly besmirched, the matter of the insurance recompense unresolved and the whereabouts of the real stones, the private secretary and the governess quite unknown, it is a matter of no great surprise that the unfortunate Warburg - neither charged, tried nor acquitted - should find a sudden shortage of patrons for his burgeoning enterprise!

"Nonetheless, my instinct tells me he is an exceptionally sound fellow for all that, but sadly the victim of unfortunate circumstance - though in truth he might perhaps be judged guilty of a degree of ill judgement and *naiveté* in accepting such a priceless consignment at face value, and without proof of its due provenance."

And with this he fell silent, leaned back in his chair and closed his eyes. I sensed his mind had already moved to other matters.

Little more of note occurred that late winter's afternoon, save for a couple of very decent mutton-wether chops with caper-berry sauce, cabbage and potatoes served by Mrs Hudson for our supper, washed down with a pretty tolerable Saint Emilion.

Holmes intimated that we should be out and about on the morrow, very likely in The Isle of Dogs, and suggested that we should dress shabbily as print workers seeking employment, and refrain from shaving for the day.

After, we enjoyed a pipe and a whisky-peg apiece by the hearth.

Over some years in the close company of my unusual friend I have discovered several weather-vanes by which I may determine his state of mind.

Should he resort to his slim, sinister velvet-lined Morocco leather case containing its gleaming surgical steel and glass paraphernalia, and the accompanying glass bottle it is a certain sign of world-weariness, boredom, and the urgent need of a conundrum to challenge that towering intellect of his.

If on the other hand he settles down for the dog-watch with his foul-smelling twelve-inch Churchwarden and two full ounces of the strongest shag from Barkers, he is likely wrestling with a problem he feels needful of the most attentive and strenuous consideration; but when he reaches for his darling Stradivarius, as he did this night after supper, it may signal ambivalent moods. Should he seize it without care for its state of tune, and scrape out harsh discordant notes, then he is better left alone.

On this occasion, however, he settled it reverently under his angular chin then, with eyes closed, lips pursed in the gentlest of smiles, proceeded painstakingly and at some length to tune it pizzicato-style; when it was perfectly to his liking he turned to me.

"Now what do you think to this, Watson? It is my own transposition from the composer's original score. I am certain you will know the piece."

He sat upright, applied a measured two strokes of rosin to the horse-hair bow, closed his eyes once more and commenced, a look of ineffable pleasure upon his face. The piece started gently enough, and almost upon the instant I knew it. Gradually the tempo increased, the familiar theme was established, then the key soared ever higher through innumerable artful variations until Holmes' slender, prehensile digits were fairly flying up and down the slim ebony finger-board.

Abruptly and dramatically he stood, and the bravura performance ended on a quartet of striking and most arresting chords of, I suspect, Holmes' own devising. "Bravo, Bravo Holmes!" I applauded quite spontaneously, and he made me a humorous mock bow. I could not then have known that the events yet to unfold the following day would make it seem, in hindsight, perhaps the most inapposite piece upon which we might have retired for the night.

It was the *scherzo* from Beethoven's 'Ode to Joy.'

* * *

CHAPTER TEN

A NEW ALLIANCE

Early next day, and mindful of my friend's counsel of the evening before, I did not shave that morning, and donned the old corduroys, scuffed boots and the ancient, musty-smelling frayed pea-jacket that was a regular member of the cast in Holmes' considerable wardrobe of disguises in which he so delighted, laid out for me the night before by my colleague.

A worn shirt lacking collar or stud, taken creased and unlaundered from the linen-basket, a threadbare tweed waistcoat and a carelessly knotted frayed muffler, topped off with a greasy-looking loafers' cap completed my attire, to the effect that my patients would have been horror-struck, and Mary would have turned me from the house.

I smiled wryly back at my scruffy reflection in the Chevalier mirror and felt sure Holmes would approve of my new *alter ego* – vanished was the flourishing Doctor of Kensington, transformed in moments into a simple, plainly-dressed, utterly ordinary and perfectly unmemorable working man. I checked my watch; it lacked a quarter of nine and hearing Holmes in conversation with Mrs Hudson through in the parlour, entered to join him for breakfast.

He was attired only slightly less dismally than I in a cheap ill-matched three-piece, shabby and shiny with somewhat frayed cuffs, and a worn billycock hat. To compensate he sported a soiled bank-clerk's round-tab collar shirt with grimy neck-tie, and had overnight magically aged by a decade, and grown splendid mutton-chop whiskers, affording an air of something resembling, perhaps, a modest aspiration to scruffy gentility.

Without so much as a frown or a raised eyebrow at our appearances Mrs Hudson finished setting the breakfast table, wryly surveyed the pair of us, gave me a cheery "Good Morning Doctor" and departed the room. I imagined, perhaps, she assumed that since I was once more back in Holmes' close company I like he, had succumbed to strange eccentricities of dress and conduct!

Between hasty gulps of coffee and mouthfuls of buttered toast and Patum Pepperium – a particular delight of his – Holmes outlined our plans for the day ahead. Neither of us knew it but they were destined to be thrown into complete disarray by the most terrible events.

"Today, my loyal friend, we are likely to enter deep and, very likely, dangerous waters. It is my notion that we travel by train as far as the West India Docks Basin."

He traced our journey with a thin white finger on a map he had beside him at the table.

"From there we shall proceed South on foot; you would agree that a pair of unemployed printers would be most unlikely to dismount from a cab in Cubitt Town!

"You shall be a compositor – just rattle on about the elegance of Times and Garamond and the declarative strength of Franklin Gothic Bold when needed, and I for my part shall play a press operator. We have been in association together for some years, but fallen upon hard times and are seeking business." I smiled at Holmes' blithe confidence in my assumed ability to masquerade as a typographer.

More sombrely he added "We shall also go armed" at which he stepped to his desk and collected his revolver; I retrieved my own from my room. Holmes resumed: "I do believe, Watson, that in those old clothes, you present an admirable and most credible printer's compositor!

He passed me a battered lead tube. "A little of this ink staining your fingers will complete the picture splendidly. What time do you have?" I checked my watch. "Why, it is still only a half after nine."

Holmes gave me an old-fashioned look. "And do you really think that your father's fine and costly gold perpetual twin rotating Tourbillion Breguet watch adorning your greasy frayed waistcoat is quite the thing for an impoverished, unemployed compositor to sport around Cubitt Town?" Realising my gaffe I hastily replaced the Breguet with the old but serviceable steel turnip watch I frequently used for timing patient's pulses.

At that moment a hammering on the street door announced an arrival. We heard Lestrade's unmistakable nasal tones in agitated remonstration with Mrs Hudson and seconds after, he burst into the room.

He looked tense and drawn with tiredness. Grimly he addressed my colleague, ignoring his strange attire. "Very well Mr Sherlock Holmes, what's going on? I think you know rather more than you let on about the affairs of Mr Henry Petch and the death of Dulcie Hobbs! You owe me an explanation and I want the truth — what 'small matter' are you assisting Mr Petch with, and how came you so swiftly to the scene of the Hobbs woman's suicide?" Holmes smiled bleakly. "Why, Lestrade, you are quite discomposed. What can possibly have occurred that should oblige me to explain my confidential investigations to you?" Lestrade glared back at Holmes. "Do you know a man by the name of Solomon Warburg, once a private detective, now a cabman by trade, Mr Holmes?"

Holmes affected to ruminate. At length he replied "I believe I may have knowledge of him — an exceptionally muscular fellow, yes? What of it?"

"Here's *what of it*, Mr Holmes; at around midnight last night he was found most savagely stabbed and beaten almost to death in a warehouse in Cubitt Town on The Isle of Dogs! He is now in critical condition in the Charing Cross Hospital and it rests in the scales of fate as to whether he lives or dies!" Holmes' countenance darkened.

"That is grave news indeed Lestrade, but how do you believe this involves me?"

"Because, Mr Holmes, I now know that Mr Henry Petch is involved in the business of printing money for the Bank of England, and also is your client; and that Dulcie Hobbs was his maid, and that you and the Doctor here appeared as if by magic shortly after the Yard was called to the scene of her suicide; and that the unfortunate Mr Solomon Warburg received a summons brought by your boy, to 221B Baker Street yesterday, and that he was found hours later almost murdered – with an indelible image of a Bank of England ten pound note impressed upon his forehead, and a fragment of a label in his clenched fist bearing the name of Portals Paper Mill! I ask you for the last time, Mr Holmes, what the Devil is going on here!

"Oh, and lest you seek to fob me off with some fancy high falutin' theory, the lad who came across Warburg swears that the near-dying man uttered just two words before lapsing into unconsciousness..."

At this my colleague looked up sharply. "And they were...?"

Lestrade looked gravely back. "The two words he spoke were '*Sherlock Holmes*' – the boy is certain of it!"

Holmes steepled his fingers beneath his chin in that most familiar manner of his, and sat, eyes closed, deep in thought for some moments.

"You are perfectly correct Lestrade, and it would be reckless of me not to concede that this is now become a very deep matter; indeed, it is so deep that before I speak with you, I must consult some exceedingly elevated persons in the very highest echelons of the treasury; I fear I am not at present at liberty to reveal to you the nature of my investigation.

"But perhaps you will take my meaning if I tell you that this is effectively a matter of State of the utmost delicacy, and rash, precipitous or ill-advised action on the part of either of us would likely plunge the national economy into financial chaos, and ruin both of our careers into the bargain!

"I make no doubt of the fact that you would end your career wearing a helmet and blue serge, carrying a truncheon once more, and I would be fortunate indeed even to secure employment cleaning the very laboratory equipment I once used in my forensic research. The wrong move at this point will merely drive our quarry deeper underground and thus confound us both even further. Indeed, it is probable that Warburg's brave but quite uninvited intervention may already have done so."

"But what I will confide to you is that Perkins, Bacon & Petch have a very grave problem, with international implications; that Dulcie Hobbs was without the merest shadow of a doubt brutally murdered; and the fact that Solomon Warburg yet clings to life can only be testimony to his astonishing ox-like constitution, else surely he would be in the mortuary as we speak, and you would be launching a double murder-hunt! He is a sound and very brave man but impulsive, and I fear in his attempt to assist he has been sorely used, and for that perhaps some responsibility lays at my door. If he lives, it sounds as if he will have been lucky to escape with his life.

"I may tell you that the stakes for which my adversaries are playing, Lestrade, are astronomically high and they will not hesitate to murder again to further their scheme. It would be wise, incidentally, to place a police officer by Mr Warburg's bed, lest word gets out that he yet lives. My guess is that he has already seen too much for his own safety.

"Now I will make you a bargain, for time is very much against us; if you will be good enough to tell me all that you know of the events of last night, I give you my solemn word that I shall speak with those higher authorities who alone can unseal my lips. Then we may pool our resources – agreed?"

Lestrade eyed Holmes narrowly, clearly pondering whether he should throw in his lot with my artful colleague, or perhaps invoke the undoubted authority of his official position and seek to compel Holmes with the force of the law to reveal his hand. After some deliberation, and clearly at his wits end over these troubling events, the little detective conceded with, it seemed to me, a degree of grudging gratitude and relief.

"Very well Mr Holmes. It is not my preferred method to reveal the details of official investigations to the public, but I think I am man enough to concede that while you and I approach these problems somewhat differently, your unusual techniques have on occasion been of value to the Force." He produced his pocketbook and flipped through it to the relevant page.

"This is what I learned..." here he grinned a little sheepishly "...and also what I have *deduced*." Holmes nodded encouragement and smiled approvingly.

"After receiving a message at the Station, I arrived in Cubitt Town shortly after midnight at Slater's Yard, hard by Saunders Ness. There, in a sort of large shed by the warehouse, I found the unfortunate, viciously battered Mr Solomon Warburg bleeding heavily from a stab-wound in the neck, seemingly dead, but the lad who discovered him told me he had been just sufficiently conscious half an hour earlier to utter your name, before finally sinking into coma. When I arrived Warburg was barely alive, with the faintest of pulses, sprawled face-down among a whole clutter of old tar-buckets and upended barrels of pitch, brushes and other builder's tools. Close by was a heavy block and tackle on a length of rope, all considerably blood-stained, from which I deduce that it may have been used in the beating.

"Here is the boy's account: he was sitting with his brother on the front step outside Chapel House by Millwall Dock, when around ten o'clock Mr Warburg pulled his cab to the side of the road. For a shilling they agreed to mind the cab and horse while Mr Warburg walked into Cubitt Town apparently on a business matter. Approaching midnight the two lads decided they had waited long enough, but eager to get their promised reward, they decided that one should go to the town and find Warburg, while the other waited with the nag and growler. The lad wisely headed for the Cock Inn, the likely source of all gossip of comings and goings." At this Holmes once again nodded approvingly.

"Here he learned that a cabman corresponding to Warburg's description – the lad gave out that he was looking for his father – had taken a small beer and then enquired of the landlord about the possible whereabouts of two gentlemen he sought, one tall, moustachioed and distinguished-looking and one, something of a heavy-weight wall-eyed bruiser.

"The landlord told the lad that he had directed his 'father' – Warburg of course – to Slater's place near Saunders Ness, shortly after which two other big ugly fellows lounging at the bar swiftly finished their ale and shortly after followed out behind Warburg. The landlord subsequently confirmed all this to me.

"I identified Warburg, of course, from the number on his still-waiting cab, after which it was simplicity itself to learn from the cab-stand that your page had the day before summoned him to see you here. I concluded that he had gone to Cubitt Town on some business of yours, but when – with the help of two officers I rolled him over – and there was a perfect impression of a Bank of England ten-pound note on his forehead, I began to see some sort of connection with

Mr Petch and Dulcie Hobbs. He also appeared to have been badly bitten, perhaps by a large dog.

"The scrap of paper in his hand meant nothing to me at first, but I learned early this morning that Portals Paper Mill makes the special paper for printing banknotes." He closed his notebook and said "And that is all I have learned Mr Holmes. What it all means I cannot fathom, but I can see you know rather more than I about this tangled affair?" My friend looked up sharply at the official detective. "Tell me, Lestrade, did you explore the rest of the warehouse after finding Warburg?"

Lestrade looked a little discomfited. "Well no Mr Holmes; you see I more or less assumed that having found the beaten man, with no culprit in view, my first job was to get him to hospital as rapidly as possible and appeal for any witnesses to the crime." Holmes emitted a "Tut" of annoyance, clearly signalling his exasperation at a lapse in basic investigative procedure that even I saw as a glaring blunder. He took a deep breath and continued.

"Regardless, I commend you Lestrade; in a surprisingly short time you have gathered the warp and the weft of the matter in your hand. I should not be at all surprised if at the successful conclusion of this business, and if you will follow my lead, you do not find yourself promoted a rank. However, as I have stated, I am as yet unauthorised to tell you how to weave the threads correctly into the web that will snare our quarry. Indeed, I myself lack a few vital strands for its completion, but if you have no objection, a visit to this Slater's Warehouse may illuminate further. After, I propose to visit the unfortunate Warburg and see how he fares. Tomorrow I shall contact you and tell all." A look of considerable relief passed over Lestrade's tired face. "For that I should be mightily grateful Mr Holmes. The man guarding Slater's place is Constable Clarke; you met him at Chiswick – he will be happy to assist you." Upon this note of compromise they shook hands and Lestrade made to leave. "Oh, one more thing Lestrade, you say Warburg was stabbed – did you by any chance find the knife?"

"I did Mr Holmes, though it wasn't exactly what you might term a knife; it was removed by the surgeon from where it had been driven halfway through his collarbone, a hair's breadth from his carotid artery. It was an odd, exotic stabbing-weapon, unlike any I have seen before – certainly foreign, oriental maybe, a short slim needle-sharp blade with a wooden handle." After Lestrade departed Holmes sat pensively for some moments, deep in thought, then sprang to his feet. "You heard him Watson? You heard him? Assume! Assume! The most basic error one may make in forensic detection is to *assume!* Had he explored further he may well have seen what Warburg saw, and on account of which was nearly murdered for his pains! That was intended as a clear warning to me!" He composed himself once more. "What do you make of the description of the knife Watson? It is very significant but it will also cause us very great difficulty, of that I am certain."

"I can cast no light upon the matter Homes; I am versed in the different wounds caused by various calibres of pistols and rifles but as to exotic oriental knives..." I shrugged. At his desk he scribbled a lengthy message on a telegraph form, summoned the lad downstairs and required him to run it along to the Telegraph Office immediately. "Now Watson, if you're still game shall we venture to Cubitt Town and see if two unemployed printers may advance their cause?"

And so it was, we departed the civilised calm of Baker Street for the unknown dangers of Cubitt Town...

* * *

CHAPTER ELEVEN

ASA BORMANSTEIN

As Holmes had planned, we exited Blackwall Railway Station and headed southward on foot. Shortly after one o'clock, we passed a forbidding derelict building, clearly once an inn, with grimy blind windows obscured by greasy-looking grey curtains like cataracts, and a peeling sign, swinging by one hinge proclaiming somewhat apocalyptically *'Folly House.'*

We continued warily south in silence, following parallel with the route of the dank and malodorous Blackwall Reach of The Thames on our left, eventually entering the hinterland of Cubitt Town after perhaps half a mile. The place crouched low, crawling, dark and menacing around the south-eastern point of The Isle of Dogs, forever imprisoned to the north by the glowering sprawl of the two huge import and export docks, with their forest of articulated cranes moving slowly back and forth at different angles like the legs of giant dying beetles stranded on their backs; to the south and west it was incarcerated by the black turbid waters of the Reach and to the east beyond, by the dismal flat wilderness of the Greenwich marsh.

On either side were expanses of wide, rank-smelling mud-banks featureless except for decrepit moored hulks and barges, many proclaiming their age and years of immobility by the fringes of black-green slime, etiolated grass and scrubby reed that crept ever-nearer, one day no doubt to overwhelm and strand them forever.

By contrast to these moribund hulks, in the wintery light I could just make out in the distance, the spidery steel skeleton of a new ironclad war-ship, rising improbably optimistically from the tangle of shipyard buildings I later learned was Samuda's Yard. Even at a distance I could see showers of red and yellow sparks cascading like fireflies, at every blow of the heavy hammers on white-hot rivets.

The further and deeper we penetrated this forbidding and alien place, the more grateful I felt for the reassuring heft of the loaded revolver in my right coat pocket. My sense of foreboding only increased as we entered the looming, closely-built, ill-lit streets; doors slammed shut at our approach, mongrel curs slunk after us baring their yellow fangs and snarling, and scowling men fixed us with baleful stares, then muttered quietly to each other with palpable suspicion as we passed by. Even disguised as we were, still plainly to these denizens of London's docklands, we were strangers in a strange land.

I murmured "It seems that our presence here is rather rattling the locals. Do you not think this adventure may be, perhaps, a little ill-advised?"

He chuckled humourlessly. "Rattling the locals is precisely what we have come to do Watson. I strongly suspect that in this unsavoury corner of our great metropolis there are several people I am most anxious to rattle; there will be a those who are aware that some out-of-the-ordinary new venture may be operating here but will be too close-lipped or perhaps too terrified to talk; there will be some who have knowledge that strangers are at work hereabouts - and where - but for inducement may tell what they know.

"And then there will be those we seek; a smaller, shadowy cadre of criminals who know *exactly* what is occurring here in Cubitt Town, and who now have conclusively demonstrated their willingness to intimidate and murder without compunction. And now they seek to hide, to vanish beneath the murk of this place.

"But they are close Watson, mark my words they are very close – I can sense them, I can feel them, and I believe I can almost smell them! But we must be on our mettle, for assuredly after Petch's visits to Baker Street, and Warburg's rather ill advised sally here, they will guess we are nearby and will be preparing for close action. Nonetheless I have no doubt that we shall..."

Holmes' *sotto-voce* conversation was abruptly interrupted by two evil-looking, burly heavyweights who stepped unexpectedly from a dark side-alley and insolently and aggressively barred our passage. I made to step left, upon which they moved to block me. I stepped right and again they mirrored my move.

They clearly intended us no good.

The taller of the two bludgers – hideously wall-eyed – held a short length of heavy iron chain in his massive scarred fist, which he carelessly and intimidatingly swung slowly back and forth. It terminated in a large, rusty padlock.

The shorter, likewise held a heavy chain except that it was rather longer.

And at the end of this chain was not a padlock, but something rather more menacing – a huge, slavering brindle dog of mongrel provenance, but undoubtedly spawned from mastiff stock somewhere in its past. Judging by the recent bruises and gashes on the thugs' faces and knuckles, both had clearly and very recently been in a violent brawl. I made little doubt that this ugly pair had most likely been involved in the murderous attack on Warburg.

Casually, but very slowly, I slid my right hand into my jacket pocket and grasped the familiar, reassuring chequered grips of my service revolver, gently eased back the hammer and at a snail's-pace, inched the heavy hexagonal barrel upward until I judged it to be dead-level with the two thugs' midriffs. I was aware that Holmes also had his hand in his coat pocket.

Dead, bestial eyes stared coldly back at us.

For guidance I glanced swiftly at my colleague; his face was perfectly composed, even a hint of a wry smile playing on his lips. Unexpectedly, he beamed amiably at the pair of thugs and in the most urbane of tones spoke: "Ah, good afternoon gentlemen, what excellent good fortune; exactly what we were looking for – local men with local knowledge; would you be so kind as to direct us to a nearby inn where we might enjoy a hearty bite and an ale or two? The Folly House Tavern appears to be long-closed. However I have heard tell of The Cock public house, but we are strangers to your fine town – perhaps you could recommend it?"

Evidently, being accustomed to intimidating, this quite unexpected response clearly took the wind clean out of their sails, for a look of hesitancy passed briefly over their brutish faces.

They glanced at each other uncertainly, unsure as to how they should respond to this polite but banal question. As if to regain the initiative, the dog-handler menacingly uncoiled a few links of the animal's chain and the giant hound strained forward.

Holmes' surprising response was to reach down and stroke the vicious-looking beast's huge head at which, to my astonishment it vigorously licked his hand, obediently sat, and wagged its tail enthusiastically. "Good boy, good, boy" murmured Holmes soothingly. Upon the instant, looking shamefaced, the thug on the other end of its chain violently hauled the errant animal back.

Wall-eye, the taller of the two bruisers addressed us truculently. "Folk like to keep themselves to themselves in these parts. They don't appreciate strangers nosing around – now what might be your business hereabouts?"

Holmes smiled blandly. "I do not see that it concerns you gentlemen in the slightest, but the fact is that we are printers by trade, come to seek employment; I had heard there might be a printing concern in the area?"

The dog-handler spoke. "There was but..."

His partner interrupted him brusquely. "There's no such business anywhere around here, so you are wasting your time." Holmes turned to me and ruefully said "Oh dear, Mr Cooper, it seems our journey today is to no avail. But thank you for your assistance gentlemen – we have clearly been misinformed. No matter, let us refresh ourselves at The Cock Inn and then try our luck elsewhere."

"I heartily agree, Mr Brown" I replied, and with this we smartly side-stepped the two drop-jawed heavies and continued on into the centre of Cubitt Town. As we walked, Holmes murmured "Don't look back Watson, but if you are thinking what I am thinking, judging by the cuts and bruises on those two fellows, then the mighty Mr Warburg gave a pretty respectable account of himself wouldn't you agree?" He looked at his watch.

We eventually found the inn a few minutes before two o'clock. It turned out to be a tolerably civilized and cleanly place, quite in contrast to its gloomy environs. I observed at this hour there were only three other customers gathered at a table by the fire, talking softly among themselves.

They looked much like respectable working men, and glanced up only briefly and disinterestedly as we entered, then returned to their quiet conversation. The landlord seemed hospitable enough, and quickly brought us a lunch of fresh-baked bread, ham, cheese and onions and a jug of foaming ale. It was surprisingly palatable. Presently the three men bade the landlord an affable farewell and departed.

Holmes invited our host to share a glass, which he accepted happily enough. "I understand there was a bad business here last night landlord – I believe I heard some poor fellow was beaten to death."

"That is correct sir, and there was I conversing with him only an hour or two before! A giant of a man, he came in for ale and enquired where he might find two acquaintances of his; when he described them I immediately directed him to Slater's Yard near the Reach-side, for I had seen two men in and out of there, exactly matching his descriptions. Shortly after, his lad comes in looking for his Pa, and so I told him to try Slater's.

"And the very next thing, I've got some police Inspector, Bulstrode or something of the sort, knocking me up at goodness knows what hour and asking all manner of questions. I don't know whether the poor fellow died, but there's a police constable at Slater's gate even now so it must be a bad business."

Holmes tutted sympathetically; the landlord resumed his litany of sorrow in a tone of mournful regret. "Not so very long ago, gents, this was a decent place, built by no less a man than William Cubitt, the Lord Mayor of London himself; in those days it was filled with cheerful hard-working families earning honest livings, and well-fed children playing on the pavements. No-one made a fortune, but there's industry here a-plenty, factories and tolerable wages for those who have the appetite for hard work; the docks, the ship-yards, cement factories, potteries, pitch, even Claridges Patent Asphalte Company on Pyrimont Wharf – most offering a fair day's money for a fair day's work."

At this second reference – to pitch and asphalt – Holmes shot me a brief, meaningful glance. I took his import upon the instant. The landlord sighed, "But for those who prefer easier, swifter gains, there's always thieving, black villainy and grievous violence and sadly this locality is becoming a bad place to be because of it."

All this while I was thinking longingly of the familiar, reassuring, gently-faded comfort of 221B Baker Street with its cosy flickering fire, mis-matched easy chairs, eclectic clutter, and my favourite old burgundy-velvet smoking jacket; Holmes murmured our thanks along with a few comforting valedictory words to our gloomy host, upon which we hastily departed his small oasis of comparative civility, which he plainly felt was drowning in an ever-deepening morass of impoverishment and social evil.

I would have been hard-pressed to disagree with him.

We departed the inn and its doleful landlord shortly before three and after threading our way uncertainly through some singularly insalubrious side-streets – I noted in passing a large establishment on the corner of Manchester Street called The Cubitt Arms – we arrived at our destination around a quarter after three in the afternoon. Dusk was already approaching as we neared the gates.

Slater's Yard was an unkempt, dismal acre of muddy scrubland, enclosed by a high dilapidated wooden paling fence, broken down in places, within which stood a two-storey brick-built warehouse, apparently derelict and chained shut, with a crudely hand-painted sign proclaiming 'DANGER – KEEP OUT'. It was fringed with the desiccated skeletons of last year's nettles and thistles, witness to years of neglect.

Adjoining the warehouse to the right was a large, shabby lean-to tar-painted shed or workshop affair; its sagging wooden doors hung drunkenly open. Beyond it was a brick-built shelter, open to the yard on one side and surmounted by a rusty tin smoke-stack; within sat a small antiquated steam engine on a brick pier, beside which was a large wooden bunker filled with coal. The slack canvas drive-belt appeared to run from the engine's pulley through a hatch in the wall into the main building.

Outside on the broken pavement, thorny tentacles of leafless winter bramble groped blindly through gaps in the rotten palings as if seeking to snare unwary passers-by and drag them inside the gloomy place; a large emaciated yellow dog, ribs protruding like a toast-rack, rooted through a pile of rotting waste, but slunk reluctantly away at our approach. On the street outside, a cold and bored-looking Policeman, the same PC Clarke we had encountered outside 64 Chiswick High Road, stood guard.

"Good Day Constable Clarke" Holmes addressed him; "I may tell you that I am now working officially with Inspector Lestrade in this little matter – and a pretty grim business it is too from all accounts?"

"Grim enough Mr Holmes if you count beating a man nearly to death with a four-pound hard-wood block and tackle and sticking him with some kind of Chinee knife. I shouldn't be at all surprised if this hasn't become a murder scene by nightfall. It'll be a miracle if the poor fellow lives out this night – you'd need the constitution of an ox to survive a hammering like that, Mr Holmes."

"Indeed, Clarke" replied my colleague sombrely. "And let us hope that that is exactly what the redoubtable Mr Warburg possesses. Now with your permission Constable, I will examine the scene where you first found Warburg. It will be inside yonder large workshop I believe?"

"That is quite correct Mr Holmes. Nothing has been disturbed, nothing removed except poor Warburg, and it's been under guard since we arrived last night."

Holmes nodded approvingly; we set off across the squalid, rutted yard, where Holmes paused several times and carefully studied the ground between the workshop doors and the pavement, which to me appeared no more than a maze of footprints and wheel-ruts of varying depths. But from his intent, preoccupied expression, I knew he had observed something of significance. We entered the dilapidated building, the scene of last night's murderous attack. A dirty amber glow penetrated through the open doors, leaching reluctantly from the nearby flickering gas-lamp on the street.

Once within and when our eyes became accustomed to the winter-afternoon gloom, two things immediately struck me most powerfully: the first was the scene of complete chaos – mute witness to the violent brutality of the attack and the desperate resistance offered by the mighty Warburg. Clearly he had been aware that he was fighting for his very life.

The second, immediately striking thing was the overpowering, all-pervading, resinous stench of pitch. Barrels and black-crusted buckets lay overturned, brushes and shovels were scattered like fallen boughs after a violent storm; a substantial pulley and tall iron tripod of some sort lay across all like a fallen tree, and tangled coils of hempen rope writhed like vines throughout the wreckage of the battlefield; a heavy wooden bench lay on its side. Embedded in a puddle of fast-setting tar was an overturned Irwin paraffin lamp and also a darkly discoloured heavy wooden block-and-tackle attached to a length of stout rope. I examined it closely, and swiftly realised that the crusted stains were not tar, but the dried red-brown of a man's life-blood.

"I advise you to have a care where you place your feet Watson." I glanced down, and sure enough there were several large pools of the still-hardening sticky stuff all around, already starting to form a wrinkled skin in the dry chill atmosphere of the building. I stood silent while Holmes surveyed the scene at length. After some time he turned to me. "What may we learn here Watson?" I looked carefully and minutely around the entire space and composed my observations.

"I would say, Holmes, that the wreckage and disorder testifies to the extreme brutality of the struggle, and further, I would suggest that in view of Warburg's obvious strength and prowess as a boxer, there were very likely more than two assailants — perhaps three or even four, two of whom we probably encountered earlier this afternoon, and were possibly the couple of heavies that the landlord saw leave the public house last night and follow Warburg, after overhearing his enquiries as to the whereabouts of Mustachios and Wall-Eye.

"They set about him and in the ensuing desperate fight, occasioned this..." - and I indicated the shambles there before us. "In conclusion I suspect that he found the scrap of the Portals wrapper hereabouts, which suggests that the printing press, plates and paper are also probably nearby, most likely in the warehouse, which Lestrade so negligently ignored."

I concluded "In short, I am suggesting that the missing plates and paper may very likely be within our grasp!" There was no answer.

I became aware that Holmes' attention was entirely elsewhere - he appeared to be perfectly transfixed by something at the other end of the building.

Abruptly, and now without regard to the tar-pools, he clambered over the wreckage to the far corner of the workshop and snatched a white envelope from where it was pinned to the wall.

I had overlooked this incongruously pristine object entirely.

With great scrupulousness he examined it and without lifting his eyes from it for a moment he replied "You are right in all of your deductions Watson, except for one - the plates, paper and press, and the criminals responsible are gone." He pulled aside an old tarpaulin which hung across far wall.

"How can you be certain Holmes? We have yet to examine the warehouse!" He looked around impatiently. "Of course they are gone Watson! The floor in here, the tracks on the ground outside yield a more reliable and account than any eye-witness might offer. They are without a shadow of doubt gone, and I have suspected it from the moment we entered the workshop. However, that they *were* here is in no doubt.

"But where are they now I wonder, that is the question?" and with this he picked up an empty, shiny tin canister from a small discarded pile in the far corner and tossed it to me. It contained a pungent, syrupy black residue.

But it was not pitch. It was something else entirely. I peered closely at the stained paper label. It was the highest-quality German black printing ink.

After peering once more behind the tar-stained tarpaulin hanging against the far wall for some minutes, Holmes carefully picked his way back through the tangle of debris, delicately holding the envelope aloft by one corner. He held it before my eyes. "By thunder Holmes – it's addressed to you!"

"Indeed it is Watson; I expected it to be so the moment I espied it. I warned you that they would know we are closing with them and here is the proof.

"It seems we were expected, but how came Lestrade to overlook this I wonder... unless it has been introduced to the scene since his departure last night?

"I doubt not I shall solve that little conundrum soon enough – meanwhile, let us see what our unknown correspondent has to say to us." He opened his small bone-handled, razor-sharp penknife and carefully slit along the top edge of the envelope.

To my surprise he did not immediately examine the contents, but stepped from the workshop into the yard where, outside in the chill early-evening air, he plunged his beak-like nose within the envelope and, eyes closed, inhaled deeply several times. He grunted softly, but whether with satisfaction or disappointment I could not immediately determine.

He turned his back toward the dull street-lamp so that its sullen glow fell weakly upon the two items he had extracted from the envelope.

One was a ten-pound note. The second was a letter, clearly much lengthier than the note Petch had received. In a low voice, lest the Constable overheard, he read:

Sherlock Holmes
I know full well that you are meddling in my affairs. You have caused me considerable inconvenience. However, you now know what grave misfortunes tend to befall those who interfere in my plans – your presence here means you know of the sad accident that blighted your blundering accomplice's attempt to spy on me. You will find a proof of that which you know we possess, indelibly marked on his corpse. You have been duly warned. Desist from your interference, and you and your scribe may

just live to enjoy a long and fruitful life. I warn you not to attempt to trace me further – you will be endangering your health and wasting your time, of which commodity you now have precisely five days, within which period you will arrange with The Bank of England to deposit in a private account at the Bank Leu AG in Zurich, the sum of two hundred and fifty thousand pounds Sterling, or the equivalent in bullion. You will appreciate that this is a mere ten-percent of the amount of money we are even now manufacturing and can distribute at will.

Failure to meet these terms will result in the market being flooded with perfect counterfeit notes, and the consequences will be your responsibility. The account number is recorded upon the enclosed bank-note. Upon confirmation that the money has been deposited in Zurich, you will be contacted with the whereabouts of the plates and paper, when they may be retrieved. Then our business will be concluded. I am certain that The Bank of England will see the wisdom of complying...

Asa Bormanstein

I was silent for some moments as I digested this astonishing intelligence. It would appear that all along the villains had never intended to pursue the risky business of circulating vast amounts of forged currency, but rather, to hold The Bank of England to ransom for a single massive payment in the sum of a quarter of a million pounds of real sterling or gold, using the crude but powerful threat of flooding the economy with a huge injection of false notes.

Unless Holmes knew considerably more than he was revealing, a possibility I would not necessarily discount, I could envision no other route available to the Bank except to submit to this blunt demand forthwith – in effect, to be compelled to buy back their own printing plates and two and a half million pounds in false money for ten percent of its face-value, in real notes or bullion.

My immediate thought was that the modest cost of complying – though still a perfectly staggering sum of money – seemed to me a small enough price to avert the unimaginable economic consequences of defiance. I was on the point of sharing these thoughts with Holmes, when quite unexpectedly, he strode swiftly to the gateway of the yard, where the bored, shivering PC Clarke stamped his feet on the pavement under the wan glow of the gas-light; the yellow dog had sneaked back to rummage in the rotting midden.

For just the briefest moment, it seemed to me that the unlikely trio, dimly illuminated in the dismal pool of pallid light, composed the most improbable *tableau* – an emaciated yellow dog seeking sustenance, a shivering red-nosed policeman seeking warmth, and a pale, gaunt detective seeking an unknown correspondent.

"Ah, there you are again Mr Holmes. Seen everything you need? Something of a battlefield in there eh?"

"Indeed PC Clarke – it clearly was a most violent confrontation. Tell me Clarke, you have been on duty here since attending with Inspector Lestrade last night?"

"Yes Mr Holmes and I'll be powerful pleased when Wickham and Langridge show up to relieve me – indeed they're late now" and he stamped his cold feet for emphasis. Holmes fixed the shivering policeman with a steady gaze. "That is well Constable. I take it then that no strangers have entered the yard or buildings, you have had this crime-scene under surveillance continuously?" The policeman shrugged uneasily. "Well, more or less Mr Holmes..."

"Hmm... tell me more about the *less* Constable."

The burly constable looked vaguely embarrassed. "Well Mr Holmes, you know... I had to answer an urgent call of... well, nature."

He gestured helplessly at the wide-open, privacy-denying wasteland around us. His voice took on a slight edge of unease, no doubt because of his knowledge of Holmes' familiar relationship with his senior officer, Lestrade.

"Honestly Mr Holmes, I was only away for a few minutes. About half after two I regret to say I was compelled to run to The Cubitt Arms to ah... answer the call and I thought there would be no harm done if after, I warmed up with a swift glass of Porter by the stove. I was back here at my post in twenty minutes, and not a second more, I swear it Mr Holmes."

The smallest quiver of a smile flickered momentarily over Holmes' lips. "A perfectly reasonable explanation constable and an even more reasonable cause to desert your post momentarily. No great harm is done; indeed, without your short absence for twenty minutes, I would likely lack a most valuable clue now in my possession. I trust you will not have too much longer to wait before your colleagues arrive. And now I bid you goodnight constable."

It lacked a quarter of seven before we arrived at the familiar entrance of the Charing Cross Hospital. We were directed to a ward on the first floor, where we found a constable seated at the door; he leapt to his feet. "Good evening gentlemen; Mr Holmes and Doctor Watson I imagine? The Inspector told me I may expect you." Holmes nodded with satisfaction. "Tell me Constable, has Mr Warburg received any visitors since he was admitted?"

The policeman thought for a moment. "Apart from Inspector Lestrade, there were a couple of burly heavies..." Holmes visibly stiffened "...but they were his two lads. The Inspector said it was all quite in order. Talk about 'like father like son', they were gigantic as well." Holmes relaxed.

At this hour the ward was hushed and dimly illuminated. Warburg's bed was instantly distinguishable among the dozen in the room, by the almighty bulk of the man under the blankets; he appeared to be sleeping calmly, propped up on several pillows, one tree trunk-like arm resting across his barrel chest, the other at his side, encased in bandages.

The mere fact that he yet breathed was testimony to a most extraordinary constitution – rarely I have I seen such dreadful injuries inflicted even after the most sadistic of beatings.

I judged he would be a very long time healing, if indeed he survived. When the perpetrators were eventually apprehended, the charges must surely include attempted murder?

I reached for his wrist and felt the pulse; it was improbably vigorous. "Something of a medical anomaly would you not agree, Doctor Watson?" I turned to see who addressed me. A tall silver-haired doctor peered at me over half-moon tortoise-shell spectacles and extended his hand to each of us in turn.

"Doctor James Moffatt; Inspector Lestrade advised me of your visit gentlemen. I am pleased to meet you, but I'm afraid I must warn that regardless of his great strength, this Goliath still tires extremely quickly; I regret I may permit you no more than ten minutes."

Our murmured discourse must have awoken the somnolent giant for he stirred, opened his eyes, and after a few moments appeared to recognise us.

Painfully, a smile broke across his dreadfully abused face. His eyes vanished as before, but this time within a grim patchwork of puffy black, purple and yellow bruises, sutures and abrasions, surrounding a savagely broken nose and crusted, torn lips.

Doctor Moffatt discreetly withdrew to the far side of the ward, while a nurse considerately brought two chairs for us. Holmes leaned close to the bedside and quietly addressed the supine man.

"My dear Mr Warburg, no-one is more heartily glad than I to see the leviathan finally wakes; do you feel sufficiently recovered to speak with us?" Warburg, with a titanic effort, levered himself up onto his good elbow; I swiftly wedged another pillow behind him whereupon he sank back gratefully with a vast sigh. Wryly he croaked "Well Mr Holmes, so much for my attempt to ascend your ladder of observation and deduction, and so much for the *'wisdom of your Solomon.'* I felt, perhaps I might have been of assistance to you in some small measure; instead, I fear I have played the part of *rosh ha-kesilim.*" Holmes smiled; quietly he murmured:

"Ah he, the Biblical Chief of the Fools. Well, I fear I must agree Warburg, you have indeed been extremely foolish, but then you have also been courageous, enterprising and resourceful; predictably you have of course impeded my investigation and yet curiously, at the same time you may, perhaps, have advanced it. Sadly, in so doing, you have paid a most dreadful price for your well-intentioned but ill-advised intervention in this affair."

Warburg chuckled weakly, causing him to cough and wince in pain. When the spasm subsided he said with a crooked grin "Indeed gentlemen, indeed I have, but do you... suppose..." he lapsed into a fit of painful coughing "...my handsome good looks are... lost forever?" He rolled his eyes upward as if to view his own forehead. "But then it now seems than I am worth ten pounds more than when I visited Cubitt Town!" He spoke slowly and indistinctly through battered and swollen lips. Holmes smiled and I laughed out loud, occasioning a stern glance from the nurse; that a man in Warburg's dismal straits could, improbably, summon up a jest seemed almost beyond belief.

"In the circumstances, you show the most remarkable fortitude my friend" said Sherlock Holmes kindly. "But you will need to rest; for now, are you strong enough briefly to tell us the bones of what occurred last night, and particularly, what you might have seen? Inspector Lestrade has already informed us of events more or less up to the moment you arrived at Slater's Yard."

"Very well Mr Holmes. When I arrived at Slater's all was quiet, and the place appeared to be deserted and in total darkness. The gates to the yard were slightly ajar, as were the doors to the large workshop. I chose this latter entry, as the main warehouse was securely locked and chained. Once inside I lit the old

Irwin lantern I had brought with me; its light is poor but even so I could make out tar barrels, tools and the like stacked around the walls.

"There was a small pile of waste-paper in one corner – when I picked a piece up, it appeared to be an outer wrapper bearing a label from Portals Paper Mill... there were three of them on the floor. I know from past experience in banking exactly what they manufacture and thought this a mighty odd item to be found in a shabby warehouse in East London. There were also empty ink cans. I decided to retain the label in the event that it might aid you in your search for, ah, your 'friend'".

"That was most astute of you Warburg, and a most useful clue. Lestrade, with some considerable difficulty, later prised a fragment of it from your clenched fist while you were unconscious."

"I am glad it has some value.

"Anyway, Mr Holmes, at that moment a dim glow suddenly illuminated the workshop; it appeared to emanate from behind a large tarpaulin hanging across the far wall so I immediately extinguished the Irwin and cautiously pulled back a corner of the tarpaulin, which, it transpired, concealed a pair of locked doors into the warehouse itself..."

"...one of which has a small glazed panel inset" interjected Holmes. "I discovered them myself only an hour or two back. They were padlocked, but it appeared that they opened into a bare and empty room."

Warburg vainly attempted to reach for his water-glass, which I passed to him. After taking a long draught he continued his tale. "Well Mr Holmes, I assure you it was far from empty when I looked in. The glass was dirty, but I could see well enough to make out the heavy who rode in my hansom to Chiswick, along with a second taller man; his back was toward me; they appeared to be in discussion around a printing press, which the second fellow seemed to be tinkering with. He may have been the tall moustachioed man you seek.

"Also, if it is of relevance, the press was most recognisably an old Koenig, driven by a steam engine in the adjacent outside shelter. I assume, now, this is a case of forgery you are investigating."

"Indeed Warburg" Holmes murmured. "Please continue."

"The rest of the story is eloquently written all over this poor aching body Mr Holmes. As you can see, they were gifted a rather large page upon which to write, and it appears they were most determined to cover it closely! I was dealt a mighty blow upon the head from behind, which momentarily stunned me – indeed I staggered and almost was felled by the force of it; fortunately my skull is as robustly constructed as the rest of my frame.

"I turned; in the dim gloaming from the street lamp I made out two heavily-built thugs, both of whom I had noted drinking in the alehouse earlier that evening; clearly they had followed me."

"You are correct" said Holmes. "The landlord himself confirmed to me that they appeared to be listening most attentively to your conversation with him; something to which you should perhaps have been more alert when nosing around foreign and dangerous parts. They followed you out only a few minutes after your departure."

Our battered behemoth nodded ruefully.

"I have a lot to learn from you Mr Holmes. To resume then, one of them was swinging a heavy block and tackle on a short length of rope, no doubt the object that almost knocked me unconscious; the shorter restrained a large and vicious-looking dog on a chain. I decided upon the instant that I had a pretty fair chance of dealing with the two heavies but the dog, I judged, would prove a far more dangerous and unpredictable adversary and eliminating it from the ruck immediately became my most urgent objective."

As I listened to this horrific account, I marvelled at the cool presence of mind that enabled him to plan his impending struggle. He continued "Having no weapon to hand, I proffered my left arm to the beast, which it immediately seized; with its jaws thus occupied I raised it off the ground and delivered my best, I may say my most famous blow, a punishing right cross, whereupon the animal fell unconscious as if pole-axed."

I considered the monumental strength required to lift that monstrous dog clean off the floor with one arm. Warburg ruminated for a moment.

"I recall it had the self-same effect upon Charley Mitchell at The White Rose, but that was just a friendly bout... anyhow, when the dog went down, the two thugs set about me with a real will; I took many severe blows from the block and tackle, but as for fist-fighting, they were lowly street brawlers; indeed I believe I was close to gaining the upper hand when I was once again attacked, from behind.

"Something sharp stabbed hard into my shoulder – apparently the surgeon removed some kind of foreign knife. The police have it now." He pointed weakly at the dressing at the junction of his thick neck and meaty right shoulder. I noted it was exactly at the medial end of the collar-bone where it joins the sternoclavicular joint, perilously close to the external carotid artery.

He continued "The outcry clearly had alerted the other two, whereupon I soon went down under an interminable welter of kicks and blows. I remember little more after that, gentlemen, except the lad finding me." Ruefully he concluded "And now here I am, painfully paying for my imprudence, and richer by ten pounds which I can never, ever spend! I declare I must be the world's first human counterfeit banknote!"

Holmes smiled at the outlandish brand across the big man's forehead. "Indeed, but I suppose you make take solace from the fact that ten pounds rarely lasts forever; inevitably it dwindles and is soon gone. Now tell me Warburg, for I know you to have a keen eye for detail, describe for me if you will, the far end-wall of the workshop when first you saw it."

Warburg screwed his eyes shut. "About twenty feet wide and ten high; brick and weather-board, being the outer wall of the warehouse, a large tarpaulin stained with pitch hanging from a beam, perhaps to conceal the doorway beyond. The three paper wrappers and several empty ink canisters in the right corner, several ladders, coils of rope and various contractors' supplies, paint and implements against the wall to the left."
"That is all? Nothing, for example, like this, pinned prominently to the wall?"

Slowly and painfully, Warburg opened his bruised and swollen eyes and peered at the white envelope Holmes had produced from his pocket. "There was nothing like that Mr Holmes, I will assure you. Even with the dim light of the Irwin, that envelope would have been illumined like the Trinity Buoy Wharf lighthouse! No Mr Holmes, I swear upon the Torah that your envelope was not anywhere upon the wall."

"That is good enough for me, Warburg, and also it happens to be the second piece of information of incalculable value that you have furnished. Now rest, my friend, for you are tired."

And indeed, the man's eyes were now slowly drifting shut. We stole quietly away, and headed back to Baker Street.

* * *

CHAPTER TWELVE

THE CHIEF CASHIER'S DILEMMA

Breakfast next morning was necessarily a hasty affair. Today was the first of the five days before the deadline set by the criminals expired. Holmes had informed me the preceding evening that he expected visitors around ten, and though the table had already been cleared, the faint savoury aroma of smoked haddock lingered yet. Save for the measured tick of the clock, the room was silent, when from behind his newspaper Holmes startled me: "How is your nose this morning Watson?" Puzzled, I set down the map of Lime house, Poplar and The Isle of Dogs I had been studying with aid of his lens, much mystified by such a very peculiar enquiry.

Drily I retorted "Well Holmes, as I am sure with your sharp eyes you will have observed, it is still here in its correct position upon my face and to my knowledge it performs its function as well as ever; it can certainly still distinguish a Fumé from a Fuissé."

"Capital! I may have need of its services later, after this agreeable but lingering aroma of smoked fish is gone." I was on the point of enquiring to what this most odd exchange could possibly refer, when Mrs Hudson entered. "Your callers, Mr Holmes" and she showed in two visitors; the first, Mr Petch – again nervous and highly agitated, as seemed his permanent and understandable condition nowadays – and a second gentleman whom I did not recognise, appearing only slightly less troubled; he was faultlessly attired in frock-coat, striped trousers high-cut in the old style, and grey silk waistcoat. Carrying a gleaming top-hat, grey kid gloves and silver-mounted cane, he looked for all the world like a well-to-do city banker – and so indeed he proved to be.

Holmes rose to welcome them. "Good morning gentlemen both; addressing the stranger he said "I am Sherlock Holmes. This is my friend and colleague, Doctor Watson, who is good enough to assist me on certain of my investigations; Watson, may I present Mr Frank May, the Chief Cashier of The Bank of England."

I realised on the instant, of course, that this was the 'higher authority' Holmes had been compelled to draw into his confidence, now that it seemed quite inevitable that Lestrade would become concerned in the matter. He addressed Holmes in a low, sepulchral voice.

"I received your wire – bad news Mr Holmes. Very bad news. Indeed, it is the worst possible news. I have two pressing questions for you. Can you find them in time? And can they be stopped?"

Standing somewhat behind him, Petch winced visibly at each word May intoned. Holmes indicated for our guests to be seated. "I believe I can find them Mr May, and they can indeed be stopped."

Succinctly he detailed the events which had occurred since Petch first presented himself at Rules on Christmas Eve; in this narration my colleague spared nothing of Dulcie Hobbs' horrible murder, the Yard's initial acceptance of it as, *prima facie*, a simple case of suicide and of the subsequent lethal attempt upon Solomon Warburg's life in Cubitt Town. Frank May, now grim-faced and pale, was evidently most deeply shocked by the account. It showed plainly in his countenance just how unspeakably alien were these sordid and bestial doings – but Holmes' bread and butter – to the civilised, evenly-regulated life of the second most powerful man in The Bank of England.

"...and that is why I convoked you here today Mr May; I had planned to apprehend the criminals responsible with absolute discretion, and with no police involvement for the obvious reasons of averting public panic and financial chaos; and indeed, until one Mr Solomon Warburg's well-intentioned but clumsy intervention, I believe you would now have had your plates, paper and any notes printed, safely back under lock and key, along with the villains. But they have panicked and moved their, ah, place of business to whereabouts at present unknown to me. And the sad murder of Mr Petch's maid and the near-murder of Solomon Warburg have all conjoined to the point where the Yard demands to be informed. They have, however, undertaken to work chiefly under my guidance, in the interests of the economy."

Petch had reverted to rocking in his chair, wringing his bony hands feverishly. The Chief Cashier straightened in his seat, composed his features and addressed the great detective:

"Very well; you will perhaps understand Mr Holmes that such unspeakable events are so far beyond my sphere of experience that I find myself completely incompetent to choose any course of action.

"But I see clearly from the discretion you have demonstrated thus far that you have an acute understanding of the implications of two and a half millions of false money being circulated. But, Mr Holmes, these men must be stopped, *whatever the cost!* Perhaps you will be good enough to tell me what options you believe may be open to us."

"It is my firm opinion, Mr May, that you have only two. The first – and I venture to suggest, by far the most preferable – is to place your complete reliance in me, without question or reservation" Holmes stated in a level tone.

"The second, as you will now read, is to pay a substantial ransom for the return of the stolen goods." And with this he handed May the Slater's Yard ransom-demand, along with the enclosed second proof. The Chief Cashier's eyes hardened as he swiftly scanned the letter. He read it aloud a second time, more slowly, and then turned his attention to the banknote, examining it at extreme close range through the gold monocle he retrieved from his waistcoat pocket. Holmes passed May his powerful lens with the aid of which the Cashier examined every part of the note in great detail.

Petch continued to wring his hands in deep anguish. His cheerless demeanour portrayed clearly his inner fears for surely outright ruin now stared him in the face. He and his business were disgraced, and they evidently would lose not only the irreplaceable business of The Bank of England, but of every other patron who learned of the scandal. Such a dismal conclusion, to me at least, appeared quite inescapable now that the matter must inevitably pass into the vulgar realm of the public domain.

Mr May looked up from the banknote. Calmly he said: "Well Mr Holmes, I am sure you recognise that this is a well-nigh perfect ten pound note; the cipher and serial number are completely nonsensical of course, but will appear quite authentic to the layman; they are correctly placed and printed, and I have not the slightest doubt that any number of these... things... will pass into circulation with the greatest of ease." He glanced at Petch, now bent over with his face sunk in his hands.

"But then that is only to be expected of the work of the finest master engraver in the country, perhaps in all of Europe. It seems we have five days before disaster befalls us. Now do not misapprehend me Mr Holmes; I am conversant with your unparalleled reputation for solving those problems which are too obscure, or too delicate to entrust to the regular forces of law, but for this matter to become common knowledge is a risk I feel I may not take.

"You say the villains have moved, yet you know not where.

"If I understand the matter aright then you cannot hunt them, for you know not whom to hunt; you cannot locate them for you do not know where to look; the police cannot arrest them for they do not know whom they should arrest; and if they flee the country, the port authorities cannot seize them, for they do not know who to seize; unless I am much mistaken Mr Holmes, lacking a description, a name and a location – save for this sole reference to an anonymous private bank account – we are powerless to deny them! How can you be confident in your assertion? Should you fail to locate them within the time they have set, the consequences would be perfectly unthinkable. No, the notion is quite insupportable; I am afraid, Mr Holmes that we shall have to pay the ransom; staggering though it is, it is a mere fraction of the costs that will be occasioned if this quantity of fraudulent money circulates freely.

"There is no other way. I shall immediately inform the Governor and we shall seek the permission of Lord Salisbury and, most likely, the Chancellor of the Exchequer too, Mr Goschen.

"I confidently anticipate they will concur with me and authorise the transfer of two hundred and fifty thousand pounds to the account number indicated upon this despicable banknote; only thus may we be assured that the matter will be drawn to a swift and, most importantly, a discreet conclusion." There was a prolonged silence.

"I see" replied Holmes laconically. "Evidently, expenditure of this vast and unprecedented scale is of no great moment to The Bank!"

"My mind is made up Mr Holmes — we must meet their demands!"

My colleague was silent for some minutes. Sherlock Holmes was quite altered when he was deeply immersed in a problem as intractable as this was proving to be. Had one only ever encountered him as the silent thinker, the supreme master of inexorable logic, the hermit-like resident of 221B Baker Street, one might at that moment perfectly easily have failed to recognise him as one and the same man. His face was flushed and intense, brows drawn tight in dark concentration and his eyes burned out from beneath them with an unrelenting hardness. His shoulders were hunched, his thin lips compressed in a tight line.

I was upon the point of suggesting that Mr May's proposal, while costly, seemed likely to be the most prudent path, when I realised that Holmes' mind was now so completely concentrated upon the matter that any comment of mine would be unheeded by him, indeed, would likely be an irritant. I remained silent.

He looked up at the Chief Cashier. "Very well Mr May; it seems that despite your attendance here, you prefer to rely upon the counsel of your own dread, rather than the considered advice of one who may modestly claim to have resolved many far more delicate and intractable problems than this, Gordian though the knot may be.

"Should you doubt my credentials, I am sure enquiries could be made."

May stared levelly at Holmes. In a low, toneless voice he replied "Oh they have been Mr Holmes, believe me they already have been..."

Holmes closed his eyes and frowning darkly, he squeezed his temples between the slim white fingers and thumb of his left hand, like a pianist spanning an octave. Abruptly he looked up at the Chief Cashier, shrugged resignedly, smiled amiably enough and returning to his natural manner said "Very well Mr May; by all means proceed, a perfectly splendid notion! I may take it, then, that our business here is done? That is well, for I have several other pressing matters to attend, for clients who generally prefer to act upon my counsel." He paused and then added, as if as an afterthought:

"However, I most strongly advise that you should authorise a far greater sum of at least, say, half a million pounds, perhaps even more, and pretty briskly too, for you will have need of it. That advice is with my compliments."

"But Holmes" I interjected, "the demand is only for a quarter of a million pounds!" He glanced at me, somewhat coolly and addressed his audience. "Gentlemen, if you truly believe that the payment of this ransom will be the end of the matter, and that you may expect a tidily wrapped, prompt delivery of the stolen items to Threadneedle Street, perhaps accompanied by a gracious letter of thanks, then you are entirely deluding yourselves!" He stood and commenced pacing agitatedly to and fro, his hands clasped behind his back.

"Understand me in this Mr May, an extortion of this vast scale is never a singular event, but rather the commencement of an insidious – possibly endless – process and I guarantee you Sir, that if this payment is made, there will undoubtedly be a further demand and no return of your plates or paper! Trust me in this matter Mr May, for I have some deep experience of the breed. They will not cease their demands until the object of their hold over the victim is retrieved or nullified – or they are arrested. Only then are they rendered impotent.

"These are not men of honour; you may just as well, with precisely the same pointless consequence, beneficently gift the money to the first impoverished beggar whom next you encounter, for assuredly you will achieve nothing more by it – save to place The

Bank in abject thrall until such time as you are compelled at great expense, to withdraw all ten pound white notes now in circulation."

"And even so, your adversaries may well yet circulate the fraudulent notes at a greater rate than you can recall the authentic ones, while remaining continuously on the run!

"And finally, do not lose sight of the fact that a young woman has been most brutally murdered and but for his quite astonishing constitution, Mr Solomon Warburg would, of a certainty, be her cold companion in death upon the mortuary slab!"

At the conclusion of these hard, plain words the august Mr Frank May, Chief Cashier of The Bank of England appeared to be struggling in a churning maelstrom of indecision; he looked exactly what he had become ~ a man of high business affairs, entirely accustomed to wielding great authority – but now quite powerless to do anything but to yield to evil circumstance far beyond his control, and to accept Holmes' counsel.

Abruptly Frank May stood and drew himself to his full height. Grimly he said "Very well Mr Holmes. If what you say is correct, it would appear that The Bank has no option but to place its entire confidence, and that of the British economy, in your abilities. I pray that they may be adequate to the need.

"Do you believe you can apprehend the perpetrators in five days? Do you have even the faintest notion where they may now be?" All turned toward the lean detective.

His eyes were closed in concentrated thought, one thin pale finger to his pursed lips in the rigid, frozen posture I knew so well — it generally signalled the fact that he comprehended rather more than did his audience and, indeed, than he was yet prepared to reveal. He looked up, a tiny flicker of a smile on his lips. "In answer to your two questions Mr May, then yes, I am confident I will resolve your dilemma within the time allotted.

"As to your second, no I do not yet know *precisely* where they are, but I know something of almost equal value..." Petch and May looked hopefully at Holmes.

"I am confident I know where they are *not!*" And upon this somewhat cryptic note he stood once more, a clear portent that the conference was at an end.

* * *

CHAPTER THIRTEEN

THE SMELL OF MONEY

After the door closed behind our guests, Holmes sank back in his chair and was silent for many minutes. I knew better than to press him at this critical juncture, for certainly he would divulge such thoughts as he felt ready to share at the moment of his choosing. I returned to my study of the map of the Isle of Dogs and its environs, striving to find some clue, perhaps some other noisome, out-of-the-way place where the villains might have gone to ground in order to continue with their wicked work.

It struck me that the speedy overnight removal of a heavy printing press and a large quantity of security paper was a not inconsiderable undertaking, even with several burly men and, I surmised, certainly a heavy wagon and strong horses. Surely they would not flee further than necessary? But looking at the map once more, I realised just what a vast warren of rookeries this place was – even within a span of just a few miles it embraced Rotherhithe and the Redriff Marsh, Stepney, Limehouse and Poplar, Greenwich and Plaistow with its great wasteland of Abbey Marsh, and southward, Peckham, Bermondsey and Deptford; it certainly seemed to me that to find a needle in an entire field of haystacks, in an entire country of hay-fields would pose a somewhat lesser challenge. And based on what subtle clue, I pondered, was Holmes so confident as to state that he would locate the press, the thieves and the priceless plates and paper within the allotted five days, perhaps even less?

He emerged from his brown study and addressed me: "It is said Watson, that the blind, being deprived entirely of their window upon the world, may demonstrate marked acuity in other senses by way of compensation, most notably the senses of smell and hearing. Piano-tuners are very often sightless, and there have been some notable perfumiers similarly challenged; I rather fancy putting the notion to the test."

Long-accustomed as I was to my friend's inexplicable and bizarre leaps of logic and my struggles to disambiguate them, I knew of a certainty from this odd statement that he was now so totally absorbed by the problem at hand, it must in some curious way bear upon the matter. "I have heard as much myself Holmes, but I fear you lack a piano-tuner or a perfumier with whom to explore the theory."

"Hah!" he cried and dived into his bedroom, to return with his black silk opera scarf. "Permit me to rob you of your eyes for a moment Watson, that we may test that discerning nose of yours. I wish your opinion upon an important matter."

Mystified, I permitted him to blindfold me, and the room became as black as the tomb, bringing to mind my insane dream on Christmas Eve of that infernal plant-house. "I am holding something under your nose; what can you determine?" I took a cautious sniff, wary of some of the noxious substances with which Holmes was wont to dabble. I detected a faint, inoffensive odour, perfectly familiar to me. "I believe I collect the smell of new paper, and printing ink Holmes. Surely this is one of those fraudulent banknotes?"

"Indeed it is Watson, but explore deeper – what more can you detect in the bouquet?" I inhaled deeply and now discerned something else, the smallest trace of a faint but familiar aroma. After a moment of hesitation I recognised it. "I do believe there is the taint of pitch about it Holmes. But then the place where it was likely printed was awash with the stuff!"

"Exactly! Capital Watson! Now indulge me a further moment- what of this?" Again I inhaled. "It seems the same again Holmes – perhaps the second note?" I sampled once more. Now I detected a subtle difference, a second undertone, but one I could not immediately place. "It is the same, but the aroma of pitch seems somehow lesser, and there is the smallest hint of something else, an unpleasant smell of decay" I inhaled again, more deeply, and then it came to me "...of rotten eggs or decomposing flesh?"

My colleague whipped away the scarf and beamed at me. "A fair description; we concur to a nice point my dear Watson! Mark that curious aroma well and remember it. A keen sense of smell can be quite as valuable as any of the other faculties in the solution of certain problems. And heightened by the complete elimination of the distraction of sight, it can be perfectly invaluable."

He strode to his desk, rummaged in the drawer and returned with a pair of compasses and an ivory rule. "This map of the Isle of Dogs is executed at a scale of one mile to one inch. Now let us more closely locate our quarry." He set the compasses at a radius of three inches, placed its point upon the location of Slater's Yard in Cubitt Town, and inscribed a circle – an area around six miles in diameter "There, Watson, within that circle is where I am convinced the villains have gone to earth. It can, I am sure of it, be no further away!"

Recalling my principles of mathematics from schooldays I was aware that the area of a circle is calculated by means of the multiplication of its radius squared, by *Pi* – roughly 3.14. I made a swift, approximate mental calculation. "I am not at all sure how you have reached that conclusion Holmes, but even if you are correct, by my mathematics that small circle embraces more than twenty-eight square miles of territory! In five days it would take a positive army of sharp-eyed men diligently to search all of it! What chance do we two alone stand of locating one small printing press?"

He smiled somewhat mischievously. "I believe we stand an excellent chance of locating it my dear Watson, for the simple reason that if my notion is correct, I do not believe we need to scour all of it!"

"But still I cannot fathom why you particularly believe our quarry to lie within this area at all." I indicated the circle, centred upon Slater's Yard. "And why this particular diameter Holmes?"

Somewhat inscrutably he replied "That remains to be proven Watson, but my thesis turns upon the reliability of our noses, the speed of a Koenig steam-driven press, and most particularly, the distance which a strong but panicked man can cover on foot in, say, an hour at his best pace, and the odd odour on the second proof. You may care to consider those factors, for they have considerable significance.

"And now I shall leave you to your own devices for I must go to the Yard and take Lestrade into my confidence, or at least so far as is absolutely necessary. In addition I intend to visit Mr Warburg. I shall return for dinner at perhaps, seven; will you join me then?"

And with this he descended to the street. I returned to my study of the map, vaguely aware of his stentorian tones summoning a cab. I allowed my mind to range freely over the disparate matters he had drawn to my attention; the curious blindfold experiment, the circle now precisely scribed on the map, the operating speed of a steam-powered printing press and the pace at which a man might travel on foot.

After much deliberation, I remained unable to organise these factors into any workable theory, or even a coherent speculation, save to estimate that a man might cover perhaps three or four miles on foot in an hour. Somewhat frustrated I set the problem aside against the hour when Holmes returned, heaped more coals upon the fire and contentedly immersed myself in Thomas Pickering Pick's excellent new volume, *Fractures and Dislocations*.

Little more of note occurred that afternoon save that Mrs Hudson brought tea at four, and at six a telegram message was delivered.

It was addressed to Holmes; I set it upon the mantelshelf and went back to my studies. He burst in at seven o'clock and seemed to be in high good humour occasioned it would appear, by his afternoon excursion; I knew of old that he would apprise me of progress in his own good time. "There you are Watson." He shrugged off his Ulster and tossed it carelessly upon the chair. "I should not wish to be out and about much later than this – there is a wickedly thick fog brewing up out there." I parted the curtains and peered out and indeed it appeared to be gathering fast, coalescing into an evil greasy shroud that hung low over the rooftops and showed dull brown-yellow by the barely visible gaslights below. Only yards along Baker Street they were obscured completely. It would be a night of rich pickings for thugs and footpads.

Despite the perpetual state of apparent chaos and disorder that existed throughout most of Holmes' papers and possessions (with the sole exception of his meticulously maintained indices of news-clippings and his fastidiously organised wardrobe) he possessed an uncanny knack of spotting upon the instant if anything had been moved, removed or added.

Thus I was not in the least bit surprised when I was upon the point of mentioning the telegram to him, he strode to the fireplace and retrieved it from the mass of paperwork piled on the mantel.

"Ah, we may expect company this evening Watson. It seems Mr Frank May requires to consult once more upon 'a matter of the greatest urgency' to which end he proposes to visit around eight o'clock this evening. I very much hope that this does not signify a change of heart to pay the ransom demand! That would be a most foolish course of action."

Presently, over a simple dinner of the thick-end of a cold ham and mustard piccalilli Holmes described his afternoon between surgically-dissected, precise bites.

"For one generally so impulsive, so disposed to leap into precipitate action at the earliest apparent clue or the first sign of criminality, Lestrade seems for once Watson, prepared to show quite remarkable restraint in this case. Initially, when I apprised him of most of the backdrop to the murder of Hobbs and the attempted murder of Warburg – who, by the by is recovering at a most encouraging rate – he was seized with his usual reckless notion of reinforcing failure with failure.

"He would have launched a nationwide manhunt complete with a detailed statement to the newspapers accompanied by a veritable deluge of, no doubt, quite unrecognisable and useless posters and handbills, largely based on vague second-hand accounts, depicting sketches of various wall-eyed thugs and a miscellany of distinguished-looking men sporting different styles of moustache!

"It is my unvarying experience that such vague images have more utility in a general treatise on anthropology!"

I chuckled at my friend's permanent frustration with what he considered to be, with very few notable exceptions, the hopeless ineptitude of most Scotland Yarders. "How then, did you disabuse friend Lestrade of his madcap plan?"

Holmes smiled happily. "Oh, I simply pointed out to him that Warburg's interference, quite apart from earning him the fearful beating he suffered, merely served to drive our prey from where we suspected them to be, to a new location yet unknown to us; indeed, they might even see fit to make good their threat and commence circulating their counterfeit notes in order to hasten the Bank's decision.

"But I believe he truly appreciated the gravity of the situation when I informed him that our client was now no less a body than The Bank of England itself, reporting directly to the first secretary of The Treasury, the Chancellor of The Exchequer, and Lord Salisbury, and it would be to those gentlemen he would become accountable; I further suggested he might conceivably fall foul of the new Act to prohibit disclosure of official documents and information, which you may be aware received Royal assent this summer and has now passed into law — although candidly Watson, that was somewhat of a bluff on my part!

"In short, I impressed upon him the many hazards entailed in haste, and the great virtues in delay; thus for a very few days at least, he is now under my advice and will stay his hand.

"Finally, I gently hinted that all the honours would still be his for I shall, of choice, remain in the wings when the last curtain falls on this drama." Holmes was clearly much pleased by the skilful diplomacy he had wrought, and I chuckled at the smooth cunning with which he had muzzled the famously headstrong Lestrade and so, tactfully restrained him from leaping into rash action. I was upon the point of asking him to explain the significance of the smell of the banknotes and the meaning of the circle on the map when the doorbell announced the arrival of our visitor. Rapid footsteps on the stair indicated a degree of some great urgency.

There was a single sharp rap on the door but before Holmes could answer, it opened to reveal Mr Frank May. His jaw was tight, his brow furrowed with concern, and it seemed to me that he too was now exhibiting all those symptoms of immense stress so familiar in Henry Petch. Clearly, the increasing strain of this grave situation was playing havoc with his nervous system. "Good evening Mr May" said my colleague. "You have done well to be so prompt in view of the great fog brewing out there." May made no comment. Without taking his eyes from Holmes he slowly reached into his inner pocket and produced an unsealed envelope, clearly blazoned with The Bank's emblem. With a hand that showed rather more than a tremor he passed it over, uttering only eight words, in the dead tone of a man speaking as from beyond the grave.

"God help us Mr Holmes, it has begun..."

* * *

CHAPTER FOURTEEN

JUDAS SILVER

Sherlock Holmes snatched the proffered envelope and having spared its exterior only the most cursory of examinations, removed the contents. What he held up to the light caused him to furrow his brow in deep perplexity. It was, it appeared to me, yet another – now the third – of the fraudulent ten pound banknotes. Eyes closed, with the closest deliberation, he raised it to his nose, inhaled several times deeply, nodded once and then proceeded to examine it minutely upon both faces with his lens. He offered it to me. "You will not require the blindfold to assay this one Watson."

I sampled its odour. It was the same rotten, sulphurous scent again, perhaps even more pungent than the sampling of the morning? Holmes returned his attention to the Chief Cashier.

"Mr May, when and how came you by this third note, for I see it was clearly not sent to you by our criminal printers?" For a brief moment I pondered how Holmes could so confidently bar it from being yet another signal from the villains. Our visitor consulted his watch. "You are perfectly correct in that Mr Holmes.

"This note was brought personally and urgently by one of the cashiers to my desk precisely two hours and thirty minutes ago. Along with other notes and coin, it had been presented for payment into one of our smaller business accounts at the Bank by one Mr Julius Kauffmann, the senior partner of Kauffmann Brothers in the Whitechapel High Street." He winced almost imperceptibly and continued in a tone of faint distaste "I am told by my staff that they are... pawnbrokers, merchants in second-hand trinkets, jewellery and... the like." He spoke the words in a low tone and reluctantly, as if they savoured of something objectionable and might choke him with their mere utterance. Holmes carefully replaced the banknote in the envelope and set it aside upon the occasional table.

"I shall, of course, require to retain this for the present. Who brought the note to your attention so promptly, Mr May, and why? Was it some curiosity about Mr Kauffmann's demeanour, or was it perhaps the banknote itself?" The Chief Cashier brightened momentarily. "That may be the only stroke of good fortune I have enjoyed today Mr Holmes. Fortunately Mr Kauffmann presented himself and his takings at the desk of one of our brightest cashiers, a rising young man, Hugh Tenbury-Ripon. It so happens that he is an ardent notaphilist, and extremely sharp-eyed into the bargain. Aware that our new issue of ten pound notes was not due to enter circulation until sometime after May this year, he examined this note rather more closely and observed that the cipher and serial number appeared to be an illogical, strange and radical departure from the Bank's secret and long-established formula.

"Pleading some small administrative query he asked Mr Kauffmann to wait momentarily and came directly to my office for instructions. He told me that Mr Kauffmann had not personally been handed the note, but that it had been accepted in settlement of a purchase by one of his employees." Holmes was attending closely to this tale of an unexpected third advent. "And what advice did you give to Tenbury-Ripon Mr May?"

"In the ordinary way of things Mr Holmes, the note would be confiscated, the depositor informed that it was a forgery and, naturally, he would receive only a receipt for it, but no manner of financial compensation whatever.

"However, in this case I judged it far too dangerous to risk a public panic by letting knowledge of this sensitive and privy information pass into the common domain.

"I instructed Mr Tenbury-Ripon to accept the note and to inform Mr Kauffmann in an offhand manner that it was merely a trivial Bank mis-print, a rare but not unique event, and therefore in this unusual case we would of course honour the note's value, and thanked him for bringing it to the Bank's attention.

"It seems Mr Kauffmann was a little intrigued but nonetheless perfectly content with this arrangement. Tenbury-Ripon knows no more than he has been told;

and even should he suspect that something is amiss, he is a loyal, highly ambitious but most discreet young man and without reservation, shrewd enough to keep the matter close; I make little doubt that he may even one day sit behind my desk."

Holmes rubbed his bony hands together vigorously in evident satisfaction. "That is excellent Mr May, extremely skilfully played if I may say, and certainly precisely what I would have advised. No needless suspicions have been aroused and with luck Mr Kauffmann will believe that nothing more notable than a small curiosity passed across his counter, and thus think no more of it.

"But now we must see if we can discover how it came into Mr Kauffmann's possession, and swiftly too. I presume that this note was presented to Mr Tenbury-Ripon, and he, passed it to you in precisely this condition for as we can observe, it has been folded in half and folded again into four at some time since it was printed, yet shopkeepers do not customarily fold their takings, but bundle them flat – is that not so?"

"Indeed, Mr Holmes. Such creasing is typically exhibited after the note enters circulation, when certain persons as are not accustomed to carrying a pocketbook – usually for the reason that they rarely if ever are in possession of a sufficient quantity of paper-money to justify such a gentleman's essential – very often fold a note and stuff it into a trouser pocket, a rather vulgar custom but commonplace enough.

However, it does seem to me, if I may say that you appear oddly satisfied with this event."

Holmes' cold grey eyes had taken on that strange appearance which I had seen on many occasions when confident that he was fast-closing with his quarry; distant and far-away as he were staring fixedly upon a remote horizon, yet curiously alive, sharply focused and intently concentrated.

From his alert demeanour, which put me affectionately in mind of a malnourished bloodhound, I felt sure that the apparently random appearance of this third note, and its creased condition had somehow significantly advanced his hunt. At that moment I would have given scant odds indeed that the criminals could elude this doughtiest of detectives.

After some thought, during which May and I remained deferentially silent, Holmes eventually continued: "I believe I may now set your mind at rest Mr May – I am confident that the appearance of this note is not an augury as you fear, that *it has begun.* Very far from it; in fact I much doubt if the criminals' principal is even aware of the note's circulation.

"We know the villains are pinning all their hopes on cowing you into handing over a vast ransom for the return of the stolen materials, or face a deluge of harmful fraudulent currency being unleashed into your carefully-balanced economy. They would not knowingly reduce the gravity and menace of their own threat. They know well that you are fully aware of their competence to print and circulate – what need is there of a third reminder?

"From what I have learned tonight, therefore, I believe I may state with considerable confidence that it is most unlikely you will be required to meet their terms. Should you be minded so to do, it would be the most needless, the most costly, and the most monstrous of travesties of all that is decent and right.

"With the appearance of this note I now feel certain that they foolishly and unwittingly have revealed their Achilles heel and it is within range of my arrow."

At this the distinguished banker appeared almost to grow in stature; his back straightened, his brow became smooth once more, his tensely clenched hands slowly uncurled, and a look of infinite relief flooded visibly over him.

"I will not enquire the basis for your evident confidence Mr Holmes, for your abilities in such delicate and sensitive matters are legend, and I can find no flaw in your logical analysis of the situation. I have read Doctor Watson's accounts of your methods of observation and deduction and though it appears to me that while they have been, on occasion, most unusual, we do find ourselves in a most unusual, perhaps unique situation. You have greatly buoyed me up."

I observed just the smallest flash of a self-satisfied smile pass almost invisibly across Holmes' lips. And while my clever friend always eschewed the public spotlight, he very occasionally permitted himself a tiny moment of self-indulgent satisfaction at the praise of those whom he considered his peers.

"You are exceedingly kind Mr May" said my colleague "but let us hold a little longer for our laurels – and certainly until the Derbies are securely upon the villains' wrists, they incarcerated and enjoying the hospitality of Inspector Lestrade's tender mercies, and your plates and paper are once more safely under lock and key. Now, if you have no further matters to bring to my attention, I shall terminate this little meeting, for there is a great deal I must set in place, for one of our five days is now elapsed."

When eventually Mr May departed, clearly somewhat more reassured than upon his arrival, Holmes collapsed limply in his chair before the fire. My friend looked drawn and care-worn, and I began to suspect that the immense responsibility of solving this case of national importance was starting to bear down upon him like the heavens upon the shoulders of Atlas. I wanted to quiz him more about the evening's unexpected development, but already he had withdrawn completely into that strange and taciturn world of his own creation, in which nothing existed for him save his extraordinary intellect, the grand engine that powered his unique deductive abilities.

"Have a care to take some rest old friend" I said gently. "There are only two ends to burn on even the mightiest candle. Sooner or later they must meet and consume it entirely." He opened his weary eyes and smiled lazily. "Fear not my dear Watson – this *is* my rest; it is stultifying inactivity that so fatigues me." And he reached for his pipe.

Silence descended once more; aware that any further attempt at conversation would be as rewarding as attempting conversation with a Trappist monk, I stole noiselessly to my room and retired for the night, leaving him to his introverted silence of deduction...

When I awoke the following morning my first chilling thought was that this was the commencement of the second day; I conceived it must have been inordinately early, for only the faintest glimmering of dawn penetrated the drape, yet strangely my watch upon the bedside table reported that it lacked only five minutes of nine o'clock. Upon parting the bedroom curtains I realised the cause; the overnight fog had curdled into a vile and impenetrable miasma, fuelled by the innumerable meagre soft-coal fires, each battling feebly against the winter chill in countless thousands of dwellings across the city. Our modest hearth was but one of the guilty culprits.

Outside, the gloomy consequence was that the windows at 221B appeared to have been swaddled during the night with dense, dirty, ochre-coloured gauze. Even at this morning hour, the street lights were still lit, but to miserable effect. Save for one or two hardy souls groping blindly through the murk on foot, the street beneath was perfectly empty; no street-vendor cried, no tradesman's wagon or brewer's dray rumbled by, no hansom plied its brisk business; such was the horrid, sinister stillness that had descended across the paralysed city.

While dressing I sombrely reflected that as a dismal consequence of this unhealthy air, my medical practice would inevitably be beleaguered by wheezing asthmatics, chronic bronchitics and every other manner of poor suffering soul certain to be afflicted by the jaundiced atmosphere, and I had no doubt that many would succumb to these noxious vapours long before the primroses next bloomed in Regents Park.

It is a sad commonplace of our modern metropolitan times.

I entered the parlour to find Holmes seated at the window, still in his night attire and dressing-gown, glaring moodily out at the sickly glow of the near-invisible gaslights in silent Baker Street below; I perceived upon the instant that he was in the vilest of humours. "Ah, good morning Holmes" I said cautiously.

Tetchily he retorted "I defy you, Watson, to present me with one single redeeming feature of this benighted morning. There is, for my purpose, nothing good about it in the least part. The hunt cannot ride with blind hounds, and hope for a kill. And no more can I! I am unsighted like Polyphemus! I am blind as Lear's Gloucester! Quite as sightless as a common bat!

How are we to comb the rookeries in The Isle of Dogs in such conditions?

"Pah! You could barely see to comb your hair in this murk; I much doubt that any cabbie would venture to take us so far without an army of torch-men to lead the way! And still time marches inexorably onward. These infernal fogs can last for days..."

Knowing that this gloomy and self-indulgent mood would serve only to obscure my friend's powers of concentration at this most critical of times, I sought to lighten his disposition. "That is quite true Holmes, but we have too, on occasion, known them to lift unexpectedly and quickly. Come; let us hope for better weather, while you tell me of your plans for the day if you will."

He glared balefully for a final moment at the fog outside and softened. "Of course you are right my wise and prudent counsellor! We must hope that the winter sun may burn its feeble way through this miserable gloom, so let us bank up the fire and I shall tell you of what I yet hope to achieve this day."

Pleased at this welcome upturn in my friend's blue funk, I loaded a generous shovel of coal upon the fire, placed the old Malacca cigarette box and some vestas upon the table between our easy chairs, and took my place alongside him before the cheery blaze. He drew deeply on his cigarette, exhaled long and slowly, and after some moments he spoke.

"Some of what I will now summarise, Watson, I readily concede, is informed assumption and some, informed deduction, and it is now that I look to you to moderate by playing the devil's advocate, as ever you have done."

I was surprised and not a little flattered by such uncommon deference shown me by Sherlock Holmes, and I sensed it signalled perhaps a rare moment of self-questioning under the weighty responsibility he had shouldered.

He continued. "Have you considered the matters I recently brought to your attention? The speed at which a strong, agitated man may walk when pressed by exigent circumstance; the rate at which a Koenig press may operate; the circle I inscribed upon the map – you have noted its centre and radius I know; and the odd tainted odours your keen sense of smell detected upon the three banknotes that have appeared thus far? To which I might add the curious matter of the threatening letter from Asa Bormanstein pinned to the wall, which strangely was not in evidence when Lestrade was present at the scene of the crime, still not there when Warburg made his ill-advised foray, yet was so prominently displayed precisely for me to discover later next day; and this despite what we believe to be a more-or-less continuous police guard upon Slater's Yard. Do not those finer points, when considered together, become highly suggestive to you?"

I had already struggled to comprehend whatever connections the great detective clearly saw between these incongruent events, but save for my earlier estimate of a man's walking speed, had failed miserably to establish any intelligent thread of logic between them; and while Holmes' notoriously acerbic comments upon my attempts at deduction had without doubt mellowed of late, there was certainly no theory which I was emboldened to advance for his pitiless scrutiny. However, of one thing I felt reasonably certain – that of all these diverse factors he had brought to my awareness, there was one which stood out quite signally.

"I regret, Holmes, I am unable to make full sense of these matters, save to opine that the most significant must be the circle you inscribed upon the map, and it is my belief that the answers to all the other strange questions have somehow directed you in its placing and size."

"You improve; I declare you improve almost daily Watson!" He lit another cigarette and after inhaling a few enthusiastic puffs, reached for the map and flattened it upon the table between us. "The circle, Watson, which is the focus of this hunt, has a particular radius and a particular centre. You may care to give further close thought to the placing of the circle's centre on Cubitt Town, its radius – approximately three miles or so, and the interval within which we can estimate quite closely that the envelope was introduced to the scene at Slater's Yard. Too, it might be worthwhile to consider why and how the letter and envelope came to be written and placed there precisely during PC Clarke's brief absence, and a few minutes before the particular moment we discovered it.

"The speed of the press becomes significant in view of the fact the letter demanded that the ransom be paid in five days, failing which the counterfeit money will be released far and wide, which implies, does it not, that it will all be printed within that period of time?"

"That is certainly possible" I replied.

"It is more than that – it is probable."

He closed his eyes, placed his elbows upon the arms of his chair, fingers steepled as always when preparing to deliver one of his pedagogical explanations "You have before you, Watson, all those data that I have. The perfect logician, and to my knowledge there is none-such, might observe a single one of these facts in its context, and deduce not only its causes, but also its likely results. The great naturalist Cuvier could describe a complete animal merely by contemplating a single bone – how I would have enjoyed an encounter with that man and his mind!

"Imagine, Watson, merely by holding a mandible in his hand he was able to pronounce with certainty:

'if an animal's teeth are such as they must be in order for it to nourish itself with flesh, we can be sure

without further examination that the whole system of its digestive organs is appropriate for that kind of food, and that its whole skeleton and locomotive organs, and even its sense organs, are arranged in such a way as to make it skilful at pursuing and catching its prey. For these relations are the necessary conditions of existence of the animal' - that, Watson, is deduction in its finest, purest, most elevated instance.

"And in the same manner in which nature binds its creations with inviolable laws both of genesis and of evolution, so I have found the world of criminal enterprise to be constrained along similar lines. When I observe one particularly singular event, it may be that I can deduce its past cause and its future consequences. As an example, do you recall our encounter here at Baker Street at the time of the case presented by the King of Bohemia? You may recollect that I startled you by observing that you were back in harness?"

"I recall it quite vividly Holmes, for you pointed out the clumsiness of our maid from the abuse she bestowed on my boots when scraping away the crusted mud, and then you correctly declared me to be back in general practice because, if my memory serves, you detected the odour of iodoform, black stains of nitrate of silver upon my forefinger, and the tell-tale bulge in my top-hat where I, like most practitioners routinely secrete their stethoscope!"

"Child's play Watson, mere child's play.

"But back to the matter in hand; research is easily had. For example, I have already established that the Koenig press – for that is what Warburg reports he saw – is capable of generating up to eighteen-hundred impressions per hour, each of two banknotes – thus, three thousand six hundred ten-pound notes in an hour – thirty six thousand pounds per hour. Thereafter the calculation of the mathematics is simplicity itself and, given the time-scale imposed, and some hours of diligent application, this indicates to me that the villains are already most likely well under way in their enterprise, and perfectly competent to realise their threat.

"Warburg observed three discarded Portal's wrappers; each contained five thousand sheets, each of which yields two ten-pound notes. We may surmise, therefore, that at that point in time, they had already printed at least three hundred thousand pounds sterling. The question is, where are they now – where have they gone to ground? Which question returns us in a most circular manner to the circle inscribed upon the map there before you."

He leaned back and became still and silent, evidently awaiting my thoughts on the seemingly intractable problem there before me. However, not only could I now perhaps see my way dimly through part of the serpentine maze of Holmes' convoluted reasoning, I suddenly realised as I looked over his shoulder, for he sat with his back to the windows, that I could now see the rooftops on the far side of Baker Street; the vile fog was giving way to pallid watery sunshine!

Swiftly I reviewed all the factors that Holmes had clearly deemed central to the puzzle and, with not a little trepidation, I hazarded all. "I judge, Holmes that the two heavies with the massive hound we encountered as we entered Cubitt Town are certainly members of the gang, and were no doubt instrumental in delivering Warburg's savage beating; they seemed much unnerved at our appearance, and presumably, while we took lunch and interviewed the landlord at the inn, they visited Slater's Yard and placed the ominous letter addressed to you. Clearly, it was designed to frighten us away, and also to be conveyed to The Bank. The fortuitous absence of Constable Clarke from his post for some twenty or so minutes no doubt made their mission considerably easier in its accomplishment. As to the rest, I need to consider more deeply."

Holmes beamed amiably. "All that you surmise is close to what I believe occurred Watson, with some notably vital exceptions and omissions. And your foretelling of the weather is just as accurate, for I observe this infernal gloom is even now lifting, and there below our window passes the second hansom since we have been seated. Let us try for a third and see what we may discover at Messrs. Kauffmann Brothers in the Whitechapel High Street..."

We eventually located the pawnbroker's establishment, positioned next door to a garish Penny-Gaff shop advertising the forthcoming exhibition of one Joseph Merrick, tastelessly billed as 'The Last Appearance of The Elephant Man'. Despite the waning public appetite for so-called 'freak-shows' I believe I will never cease to despair at man's vile and salacious interest in viewing the maimed, the deformed and the slow-witted, for the sake of vicarious amusement and entertainment.

Had I the requisite skills in attending to such specialised medical needs I believe I should have wished to rescue any human-being in these desperate straits from such a miserable, humiliating and sickeningly debased existence. Holmes broke into my sombre chain of thought. "Mayhap one day the human race will become a kinder, more civilised species, Watson. Until that time, I fear we must bear such unpleasantness and hope for a more enlightened age. Come; let us see what we may learn at Mr Julius Kauffmann's emporium of debt."

For all its modest exterior, Kauffmann Bros was surprisingly well-appointed within. I surveyed our surroundings as the clanging of the large brass bell upon the door subsided into reluctant silence. There were no other customers. The place smelled of dust, floor-wax, metal polish and the melancholy remains of other peoples' lives. To left and right were glass-fronted cabinets rising the full height of the shop, filled with the most amazing variety of articles, all, I supposed, testimony to lost fortunes, hard times, broken relationships and dire straits.

With a pang of sadness I perceived upon the instant a waste-paper basket fashioned from the dried foot of an elephant, quite crammed with sticks and walking canes of every conceivable style and taste, standing sentinel over piles of gold and silver watches, chains, rings, cravat pins and the like. Another cabinet was filled with further sad remains of long-dead pachyderms – entire six-foot tusks of finely incised ivory, paperweights, delicate fan-tracery screens and inlaid boxes, all surrounded by a small menagerie of intricately-carved netsuke.

Another display was filled with musical instruments sufficient, it seemed, to equip a small symphony orchestra, and a further, with workmen's tools – another reflection of the trying economic times borne by the ordinary working man.

Across the full width of the far end of the shop was a worn dark-wood counter, surmounted by a stout brass grille that extended to the ceiling; behind it were three counter-stations, much as one might find in a bank. Two were occupied; one by a slight, elderly, frail-looking patriarch of Hebrew aspect, the other by a sturdy looking lad of perhaps five and twenty years who appeared to be deeply engrossed in sorting pledge-slips and the like. Both wore yarmulkas. The older man greeted us with a sad, gentle smile.

"Good afternoon gentlemen; welcome to my small kingdom of Paradise Lost. Have you come to relieve me of some other soul's unredeemed pledge, or are you perhaps come to add some item to this world of indebtedness?"

Holmes paused. "Mr Kauffmann? Mr Julius Kauffman?" The elderly gentleman vanished momentarily from his station, and promptly reappeared inside the shop through a cunningly concealed door, secured no doubt with locks of the highest security, judging from the series of clicks and snicks as keys were turned and bolts slid back.

"I am he; how may I help you? I believe I may claim that my advances are more generous than many, my interest charges more lenient than most, and my sales of unredeemed pledges are priced to yield little more than a modest return on my outlay."

Holmes smiled genially. "I am sure that is all true Mr Kauffmann, but our business today concerns another matter. I am Sherlock Holmes; this is my colleague Doctor Watson and we are here on an altogether different matter. It is in connection with your recent visit to The Bank to deposit your takings; you will perhaps recall some trivial irregularity concerning the ten-pound note which you presented yesterday?"

Kauffmann frowned in puzzlement. "There is no need in the slightest for concern Mr Kauffmann; The Bank has merely asked me to investigate the circumstances whereby a mis-printed proof-note came erroneously and prematurely to enter into public circulation — a careless administrative error of The Bank's own making I feel sure, and easily resolved.

"I understand that the note in question was not tendered to you but to your assistant? Perhaps I might speak with him about the transaction concerned?" The little pawn-broker relaxed somewhat. "Mr Meyer, will you attend out here please." The young man left his station and reappeared through the concealed door. "Meyer, this is Mr Sherlock Holmes. He is acting for The Bank in the matter of the mis-printed ten-pound note I mentioned to you. You will recall that you accepted it. Please be good enough to relate to Mr Holmes the circumstances of the transaction." At the mention of my colleague's name the young man's eyes widened.

"Mr Sherlock Holmes? *The* Sherlock Holmes? Why, I hear of Sherlock Holmes everywhere! I'll be honoured to assist." He sounded his silent aitches. "It was the day before yesterday Mr Holmes; business was very slow and I was minding the shop on my own while Mr Kauffmann was out on a valuation. For the longest time I had been watching two fellows peering in the front window at the display of silver; burly, ill-looking ruffians, shabbily dressed and marked with cuts and bruises they were.

"The shorter of the two had a very large, fierce-looking dog of some sort on a chain. The larger appeared to be pointing at a particular item in the window, whereupon there seemed to be an altercation between the two, the smaller, seemingly attempting to dissuade the larger from his purpose. Eventually the bigger man had his way and entered the shop; he appeared to me to be somewhat ill at ease, rather nervous. His eyes went in different directions so you didn't know which one to look at."

Holmes made no sign of recognising this increasingly familiar description, or of the fact that we two had almost certainly encountered the pair ourselves only recently in the grimy Streets of Cubitt Town. Holmes remained silent.

"Anyway, he asked to examine a bracelet comprising thirty linked flat disks of silver, which I retrieved from the window case. It was a reasonably substantial item, priced at two pounds ten shillings but he seemed not in the least deterred by the cost, and further asked if we could have the bracelet engraved for him, which is something we offer through the services of a nearby man. I duly wrote down the words he required to be engraved, and he dictated a local address where it was to be delivered upon completion. It was the address of a woman; I think perhaps a sweetheart?

"What with the additional engraving requirement, I naturally insisted on payment in full before proceeding any further with the commission. He paid with a new ten-pound note which had been sharply folded in four. Being such a large denomination of note

I examined it closely though discreetly and it appeared to me to be good; I gave him his change and he departed."

At this intelligence Holmes' cold grey eyes blazed with excitement, like white-hot coals on a smithy's forge. "Tell me Mr Meyer, when was the bracelet to be delivered? Do you still retain the slip upon which you recorded the details of the transaction?"

"I do Mr Holmes, excuse me one moment" and he darted back through the secret door, to reappear some moments later, flourishing a yellow flimsy which he proffered to us; Holmes snatched it and scanned it eagerly. "May I retain this Mr Meyer – it is of considerable significance; I note the bracelet was to be delivered this morning." The young man looked uncertainly to Kauffmann for approval. The pawnbroker nodded his acquiescence, and so with suitably fulsome thanks all around and many reassurances, we departed the premises of Messrs Kauffmann Brothers. Outside on the pavement once more Holmes consulted the yellow slip with evident satisfaction.

"This is quite excellent Watson; we shall now walk a short way to Narrow Street in Limehouse. Do you recall what I told you after we visited Dulcie Hobbs' rooms – the wisdom of the Yard – *if you ask whichever officer of the establishment how they take most villains, he will tell you – at the houses of the women*' and so it proves to be, time and again. It is their eternal weakness and thus it plays to our strength." We walked south towards the river for some minutes before Holmes spoke again.

"I am not entirely taken by surprise at what we have learned from young Meyer but now in knowledge of our next destination, with hindsight, I would have wished that one of us were armed." I patted my coat pocket. "Never fear Holmes; after our horrid discovery at 64 Chiswick High Road I privately resolved to keep my revolver loaded, close at all times, and upon my person always when out and about until this business is done."

"Stout fellow" he murmured, and strode on. No matter what danger might lie in wait, I could not wish for anything better than to be associated with my friend in one of these strange adventures which were the ordinary condition of his existence.

Whatever odd fading vestiges of gentility might have existed here and there in Whitechapel High Street vanished rapidly as we headed south, giving way to the meanest, vilest streets I believe I have ever walked, and in this I would include the most impoverished villages I encountered in Afghanistan, many of which would put this foul place to shame.

Seemingly derelict houses leaned crazily into the ever-narrowing streets at impossible angles, more or less according to their degree of dilapidation and neglect. Only lines of grubby washing, the odd wisp of smoke from a chimney pot, and freshly-strewn garbage upon the street outside the doors betrayed the fact that these noisome hovels were inhabited by human beings.

On street corners and in dark doorways, gangs of menacing-looking ruffians muttered in low voices, turning their backs as we passed. On one occasion we were followed for a short distance by the sounds of foul oaths and coarse laughter. Unimaginably dirt-encrusted urchins played in filth, indifferently watched from doorsteps by slatternly gossiping women; I shuddered at the abominable lives eked out by these sad creatures of the under-world, and all the while the air became more noxious, heavy with the evil reek of bad water, decay, and years of accumulated human waste.

I thought I detected a strong whiff of the same decayed odour on the counterfeit notes, but it may have been my imagination, in an entire world of decay.

Treading with some care through the mire of the streets, we eventually arrived at the rotting door of number 11 Narrow Street. A stained, peeling, crudely written scrap of card nailed to the door proclaimed in childish characters the proud occupant of this dire place to be:

DAISY GOODCHILD (Miss).

Holmes wrinkled his nose in distaste; cynically he muttered "It would seem that Daisy Goodchild, despite her apparently ardent admirer, still wishes casual passers-by to know that she is yet unattached..."

He made to knock upon the grimy, sagging door with his bare knuckles, thought better of it, and fastidiously rapped with the soiled ferrule-end of his walking cane. Within, a child mewled shrilly and was silenced with a harsh shout and what sounded like a sharp blow, after which there was silence for some moments, followed by cautious footsteps approaching the door. After a short pause the handle turned and the door creaked open a mere crack to reveal in the gloom within, a suspicious eye peering out at us... I gripped the comforting butt of the heavy piece hidden in the pocket of my Ulster. Querulously a woman spoke; "Who's there? Sidney already paid the rent if that's what yer come for." Hearing a female voice I eased my grip on the revolver.

Abruptly the door started to close; Holmes' foot moved swiftly to wedge it open. "Miss Goodchild – there you are in error! We are not come to ask for money, but to pay what you are owed. If I may explain..." The solitary eye peered out more hopefully, and slowly the door squealed fully open to reveal a not unappealing young woman, save that her other eye was quite as black-and-blue as both of Solomon Warburg's had been after his savage attack. The sour odours of unwashed bodies, linen long overdue for laundering, stale food, tobacco and alcohol wreathed evilly out to assail us.

As the woman stepped forward I noted the silver bracelet looped around her left wrist.

Suavely Holmes continued: "Miss Goodchild I presume? I represent Kauffmann Brothers, the respected jewellers in Whitechapel where your friend recently purchased a gift for you – a Mr Sidney Belton I believe? Ah, I see it has already been delivered to you – is all to your satisfaction? It certainly looks charming if I may say so." The creature essayed a coquettish simper, which appeared perfectly grotesque from behind the blue-black blood-engorged, discoloured eye. My friend resumed: "It appears that Mr Belton was inadvertently handed rather less change than was correct, to the amount of two pounds and fifteen shillings – a most unfortunate oversight on our part, for which I apologise. We are come to return it if you would be good enough to provide me with your friend's address."

Upon the instant a clever, cunning look passed across the woman's face. "Two pounds and fifteen shillings you say Sir? A sizeable sum. Well you can hand that to me now if you please." Holmes gave her a pained, apologetic smile. "Would that I could Miss, for it would save me valuable time of which I have very little to spare, but the fact of the matter is that the receipt is made out to Mr Sidney Belton, and it is our strict business policy that such returns may only be made to the purchaser. If you could just give me his address we can clear the matter up forthwith..." Cowed by Holmes' authoritative tone, she yielded. "You'll find him across the river on Jacob's Island; number 30 Jacob Street, by the tannery, hard by Tan's Yard."

Gravely he thanked Miss Daisy Goodchild and we departed that vile place. The fog was once more closing in like an oppressive brown blanket falling from the murky sky; we decided to return for the night to the warmth, safety and comfort of our familiar rooms in Baker Street.

Mere days now remained until the criminals' grave threat would be made real, and millions of pounds of counterfeit sterling currency fed like a sinister and lethal poison into the nation's economy...

After a slower than customary journey through the thickening fog we eventually attained Baker Street somewhat after eight o'clock, where we wreaked hearty havoc upon a scratch supper of chicken broth and a cold game pie with buttered greens. Quietly Mrs Hudson entered, banked up the fire, cleared the remains of our meal and departed, uttering a small sigh of exasperation at the state of our boots which I had placed outside the parlour door for the boy to attend to.

In our customary chairs before the flickering coals once more, Holmes spread a large-scale map of South London across his knees and proceeded to examine it minutely, while I sought through the pages of Dickens' 'Oliver Twist' for the passage I recalled which so vividly described our afternoon's adventure in this seamy part of the Capital, for I found I was deeply affected by the abominable circumstances of that ghastly place, and the mean lives its denizens eked out there... I found the passage I sought:

"...crazy wooden galleries common to the backs of half a dozen houses, with holes from which to look upon the slime beneath; windows, broken and patched, with poles thrust out, on which to dry the linen that is never there; rooms so small, so filthy, so confined, that the air would seem to be too tainted even for the dirt and squalor which they shelter; wooden chambers thrusting themselves out above the mud and threatening to fall into it - as some have done; dirt-besmeared walls and decaying foundations, every repulsive lineament of poverty, every loathsome indication of filth, rot, and garbage..."

Abruptly, Holmes set aside his map and turned to me. "You are much impressed by what we saw today Watson, for I observe you are deep in the works of one of our keenest observers of the criminal classes – Dickens' 'Oliver Twist' if I am not much mistaken. Let me guess, might it be the passage where Sykes meets his gruesome but well-deserved end in the poisonous mud of Folly Ditch?" I nodded.

"Indeed Holmes. I confess I am depressed and startled at observing intimately, such deprivation, such degradation, at witnessing human beings living at the lowest believable level, faring no better than beasts of the field, and in this modern technical age of wonders, electric illumination, the telegraph, medical advances unparalleled... the rookeries of Seven Dials seem almost wholesome by contrast."

"Then tomorrow dear friend, I fear we must steel ourselves for a far more unpleasant ordeal, for we go to hunt our quarry in his lair, and it is concealed in an environ considerably more dreadful than that which you witnessed this day." I shuddered involuntarily, and then with a start, understood the full import of Holmes' words. I realised that he now knew full well where the criminals were located!

"How long have you known this matter Holmes?"

He stepped to the mantel, retrieved his bulging Persian slipper and favourite foul briar, arrayed them alongside the vestas and cigarette box and reseated himself, now upon the soft old Turkey carpet before the mellowing fire.

I concluded that he was preparing for an all-night sitting; *quite a three-pipe problem* as he had once pronounced to me. "How long? Well, I have had suspicions from the very moment we received the second proof. They were then reinforced by several apparently small but vital factors – among them, the precise time the blackmail demand appeared on the wall at Slater's Yard after we encountered the two thugs, particularly the odour of the third proof presented to us by Mr May, and subsequently the yellow slip so fortuitously provided by young Mr Meyer; it is lying there upon my desk."

He sat silent for a long moment, his long arms folded, chin sunk upon his chest. He appeared to be striving to recall something.

Suddenly and to my surprise he sombrely intoned: *"Thirty pieces of silver burns on the traitor's brain; thirty pieces of silver! Oh! It is hellish gain!"* I eyed him with considerable curiosity and waited; Holmes was not a natural poet. "It occurs to me, Watson, that it is close to two thousand years since the last notable betrayal for a mere thirty pieces of silver." He passed me the yellow slip. I read it and understood;

> *Sold to Mr Sydney Belton: One ladies' silver bracelet, thirty roundels and links. Overall weight four ounces - £2.15s Engraving: 'To My Daisy from Her Sidney' (4s.11d)*
>
> *Cash received with thanks: £2.19s.11d*
>
> *Deliver to: 11 Narrow Street (A.M.)*

I looked back at Holmes. "Clearly Belton must have been so maddened by the sight of so much easy money that he secretly purloined a counterfeit note in order to indulge his romance, or perhaps to make amends for the consequences of his violence!

"Then his overweening greed has betrayed his master's whereabouts for a paltry thirty pieces of silver! Surely Holmes, all we now need do is observe him at his lodgings and follow wherever he goes, for assuredly he must eventually lead us to the lair?"

My friend applied a match to his briar, puffed steadily for some moments, and at length, from within a dense cloud of pungent tobacco smoke uttered in a tone of the deepest satisfaction;
"Judas Silver..."

* * *

Chapter Fifteen

THE VILLAINS ARE TAKEN!

I rose early the following morning – three days now remained until the ransom demand expired – only to discover that Holmes had breakfasted sparingly and departed at what must have been a most ungodly hour. The measureless amounts of intellectual and physical energy he continued to invest in this most demanding of investigations surely could not be sustained with tea and toast alone, yet such appeared to have been his meagre repast that bleak and foggy morning. An egg and three rashers of bacon remained cold, congealed and quite untouched upon his plate.

In something of a reflective mood, and wishing for a quiet morning, I resisted the urge to call down to Mrs Hudson for breakfast; instead I buttered a round of toast, heaped the bacon and fried egg upon it and topped it with a second slice, generously spread with mustard. Ruminatively I munched my cold sandwich beside the fire, and pondered when and how this adventure might finish. That it would end soon seemed assured, for I was certain that Holmes now knew precisely where the chase would be concluded. As to the finish, I was by no means as confident.

It was clear beyond all doubt that at the final *dénouement* we would be confronting the most desperate of London's villains, who had already furnished ample proof of their casual indifference to inflicting savage violence, pitiless torture and calculated murder upon those who stood in their path. These men, and we knew not how many they numbered, would stop at nothing to achieve their end.

Idly I wandered to the window and gazed down at the street below. There was little to divert me there; a cabbie appeared to be arguing good-naturedly with his newly-alighted customer – perhaps a disagreement about the fare; three elderly women stood gossiping in a group, apparently comparing their purchases; a pair of tough looking characters idled in a doorway opposite, talking behind their hands. I observed them sneaking swift furtive swigs from a shared spirit bottle, and none too covertly either. Were they, too, spying on 221B? I noted that the fog was now little more than a heavy mist, and the gas-lights had been extinguished.

Returning to the hearth, I perceived a drawer to Holmes' desk was, rather unusually, left open; it was the one where customarily he kept his revolver; the drawer was empty. There was a further notable absence that morning; the walking stick that Holmes had elected to take with him was the silver-handled killer, the elegant medlar-wood cane which artfully concealed a slim and lethal razor-edged Solingen steel sword, a weapon of which he was a master, and to whose skill at least two men who foolishly had challenged him could testify.

I certainly did not have need of Holmes' singular skills of observation and deduction to divine what dark manner of business he had embarked on alone this morning; clearly it was likely to be warm and perilous work.

(I will confess that I felt a little hurt that Holmes had ventured out and about on dangerous business without alerting me; I felt that natural concern for a valued friend and colleague who may perhaps, for the first time, have taken solely upon himself a danger better shared by two.) I resumed my study of Thomas Pickering Pick's *Fractures and Dislocations*.

It was around a half after four in the afternoon that the parlour door opened to admit – quite unannounced – a thin, exceedingly grubby-looking, shabbily dressed and heavily bearded man. He wore a greasy, shapeless knitted Monmouth cap and a patch over his left eye. With a drunken belch he lurched unsteadily across the room and stretched out upon the sofa. He not only reeked of the sewer – the rank juniper-sharp stench of cheap one-shilling gin assailed my nostrils instantly. "Good God you dirty scoundrel!" I roared. "What the devil do you mean by this intrusion? Explain yourself this instant, else I shall summon an officer and have you arrested for trespass! This is the private residence of Mr Sherlock Holmes and unless you have a satisfactory explanation for this outrageous behaviour you will shortly find yourself spending the night in rather more confined accommodation and on something considerably less comfortable than that couch!"

This noisome, one-eyed, gin-sodden spectre lay slack-jawed and inert, a thin trail of saliva leaking from a corner of his mouth into the filthy beard, eyes closed and snoring coarsely; he appeared to have lapsed into complete unconsciousness. Now in a considerable fury I strode to the open door and bellowed down the stairs "Billy, down there! Fetch a constable upon the instant! Tell him a drunken vagrant has forced his way into Mr Holmes' rooms!"

"Very good Doctor Watson!" he piped and I heard the street door open but before I could turn, a most familiar voice behind me murmured "You may call him back; forgive me my dear Watson, but you know my small *penchant* for the theatrical; however, I am reassured once again that if I can bamboozle my close friend, then I have remained safe from detection today!" In amazement I spun around, to see a smiling Sherlock Holmes now fully alert and sitting quite upright, eyes shining with excitement, eye-patch gone, peeling the remnants of the vagrant's beard from his lean jowls and fastidiously wiping his chin and cheeks with a tattered, grubby kerchief; he made to stuff it back into the pocket of the grimy ankle-length overcoat, then with evident disgust he balled it up and hurled it upon the glowing embers.

He stood, unbuttoned the gin-reeking coat revealing the sword-stick hanging concealed within, and cast it on the carpet behind the couch along with the coat. The revolver he returned to the drawer without comment, together with a half-empty bottle of gin. Beneath the dreadful outer garment, he was, if it may be imagined, even more disreputably attired. I watched perplexed as he calmly seated himself at his desk and proceeded to write a lengthy telegraph message, and a somewhat shorter letter, which he sealed in an envelope.

The boy in buttons below responded promptly to Holmes' brisk summons shouted down the stair-well. "Billy, here is half a guinea; take a cab with all speed – there is not a second to lose; despatch this telegraph most urgently, and be certain to point out to the clerk that it is addressed to M. Louis Lépine at the *Sûreté* in Fontainebleau, which is near Paris. Be most emphatic on that point. Then proceed with all haste to The Bank of England in Threadneedle Street and hand this letter to the Sergeant-at-Arms; tell him to be sure to hand it to Mr Frank May in person this day, without a moment's delay." The boy darted smartly from the room and clattered down the stair; a moment later I heard his piercing whistle, shortly followed by a cabbie furiously whipping up his nag.

I turned back to Holmes. "You have clearly been out upon perilous business have you not? Had you woken me, I might perhaps have been of some small assistance."

He did not reply immediately, but gazed for several moments into the grate in that peculiar introspective fashion which was so characteristic of him, at the tiny streams of incandescent sparks which chased each other around the coarse, charring weave of the filthy rag, like frantic fiery ants in a tiny maze of warp and weft. "There before us in the coals Watson is the perfect metaphor of the official Force at work; so many busy little bright sparks racing hither and thither, randomly pursuing any and every avenue open to them, with no idea where they may lead; observe how they cross each other's paths, collide head-on or their trail merely goes cold, but all peter out to no practical conclusion."

I smiled at this fanciful, but apt analogy and waited for his account of his day's doings. He continued "As you have no doubt remarked, I did indeed venture out heavily armed, for today I entered deep into enemy territory – if you will, for the purpose of espionage, of intelligence-gathering. But my chief, most reliable weapon was this rather pungent disguise; in much the same way as you may best conceal a secret letter in Her Majesty's postal system, or a needle in a sewing-kit of needles, so quite the best way to hide a drunken idler who wishes to observe, without himself being observed, is among numerous other drunken idlers, all of whom sit gazing aimlessly and blankly at trivial events and objects.

"Indeed, I know for a fact that on several occasions I was charily watched by my quarry, but I was not noted in the least bit and as matters transpired, I was not in any great danger. I even engaged with others of the underworld; they clearly took me to be one of their brethren, as habitual drunks will, and for a suck on a bottle of the British stupefacient, shilling-gin, were most happy to talk about – as best they could – what events they had observed, or could recall, over the past few days.

"A most illuminating if malodorous lot they were too; but between them their inebriated ramblings unwittingly were the *tesserae* of a small mosaic of important data I have pieced together. But I caution you it is a wicked, closed place Watson – in all probability the worst, most dangerous rookery I have ever had the misfortune to visit, and the villains' present location is virtually an unassailable fortress.

"Should you be interested to know more of this foul and perilous place I would recommend you consult Henry Mayhew's excellent collected jottings on poverty and the London poor – an invaluable insight into the sad but natural environment of many of the criminal classes." He extracted a slim cloth-bound volume from the bookshelf, sought for a page and passed the book to me. "And should you not be deterred by my description of this place, Mayhew perhaps offers a more vivid account..."

I read the proffered page with growing horror – and this was the place my friend had visited quite alone...

"*...the water was covered with scum almost like a cobweb, and prismatic with grease. In it floated large masses of rotting weed, and against the posts of the bridges were swollen carcases of dead animals, ready to burst with the gases of putrefaction. Along its shores were heaps of indescribable filth, the phosphoretted smell from which told you of the rotting fish there, while the oyster-shells were like pieces of slate from their coating of filth and mud. In some parts the fluid was as red as blood from the colouring matter that poured into it from the reeking leather dressers' close by.*"

I looked up at Holmes, aghast. "It is indeed a grim place Watson but happily, I believe we may be able to seize our quarry without the necessity of laying siege to their lair, which would assuredly involve significant personal danger and doubtless considerable violence. There is an easier way, but regrettably we shall be compelled to call in Lestrade and his bright little sparks; however for the present, Watson, do you bank up the fire while I remove this noisome disguise.

"You would be perfectly astonished at the difficulty it caused me when I decided to take tea in Belgravia – it required a good five minutes of earnest persuasion before I could gain admittance to a respectable establishment" and with this odd comment he stepped into his room. "Pshaw!" I called after him.

"Tea in Belgravia? A likely tale! Dressed like that I doubt you could have gained admittance to the workhouse!" I chuckled to myself as I attended to the fire. The rag continued to smoulder.

He returned ten minutes later in his favourite old mouse-coloured dressing gown. I was applying a match to a cigarette when the door opened to admit Mrs Hudson, followed by an all too-familiar figure. "Excuse me Mr Holmes, but Inspector Lestrade wishes to speak with you." We both turned in some surprise. "Good day Inspector" said Holmes affably. "An unexpected pleasure – you have news?"

Lestrade's next words caused Holmes' eyebrows to shoot heaven-ward, and left me in stunned amazement. "Oh I have news alright Mr Holmes; my word yes I do indeed have news – the very best of news! The villains are taken! The case, d'you see, is all but solved, for today I arrested the culprit and his chief accomplice – even now they are in custody! One of them even had a loaded six-barrelled barker in his pocket." I glanced at Holmes in astonishment at this momentous announcement. I swear he winked at me, but perhaps it was just an involuntary flicker of his eyelid; he stood and grasped the Yarder's hand, pumping it vigorously. "Well done Lestrade, well done indeed! I will own that even an amateur like me does not take much pleasure in being bested, but nonetheless, I offer my heartiest congratulations!"

Lestrade basked in this rare moment of victory over Holmes the amateur, Holmes the dabbler, Holmes the madcap theorist, for such he perceived my great detective friend to be. "Come Lestrade, draw a chair to the fire and tell all – I am certain that Watson will be as entertained as I to hear your resolution!"

Lestrade seated himself, pursed his lips and steepled his short, stubby fingers beneath his chin; I was amused to note that he appeared unwittingly to be imitating the master.

After a theatrical silence, he began rather self-consciously; "Well, if I may say so Mr Holmes, I'm really a little surprised you didn't see what was going on right under your nose, perhaps on account of all that theorising and observing and deducing you're so fond of, but you see this wasn't a *theoretical* crime and it wasn't *observed* so I don't see there's much *deducing* to be done." He loaded these words with as much thinly-veiled sarcasm as decent manners would permit.

Holmes smiled ruefully and nodded, apparently in acquiescence.

"You see Mr Holmes, the Force deals in *facts*, not *theories*, and the *fact* of the matter is that the perpetrator of any crime must have three most important qualifications; the *means*, the *motive*, and the *opportunity!*" My friend pondered this illuminating revelation as if he had been presented with a new and startling, hitherto quite unconsidered notion which had never before struck him.

"Now the point is, Mr Holmes, while you have been busy *theorising* I have been hard at work doing some good old-fashioned plodding detective work – you know the sort of thing; questioning suspects closely, corroborating statements, establishing alibis; perhaps not to your strange tastes, but I assure you it cannot be beaten for yielding sound results. And the fact of the matter is that there were only two people in all of London who had the means, the motive and most importantly, the *opportunity* to commit this audacious crime at the precise time it occurred..."

"So with or without your assistance Mr Holmes, and with all due respect, I do believe I may anticipate some small recognition from my superiors! Chief Inspector may yet be my next rank." Holmes beamed radiantly at Lestrade. "Splendid news Lestrade! I give you joy of it! And as you well know, nothing delights me more than to see a true villain fairly and squarely laid by the heels by a better man!"

Holmes gazed for a moment at the fragment of rag in the grate; a single spark still crawled blindly around the threads of black, charred fabric. He looked up and fixed Lestrade with a kindly smile.

"Then I presume you have now not only the criminals under lock and key, but also the stolen plates and paper, and any currency already printed?" Lestrade shifted in his chair. Equivocally he answered "Not quite at this precise moment Mr Holmes; they are still stubbornly denying any involvement in the matter

– but then again they would, would they not? They'll be singing like canaries in a day or so; I know from long experience when a man is guilty – and mark my words, these two are as guilty as blackest sin – the only pair who could possibly have pulled off the caper – and I'll hear the truth of the whole matter soon enough."

Holmes turned and gazed vacantly at the window, a droll expression on his lean features, and with that so-familiar gesture of a bony fore-finger to his pursed lips said in a perfectly neutral tone "Oh, of that Inspector, I am more than certain, but then, after all, you do have the reputation of being one of the brightest sparks at The Yard." Involuntarily my eyes darted back to the fragment of charred rag in the fire.

I watched as the single remaining spark sputtered into extinction.

Holmes' words appeared to please Lestrade greatly; he rose, rubbed his hands together in satisfaction and said "Well then Mr Holmes, I'll be off now, for I have some more questioning to do to tidy up the case. If you watch the papers over the next day or so I'm sure you'll read the full details." Holmes and I rose from our chairs. "Just one more thing, Lestrade" said Holmes; "precisely who do you have under arrest?"

"You still can't *deduce* Mr Holmes? On suspicion of aiding and abetting a felony, and conspiracy to steal we have arrested a real bad'un – one Sergeant Jacob Gunton, the watchman on duty at Perkins Baker & Petch at the only possible time of the robbery." My colleague's eyes opened wide in astonishment. I made to speak but he stilled me with a tiny gesture. "Good Heavens Lestrade, you truly amaze me. But if Gunton was an accessory, who was his principal, the mastermind behind the affair?"

"Ah, now Mr Holmes, I rather expect I shall startle you both." Holmes stared at the burned-out scrap of rag in the grate and murmured "I am sure we may depend upon that."

Lestrade retrieved his coat from the back of his chair and replied flatly: "On suspicion of theft, conspiracy to forge currency of the realm, and of uttering said forged currency, I am holding Mr Henry Petch of Messrs Perkins, Baker & Petch; there will likely in due course be added the grave charges of murder and attempted murder. I fear you have been duped by your client." There was a lengthy silence.

"Good Lord Lestrade, I am more than startled – I am almost speechless. But perhaps you will allow that such an outlandish outcome is one which I could never have imagined in a lifetime of investigation. Why, I must be blind! I tip my hat to you!" Lestrade smiled thinly.

"That's as maybe Mr Holmes, but it would do no harm perhaps to bear in mind my little motto – Means, Motivation and Opportunity: you won't go far wrong. Meanwhile, I expect you have other cases to, ah, *theorise* over..."

Holmes beamed. "Indeed, as it happens, I have Inspector. Even now I am pondering a curious matter which has only very lately come to my attention. In the unlikely event that I ever fathom it out I expect Doctor Watson may perhaps one day fancifully publish it as *The Adventure of The Demented Inspector.*" Lestrade departed, looking distinctly puzzled. Holmes sat silent for some time, eyes closed, frowning.

Abruptly he barked "I will not have it! It just cannot be! If Lestrade were to be given the slightest credibility, then Petch has deceived me! But consider, Watson, are we soberly to believe that a frail septuagenarian and a one-armed, hook-handed, sixty-five year old invalided soldier between them spirited away two dozen heavy boxes of security paper and the printing plates without being observed?"

He paused. "Sadly, however, Lestrade's deluded conclusion will soon be vindicated in his own mind. He will shortly be more confident than ever that he holds the culprits, for unknowingly he holds most damning evidence."

"I quite agree it does seem most improbable Holmes, but you must admit that they certainly had the opportunity. The means could easily have been hired labour – Mustachios and Wall-Eye – and the motive is self-evident – vast financial gain."

My companion snorted. "Nonsense Watson. Petch is in his twilight years, he has all a man could wish for – a fine house, ample money, a comfortable marriage and his beloved orchids; no, there is no motive there. Consider further, could two elderly men, with only three arms between them conceivably have subdued Dulcie Hobbs, and then lifted her several feet up to a hangman's noose?

"And might they credibly have been two of the four who attacked the mighty Warburg? I rather think not. Warburg was stabbed in his right shoulder from behind and Gunton lacks his right arm – it would be a most unnatural action for a left-handed man, who, from behind, would surely aim for the left carotid?

"And Petch has only strength sufficient to scratch on metal shims and snip at orchids. But sadly, although Lestrade does not yet know it, he will soon be parading his trump card, his proof absolute. Just as soon as he learns the nature of the weapon removed by the surgeon he will be certain he has his man!" I was deeply puzzled. "But how can he have taken the wrong men, yet possess proof absolute of their guilt? The two notions are quite inconsonant."

By way of answer, Holmes darted from the parlour and took the stairs down, three at a time. I heard him ask Mrs Hudson a question; he returned shortly, waving the bone from the ham we had so recently demolished, along with a butchers' chopping board.

Mystified, I watched him as he placed the heavy board upon the dining table and positioned the thick, bare ham-bone perfectly centrally on the wooden slab; he strode to his desk, retrieved the needle-sharp Balinese kris and joined me at the table.

"Would you agree that this bone is not so very different in thickness from a large adult male's clavicle?" I had to agree that it was so. "And while this weapon does not precisely match Lestrade's description of the one removed from poor Warburg's collar-bone, it is slim and extremely sharp is it not?" I nodded.

"Petch, I estimate, is now in the latter part of his seventh decade, thin and frail. You, Watson, are little more than half his years and pretty hale?" Puzzled, I nodded. "Then do me the goodness of driving the blade, I believe Lestrade said – *halfway through the collar-bone*? Perhaps toward the thicker medial end where it would connect with the breast-bone, for that is where Warburg was stabbed." I raised the knife above my head, took careful aim, and drove down with all my force.

The bone did not break; I did not leave the knife deeply embedded; I succeeded merely in removing a splinter and occasioning a deep scar upon its surface. I attempted the bizarre task a second time, to no greater effect.

"I take your meaning Holmes; clearly neither Petch nor Gunton could feasibly have stabbed Warburg. However, Lestrade concedes he has never before seen the odd type of weapon used in the assault. Perhaps in the hand of a different man it would pierce the clavicle? We should need to examine it, should we not?" He shook his head.

"That is quite unnecessary; I have already seen many like it – as have you, and Lestrade's description positively confirms the matter, which is what will shortly make matters appear so black for Petch. He has not the strength for the crime, his alleged accomplice has not the limb for it, and yet..."

"Then what damning proof is Lestrade unknowingly holding?"

Gravely he replied "From his perfectly explicit description, the curious weapon that was so cruelly embedded in Solomon Warburg's neck was, and I make not the slightest doubt of it... *an engraver's burin...*"

* * *

Chapter Sixteen

A Call to Arms

The following morning around ten, day four of our five-day deadline, Holmes stood in silence at the window, gazing out into the gloom; I was mulling over the startling new intelligence delivered by Lestrade the previous afternoon.

"If you truly believe that what you say is correct Holmes, then flimsy though Lestrade's case appears, may not two innocent men at the very least be sent to trial for these grave charges? And even with an acquittal their reputations will be irretrievably damaged." He turned and laughed drily. "Not in the least; Gunton and Petch are perfectly safe in the custody of the law – Lestrade's imagined 'case' is so transparently and evidently circumstantial that no jury will ever convict. And furthermore, I do not merely *believe* that what I say is correct – I *know* it to be so, for I now have seen the faces of the two gang-leaders, and more than that – I know precisely where they are! I have seen them with my own eyes Watson! Wall-eye and Mustachios! Indeed, I have suspected their present location since the appearance of the second and third proofs. We shall introduce them to friend Lestrade within hours."

He dived for the map upon which he had earlier inscribed the circle, and after a moment's deliberation, scrawled a small cross, barely more than a mile and a half or so west of Cubitt Town. Strangely, the cross was placed in the river, hard by a salient of land in Bermondsey called Jacob's Island, on the southern side of the Thames. Time was now fast running out until the expiration of the deadline set in the Slater's Yard note, when the criminals' threat would be made good; I wondered, might Holmes be cutting things a little too fine? And yet he appeared perfectly sanguine.

"Then despite the dangers, should we not make all haste to this Jacob's Island, for time is now surely against us Holmes?"

"Indeed it is Watson, but do you feel so valiant that you and I alone shall take on six burly, desperate and heavily armed ruffians at night, at least two of them murderers, anchored in the middle of the Thames on the lately renamed *SS Betania*, moored in a fast-running tide of poison, for that is where I tracked them to.

"No, that is not the way; it is a fortress. So like our own noble Iron Duke, I have invited our enemy to join battle on the ground of my choosing – and like Wellington, I choose the high ground. I also feel that we should recruit some assistance"

"Then you do mean to call in The Yard? Lestrade is already convinced he holds the culprits." Holmes laughed mirthlessly. "No Watson, just for today we shall leave the ardent Lestrade to his fruitless interrogations, for he will by now be quite certain he has his man. We shall work an altogether different way." I looked at him quizzically. "And what way might that be Holmes?"

He grinned and said airily "Why, the very simplest way; I have cordially invited Mr Bormanstein and the rest of his unlovable crew to pay us a call tomorrow at midnight, and at the same time to have the courtesy to return all those items which are not rightfully his!" I was dumbfounded at this apparently nonsensical notion. "You are seriously suggesting that they will see the error of their ways, play the white man and do the decent thing; that they will pack up the paper, any currency printed together with the plates, and then politely deliver them into your custody?"

He pondered for a moment; a tiny smile played on his thin lips. "Yes, I expect something very much along those lines; I can be extremely persuasive you know, Watson." I shook my head in bewilderment. It seemed to me that the inexorable pressure of this case, the dire consequences of failure, and the relentlessly-approaching deadline might be proving altogether too heavy a burden for my friend. "But Holmes..." I said quietly "...in the improbable event that they accept your 'invitation' is it not more likely that they will attend on an assassins' mission? Are you so determined to play Daniel and invite the lions into your own den? We are but two; they by your own admission are six or more, and proven killers. There is a world of difference between bravery and fool-hardiness! How in Heavens could we defend ourselves against such odds?"

"Why of course Watson, we shall raise an army."

The rumble of a growler halting below our window announced a visit. Holmes raised the sash window and called down to the street "Come up directly gentlemen!" Several pairs of heavy feet tramped up the stair, shaking the very floor beneath us. To me he added with a mischievous smile "Here, if I am not very much mistaken, comes the infantry." I waited to see what this thunderous arrival might herald; I had not long to wait, for the door opened to admit the formidable, beaming visage of Mr Solomon Warburg (still discoloured but seemingly much healed), followed by two huge, amiable-looking young men of open, handsome countenance – both well over six feet in height and perhaps seventeen stones of solid muscle apiece – unmistakeably identifiable by their features as his sons Joshua and Samuel. With their arrival, the parlour immediately became rather crowded and appeared considerably smaller.

"Joshua, Samuel, I have the honour to present Mr Sherlock Holmes and Dr Watson" announced Warburg the senior with a note of pride. Holmes and I extended our hands in turn, to observe them completely engulfed within our guests' ham-like fists. "Thank you for attending gentlemen; please be seated." I watched with interest and not a little concern as the sofa visibly bowed and a fireside chair creaked most alarmingly under the strain. Holmes perched upon the corner of his desk; I took a seat on the old ottoman and waited; our guests looked expectantly at Sherlock Holmes. "We are not quite all met gentlemen – we lack one more..." at which a slow and ponderous tread sounded on the stair. "...And I do believe this is he, our heavy brigade..."

There came a timid, almost nervous tap at the door. "Come!" cried Holmes. Cautiously the door was inched open to reveal the Perkins, Bacon & Petch night watchman, Private Jeremiah Shadwell. He ducked his head as he entered the crowded parlour. Warburg the senior was undeniably big; his two sons were giants; but by comparison, Shadwell was truly a colossus; I estimated perhaps six feet and seven or eight inches in height, and fully twenty stones in weight, without a scrap of spare upon him. He appeared somewhat overwhelmed by the assembled company and waited shyly at the doorway. "Come in Private Shadwell, and be most welcome. Perhaps you could be comfortable on, ah..." Holmes cast warily around for any remaining unoccupied item of furniture that might stand some small chance of bearing the weight of this mountainous man "...Ah, over there, in the corner." He indicated his cleared chemical bench which, though stoutly built of heavy old teak timbers, still squealed alarmingly in protest as the behemoth took his place; he declined refreshment. The Warburg clan examined the arrival with friendly but professional interest, as bloodstock agents might size up a strong yearling at Tattersall's; it seemed they were suitably impressed with what they observed. Private Shadwell made his duty to Holmes, his new-found 'senior officer' in the old-fashioned way by raising two knuckles to his forehead, and then he nodded awkwardly in the general direction of the Warburgs.

I, meanwhile, was striving to reaffirm my faith in the dependability of solid London town-houses, particularly the floor joists and their ability to support the combined weight of this extraordinary group that Holmes had summoned. Wryly I considered that if my faith turned out to be misplaced, we should all shortly join Mrs Hudson in her private rooms below at some considerable velocity, and no doubt to her very great astonishment and displeasure.

Holmes resumed. "And now to business gentlemen. I am inviting you today to consider embarking upon an unusual adventure which you should know will not be without danger; you may not be aware yet, but you are all involved already, as I shall make clear. Tomorrow night we intend – that is, Dr Watson and I, to apprehend six, and possibly more, men. They are large, dangerous, desperate – and very likely armed. We would much value your assistance. There is no guarantee of reward or even of glory, but if we succeed, you will have fended off a grave threat to Great Britain and The Empire." Solomon Warburg glanced around at the other three giants and murmured "Two against six is not very favourable odds for you and the Doctor Mr Holmes – but should we join with you, I fear they will worsen..." he brightened and his eyes vanished momentarily "...for them." My colleague smiled broadly and continued. "Now should you be curious as to why I have invited you all, then look around at your peers, and see that we have already met our first requirement – strong, brave and honourable men who can handle themselves, if it comes to it, in a desperate ruck." The group briefly appraised one another once more and a low growl of approval hummed through the room.

"There is a further reason why you may choose to disturb your quiet ordered lives by unnecessarily involving yourselves in this dangerous adventure – you all have an interest in its successful outcome.

"You, Private Shadwell, know as well as I do that your senior officer, Sergeant Jacob Gunton is a fine, well-regarded and honourable man who, like you, has served his country with great valour and should not falsely be in custody for mean theft and for abusing the great trust his employers placed in him.

"And Mr Petch, your benefactor and employer, a kindly old gentleman of arts and flowers – is he to hang for a murder that he could not possibly have committed?" Our little army looked up in some surprise. "Oh yes gentlemen, these villains have killed; murder, most callous murder has been done purely to silence a foolish young woman of tender years! At least two of these men are irreducibly evil, quite devoid of morals. And surely, gentlemen, is not moral choice the fundamental element of human conduct, lying as it does, at the very heart of humanity itself?

"And as for you, Samuel and Joshua Warburg, would you not relish the opportunity to even the score with the cowardly villains who so mercilessly attacked your father and came within a hair's breadth of leaving you orphaned?"

They made no comment; but around the crowded parlour I noted eight mighty fists resting on eight tree-trunk knees tighten until forty giant callused knuckles showed white. Holmes moved to the conclusion of this extraordinary and unprecedented speech. His audience appeared spell-bound and, in truth, I too was caught up in his oratory. I had never before heard the like. Holmes was skilfully uniting them as a fighting brigade.

He continued. "And finally, gentlemen, there is one further, one crucial, and for me and my loyal colleague here – one rather old-fashioned reason to undertake this hazardous task..." All eyes were fixed on the tall, gaunt detective, now standing before the fire.

"...And that is, to serve our country. What I will next tell you, gentlemen, is very likely subject to the new Government Secrets Act, now passed into law. If you decide to remain in this room and hear me out, you must understand that what you learn may never leave this room or pass your lips, under pain of imprisonment.

"Should you feel you are unable or unwilling to comply for whatever reason, you are perfectly at liberty to leave this moment, and no-one will think the less of you. However, now is our only chance to seize the real criminals. I shall smoke a pipe while you confer." Holmes and I moved discreetly to the window seat; he lit his pipe; I the last Turkish in the cigarette box.

He had barely got his little meerschaum furnace up to temperature when our unusual militia concluded their murmured conference. Warburg the senior turned to Holmes and cleared his throat, at which all four leviathans slowly and solemnly twice nodded their agreement in our direction. My colleague smiled with deep satisfaction; "That is quite good enough for me gentlemen, and no less than I expected." He returned to his place in front of the mellowing embers in the grate. "Very well; bearing in mind you are now all sworn upon your honour to absolute secrecy, I will tell you that a band of extremely desperate men have stolen the new printing plates for the Bank of England's £10 notes. They have also seized sufficient of the special watermarked paper to enable them to create two and a half million pounds in counterfeit currency. They have already sent us an earnest of their intent to wreck Great Britain's economy; they wish to blackmail The Bank of England into paying a vast ransom for the return of the stolen plates and paper. If the government refuses, and they release that fraudulent money into circulation, every working man's wage, and his family will suffer; panic will spread like wildfire in the stock exchange, and the world-wide reputation which the British Pound enjoys will be in tatters. For reasons of their own, the police have mistakenly arrested two good men; tomorrow night we will rectify that error."

He passed one of the three counterfeit notes in his possession to Warburg who ruefully examined it and unconsciously rubbed the fast-fading image upon his forehead; he passed the note to our new band of brothers-in-arms for inspection. Private Shadwell appeared quite bemused to be holding so large a sum of money in a single note, counterfeit or not. Holmes continued his exposition.

"I have set the dependable Mr Warburg to instruct you in your particular roles; after all, he alone of us has uncomfortably close experience of these blackguards; I have already briefed him in great detail. He is now your commander and will tell you how and when to approach the building, your battle-stations, and what actions to take at my signal. Heed his words closely, and with luck and fortitude we shall take these villains and their ill-gotten gains! Tomorrow we fight for justice and decency, for our great British economy and our government, and perhaps far above all else gentlemen, for Queen and Country..."

At Holmes' final words something rather comical, yet a little touching occurred; mayhap as a result of his time spent serving in the officers' mess at the loyal toast, Private Jeremiah Shadwell sprang to his feet at full parade attention, thumbs perfectly aligned with the seams in his trousers and loudly declaimed "For Queen and Country!"

After a rather uncertain pause we all rose and joined in the loyal toast, variously with salutes, tea-cups and a life-preserver; in the case of Sherlock Holmes he was compelled to raise his meerschaum pipe, and for me it was perforce the only thing to hand - a half-smoked Turkish cigarette. Nonetheless, it sufficed to dignify the moment. He moved to his conclusion. "And finally gentlemen, there is to be no killing, unless you perceive your life to be in immediate and mortal peril.

"Doctor Watson and I shall carry pistols in the event they may be needed, as will the police. You may carry such protection as the law permits – and use such force as it reasonably allows." As if in an afterthought he added, perfectly solemnly "...or such as you see fit in the heat of the moment - but be discreet, though I do believe we may dispense with the Queensbury Rules on this occasion." At this, broad grins broke out all around the room; three life-preservers and a set of black iron knuckles were briefly produced, only to vanish with equal speed - in the hands of these four giants, potentially lethal weapons. Holmes affected not to notice them but for the smallest instant a tolerant smile of approval illuminated his gaunt features.

"And now my friends, Dr Watson and I must leave for an important engagement in Threadneedle Street. Mrs Hudson will shortly bring refreshments; when you are done, the boy downstairs will show you out. Until we meet tomorrow evening gentlemen, I bid you good-day. Attend closely to Mr Warburg's directions, and I doubt not gentlemen, that together we shall prevail..."

Below on the street, Holmes hailed a hansom. "Threadneedle Street, driver, The Bank of England, as quickly as possible!" Clearly he had some pre-arranged appointment. I glanced slant-wise at my companion; his face had assumed the fierce, intent appearance of a wolf closing on its prey after a long and arduous chase...

At Threadneedle Street the Master-at-Arms escorted us through the empty cathedral-like banking hall, pursued by a hundred echoes of our own footsteps. Beneath our feet I knew was stored the huge reserve of gold bullion that guaranteed all the Sterling currency in circulation. The office of the Chief Cashier of The Bank of England was a surprisingly modest affair, elegantly furnished but little more spacious than the parlour at 221B; a drawn and tired-looking Frank May sat alone at his desk in a pool of light, reading by the wan yellow glow of the single globe.

Wearily he rose at our entry; "Good evening Mr Holmes, Doctor Watson; please be seated." He fixed us with a stern look.

"This is all damnably irregular Mr Holmes; indeed, I cannot recall a situation to compare in all my years in banking and to be quite candid with you, it appears to me to have all the elements of a desperate last throw of the dice. It is altogether quite without precedent!"

Sherlock Holmes steepled his thin white fingers and gazed intently at May. "I am certain it is, but is not the situation in which you find yourself also quite without precedent? Do not desperate times call for desperate measures?"

May sat back in his opulent leather chair with a look of resignation and sighed deeply. "You are right Mr Holmes. Very well; to business then; I have, as you requested, communicated with Herr Balmer at The Bank Leu in Switzerland and he has, to my great surprise, agreed to comply with your unusual request. As you can see for yourself, it is done."

He passed across a telegraph message which Holmes scanned eagerly then, with a chillingly feral grin, pocketed it with evident satisfaction. "And what of the other matter, Mr May, the, ah, paperwork... I trust that is all in order?"

The chief cashier looked pained; "Ah yes, that. It is here..." and he retrieved a large brown cardboard box-file from beneath his desk. "Do you have suitable security about you gentlemen?" Holmes looked across at me. "Doctor Watson here is armed. Watson, be a good fellow and take charge of this would you?" May reached beneath his desk once more; "I believe this was a further requirement Mr Holmes?" Bemused, I watched May hand Holmes a bulky canvas bag and what appeared to be a receipt of some sort across the polished desk-top; Holmes appended his signature to the document. We stood and May solemnly shook hands with each of us. "Godspeed gentlemen and I pray for a successful outcome - the fate of the nation's economy now rests in your hands."

And so we departed The Bank of England, I carrying my evidently precious burden, Holmes bearing the canvas bag and whistling tunelessly. I knew better than to quiz him for the present. Once back at Baker Street he relieved me of my mysterious burden and placed it upon the dining table, along with the bag.

When I tentatively enquired about the contents, he replied offhandedly "Oh these, Watson, merely bundles of exceedingly dull financial papers; those with an interest in such things might find them perfectly fascinating, but I am certain that were you to read even a dozen of them you would become bored to distraction – they all say much the same thing."

He slid the cardboard box across to me. "Here, see for yourself." The box was a large double folio-sized cardboard file; the lid secured by a strong cord wound around two stout bone buttons. I unwound the string and lifted the lid; I was silent for some time. I looked up at Holmes; a quirky little smile flashed over his face. "Interesting reading, eh?"

"Is this real?"

"Oh yes Watson, it is perfectly real"

"This is a fortune! Good Lord, there must be tens of thousands of pounds here!"

"One hundred thousand to be precise."

"Then The Bank proposes to pay for the return of the plates and paper?"

"We may not expect Mr Bormanstein to return them for no gain at all. But worry not Watson, this is merely for show – a theatrical prop I trust – it is my bait; I would prefer not be compelled to hand it over, but a rat-trap with no bait catches few rats." I shook my head in wonderment at this extraordinary *volte-face*. It seemed not the triumphant end I had hoped for; as I went to my room I reflected that while Holmes was an undoubted prodigy in the field of criminal detection, perhaps even he had his limits, faced with such an intractable situation.

* * *

CHAPTER SEVENTEEN

A RAT-TRAP IN BELGRAVE SQUARE

While shaving early next morning – the final day of the deadline – I overheard Holmes in quiet conversation with a visitor; a moment's concentration on the *basso profundo* voice of the caller confirmed that it was Solomon Warburg. I understood none of the murmured discussion except Warburg's parting words:

"Until later then, Mr Holmes."

My colleague laughed quietly, the parlour door closed, then silence reigned until I heard Mrs Hudson's morning greeting as she entered to set breakfast; I adjusted my collar and entered the parlour. Holmes was already attacking a large kipper; "Most timely Watson – yours is still warm under the cover." I was mystified by his calm, confident mood at such a critical hour. He paused; "Today is the judgement day – you are still with me?" For answer I placed my revolver beside my plate; "Of course Holmes; Mary returns from Cambridge tomorrow evening, but even were she to return earlier, I could never forgive myself if I allowed you to face this peril alone, even with your burly welcoming committee.

"I have some private matters to attend, and several tedious house-calls I must make today in Chelsea and

Kensington, but I shall return around nine if that accords?"

"That will do splendidly Watson but be sure not to be much later; I myself shall call on Lestrade and apprise him of our guests tonight; I am certain he will attend, for we know he will never recover the stolen plates and paper from the blameless Petch and Gunton and they, I am sure, are quite as bewildered as Lestrade is deluded! Perhaps after, I may make a few small purchases, try my hand at the tables of The Bagatelle Club and then take tea in Belgravia" with which odd announcement he returned his attentions to demolishing his kipper.

Holmes rarely shopped or took tea out, and never gambled, much preferring to deduce the outcome of a circumstance, rather than leave the conclusion to pure chance. Little more of interest occurred that morning save that Billy showed Wiggins, the self-appointed leader of the Baker Street Irregulars up at noon. He appeared most excited as he delivered his message in breathless gasps.

"It was just like you said it would be Mr 'Olmes – Mustachios, the toff went to the telegraph office spot on ten an' picked up two messages. I got just the quickest peek at them as the clerk handed them over. One was quite short, just a few lines, an' the other was all down the page. 'E seemed most 'andsome pleased wiv 'em.

"Pretty nippy-like he legs it back to the river an' one of 'is big geezers – the one wiv' the squinty eyes – rows him out to the big boat at best speed; then 'e starts ordering all the heavies about, right toplofty, 'ollering at the top of 'is voice an' pretty soon they starts to load lots of 'eavy-lookin' boxes in the boat an' rows 'em over to a wagon on the quay; I 'eard 'im shout to be loaded in time to be in town by midnight. Then I legged it back 'ere as fast as I could wiv the news."

"And the other errand?" The urchin reached within the capacious pocket of his ragged, oversized coat and produced a flat, evidently weighty package folded within brown paper.

"Ah yes Mr 'olmes – Mr Kauffmann sends his best regards and 'e 'opes 'e done it right. I told 'im that you wanted it just like in a mirror, which 'e thought most 'stremely strange." Holmes unfolded a flap of the wrapping and peered within. He smiled and said "That is very satisfactory Wiggins – you have done well." A moment later and a florin richer, the grubby little fellow dashed down the stairs to vanish into the labyrinth of London' streets.

A fierce gleam of excitement appeared in Holmes steel-grey eyes. He thrust a pale, sinewy hand out, palm-up. In a low, exultant tone he said "I have them now Watson; I have them right here..." and the bony fingers closed inexorably into a vice-like fist, the startling strength of whose grip I had seen demonstrated more than once in the past.

"My trap is baited and ready to spring – I will take them tonight!"

I departed to attend my first call in Knightsbridge; it was a full hour and a half before I was released by my irascible patient – the hugely florid Brigadier Grenville-Wyatt who grumbled (despite my best ministrations) that his gout was worsening, and became quite testy when I suggested that an entire bottle of Cockburn's port *per diem* was perhaps excessive; later in Kensington the widow, Mrs De'Ath, an enthusiastic and accomplished hypochondriac, despite her enviably robust state of health appeared morbidly determined to live up to her family name and positively would not let me leave until I prescribed something different, something novel; in desperation I suggested violet cachous from Benedict's Confectioners and charged only a half-crown for my consultation; (amusingly, just two weeks later Mrs De'Ath earnestly assured me that the innocent and entirely ineffectual cachous had quite cured her grave symptoms, and proceeded to upbraid me for not having prescribed them earlier! Ho Hum...) I felt certain that Holmes must be enjoying a livelier afternoon than I!

As matters turned out I returned to Baker Street a few minutes before nine, when I encountered Holmes seated at his desk, meticulously cleaning and loading his revolver. "Ah Watson; good to see you back; and how has your day been?"

I shrugged resignedly. "Oh, it was perhaps only slightly more absorbing than attending last week's all-night sitting debating the proposed redrawing of several London Borough boundaries."

"I am sorry to hear it, for I by contrast have spent a fascinating afternoon on a jigsaw puzzle – you have no idea how gratifying it is to locate and place those crucial few pieces over which for days, you have puzzled how to fit into the emerging picture! However, enough of this chatter – we must make ready to welcome our guests in a fitting manner" and he reached for his coat, hat and revolver.

"He called down for a cab, and then retrieved a gleaming new Gladstone bag which I had not previously noted, from beneath his desk; it was equipped with a heavy steel chain and a thick bracelet to lock upon one's wrist. I presumed it contained the humiliating ransom to be paid.

"Then we are to depart Holmes?" at which he said wryly; "Surely you did not imagine that I planned a Brick-Lane booth-brawl here at Baker Street! I doubt that we would have lodgings beyond tomorrow if that were to be the case; no, Watson, I have chosen an altogether more congenial meeting place, and Mrs Hudson shall be spared considerable distress. Come; get your coat, for unless I am much mistaken that is our driver below."

Travelling into town I quizzed Holmes as to the reason for our leaving Baker Street at a little after half-past nine for a midnight rendezvous, unless it was to be a good distance away. "Not in the slightest Watson; in fact it is not far away at all, but we are dealing with wary, experienced and dangerous men. I am certain that they will arrive before the appointed hour and keep a circumspect watch on the place for at least an hour, perhaps more, lest they be drawn into a trap. Unknown to them we and our hidden army shall be in place long before midnight, and waiting to welcome them appropriately."

Shortly, we entered that most exclusive, most expensive acre of London - Belgrave Square, where we alighted on the north side opposite a large grand house; like many of its neighbours it was extravagantly ablaze with light. Our arrival passed quite unnoticed among the gaiety of promenaders and the myriad fares arriving and departing in this centre of London's high-society.

As I paid off the driver, Holmes nodded briefly in the direction of two very heavily-built gentlemen, dressed for the opera or theatre, seated on an elaborate wrought-iron bench beside the garden-square directly opposite the splendid mansion. A brightly-illuminated brass plaque beside its stone pillars identified it as Eaton House.

The two muscular theatre-goers resumed their quiet conversation; Holmes took my elbow and guided us away from the mansion, then crossed the street, at which point we doubled back until we arrived at the coaching entrance beside Eaton House; after a careful glance around, we strolled casually into the dimly-illuminated coach-yard. I froze as a monstrous silhouette loomed from the shadows; instinctively I reached for my revolver.

"Easy, Watson" Holmes murmured.

Softly he said "Good evening Private Shadwell; you understand your duty tonight?" The colossal soldier's improbably quiet voice replied "That I do Mr Holmes Sir, never fear."

"That is well Jeremiah; then stay alert for the sign."

My companion clearly knew the lie of the land because he guided us swiftly and unerringly through the gloom of the yard to a low arch at the far side by the stables and then to the left along a path bordering wide lawns, when we arrived at what I guessed to be the tradesmen's entrance at the rear of the house. A few paces beyond, a great wash of light issued from a long array of glass doors in the French style, all leading onto the velvet lawn and the trees beyond. Elaborate wrought-iron shutters were open, but folded back against the sandstone walls. The merest glimpse through the windows told of an exceptionally opulent interior. We were admitted by the butler – a sallow, lugubrious-looking fellow who introduced himself as Balthazar; he ushered us through into a large and magnificent inner hall where we encountered Inspector Lestrade and a burly constable – both armed – and the mighty Solomon Warburg.

After a murmured discussion concerning the detailed dispositions of the men, Holmes concluded "Remember gentlemen, the trap is now baited and set – if we are to catch our rats in the act this night it is quite vital that you do not enter the library until I sound my whistle; the Doctor and I shall be observing progress closely from within the adjoining writing room at the far side. I think it probable that no more than three will enter the house; the others will most likely be on guard by the wagon at the front entrance. "They will be... taken care of by my men in the square. Should Bormanstein set his thugs outside the study door, then take them quietly at your first opportunity. There will now be something of a delay until midnight, for I am certain the house – if it is not already being watched – will shortly come under discreet surveillance by our guests, and will remain so until the appointed hour. Are we all clear on this gentlemen?" The reply took the form of three grim, determined nods.

"Then let us to our places; until midnight men, and not a sound before!"

Balthazar gravely opened the large double doors into the deserted library of this magnificent mansion – but whose was it? With the exception of our taciturn guide, we had encountered no other occupant, nor indeed, the master of the house. What brief glimpses I had seen of this splendid establishment were impressive, but upon entering the library I was astounded – it was a veritable temple in celebration of the most perfectly refined taste, the most costly of fine antiques, and the most superb *objets de vertu*. The walls were hung with a collection of the great masters – I counted several by Raphael, three Holbeins, a Breughel, four small Rubens and even a Titian. A large antique Tabriz silk carpet lay upon the marble floor; a log fire blazed in the grate.

There were perhaps a dozen small Leonardo Da Vinci sketches while to the side of the magnificent marble fireplace, within a thick glass case was an early Gutenberg bible. One wall was devoted to shelves of rare volumes and manuscripts – another to ebony and cut-glass showcases crammed with exquisite, eggshell-thin, translucent Japanese porcelain of unimaginable age and value.

To the rear of the room, the garden side, were fragile, intricately crafted glass-panelled doors – the French windows I had observed earlier; I noted on the right, an open door which clearly led through to the writing room referenced earlier by Holmes. Diagonally across in one corner, close to the writing-room door, sat a large, highly-polished rosewood desk upon which rested an open book; the room smelled opulently of beeswax, fine leather and costly cigars.

The overall impression was of overwhelming wealth, discreetly displayed in the finest taste.

While I gazed from the doorway at this breathtaking display of affluence, Holmes spoke quietly to the butler who then proceeded to dim the gas lights one by one, then departed closing the doors behind him. In the near darkness I watched Holmes step to the desk, and place the Gladstone bag beneath it; from here I saw his lean silhouette move to the window onto the square, where stood a small occasional table upon which rested an ornate reading lamp and a polished cedar-wood humidor; he knelt down and motioning me to follow suit, repositioned the lamp and humidor, then turned the light half-way up again. The table was now brightly illuminated, while a much softer glow spread across the desktop. The corners of the library were in deep shadow. Evidently he did not wish us to be observed from the garden or from the square.

"I believe that completes our preparations, Watson; I think we may now retire to await our visitors" and he scuttled on his hands and knees, crab-like into the darkened writing-room; I followed suit. It was similarly richly furnished. With difficulty I checked my watch in the deep gloom – it was now well after a half past eleven o'clock; minutes now remained until we confronted whoever was behind this crime. Holmes pulled the door to, leaving a crack perhaps four inches wide through which we would watch events in the dimly illuminated library. From our vantage point we could observe the desk, the small table with the brightly-lit lamp and the humidor by the window onto the square, the entrance doors on the far side of the library, and four of the six French windows to the garden.

Perhaps fifteen minutes later the front door opened and closed; after a murmured conversation in the entrance hall a tall elegantly-dressed figure entered the library. He looked somehow familiar but when he entered the pool of light at the window there was no further doubt – it was the cultured criminal, Otto Dietmar von Huntziger. I peered, astonished, at Holmes in the gloom; he shook his head, one finger to his lips; clearly, von Huntziger was a player in Holmes' trap; I remained silent. The robber-baron opened the humidor and selected a cigar then appeared to change his mind, replaced it and strolled to the desk. He glanced down and reached for the Gladstone bag, which he briefly opened. He made no comment except to emit a low whistle; having replaced it he seated himself, and became absorbed in the book which lay open before him. Without looking in our direction he said very quietly "Good evening Mr Holmes, Doctor Watson; welcome to my modest house. I see all your arrangements are in place."

Holmes made no answer for he knew perfectly well that von Huntziger was aware of our presence in the darkened writing-room. Von Huntziger continued in a low tone, his eyes never leaving the book "Like me, it seems you play for very high stakes Mr Holmes. I wish you good fortune... but even now I do believe I hear your guests arriving; I am fully prepared for my part."

My companion replied "I am extremely glad to hear it, Count" and the room fell silent once more. This was the first I had heard of von Huntziger's titled lineage. We waited in perfect silence; I heard the rumbling sound of a heavy vehicle pull up and halt outside the mansion; I stepped silently to the writing-room window that overlooked the square; a tarpaulin-covered wagon had parked, guarded by three very burly men.

I became aware that my heart-rate was increasing significantly and eased the heavy service revolver from my coat pocket. In the outer hall the butler admitted further arrivals – a moment later he led them into the library; there were three. The first was the wall-eyed brute Sidney Belton, who had spied on us at Baker Street, accosted us in Cubitt Town, and bought thirty pieces of silver for his sweet-heart; the second was his companion, the shorter bruiser, whom we had last encountered at the far end of an iron chain, restraining a monstrous mongrel hound.

After a short delay a third man entered. He was tall, lean but obviously strong and muscular, tanned and dark-complexioned with heavy military-style Mustachios; I estimated him to be of the order of fifty-five or perhaps a little more – without question it was the mysterious man in my nightmare – the same whose description we had now heard so many times. He gestured for wall-eye and the dog-handler to wait outside the library door.

Mustachios may have had the outward bearing and attire of a gentleman, but he had the countenance and aura of a criminal. With a thrill of horror I realised that I was mere feet from the man who had stolen the plates and paper, blackmailed The Bank of England, cold-bloodedly executed Dulcie Hobbs, murderously attacked Warburg, and now arrogantly attended Belgrave Square to collect his reward.

Mustachios was Asa Bormanstein!

He approached the desk; "Count Otto Dietmar von Huntziger I presume?" and he extended his hand.

"Good evening Mr Bormanstein." Von Huntziger appeared not to notice the gesture, instead closing his book and clearing the desktop. "Please be seated. As you know, I have been wired by your, ah, colleague, Professor James Moriarty, with an intriguing offer to sell certain items; he is not unknown to me. I confess I am interested, if the items are as described." Holmes and I peered out from our hiding place as Bormanstein stared fixedly at von Huntziger.

Coldly he replied "They are precisely as described Count – we have for sale the authentic new plates for the ten-pound note issued by The Bank of England; outside stands a wagon loaded with a significant sum of money already printed, and the correct paper sufficient to print a total of two and a half million pounds in Sterling."

Von Huntziger laced his fingers behind his head and leaned back languidly in his chair. "I am quite sure that is so Mr Bormanstein, but we both know the authorities are scouring the country for whoever holds the plates; possession of these items is likely to be a hazardous business and the waters are already, shall we say, muddied by your activities. Also, my intelligence agents tell me that Mr Sherlock Holmes has taken a great interest in this affair; I know from experience that he is not a man be regarded lightly - he who comes within Holmes' scrupulous purview does not rest easy in his bed and I, for one, enjoy my sleep. The risk, for me, now becomes considerably greater."

At the mention of Holmes' name, Bormanstein's countenance darkened almost to the point of lividity. "You are attempting to negotiate, to bargain? This is not some Arab bazaar, von Huntziger! You speak of Holmes!" he snorted; "Holmes the amateur detective? He knows nothing! I have outwitted him at every turn; you need have no fear of him. His feeble attempt to interfere in my affairs amounted to little more than despatching a large muscular fool to snoop around my premises; I can assure you my men made a lasting impression on him!" He smirked at his own jest. "As to the police, they have arrested the old man who engraved the plates, and his watchman as accomplice; my informers tell me that Scotland Yard are certain they have their culprits."

Von Huntziger acted his part as consummately as a seasoned thespian; "Ah, now I was not aware of that development; then the offer becomes substantially more attractive. Let us discuss the matter further."

Disdainfully Bormanstein replied "I was not under the impression that there was anything further to discuss; Professor Moriarty has proposed a price of one hundred thousand pounds – you have accepted; I had presumed you to be a man of your word, a man of honour?" There was a short silence. Ambiguously, the robber-baron replied "I believe I am no less honourable than you, Mr Bormanstein."

"Very well then; you have the money?" For answer Count von Huntziger reached beneath the desk, placed the bulky Gladstone bag on the desk in front of Bormanstein and opened it wide, displaying the three-inch high bundles of crisp new ten-pound notes stacked within. Bormanstein's basalt eyes gleamed; he selected a bundle, professionally riffled through it like a card-player checking his stake, and replaced it.

Von Huntziger smiled; "You wish to count it?"

"Do I need to? You would be a fool to try and deceive me – and were you to attempt such foolishness your health would certainly – and very swiftly – take a turn for the worse; neither of us has attained the positions we enjoy by behaving like fools. No, Count, I am quite confident I will leave tonight with the precise, agreed sum."

Von Huntziger smiled and closed the locks; Bormanstein reached across to take possession of the heavy bag; with a frown the Count swiftly withdrew it from the desk-top and placed it back on the carpet beneath the desk. "Are you not perhaps being a little precipitate Mr Bormanstein? If I remember aright, there are two elements to a contract – you have now seen and verified the payment. Perhaps I might be permitted to view the item for which I am paying so large a sum?"

Bormanstein shrugged indifferently, opened his attaché case and laid a chamois leather packet on the desk. He leaned back and watched as von Huntziger reverently unfolded the soft skin to reveal gleaming mirror-polished steel, shining dully in the subdued light that glowed upon the desk-top from the nearby table-lamp. Von Huntziger looked up; "They are indeed beautiful – a work of art, would you not agree?" Bormanstein made a bored, dismissive gesture. "I myself do not see beauty, von Huntziger; what I see is power; it is mere base metal – its beauty lies in what it can do for a resourceful man."

"Perhaps you are right. Would you object if I examine them under better light?" Coldly, Bormanstein replied "So long as they remain in this room – you know full well they are perfectly genuine."

"I am sure you are correct, but nonetheless..." von Huntziger gestured down at the Gladstone bag, "...that is a not inconsiderable sum." From the entrance hall came the sound of several soft thuds, the sound of something heavy falling and a muffled oath; Bormanstein tensed and looked up, alert.

Von Huntziger chuckled; "Please do not concern yourself Mr Bormanstein; that is merely my famously clumsy man-servant Guenther, bringing in logs for the drawing-room fire. He foolishly attempts to carry many more than he can manage but he is elderly, and invariably drops them at the doorstep." Bormanstein relaxed.

I confess I was struggling to understand why Holmes was permitting this deception to play so long; surely it would have been more prudent to have seized the criminals the moment they entered the mansion?

I concluded it could only be because he was assessing his foe, measuring his strengths and weaknesses, and was gleefully anticipating the gratifying moment when he sprang his cunning trap...

Von Huntziger picked up the parcel, stepped to the small window table, drew the curtain wider and having moved the humidor and turned up the lamp to full brightness, examined the gleaming steel plates anew under the brilliant glow of the incandescent globe; after considerable and close scrutiny he murmured over his shoulder "They look good, very good Mr Bormanstein."

"Why should they not? They are the genuine plates for The Bank of England. Let us not quibble Count; we are both busy men. You have seen the plates – give me the money and our business here is done."

Outside in the square I caught the sound of hoarse shouting, grunts and blows, a brief scuffle, then silence

– no doubt late-night revellers who had indulged rather too freely after a night at the music-hall?

Von Huntziger grinned cheerfully; "As you say Mr Bormanstein, we are both busy men and neither of us is a fool; and we are both men of our word. The goods are, indeed, exactly as offered – I am quite satisfied." He selected a cigar and spent some time cutting it and lighting it to his satisfaction. Bormanstein watched von Huntziger, then turned back to the desk and resumed drumming his fingers impatiently. Von Huntziger closed the humidor, re-wrapped the plates, returned to his chair and positioned the leather parcel on the desk between the two of them.

He reached down for the heavy Gladstone bag with its steel chain and bracelet from beneath the desk and placed it in front of Bormanstein, together with a small steel key; Bormanstein unlatched the bag and glanced at the contents a second time. Satisfied, he locked it.

Surely now Holmes would sound the alarm? Bormanstein sat with a fortune before him; the priceless package of plates lay on the desk only inches from von Huntziger's grasp – now was the time to strike! I glanced at my friend – he appeared to be transfixed by the unfolding events; his knuckles gleamed white in the gloom against the blue-black steel of his revolver.

In his left hand he held the police whistle which would signal the joining of battle; yet still he did not move, utterly concentrated as he was upon the drama playing out before our eyes.

"I believe, Count von Huntziger, our transaction here is concluded; the paper stands outside; you have the plates; I have the payment" Bormanstein said tonelessly, and snapped the heavy steel bracelet shut upon his left wrist. Only the key, a blacksmith or a butcher's cleaver could now separate Bormanstein from the Gladstone bag. He stood, nodded curtly to von Huntziger, and turned to leave...

The shockingly shrill blast of Holmes' whistle momentarily deafened me and almost stopped my heart. We burst into the library at the same instant as the far doors crashed open – Lestrade, his officer and Solomon Warburg cannoned into the room almost simultaneously; Holmes levelled his gun at Bormanstein, who stood motionless beside the desk, holding the Gladstone bag; for several seconds the library was a tableau, a frozen photographic moment. Bormanstein glared malevolently from von Huntziger to Holmes and back. His dark eyes darted frantically around the room – there was no escape." Angrily he shouted for his thugs; "Belton! Clarke! In here immediately!"

Icily Holmes said "Do not look for help from that quarter, Bormanstein; all your gang are taken!"

Lestrade now addressed him in a formal manner: "Asa Bormanstein, I arrest you on suspicion of conspiracy, breaking and entering, robbery, forgery and uttering counterfeit currency, and also on suspicion of assault with a deadly weapon and the murder of..." he got no further. Like a striking cobra, in a single lightning motion Bormanstein snatched the leather parcel from the desk and thrust it into a capacious coat-pocket; he spun around and something appeared to shoot from his sleeve - for the briefest second I saw him levelling a small nickel-plated derringer directly at Holmes' head. Instinctively I hurled myself sideways and barged him to the floor; Bormanstein's pistol emitted a sharp, flat crack and a spit of brilliant yellow flame at the same instant as Lestrade's heavy police revolver boomed deafeningly in the confines of the library.

He appeared to miss for the delicate bevelled glass of a showcase shattered some inches to Bormanstein's left, along with a quantity of priceless Japanese porcelain. Then in one great bound, with a furious snarl of mingled rage and triumph, and a malevolent backward glare of purest hatred, Bormanstein crashed through the French windows and with quite astonishing speed for a man of middle years, raced across the lawn and vanished in the blackness beyond. A moment later we heard a shouted order, the sound of a horse being savagely whipped up, then a carriage raced away into the night at a furious pace.

The room fell silent as the tomb; all eyes turned toward Sherlock Holmes who was in the act of picking himself up from the rich silk carpet. Abruptly the single remaining, intact pane of glass balancing precariously in the skeleton of the ruined door-frame fell to the stone pathway below and shattered into a hundred pieces – as if in mocking judgement upon the failure of Holmes' elaborate rat-trap.

At the end of the chase, though we were unhurt, he had lost. The bait was taken, the trap had been sprung – and it was empty. Holmes slumped into a chair and sank his head in his hands; I glared at von Huntziger who appeared to be enjoying a degree of schadenfreude, seemingly deriving some pleasurable amusement from Holmes' discomfiture. "If you care to look behind you Mr Holmes, you will observe that the good Doctor has just done you a very great service." Holmes turned – directly behind where he had been standing, precisely at head-height, was a marble bust of Socrates in an ornate alcove. It appeared to have acquired a third eye exactly between the two original orbs. Holmes gripped my shoulder tightly, stared hard at me and nodded slowly.

Lestrade spoke, surprisingly kindly. "I'm truly sorry things turned out this way for you Mr Holmes. But perhaps you overplayed your hand this time? Maybe you should have let us take him as soon as he entered the house? True, I arrested the wrong men by mistake, but I have sent instructions for their immediate release; however it would appear you have let the plates, the money and the real villain slip clean through our fingers, just when we had him in our grasp. Perhaps it would be as well if we manage this case from here-on in?"

Holmes was silent for a space. "Well gentlemen, I do confess I had not anticipated our visitor leaving so abruptly through the French windows, particularly without troubling to open them first; however, beyond that small matter, I think affairs proceeded tolerably! We have at least taken the gang, the paper and any notes they have printed."

I was trying to fathom in what possible way the outcome of the affair could be termed 'tolerable'. Lestrade cleared his throat; "In your position, Mr Holmes, I much doubt I would be looking forward to explaining events to The Bank of England. And what you'll tell Mr Henry Petch I have no idea. To think that you had all within your grasp and let it vanish. We truly should have acted earlier."

A moment later I heard the rumble of the heavy wagon being driven around into the coach-yard, after which the massive iron gates clanged shut. Several more officers arrived outside with a Black Maria and the five toughs were bundled aboard under Lestrade's watchful eye while Huntziger puffed contentedly at his cigar, still with that odd smile on his face. Holmes spoke quietly with Lestrade, while the butler silently entered, carrying a large coverlet of some sort which he proceeded to secure over the shattered window-frame against the cold night air, precisely as Petch had done, to protect his precious orchids at the commencement of this strange adventure.

Holmes looked across at Solomon Warburg who stood silently by the library doors, nursing bruised knuckles. "Lestrade tells me that you right-royally evened the score with the wall-eyed Belton who attacked you, as did your boys with the wagon crew outside."

The doughty Warburg smiled with deep satisfaction; "Indeed I did Mr Holmes; he tried to stick me with another of those infernal steel spikes of his; but I doubt he'll talk boastfully of our encounter after tonight!" Holmes murmured "Ah, the *second* missing burin..."

He added wryly "I understand from Inspector Lestrade that there may be considerable doubt he'll ever talk again – it seems that knuckle-duster of yours fractured and dislocated his jaw and removed several of his teeth!" Warburg's eyes widened in surprise; he examined his massive right fist in wonderment.

"Well I never, Mr Holmes; my right cross must be better than ever, for you see, I did not even use the steel knuckles..." Homes and I travelled back to Baker Street in silence. I concluded he was likely weighing the miserable consolation of capturing five of the gang, against the disastrous loss of The Bank's money and plates from under his nose, and his failure to take Asa Bormanstein.

And now the deadline had expired.

Chapter Eighteen

JUSTICE IS SERVED ON A PLATE

Next morning, with some trepidation I opened my bedroom door and peered cautiously into the parlour; Holmes was working at his desk.

"He is an arrogant, impertinent and over-reaching dog, Watson! He exhibits an irrational and unhealthy veneration for his own intellect, which borders on megalomania; he is almost certainly more than a touch mad, and like every mad dog, should be handled with great caution..." declared Sherlock Holmes coldly "...and put down as soon as is practicable."

Cautiously I enquired "To whom do you refer?"

"I refer to the loathsome and dangerous creature who calls himself Bormanstein. Last night he overplayed his hand – he thought to outsmart me, to make a fool of me Watson, but I was prepared and I will have my revenge!" and he continued ordering slugs of lead type in his compositor's rack.

I remained diplomatically silent while my companion worked industriously with his metal letters, roller and ink and several pieces of paper, though as to his purpose, and even whether it bore upon the case currently at hand, I could not guess.

I could think of nothing uplifting to say – the atmosphere in the room seemed to be weighed down with the heavy burden of failure, and of Holmes' close brush with death at the hand of the evil Bormanstein.

My thoughts lightened when I recollected that this was the evening of Mary's home-coming from Cambridge, and I turned my thoughts to some manner of celebration for her arrival. I was deciding between The Café Royal and Simpson's in The Strand when Holmes turned towards me. Sombrely he said "I will, of course, have to account for the outcome of last night's *fracas* Watson, to which end I have convoked Mr May, Mr Petch and Lestrade here in..." he looked over at the clock "...about thirty minutes – I have a lot to explain as you know. You may imagine it is likely to be a somewhat complicated meeting; accordingly I will perfectly well understand should you prefer not to be present."

I had observed Holmes, day and night, applying himself tirelessly to this intractable case – I was not going to abandon him in his hour of need. "I would prefer to remain if I may Holmes, if only to see fair play." He smiled warmly but said nothing.

"Anyway," I continued "Bormanstein cannot elude you indefinitely – we know his identity, we have seen his face, his gang is taken – he is now a hunted man, alone and on the run, armed with nothing but a bag of money and a parcel of useless steel plates. He will surely make a slip, and we will be waiting to pounce!"

"Watson my dear old chum, I do believe you are quite as durable as the engraved steel plates he carried away – and without doubt, infinitely more valuable than the money."

I was much affected by these words from a man whose opinion I so greatly valued. At precisely eleven o'clock I heard a hansom arrive below, followed a few moments later by a second. Holmes seated himself at the dining table with his back to the window, interlaced his fingers and waited in silence.

The parlour door opened to admit Mr Frank May, chief cashier of The Bank of England, Mr Henry Petch, master engraver and partner of Perkins, Bacon & Petch, and a few seconds later, Inspector Lestrade of The Yard.

"Please be seated gentlemen." They joined Holmes at the table; I took the remaining chair. Frank May spoke first. "If I am correct Mr Holmes, last night the clock ran out on the criminals' deadline. I believe you have called us here to report your progress; have you the Bank's money?"

Petch added "Have you recovered the plates Mr Holmes?"

Lestrade joined in "And where is Asa Bormanstein?"

Holmes held up his hands, palms out. "In order if you please gentlemen. No doubt, Mr May, you refer to a heavy Gladstone bag containing a quantity of Bank of England ten-pound notes provided by you; the last I saw of that, it was shackled to the wrist of a notorious criminal – also a murderer – fleeing into the night." He turned to the old engraver:

"Sadly, Mr Petch, even having been paid, Bormanstein still coveted the finely engraved steel, for he snatched the leather parcel before making good his escape.

"As to your question, Inspector, I regret to say that at present I have no idea where he is – losing his trail is my greatest regret, but I will find him gentlemen; in time, I will see him taken – if he does not hunt me first."

A frosty silence descended on the meeting. Below on the street I heard a growler pull to the kerb.

Coldly May said; "Then you have signally failed, Mr Holmes, and you have cost The Bank one hundred thousand pounds into the bargain. Your desperate last throw of the dice has come to nought." Holmes looked intently down at the carpet.

"And the plates are gone, probably forever" added Petch. Holmes studiously examined his fingernails.

"I have researched diligently, and his name is not on any record of known criminals" Lestrade concluded the cheerless litany.

Before Holmes could reply there came a soft knock upon the door. "Excuse me a moment gentlemen" – he strode across the room and opened the door. I heard a brief murmured conversation, a low chuckle and Holmes returned to the table bearing a sizeable cardboard box. He peered inside it and said irritably "Is it not annoying when other people's goods are delivered in error to your address? This is surely not mine" and he opened the lid wide. Holmes' face was sombre but I noted his eyes were alight with barely concealed excitement.

"Ah, I see this is possibly your property, Mr May" and theatrically, like a prestidigitator revealing the vanished lady he set ten three-inch thick bundles of crisp new Bank of England ten-pound notes upon the table before The Chief Cashier.

Again he peered within the box. "Aha! There is more – mayhap some belated Christmas cheer – perhaps this yours Mr Petch?" and he placed an evidently weighty, chamois leather parcel in the gnarled hands of the master engraver. Neither visitor spoke. Frank May fanned the corner of one stack of notes and nodded with deep satisfaction; Henry Petch slowly and incredulously unfolded the leather parcel whereupon a look of ineffable relief and joy flooded his careworn face. He looked up at Holmes; "And the Portal's paper?"

"That is safely under guard in the custody of, shall I say, a trusted... associate." The room fell silent once again; the Hampson clock ticked softly in the corner.

I beamed with delight – Sherlock Holmes had not failed; far from it, he had conjured a great triumph!

But how he had contrived it was a mystery to me. Lestrade alone appeared somewhat vexed and deeply puzzled – he shook his head in bewilderment.

"I'm sure I don't know how the trick was done Mr Holmes, but it seems yet again you have pulled the rabbit out of the hat. I know I saw the bag – I saw it secured and locked on his wrist; I saw the plates on the desk – and I saw them taken!"

"Come come Lestrade, it was you and I *in concert* who pulled the rabbit from the hat! I merely acted in, how shall I put it, an advisory capacity; this collar is fairly and squarely yours; you already hold the gang – you have retrieved the priceless plates, The Bank has its money intact – less £100 – I'm sure it will not be long before you apprehend their principal!"

This statement was emblematic both of Holmes' generosity of spirit, and his natural instinct to shun the public spotlight. His work was, for him, its own reward.

"If you are amenable, Lestrade, I will call at the Yard tomorrow morning at, shall we say, eleven o'clock, and I shall tell you what I know of this business." The detective looked at Holmes narrowly. "And exactly how much do you know Mr Holmes?"

"I know all Lestrade, I know all."

The Inspector bade his farewells and departed in high good humour, evidently well pleased with his unexpected good fortune – perhaps promotion was yet within his grasp.

Frank May studied Holmes shrewdly; "There is rather more to this affair than meets the eye Mr Holmes, and certainly considerably more than you are telling, of that I am convinced." The merest suggestion of a smile flickered briefly across Holmes thin lips. "Ah Mr May, I'm afraid there you must allow me my little trade secrets." The chief Cashier paused, then laughed drily. "Very well Mr Holmes; I suppose I shall just have to restrain my curiosity until Doctor Watson records the affair in one of his excellent accounts!" He glanced across at Henry Petch who appeared still to be dazed by the dramatic and unexpected return of his precious plates. He addressed me "Perhaps, Doctor, you might simply entitle it *"Sherlock Holmes and The Master Engraver"*, for that is where the whole affair started and finished!"

I smiled. "Perhaps I will, Mr May, perhaps I will at that."

"I believe there is a final piece of business between us Mr Holmes" said The Cashier; "You have rendered a service of inestimable value to Perkins, Bacon & Petch, to The Bank of England, to the country and likely, to the Empire. I am authorised to settle your account immediately; no doubt you have incurred significant expenditure in the course of your enquiry, and there is the further matter of your professional fee – I shall not require an accounting. I trust this will be adequate to cover any expenses." I watched in disbelief as May pushed across one of the thick bundles of notes – ten thousand pounds "And in view of the scale of the disaster you have averted, I feel this perhaps to be appropriate remuneration for your professional services." He passed across a second bundle – a total of twenty thousand pounds! May slid across a receipt upon which Holmes scrawled his signature.

My colleague gazed impassively at the fortune before him. "That is more than adequate Mr May – indeed it is a very great deal of money..." he laughed briefly "...but then I *was* playing against the man who tried to break The Bank of England, and his stake was considerably higher than mine!"

"My renewed and most sincere thanks Mr Holmes, and you Doctor Watson; I shall now take my leave and return this to our vaults; it is possibly the largest, short-term cash advance, free of interest, we have ever made!"

Holmes reached once more into the cardboard box. "Then you will perhaps find this useful" and he handed May an empty, brand-new Gladstone bag with its security chain and a key. "Oh, and these too." He passed the Chief Cashier the three counterfeit notes we had acquired during the course of our investigation. "The man who delivered this parcel awaits you on his growler below; it is equipped with dark-blinds; he is entirely to be trusted – he nearly lost his life in the course of assisting me. You will note he is more than muscular enough to ensure your safe journey back to The Bank with such a precious cargo."

When the door had closed behind Frank May, Holmes turned to Henry Petch, who sat, gently smiling, both sinewy, age-spotted hands gripping the precious parcel tightly, as if at any moment it might again be snatched from his grasp. "I apologise for my, perhaps, theatrical revelation Mr Petch; my colleague has on occasion upbraided me for being unnecessarily dramatic." Petch clutched his parcel even more fiercely and replied like a naughty schoolboy confessing to a minor crime "Think nothing of it Mr Holmes; truth to tell, I myself have been known somewhat mischievously to introduce a quite needless but flamboyant piece of scrollwork into my plates for the sheer exuberant devilment of it! But in more serious vein, I have a few questions to which I must have answers."

Holmes gestured for the elderly engraver to continue. "If the criminals employed keys, then whose did they use? As you well know, there are only four sets in the entire world. How did they enter our premises and violate the safe and the paper-store, and by what means did they contrive to remove such a large volume of material under the watchful eyes of Gunton and Shadwell? And how came these miscreants to know of the existence of the plates in the first instance?"

Holmes sat for a moment, eyes closed in thought, organising his thoughts. "As I deduced from the start Mr Petch, they did, indeed use keys. But you are mistaken when you state that there are only four sets in existence; there *were* four – there are now six!" and he handed Petch his set of glittering zinc keys attached to a small steel ring. The engraver's eyes opened wide.

"Then whose are these?"

"They are mine, but in a roundabout way, Mr Petch, they are yours!"

Petch fumbled for his watch-chain; "There you are in error Mr Holmes; here are mine in their customary place. These are new – all our locks have been replaced."

Holmes nodded and continued "The fifth set used by the criminals was made in exactly the same manner as I contrived this sixth set. *What one man can devise, another can discover?* You will recall I took your keys to my work-bench yonder. I made perfect impressions in firm-grade modellers' clay, in exactly the same way as did Bormanstein, but he used glazier's putty, when spuriously repairing the orchid-house whose destruction he himself had organised the previous night. While you were away seeking a workman, and your wife was lured out on a wild-goose chase to Doctor Bentinck's house, your maid Dulcie Hobbs – treacherously insinuated by Bormanstein using false references – removed your keys from your bureau and passed them to him, probably through the study window. The job took mere seconds. They were compelled to resort to this extraordinarily elaborate subterfuge, having previously searched your partners' houses in Harrow for their keys, but to no avail as they were both away travelling and had their keys with them.

"The impossible coincidence of your orchid-house being randomly vandalised one night, and two workmen appearing the very next morning in your predictable absence, with all necessary supplies and equipment, alerted me instantly.

"As to how the villains entered your business premises, why, by the normal method; you and your partners hired them, then allowed them in. They rang the bell, were admitted by the watchman, a record was entered in the day-book, and the villains set about their criminal enterprise!"

"Then you know their identity Mr Holmes? Surely the police can find the leader and seize him?"

Holmes chuckled wryly; "You already know his identity Mr Petch – for you and your partners paid him for his services – Mr Orman of Orman's Roofing Contractors, alias Mr Asa Bormanstein!

"I have no doubt he offered a guarantee that he would best any other estimate you may have had for the works. By contracting with him, your hard-nosed partner in charge of purchasing unwittingly gave him free access to your premises, inside, outside, and on the roof, which is where he and his gang entered.

"Once up high and out of view, it was a simple matter to remove the appropriate section of the roof, climb down directly into the paper-store and using the innocent gantry and block-and-tackle which hoisted their tar-vats up and down, haul the paper out of the store and thence down to their wagon, out of sight of the watchman, at the rear of the premises.

"To steal the plates they simply unlocked the paper-vault from within, sauntered through to your private office, much as I did using those" he gestured towards the key ring "where they used their counterfeit key to unlock the safe. If you look carefully you will find I left my calling card within – *Mr John Watson, Surveyor.* Upon leaving, one of them, probably the wall-eyed Belton seized two of your burins, perhaps because they appealed as weapons; a colleague of ours was later stabbed with one of your engraving tools. He survived two such attacks and is well."

Petch appeared deeply upset by these revelations. "However, you have not yet told me Mr Holmes how these impious men gained their shockingly detailed intelligence."

For several moments my colleague sat deep in thought. "Here we touch upon a rather delicate matter, Mr Petch, and I cannot advise upon it, though I have my thoughts. You will recollect when first we met I asked you to describe your partners candidly. I recall one was a keen card-player at The Bagatelle Club, and also enjoyed – perhaps rather too much, a glass or mayhap even, several? It is well-known that ardent spirits and gambling go together ill; even worse when they occasion garrulous talk.

"I visited the Bagatelle Club and learned from the steward that early in November your associate had lost a very large sum of money at the tables and was consoling himself in his customary way. It seems he fell into conversation with a tall, moustachioed player who plied him most generously with whisky; that man we now know as Asa Bormanstein. For a guinea, Barker, the head steward intimated to me that your colleague was volubly forthcoming on all matters, your business, your private addresses, your search for a contractor, Mrs Petch's requirement for a new maid, your opening and closing days over Christmas – all were freely volunteered. Most damning of all, he displayed his keys and, it seems, indiscreetly boasted of the importance of each, and what they guarded.

"But if, as I suspect, he is a valued colleague – perhaps a quiet word or two would suffice? In view of the calamitous consequences he occasioned, I doubt he will repeat the error." Petch smiled ruefully to himself.

"I believe perhaps we may take your advice Mr Holmes; after this dreadful business, I too doubt that such an indiscretion would occur again" and he offered his curiously evolved right hand.

Holmes and I shook it warmly and thus it was that Mr Henry Petch, aesthete, lover of rare orchids, and the master engraver of Perkins, Bacon & Petch left 221B Baker Street, perfectly content and clutching his beloved plates tightly to his chest. With the parlour silent once more I resolved to quiz Holmes on those several matters still opaque to me. He was more than pleased to comply, for he knew that in me he had his most appreciative audience.

"Let us relax with a pipe by the fire Watson and I shall briefly relate, if you wish, the entire sequence of events for you. And, infinitely more challenging to the critical faculties of observation and deduction, those small facts that the common man overlooks, but which damn a villain just as well as his confession."

And so, with that meticulous concision of narration I enjoyed so well, he proceeded to complete the puzzle for me...

"A losing night at the card table, strong drink and black melancholy can play the very devil with some men's discretion..." he began surprisingly. "But for that night's random sequence of events, the theft – and a tragic and needless murder – almost certainly would not have occurred.

"Consider, Watson: a man is brought low by a night's heavy gambling losses; he is drowning his sorrows in a bottle when quite by chance he encounters a stranger. They fall into conversation, he feels diminished and seeks to restore his rank; through sheer hubris he attempts to prove his station in life by displaying his valuable keys, and the vast responsibility and authority with which they endow him. The stranger – Bormanstein as he claims to be – plies him with ever more refreshment and he becomes ever more indiscreet.

"Like a willing lamb to the slaughter he unwittingly delivers every data necessary to commit the crime: the firm's name and those of the other partners, their domiciles and pastimes, their holiday closure dates, the search for a roofing contractor, Petch's hunt for a suitable maid and much more, no doubt.

"In short, as Lestrade might say, Bormanstein has been gifted the means, the motive and the opportunity.

"Now he must work swiftly; he conjures together a team of criminals and wins the contract at Perkins, Bacon & Petch simply by guaranteeing to beat the lowest price – it is immaterial to him whether he makes a profit or a loss – the prize is unfettered access to the premises for several days. But now he must also gain access to a set of keys; from his encounter at The Bagatelle Club he knows two of the partners are abroad in France and Ireland respectively, so he enters and searches their houses in Harrow but to no avail – Perkins and Bacon have their keys with them; hence the account we observed in the news-sheet concerning two burglaries in Harrow, but with no theft occasioned.

He now has only one recourse – Henry Petch's keys; for that he requires an accomplice within Mr Petch's residence; also he needs Petch to be absent for a day; hence the magical arrival upon the scene of Dulcie Hobbs' with her perfect but quite absurd letter of recommendation from the non-existent Baroness Amanti, resident in the untraceable French village of

Obânes St-Amarin; shortly after, the orchid house is vandalised – it was a near-certainty that such a disaster in deepest winter would send Mr Petch scurrying in panic for a glazier.

"The utterly improbable appearance next morning of a competent glazier, Mr Nathan Madgwick and his 'assistant' Mr Asa Bormanstein, coincidentally equipped with all necessaries – including putty of course – miles from his yard in the Clerkenwell Road defied all belief and set me at the very highest alert. Then when I examined Petch's keys and detected traces of putty, both by scent and by microscopic examination, it merely confirmed to me that impressions of the keys had been taken in Petch's absence. Again, the price charged for the glazing work done was improbably low but immaterial – Bormanstein's reward was five minutes alone with Petch's keys and a large slab of firm putty – thanks to the treacherous services of the late Dulcie Hobbs.

"The date is now the 19th of December, and Bormanstein has his impressions.

"It was not until some days after – the evening of the 24th – when Henry Petch called upon us, that I made my own impressions with the modelling clay which I habitually use to secure equipment at my bench. Bormanstein has already made his keys and the robbery is long accomplished. The crime, you see, occurred three days prior on Saturday the 21st."

I calculated there was a lapse of some five days between Bormanstein gaining his impressions on the 19th and Petch reporting the robbery on the 24th.

"How can you be certain the crime was committed precisely on the 21st, Holmes?"

"Come Watson, there are three compelling facts which make the 21st of December the likely date. The first is the time needed to make the keys – you recall it required the highly skilled criminal-locksmith, Isaiah Pollitt, more than a full working day to complete the task over at the bench there; it could not have been achieved earlier. And second, on the Saturday, the criminals could be reasonably assured that there would be no-one on site except the watchman and themselves."

I pondered the irrefutable logic of this. "And the third fact?"

"The organ-grinder, Watson! I doubt he earned much on a deserted Fleet Street on a bitter December 21st, for such it was as Gunton complained to us. And yet it seems this kind-hearted street musician played his machine for some considerable time, apparently for Gunton's sole entertainment. Does that not strike you as odd?"

"Perhaps he was finishing his work for the day and chose, in true festive spirit, to raise the spirits of a bored old soldier on his watch?"

Holmes chortled. "...and to Gunton's delight, obligingly played *The British Grenadiers'* at full volume for him every time he left the watchmen's hut to make his round of the site?" Realisation dawned; "Good Lord Holmes, then the tune was a warning to Bormanstein and his accomplices to be alert – that Gunton was out on his round?" My colleague shrugged and spread his hands expansively in acknowledgement. "A simple alarm signal, but well-chosen to fool a sentimental old ex-military man."

"And now, Watson, events move apace. They set up their illicit press in remote Slater's yard and start work. By that time I had Dulcie Hobbs under the closest observation; young Wiggins, who I set to watch her rooms, reported the number of the hansom that delivered Bormanstein and Belton in Chiswick on the night of her murder. The time of their arrival was confirmed by the landlady and by the time we know ashes to have been scattered upon the path; they can have been the only other people to enter her lodgings that night; their cinder-dusted footprints in her room and upon the table where they climbed to secure the hangman's noose placed it beyond doubt. Hobbs' shoes were free of cinders because she had arrived home before they were scattered.

"I then summoned Solomon Warburg – you will recall his impressively insightful deduction as to the villains' likely destination that dark fateful night. Imprudently he later ventured there alone, almost at the cost of his life and unfortunately in the process, drove the gang deeper into hiding; now we knew not where they were."

"That brings me to my next question Holmes – you appeared to be more taken up with the smell of the money, than its appearance? How did that bear upon matters, for it seemed to me, I cannot fathom how, that it somehow determined the circle of precisely three miles radius which you inscribed on the map, centred upon their hide-out in Cubitt Town. I recall you said to me something very like *within that circle is where I am convinced our wicked foes have gone to earth. It can, I am sure of it, be no further away.* Then within hours you returned in the guise of a disreputable drunk, reeking of gin and decay, having spent the morning observing the villains on this SS Betania moored at Jacobs Island – precisely within your circle!"

In that so-familiar pose, thin white fingers steepled beneath his angular chin, he responded "Do you recall, Watson, once I told you that I allow all my senses free rein; sight, sound, smell, touch, even taste; the results of their observation go into the crucible of deduction, and when the clinker of deception is cast away, there remains the lodestone of truth? You may also recall I invited your estimate of the distance a strong man in a state of agitation might walk in one hour?"

Still I could make little sense of his explanation; I shrugged, bewildered.

"Consider, Watson! We encountered Wall-eye and the dog-handler upon entering Cubitt Town shortly after one o'clock; after our lunch at the public house we walked to Slater's yard where we discovered the blackmail demand and the second proof pinned to the wall sometime after three; Warburg swore on the Torah it was not there the night before; had it been, I'm sure even Lestrade would have noticed it. The yard was under continuous police watch from midnight; Constable Clarke assured us that he had left his station for no more than twenty minutes. The entire time elapsed was little more than two hours between our encounter with the heavies and the appearance of the ransom note. After we left them I surmised that one raced to warn Bormanstein at their new hideout, that strangers were asking strange questions; I would imagine the other – probably the dog-handler, remained to observe and follow us.

"Bormanstein now wrote his demand and over-printed a bank-note with his Swiss account number as the serial – the heavy raced back with it. Fortuitously for them PC Clarke was absent for some minutes at The Cubitt Arms public house and that was when they placed their note, in full knowledge that we would shortly appear on the scene.

"Hansoms are virtually unheard of in Cubitt Town; their horse and wagon was already gone, so I deduced that the alarm was raised by a man travelling on foot – one hour out and one hour back. A fit man can achieve, perhaps four miles in an hour- but Bormanstein had to prepare his demand – more time elapses – hence the radius of my circle – Wall-eye, or Sidney Belton as we now know him, could not have travelled further in the interval!"

I sat entranced; how did this unusual man spin such fragile strands of deduction, then weave them into a deadly web as strong as steel? Holmes continued with his gripping and illuminating lecture.

"The odour of an object may tell us as much as its appearance; consider, Watson, let us suppose you receive a letter from an unknown person; it smells of rose-water – your conclusion would be..?"

"That it was likely sent by a woman." He nodded.

"Next you encounter a man who smells faintly of fish?" I started to see where my friend was leading me,

"Why, that he is probably a fishmonger, or has lately handled fish."

"And a recently printed banknote that bears the smell of pitch?"

"That it was created, or has been in a place – Slater's Yard – thick with the stuff?"

"And now a second, the ransom demand, which smells the same but with a faint hint of sulphurous decay, of rot? I refer of course to the note you kindly assayed blindfolded." Now I was upon uncertain ground. "That it was printed at Slater's Yard but has moved elsewhere and acquired this new scent?"

"Exactly Watson! And the third proof, presented at Kauffmann Brothers in payment for thirty links of silver, then brought to us by The Chief Cashier, smelled most strongly of that same rotten-egg stench of decay.

"There is only one type of establishment in the world that creates that distinctive, vile smell, Watson, and they invariably are located near water where they discharge the foul and pungent effluents of their industry; the simplest research indicated that there is only one such establishment within my deduced circle of hunting-ground – you will recall that the wall-eyed Sidney Belton, the same who foolishly stole the third bank-note to buy his sweetheart a keepsake, lodged at number 30 Jacob Street hard by Tan's Yard in Bermondsey, at Jacob's Island. His purchase – the Judas silver – confirmed my every suspicion because the note he used smelled powerfully of... *a tannery!*

"The press the criminals employed requires to be driven by a steam engine, hence the reason why I concealed myself among the unsavoury ranks of the drunks and idlers of Jacob's Island to watch the only source of steam power thereabouts – the newly renamed SS Betania, in lamentable condition – anchored motionless, adjacent to the stinking outlet gutter from the tannery, but curiously still making steam. There on her deck, I observed Bormanstein, Belton and the other heavies from time to time, and they were unquestionably set to repel all boarders! It was, as I have said Watson, a fortress defended by a fast-running moat of noxious effluents."

I now understood why Holmes had called his own ground for the final confrontation, but how in heavens did he entice Bormanstein to Belgravia? And why von Huntziger's lavish Belgrave Square mansion, why von Huntziger's involvement at all? I pressed my friend further.

"Bormanstein attended, Watson, simply because he could not stay away! – I persuaded Mr Frank May to telegraph Herr Balz Balmer of The Bank Leu in Switzerland, requesting him to send a perfectly deceitful telegraph message from Switzerland, for collection by Bormanstein, stating that the ransom from The Bank of England had been deposited in his account! Herr Balmer complied to protect both the Bank Leu AG and The Bank of England. That telegraph, incidentally, was the shorter of the two messages that young Wiggins saw Bormanstein collect with such evident satisfaction.

"The longer of the two messages was an instruction drafted by me, sent to Louis Lépine and then as I requested, duly forwarded by him to the Bermondsey telegraph office, again for collection by Bormanstein; but to Bormanstein it appeared to have been sent by Professor Moriarty from Fontainebleau. Had Bormanstein replied and queried the content, the vigilant Lépine would have intercepted his message and repeated the instruction more forcefully."

It appeared that Sherlock Holmes' artful cunning knew no bounds.

We were interrupted briefly by Mrs Hudson who set out a very civilized luncheon of boiled beef and carrots, mashed potatoes and cabbage of which I was mightily appreciative, having missed breakfast entirely.

After a short interval I resumed my questioning; "Then what exactly was the content of the message purporting to be from Moriarty to Bormanstein? It must have been extraordinarily compelling."

"It was – it confirmed that Moriarty had made an agreement with von Huntziger to sell on the stolen materials for a further one hundred thousand pounds."

"And why did you issue the invitation to meet at von Huntziger's Belgravia mansion of all places?"

"For the simple reason that to be believable, Watson, Moriarty's supposed instruction to sell on the plates and paper had to name as the buyer a known and wealthy criminal, with the means to pay the fabulous sum of one hundred thousand pounds. Count Otto-Dietmar von Huntziger is just such a man.

"Bormanstein was aware of von Huntziger's *curriculum vitae*, as was Moriarty, and concluded that the professor had contrived a means of further capitalising on the stolen goods. They were now becoming too dangerous to possess. And you will recall I warned Mr May that the simple payment of the ransom demand would not ensure the safe return of the plates.

"The telegraph, apparently from Moriarty, simply assured Bormanstein that the ransom had been received from The Bank of England, that the game would soon be up, and that he had contrived a final and highly profitable throw of the dice which would increase their total gain by a further hundred thousand pounds to the enormous sum of three hundred and fifty thousand pounds – enough to fund a criminal empire for decades.

"Hence Bormanstein dutifully appeared precisely at midnight at Eaton House, Belgrave Square, exactly as I bade him. I did tell you, Watson, I can be extremely persuasive!

"Von Huntziger, for his part, was more than pleased to join in the plan, particularly when I suggested that his cooperation would almost certainly occasion an attack of amnesia on my part in connection with the stolen Hartz sapphires!" He chuckled. "It so happens that as unresolved cases go, my heart would not truly be in any further investigation, for I know the previous owner of the stones obtained them by a cruel deception amounting to extortion; at least von Huntziger obtained them through artistry and skill!

"Then there remain just three unresolved puzzles for me, Holmes; how came it that I observed the Gladstone bag of money upon the desk, we saw Bormanstein riffle through a stack of notes, check the bag a second time, shackle it to his wrist and flee, yet today you have handed it back to The Bank?"

"By the childishly simple expedient of a second identical bag beneath the desk – I purchased two; the Count first displayed the bag containing one hundred thousand pounds in genuine currency – it had to be genuine to stand up to the close examination to which Bormanstein would undoubtedly expose it. Von Huntziger removed it from the desk momentarily until he had examined the plates, then artfully re-presented the second bag which contained ten bundles of unprinted Portals paper, each topped-off with a genuine note, each bundle being secured with an official Bank of England paper band.

"This second bag with its deceitful contents was delivered to von Huntziger earlier yesterday by Warburg, and was already concealed beneath the desk when I placed its twin, containing the genuine payment, alongside.

"Had Bormanstein troubled to make more than a perfunctory examination of the second bag, he would have found that what he accepted was ten bundles of plain, unprinted Portal's paper, and ten, ten-pound notes. But he saw what he expected to see. For all his pains he has earned exactly one hundred pounds! And amusingly, I noted he neglected to take the key which unlocks the bracelet, which will annoy him still further!"

I smiled at the audacious simplicity of the means with which Holmes had tricked the criminal mastermind. "Then what of the plates, Holmes? What on earth was in the heavy leather parcel that Bormanstein snatched?"

"Why, finely engraved plates of highly-polished steel of course! However I doubt that he will trouble to print from them.

"They were fabricated to my order by Mr Julius Kauffman and his engraver – the same who inscribed the thirty-link silver bracelet purchased with the third, counterfeit note. I am sure they are not as accomplished as Mr Petch's delicate work, but they were the correct size and weight, and wrapped in chamois leather, they served to deceive. I had all along anticipated that Bormanstein would attempt some form of double-deal, and thus defeated his last-minute change of heart.

"I placed them in the humidor upon our arrival.

"At this point we have the adroit Count von Huntziger – and his rare skill with *legerdemain* – to thank; he is most accomplished in the deft removal of valuable articles and their invisible substitution with others; I am certain it has served him in the course of his profession; you might have observed he spent an unusually long time in preparing and lighting his cigar!

"In the process it was, for him, an effortless move to change the substitute plates for the real, re-wrap them in the leather outer and return them to the desk." He paused, a mischievous smile on his face.

"However, as I say, I somehow doubt that he will trouble to print any impressions from the plates he snatched. You see, Watson, from the very beginning Bormanstein has been taunting us, he has been parading his true identity at every opportunity, for he is of that arrogant breed that believes his intellect is superior, that he is beyond the reach of the police but more arrogantly still, that he is beyond the reach of Sherlock Holmes!

"He is undoubtedly a clever man, he is certainly a very dangerous man, but on this occasion with his effrontery he has quite overreached himself!"

He turned to his desk and from his printers' tray, selected a number of the lead type-slugs, which he trickled into my open hand. There were fourteen in all; I arranged them in order – there were three A's, a single B, E, I and M, two N's, an O, an R, two S's and a T.

I looked up quizzically at my friend. "What am to I do with these Holmes?" He handed me the slips of paper I had seen him printing earlier that morning. "Well, Watson, with those characters you could compose this...

BARONESS AMANTI

"...or this...

OBANES ST AMARIN

"...and this too...

ASA BORMANSTEIN

"...oh, and you can even re-order them to spell out his *real* name...

SEBASTIAN MORAN...

"-or as he prefers to be styled, Colonel Sebastian Moran, formerly of the 1st Bangalore Pioneers, son of Sir Augustus Moran, the sometime Minister to Persia. You may recall he was on my list of Moriarty's suspected associates? You may also recall the butt of an *Indian* cigar I discovered upon the hearth in Dulcie Hobbs' rooms?

"And his supreme arrogance goes further – his first name – Sebastian – also provided the characters for: SS BETANIA and his second readily becomes ORMAN of Orman's Roofing Contractors – what extravagant vanity!

"Like his colonel-in-chief, Moriarty, he too was a scion of a good family, Eton and Oxford educated and, like Moriarty, he has turned very much for the bad – in fact I now believe him to be Moriarty's right-hand man, his senior lieutenant; it is rumoured that Moriarty pays him an annual stipend of sixty thousand pounds; henceforth I shall certainly regard him as the second most dangerous man in London! I am confident I have not heard the last of him, for certainly I have made a most ruthless and deadly enemy."

"Then what, exactly, was engraved on the plates he made away with?"

"Ah those, Watson; I decided to gift him a small keep-sake as a reminder of our first skirmish, and the man who bested him at the end..." and he passed me a sheet of Portals bank-note paper.

"What you hold is, admittedly, a rather crude but still legible impression I made with my somewhat

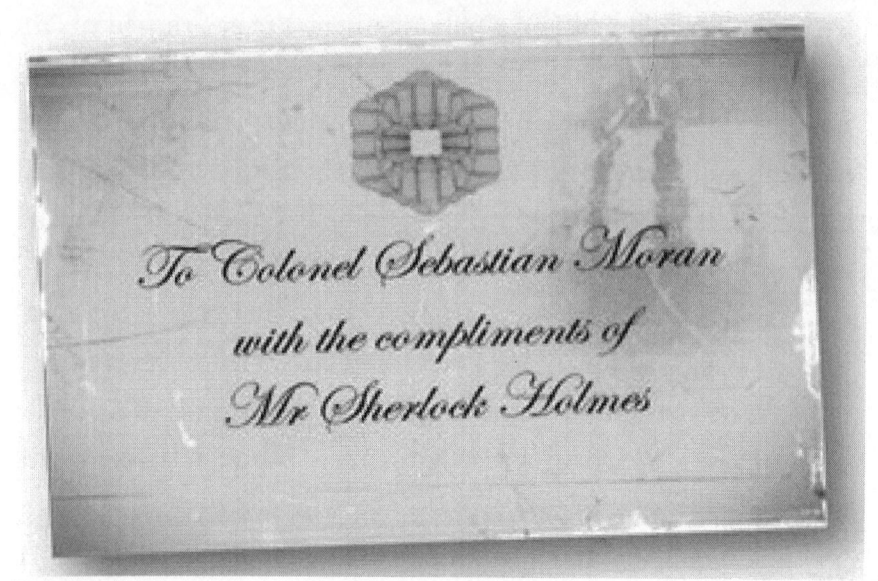

To Colonel Sebastian Moran with the compliments of Mr Sherlock Holmes

limited printing apparatus... do you not think he will treasure it?"

I burst out laughing. "Masterly Holmes, quite masterly! Indeed this investigation has been the most magisterial example of your science I believe I have had the privilege to observe."

He looked at me through a dense blue cloud of smoke and smiled. "Elementary, my dear Watson" he said cheerily, a sentiment he had never before in all our adventures together expressed in those particular words, and was never again to repeat; to other spectators it might perhaps have sounded hubristic, but for me it simply confirmed how completely fulfilled and at ease he was immersed in his abstruse but indisputably precise science of observation and deduction.

Beyond the intellectual stimulation he derives from his cases, where does he find, I wondered, that cerebral paradigm he so craves, and in company with a like intelligence? Certainly not at my door – I am at most, the willing whetstone upon which he very occasionally hones his mind; the Boswell who informs ordinary folk of the workings of this man's stellar mind; the flint from which rarely he may strike the odd small spark of inspiration with his hard, steely intellect. I could think of only two beings on the entire planet that were qualified for the role.

Mycroft, his elder brother, who Holmes readily acknowledged as his equal – on occasion even his master – is undoubtedly the foremost to come to my mind and it is possibly only Mycroft's innate indolence that saves Holmes from being bested by a superior contender in his unique field. I have witnessed several encounters between these extraordinary siblings, often when they may not have met each other for a year.

To the casual onlooker they would appear to be speaking in some arcane, unintelligible code, or even appear as two bewildered lunatics exchanging disconnected and quite incongruent phrases.

As an exemplar I paraphrase one such exchange (as best I recall it) over luncheon at The Diogenes Club and this after almost a year without meeting each other:

MH: "What do you make of the two strangers at the far corner table?"

SH: "The retired stockbroker or the cashiered army man?"

MH: "The bachelor."

SH: "Ah, he. Lives in the country, rides to hounds, starting to suffer from gout. Been in the Far East for some considerable time. Still partial to opium I suspect. Just come into a pretty substantial sum..."

And so it would go.

There is, I dread, just one other being of like intellect against whom I fear he will one day relish to test himself. I pray that day will never come, for I refer of course to that monstrously dangerous embodiment of criminal genius that is Professor Moriarty; but should my friend one day seize upon the notion of combating Moriarty, I will feel the very greatest foreboding as to the outcome...

Now today, even after several years in Holmes' close company, I feel I know almost nothing of his private milieu and past, and such minutiae as I have learned, I have gleaned with approximately the same ease as was I pulling a stubborn tooth. Those few things I have discovered are perfectly disparate in their extremes. To save his life he could not list the planets in their order from the sun; indeed he was cheerfully oblivious even of the fact that our Earth rotated annually around our star, and when I apprised him of this interesting matter, he cared not a whit because it availed him naught in his daily proceedings.

"I am sure you are perfectly correct Watson, but even were we all to rotate daily around Nelson's column, the knowledge is as valueless to me as knowing the precise number of grains of sand in the Sahara Desert!" was his blithe reply.

And yet I have observed him glance briefly around the study of a man he has not yet encountered and by observation and deduction alone, accurately divine his age, resources and place in life, his marital circumstances, profession, stature, medical afflictions, interests and vices. He has in several instances declined to act for tremendously wealthy supplicants whose motives for seeking his assistance he deemed unworthy, no matter the fee offered.

Too, I have known him compassionately to accept commissions from distressed poorer folk of humble station – with no expectation of recompense whatever – purely for the intellectual satisfaction of resolving their distressing dilemma and easing their anguish.

To my certain knowledge, with the exception of his brother Mycroft, I am the sole friend and confidant of this strange and singular, uniquely clever, subtle and talented bi-polar man; his disposition can metamorphose from high passion into the bluest funk in a moment. On rare occasions he can to me, be as transparent as the window through which, even now, I gaze vacantly down at Baker Street ~ on others more impenetrably obscure than obsidian.

He can by turns be so supremely confident of his undoubtedly superior intellect that it may be taken by many as utter arrogance, or he may be as full of self-doubt as a life-long atheist on his death-bed preparing to draw his final breath before passing through the great divide into the uncharted dark unknown beyond.

I love him as a brother, and yet he remains no more than my closest acquaintance. I respect him as my father, yet lack the nearness that should spring from that matchless, familial blood-bond.

Today I probably know him better than any man alive. But still he confides so little.

And thus Sherlock Holmes is still to me, and for all I know may well remain as long as I live, an eternal and unfathomable enigma...

John H Watson MD: April 1891, London SW1

If you have enjoyed reading
'Sherlock Holmes & The Master Engraver',
read on for a sampler of the second
adventure in the series, 'Sherlock Holmes & The
Murders on the Square',
to be published later in 2013...

SHERLOCK HOLMES & THE MURDERS ON THE SQUARE

Ross Husband
Copyright © 2013

–CHAPTER ONE–

A BODY OF EVIDENCE

Of all the strange cases in which Sherlock Holmes and I have been involved during the years of our intimacy, surely one of the most bizarre, the most outlandish – the most *outré* as my friend might playfully term it – commenced as these matters so often do, with the most trivial of events.

While he was generally mindful of the need of resources sufficient to maintain a tolerable degree of quality in his daily life (in an abstracted sort of way) Holmes lived mainly for the love of his art, rather than for the acquisition of wealth, and refused to involve himself in any investigation which did not tend towards the unusual, and even the perfectly fantastic.

As we were shortly to discover, the case of The Murders On The Square would live up to his expectations in the very highest degree.

On a warm late-July morning in 1885, shortly after breakfast we were seated comfortably in the parlour at 221B Baker Street where we roomed together on the first floor; Holmes was poring intently over the agony column in The Times and others of the more sensational news-sheets, as was his custom; I was deeply engrossed in a complex but fascinating paper lately delivered at a conference of The Royal College of Surgeons by the eminent physician Sir Edward Runciman, describing his novel treatment for the intractable problem of pulmonary embolism.

A sharp rap on the door heralded Billy, the page, with a telegram for Holmes; he opened it immediately. I returned to my studies, only to be interrupted again after a short pause.

"It seems that a large leather travelling trunk was found in Trafalgar Square yesterday, Watson."

"Mm?" I looked up, distracted. At something of a loss as quite to how to respond to this extraordinarily banal piece of information I replied "A humdrum enough mishap Holmes – no doubt it has been conveyed to the lost property office in Paddington or the like and its careless owner will perhaps claim it in due course. I make no doubt dozens of trunks are mislaid in London every year" and I returned to my reading.

Another short pause ensued...

"I'm sure you are right Watson, but then is it not so frequently the humdrum that presents the quite extraordinary?" There was a short silence, then he resumed "For example, I doubt very much that many carelessly mislaid steamer trunks contain the body of an expensively-dressed gentleman in his late seventies, folded neatly in three, wearing heavy prison leg-irons and sporting a garden weed in his buttonhole."

I set the paper down upon the instant and gave my friend my entire attention – he never jested about such matters. "Good Lord Holmes!" I noted his eyes were alive with excitement – he clearly scented the prospect of a case entirely to his liking. "Who is the dead man; how did he meet his end? And whence comes this news?"

"At present I can answer only your third question – this intelligence comes from Inspector Tobias Gregson, one of the sharper tools in the Force's box. He invites us to attend at the police mortuary; as there is a body involved I can think of no better-qualified companion than Doctor John H Watson MD – I would much value your experience if you would care to accompany me."

For me, nothing raises the pulse or tests the mental faculties more than the dispensation to assist Holmes on a case, particularly one as strange as this promised to be. "Of course I am entirely at your disposal Holmes – nothing would please me more; when do we depart?" He leapt to his feet and rubbed his hands in glee. "When else Watson – upon the instant of course! The matter is too serious for hesitation... *Carpe diem!*"

To the common man, a mortuary is a dismal place, a place to be anticipated with great trepidation, particularly when we know it to be the penultimate halt before our final interment in a cold, dark grave, and whatever fearful mystery awaits us beyond.

It is a place of limbo, a way-station to the unknown.

But to Holmes and for me, from our quite different perspectives, it can be a place of the liveliest interest. As a medical man, ever since my student days spent examining and dissecting cadavers, I quickly discovered it can be a veritable seminary of mortality, a source of much scholarship and invaluable research; and for Sherlock Holmes, certain of its more macabre inmates may offer a dark treasure-house for his singular skills of observation and deduction.

And *de facto*, any cadaver that makes a cheerless final journey to the police mortuary, rather than a tranquil passage to the lily-wreathed undertaker's parlour, most likely has a dark and sinister story to tell for those able to read it.

In the inner office a grave-faced Inspector Gregson greeted us. "It is extremely good of you to attend Mr Holmes, you too Doctor Watson. I'll be mighty grateful for any insights you can offer on this pretty little problem – for it has me completely foxed. We don't yet know his identity or where he comes from. We don't know even how he died. And as you shall see, there will be some small difficulties in performing a post-mortem. Shall we go through?" and he indicated the double doors that led to the morgue.

Through the bulls-eye glass in each I caught occasional glimpses of pathologists and their assistants at work and once, when the doors opened briefly, the top of a newly-trepanned skull being removed.

"Indeed we shall" replied Holmes "But first, if you will Inspector, be so good as to relate the circumstances preceding the trunk's arrival here." Gregson flipped open his notepad. "Very well Mr Holmes. Yesterday in the late afternoon a large brown leather steamer-trunk was observed beneath the head of one of the new lions in Trafalgar Square; it was subsequently transported here last night. It had appeared to be quite unattended and a member of the public called it to the attention of a passing constable who noted that it was securely padlocked and fairly heavy; it bore no labels or identifications whatsoever. The constable detected a strong smell of corruption issuing from within it and, becoming deeply suspicious, arranged for it to be carried here where it has remained since."

Holmes produced his slim leather-bound notebook and pencil. "Who reported the abandoned trunk?"

Gregson consulted his jottings "One Mr Benjamin Skerritt; I have his address – 17a, at the top of Upper St Martin's Lane. Yesterday he was feeding the pigeons on the square as is his custom every day; around five o'clock in the afternoon he observed two men alight from a growler; they unloaded the trunk and placed it directly beneath the head of one of Landseer's lions.

Apparently the two then seated themselves upon the trunk for some minutes, in conversation; Mr Skerritt continued feeding the birds but when next he glanced up, the two men had vanished, leaving the steamer-trunk unattended beneath the lion. When it became apparent it had been abandoned Mr Skerritt brought the matter to the attention of PC Burke who was passing by on his beat."

"Did Benjamin Skerritt furnish a description of the two men?"

"He did, Mr Holmes, but he is an elderly man - his sight is poor due to cataracts in both eyes; beyond the fact that he estimated them both to be in their early or middle sixties, respectably dressed and swarthy or sun-tanned, he could offer little more." Holmes made rapid notes in his book. "Ho hum" said he, "Not a lot, but better than nothing I suppose. In view of the exceptionally warm weather I have no need to ask why PC Burke's suspicions were aroused." Gregson wrinkled his nose in distaste.

"Indeed Mr Holmes; and the air in there gets worse by the hour."

"You have my sympathy. I trust the body still rests within the trunk, untouched?" Gregson nodded; "It does indeed Mr Holmes. The instant I lifted the lid and saw the contents I felt certain that I should appreciate your observations, and yours too Doctor Watson, and I know from our past association that nothing ruffles your professional feathers as much as a crime scene needlessly disturbed!

"We have confined ourselves to severing the hasps of the padlocks and opening the lid; I gave strict instructions that nothing was to be touched until your arrival." Holmes nodded his approval at the Inspector.

"Excellent Gregson; I was in little doubt that I could count on your admirable judgement in such a matter. Shall we..?"

The Inspector ushered us through the double doors into the cool, tiled morgue. It was clinical and perfectly utilitarian as such places must be; worn, much-mopped grey linoleum floor, walls tiled drab green to shoulder height, dull cream above. The air was heavy with the pungent odours of coal-tar soap, carbolic acid, formaldehyde - and death.

There were six waist-high stations; each consisted of a heavy white-glazed slab seven feet by four with a faucet and deep runnels that drained into an adjoining basin and gutter. Three were in use; the trepanning I had earlier observed, a further whose incumbent was clearly in train of having the major viscera removed, and on the third, what I guessed to be a recent arrival, unattended but covered with a blood-stained cotton sheet; from the profile I judged it to be a woman.

Beside the fourth slab stood a trolley, upon which rested a very large, new-looking brown leather steamer-trunk of plain, almost rustic manufacture. Two burly mortuary attendants waited close by; there was no requirement for Gregson to point out the object of our enquiry. Holmes removed his coat, handed it to one of the attendants and proceeded to examine the trunk closely from all sides; he repeated the exercise using his powerful lens, apparently paying particular attention to two areas of the lid, one at each end; throughout he muttered quietly to himself, as if committing notes to memory. He also took considerable note of the two severed padlocks.

At length he appeared satisfied that he had gleaned all that he could, and gestured to one of the attendants to open the lid, at which point his companion offered us nostril-sized wads of cotton waste impregnated with camphor oil – an essential when in close proximity with a cadaver entering the early stages of decomposition. Gregson took the same precaution.

When the trunk was opened, even through the prophylactic wads of camphor-soaked cotton, we were quickly assailed by the powerful, sickly-sweet odour of the onset of corporeal decay. Holmes, Gregson and I gathered closely around and peered at the body; it was that of a man in his late-seventies or thereabouts, impeccably clad in an expensive, clearly bespoke suit, silk shirt and necktie, and sporting costly hand-made patent leather shoes.

The corpse lay on its left side, in a foetal position, chin sunk low on the chest, thighs drawn tight up to the rib-cage, the arms wrapped closely around the knees.

It had clearly required some considerable effort to manoeuvre it into the confines of the trunk, particularly weighed down as it was with a massive pair of clearly-visible, heavy prison-style leg-irons, which must have weighed thirty pounds or more. The shins of the cadaver were cruelly chafed and lacerated from the irons. At this early stage in the examination I could observe no external wound or other cause of death.

Holmes made a lengthy and painstaking examination of the body, then gestured to the attendants to lift it onto the slab; the degree of rigor mortis present was immediately apparent, for when they had wrestled the cadaver free from the trunk, it stubbornly retained its foetal posture. The heavy chain between the rusty leg-irons clanked dismally upon the cool mortuary slab.

While Gregson and I stood by in silence, Holmes scrutinised the frightful object at close range through his lens. Oddly at variance with the man's affluent attire was the flower in his buttonhole.

It was not a rose; it was not a camellia, nor even a carnation.

It was something much meaner - a withered dandelion.

After several minutes Holmes turned to me; "Your views Watson?" Experimentally I attempted to flex the cool, rigidly-clenched fingers, then a near unbending arm, and considered my opinion. While not trained as a pathologist, I have considerable experience of death, gained during my time as an army surgeon in Kandahar serving with the 5th Northumberland Fusiliers.

Rigor mortis generally commences within two to six hours of death; over the next four to six hours, it spreads to the other muscles, then gradually dissipates until approximately forty-eight to sixty hours after death; but when conditions are warm, as those we had enjoyed for several days now, the onset and pace of rigor mortis are considerably hastened and markedly exacerbated.

Holmes awaited my opinion, for he knew full-well my experience with cadavers retrieved from the field of battle up to a day or even more after the action, in all weathers and temperatures.

I suspected I also observed a second, or should I say a parallel condition – it is a rarely-seen occurrence, generally termed cadaveric spasm or cataleptic rigidity – which occurs at the precise moment of a particularly violent death, anticipated by the victim. This man's fists were unusually tightly clenched; the face presented a hideously contorted rictus of fear, symptoms entirely consonant with an extremely vicious death, certainly foreseen by the victim, under brutal physical circumstances and intense emotion, though I could not, as yet, see the cause of his demise.

I spoke; "In my opinion, the matter stands thus, Holmes; I judge this man to have been deceased for around thirty-six to forty-eight hours – sixty at most. And while I see no apparent cause of death yet, I am pretty certain that we will discover that he died very violently, and that he was aware of his impending fate seconds before he expired. From the fresh abrasions on the ankles I think it very likely he wore the leg-irons for some hours or even days before his death. When the cadaver is straightened we may learn more."

Holmes nodded in the deepest satisfaction. "That is excellent, quite excellent." He motioned for the morgue attendants to commence straightening the body. We stepped outside for a lungful of clean air while they proceeded with their grisly manipulations.

"Your attendance is most valuable Watson – you have confirmed my every suspicion from the instant the lid of the trunk was lifted; this is no clandestine or casual disposal of a body; thus, beyond doubt the man did not die of natural causes – it is a murder, and a very bizarre and public one at that! I am certain that we shall learn the means of the killing very shortly."

Some fifteen minutes later the heavy doors to the mortuary creaked open; a sombre-faced Inspector Gregson spoke gravely "Mr Holmes, Doctor Watson, there is something I think you should see..." We replaced our camphor wads and returned. The muscular attendants had completed their brutal work; the cadaver now lay upon its back, more or less straightened, though the arms still curled forward and out as one desperately begging in supplication; I observed the massive scarlet-black lividity on the left side of the face which generally confirmed my estimate of the likely time of death.

As to the cause of the man's horrific demise, it now had become hideously and shockingly evident; it did not require a skilled pathologist to observe the curious, gleaming steel contraption that had been driven through the costly jacket lapel, deep into the heart beneath.

I peered over Holmes' shoulder as he examined the strange implement with his lens. To me it appeared rather as the apex of a narrow letter A, or perhaps the base of an inverted letter V.

At length he straightened and turned. "Gentlemen, in all the annals of violent crime, the use of this weapon is, in my experience, quite without precedent.

"It is a large, very new pair of steel dividers or compasses, of the sort associated with mathematicians, cartographers and ships' navigators..." he paused, reflectively, "and mayhap... others. That is certainly most noteworthy, but of one thing we may be sure – whoever drove that instrument in so deeply was assuredly a determined and powerful man." Gregson nodded grimly. "Perhaps one of the two men that Mr Skerritt reported seeing at Trafalgar Square, Mr Holmes?"

"I dare say you are right, Gregson, indeed it is likely. Ah me – it's a wicked world, and when a vengeful man turns his thoughts to murder, it's the worst of all.

"Now I have no doubt that you will proceed to a full post-mortem examination, but my instinct is that we shall learn little more as to the cause of death. Doctor Watson, whose experience I greatly trust in these matters has established the *minima* and *maxima* of the likely time of the man's demise and the method is all too clearly visible before us.

"With your permission Gregson, now that they are accessible, I shall search the pockets for anything that may aid us in identifying the man?"

Gregson readily nodded his acquiescence and with a gesture, dismissed the two attendants. With infinite care Holmes eased the jacket buttons free and explored within; I noted the tailor's label – it was Gieves, one of London's finest. After some moments of delicate probing he produced two items; an expensive-looking calfskin pocket book bound with worn gold corners, and a gold pocket watch and chain, Geneva-made, clearly of preeminent quality.

He examined the exterior of the wallet. "Vintage, perhaps thirty or forty years old; very fine grade leather; sometime in the past it has been immersed in water – observe here on the leather the heavy staining, and again extensively on the silk lining." Within the pocket book was a substantial sum of money in note; Holmes counted out fifty-five pounds.

"Clearly gentlemen, we may immediately discount robbery as a motive." The pocket-book contained just two more items; one was a timetable of White Star Line arrivals in Liverpool for the past three months of May, June and July; the other an unused first-class return rail ticket from London to Enfield, dated for travel on the 22nd of July. Holmes removed all the contents and peered carefully for some considerable time deep within each of the silk-lined compartments, but he produced nothing more.

He then proceeded to scrutinise the watch with his lens; "Aha, there is some small, fine, much worn engraving here...

> *With Gratitude from TBS & NH - 1872*

Obscure gentlemen, yet I have no doubt, informative in due time." The remaining pockets of the costly suit yielded three further objects; a white silk handkerchief bearing a small faint green stain, nine shillings and eight pence ha'penny in coin, and a compact, short-barrelled 32-calibre Smith & Wesson revolver. It appeared to be brand-new.

Expertly Holmes flipped the cylinder open and sniffed it; it was fully-loaded. He placed it beside the other exhibits and looked up from his strange harvest.

"And that Gregson, at this stage, appears to be all that our rather taciturn guest is prepared to reveal." He paused reflectively. "Yet he is not perhaps, quite as secretive as he seems." Holmes returned to the trunk and peered inside.

"Oho, gentlemen, now what have we here? It seems we have one more exhibit in this dark affair. I do declare few cases could afford a finer field for the acute and original observer."

He reached within and produced what appeared to be a small, flattish rectangular sliver of polished bone or ivory, perhaps four inches by two. Gregson and I approached while Holmes subjected it to a detailed examination with his lens. I peered more closely.

"Why Holmes, what the Devil is this – it appears to be scratched with symbols and childish drawings – runes and stick figures or some-such?" Gregson looked as perplexed as I. Holmes frowned darkly, his lips tight and pursed.

"I do believe you are correct Watson. What, I wonder, shall we make of this curiosity, and how came it here? But clearly it is present for a reason. So strange in its inception and so dramatic in its execution is this slaying Inspector, I would suggest that you do not release too much detailed information for public scrutiny. In that way, when we take our man, we may be sure that he, and only he, may corroborate those most singular details we have observed today." Once more he paid close attention to the odd sliver of bone; a thought appeared to strike him.

Abruptly he heaved the heavy steamer trunk onto its side and proceeded to examine the base with his lens at some length. I noted that he became particularly excited by several longitudinal, broken black lines which were erratically imprinted on the underside; oddly, he ran the point of his pocket-knife along the length of one of the lines, carefully wrapped it within his handkerchief and placed it in his pocket.

He then ran his thin white finger along the underside of the roughly-cut, raw leather edge inside the lid until he located a loose ragged shred, perhaps three inches long and an inch wide. "Would you have an objection to my removing this small sample Gregson? It will be most significant in advancing our investigation." The bewildered detective shrugged, uncomprehending, but gestured his agreement to proceed, whereupon Holmes severed the shred of leather and a shaving from the wooden frame to which it was glued, and placed them along with his pocket-knife within his kerchief.

Apparently satisfied, he said "That is all, gentlemen."

He glanced at his watch – a certain sign that he had learned all there was to be discovered.

"If there is nothing more Inspector, I should like to retain these items for a few days, and return to Baker Street where I shall ponder the matter further."

The stocky policeman nodded gratefully; abruptly Holmes' face illuminated like a beacon; "But surely you will allow, Gregson, there is nothing more stimulating, more challenging to the curious intellect, than a riddle such as this? I am grateful to you for bringing it to my attention"

Gregson scratched his tousled blond mane and eyed Holmes dolefully.

"Perhaps it is stimulating for you Mr Holmes, but I fear it is my job to get to the bottom of this dark riddle, and pretty sharply too. Can you give me any direction at this early stage?" The lean detective looked across the corpse at Gregson.

"Sadly, very little Inspector, beyond the obvious that this man is either a doctor in practice, or more likely, is now retired; he was extremely successful in his day, and he used a flexible broad steel nib and an unusual colour of dark green ink when writing his prescriptions.

"His middle initial is J.

"Oh, and one other thing, he learned some unnerving news recently that gave him reason to fear for his life. He intended to travel to Enfield on the 22nd but as we now observe from the unused ticket, did not choose to, or did not live to make the journey in time.

"Beyond that, I regret I can divine little more at present except that the trunk is of foreign manufacture, the leather and the wood from which it is constructed are of a type quite unfamiliar to me, it has at some time recently travelled on a large sailing ship in very hot climes, and the padlocks are English, from Willenhall."

Gregson stared in astonishment, as did I. Quite bewildered, he shook his head in puzzlement. "You are too many for me when you begin to get on your theories, Mr Holmes."

"Oh, and two more things Gregson; I think this sliver of scratched bone is of the very greatest consequence – it is scrimshaw. And when eventually we seize the perpetrator of this slaying, I believe it likely we shall find he is a classicist, a man of considerable learning, and has a knowledge of Greek." Upon which enigmatic note we departed; Holmes directed our driver to Baker Street.

$$\boxed{\alpha\beta\gamma\delta}$$

–CHAPTER TWO–

DÉJÀ VU

Over the ensuing week or more, as the calendar progressed from July into August and the temperature steadily rose, Holmes became increasingly energetic, disappearing for one or two days at a time, only to return and spend hours in silent thought at his desk, or dash off telegraph forms, then vanish again. He explained nothing of his activities to me. There was a notable surge in the number of letters and telegrams addressed for his attention.

As it happened, my small practice was growing busier – hay-fever and prickly heat-rash being notably frequent complaints – and so it was that our paths crossed but infrequently during those furnace-hot summer days.

I returned to our rooms late one afternoon – my notes remind me it was August the 5th – to discover Holmes seated at his desk, intently studying a telegraph message. His face was grim and troubled, yet there was a dangerous gleam of exhilaration in his cold grey eyes. "Ah, you are returned Watson. Better timing I could not wish for. I have no doubt you recall our man in a trunk? – do you have the stamina for a further visit to the morgue?" I was startled.

"There is another murder, Holmes?" In times past, I recall my friend had described some murders as 'sequential' or 'repetitive' but never yet had I recorded such a case in the course of my association with Sherlock Holmes.

"There is indeed."

"Is it a similar killing?"

"It is rather more than similar Watson. It is a perfect and precise encore; we have a second unfortunate, murdered in exactly the same manner, and packed in an identical steamer-trunk."

"When was it discovered..?"

Holmes' eyes hardened like adamantine flakes of newly riven flint.

"The trunk was reported around dawn this morning, by a street-washer."

"Where was it found?"

"Directly below the jaws of the second of the four lions on Trafalgar Square." He paused. "Shall we return to the necropolis?"

I called down to the boy in the hall to summon a cab; the journey to the mortuary passed in silence – Holmes was evidently deep in thought as he pondered this second appalling disclosure. As before, Inspector Gregson anxiously awaited us, his bluff features creased with concern. He greeted us with a grave nod.

Upon entering the mortuary I experienced the most unsettling instance of *déjà vu* – once again, beside the same mortuary slab stood the battered metal trolley, surmounted by a second brown leather steamer-trunk – to my eye it appeared identical to the first; beside it waited the same two burly attendants, talking quietly. Once more, the padlocks had been cut and hung impotently from the hasps on the trunk.

For a second time the ritual of the camphor-impregnated wads of cotton, the close external examination of the trunk and the locks, and again Holmes removed his coat; not a word had passed between the three of us since our arrival. At a gesture from Holmes the two burly attendants wrestled the corpse from its heavy leather sarcophagus and placed it upon its back on the mortuary slab; the man was taller than the first, and it evidently required considerable effort to liberate his remains from the tight confines of his coffin.

His contorted, discoloured, desiccated face was adorned with a substantial white beard; blue-bottles had colonised the trunk and their determined rear-guard buzzed in a small angry cloud around the sickly-sweet smelling remains.

This man was not wearing leg-irons; horrifically however, the back of his jacket was diagonally striped with seeping dark stains of dried, crusted, blackened blood. I could conceive of only one feasible explanation for such a bizarre manifestation, yet surely it could not be...?

Decomposition and desiccation were significantly more advanced than we had observed in the first instance, and the effects of rigor mortis were all but gone; the greater the period since death, the harder it is to be precise about the timing, but I judged the man to have been deceased considerably longer than the first – maybe up to ten days, possibly even twelve.

He was around seventy years of age, again expensively dressed.

From the severe distortion and lividity of the left side of the face, it was evident that the body had rested within the trunk almost since the moment of death.

Still, the mortuary remained silent; I looked up at Holmes who raised an interrogative eyebrow.

I answered his unspoken question; "Up to ten days, perhaps even twelve; the man was certainly placed in the trunk immediately after his demise, where he has remained until this moment.

"I observe residual signs of cadaveric spasm once again."

A soft Irish brogue voice spoke from behind us. "I agree entirely Doctor Watson; in my opinion your assessment is exact." We turned to the new arrival.

He introduced himself "Doctor Bryan O'Brian; for my sins I am the senior pathologist in this dismal place." Holmes and I briefly shook hands with him – I was pleased to hear my judgement endorsed by an expert in matters of the dead.

Inspector Gregson gestured to the waiting attendants, who heaved the body onto its back and proceeded to straighten the awful object into something more closely resembling the man it once had been; again the dreadful moment of *déjà vu* – the apex of a pair of mathematician's steel dividers gleamed brightly on the left breast, driven deep into the heart. He was resplendently bewhiskered and wore a large, square-cut, grey beard. Unlike the first victim, he retained a full head of silver hair.

In his buttonhole, chillingly, was again a shrunken yellowish-brown flower, still just recognisable as a withered dandelion.

Holmes gestured at the body on the slab; "May I, Inspector?" and for the second time he proceeded to rifle the pockets of a dead man.

They yielded a gold fob-watch on a chain, a leather pocket-book containing forty pounds in note, seven shillings and nine-pence in coin, and a second plaque of bone with yet more childish drawings scratched upon it.

Holmes selected the gold watch from his haul and proceeded to examine it closely with his powerful lens. After some long moments he passed the watch and lens to me. "What do your eyes make of that, Watson?"

I peered closely at the worn back of the case and was just able to make out the tiny engraved characters:

We observe the Laws And Ordinances

There was one further item – a folded, handwritten slip of paper, unsigned, in the wallet.

The message, written in green ink, was as terse as it was obscure:

> *TH, Victoria House, Botany Bay*
>
> *He is coming! For Jesus' sake, do not go On The Square! Be cautious!*

Inspector Gregson looked hopefully at Holmes. "It seems that this message is perhaps the first lead we have Mr Holmes – it is written in green ink; might it be from our first victim, and is this man TH? If so, very likely we have an address for this second fellow, do we not? Perhaps the two share something in common."

"I am sure you are correct Gregson; note the initials – *TH* – on his signet ring. That they knew each other seems very likely; certainly the note is a dire enough warning, but it did not save him – he clearly was not sufficiently cautious, and ended up on the square, regardless.

"And from what lies here before us we may conclude that whoever the 'he' is, referenced in the note, is undoubtedly already here; but whence has he come, I wonder, and what bitter bad blood exists between him and the two men found on The Square that could move a fellow human-being to do such dreadful and elaborately theatrical murder?

"I can think of only one emotion that could be the driving force for such inhuman barbarity – revenge, for a very grave wrong. Incidentally, Gregson, I believe you will find at the post-mortem examination that this man was cruelly scourged before he died..." These words chillingly confirmed my own horrid intuition about the thin, dark, crusted, diagonal bloodstains showing through his jacket. Holmes broke off and strode to the trunk on the trolley. Abruptly he tipped it onto its side and stared at the base – once more, the same broken black lines, imperfectly imprinted, showed dark against the brown leather. He made no comment upon his discovery, but continued: "So, gentlemen, what may we make of a second elegantly-dressed man, this one from Botany Bay, being found flogged and murdered, in a trunk in Trafalgar Square?

"It is a conundrum within a conundrum, a knot within a knot; but conundrums can be solved, and the most Gordian of knots may be unravelled with sufficient application. But of one thing I am certain –

the killer is issuing a clear warning, an announcement, otherwise why this Barnum and Bailey production – why did he not seek to conceal the murders and the bodies? And for whom, I wonder, is his warning intended?"

"In that connection I believe I may have an idea."

Gregson spoke. "I am of the same general opinion Mr Holmes, but at your suggestion I have forbidden the release of any details of the killings; it therefore seems to me likely that at present, the only person apart from us, who knows of these crimes is the perpetrator."

Tentatively he added "It further occurred to me that the dead men might perhaps have appeared among recent additions to the missing persons list, but I can find no descriptions that match, and no-one has come forward recently to report anyone resembling either of the victims, as having vanished." Holmes eyed the Inspector approvingly. "And your conclusion, Gregson?"

"Evidently either that they lived a reclusive lifestyle – perhaps they were bachelors or widowers, or newly arrived in England from foreign parts – and hence they have not been missed."

My colleague nodded his agreement with manifest satisfaction. "Excellent! Now with your permission Inspector I would like to retain the watch, the note and this scrap of bone with its odd scratchings – I feel it has more to tell than may at first be apparent, as indeed did the previous one. We may note that the drawings differ somewhat from the first example, and I am quite certain that they contain a message for someone...

"For your part, Gregson, I feel it may now be timely to step up police patrols, day and night on Trafalgar Square – if you can spare the men, I would recommend a continuous watch – and also it is now time to release the barest details of these murders; they may just flush out the killer or new witnesses, and thus save two more lives."

There was a long silence while I digested the import of Holmes' matter-of-fact statement. Gregson and I looked at him, aghast. "You think, then, this is not the end of it – you believe there will be more?" I said incredulously." Holmes laughed mirthlessly. "Of a certainty, Watson! Whoever perpetrated these bizarre murders has the whole of London and beyond in which to dispose of his victims discreetly. Yet at the clear risk of detection and capture, he has chosen the very particular and public location of Trafalgar Square – and, I am sure, for a very particular reason. I am convinced there is a symmetry, a grand design and architecture, behind these murders.

"You see, gentlemen, while the elderly Mr Skerritt feeds his pigeons, I do believe the killer is feeding Landseer's lions on The Square – and two yet remain hungry..."

$$\alpha\beta\gamma\delta$$

AUTHOR'S NOTE & ESSAY

FIRST of all, do not read this essay before the book – it contains spoilers! *The Master Engraver* is, quite patently, a work of pure fiction and pastiche. I have not attempted slavishly to emulate Sir Arthur Conan Doyle's unique style; but then, how could I? And perhaps as much to the point, why would I? I doubt much that I could impersonate perfectly to the complete satisfaction of the countless thousands of erudite Sherlockians and Holmesians around the world. Consider...

...Conan Doyle was a medical man, sometime ophthalmologist, accomplished and prolific writer, latter-day spiritualist of the 19th and early 20th centuries, and creator of his own unique, timeless and charismatic *dramatis personae*, Sherlock Holmes and Doctor John Watson and others.

I, by contrast, am a retired script writer, film director, marketing consultant and English scholar of the 21st century, attempting respectfully to lure our favourite characters out of well-deserved retirement for some more adventures, to make them perform again before a seasoned audience of highly knowledgeable and, I make no doubt, sceptical critics.

My humble credentials for the task at hand are Oxford University Board scholarship in the English language and its etymology, a professional career in PR and marketing, film writing and directing, but most of all, a fifty-year-long deep affection for the entire canon of tales, brilliant, good, and some perhaps not quite so good.

So what I have offered in this authorised continuation series is my interpretation, appreciation and understanding of Conan Doyle's splendid characters set in his evocative, nostalgic and stylish – but more often deeply impoverished, brutal and dirty London, in a manner which I hope readers will find sympathetic, respectful and perhaps reminiscent of the original works.

Too, I have attempted to explore further the symbiotic relationship and strange chemistry that might perhaps have existed between these two such disparate fictional friends, mayhap presenting a somewhat mellower, less autocratic and kindlier Holmes, and a Watson who, though still constant in his bravery and steadfast loyalty, is after many shared adventures no longer continually amazed and dumbfounded by his friend's uncanny intellect.

You may feel that it is highly impertinent to attempt a revival, and yet recent TV and film has done just that and was, I believe, well-received, albeit perhaps mainly by new or younger fans. I, however, have attempted to stay with the period and, as best I can, with the original characters; for myself, like many Holmes fans, I feel they will never be better or more vividly realised as any other than the impeccable portrayals by the late, great, Jeremy Brett and the equally perfectly-cast Edward Hardwicke. In my story there are no laptops, emails or iPhones. Our hero still dresses for dinner, communicates by letter and telegram, travels by hansom cab and steam train, paying in sovereigns and guineas, and Mrs Hudson still discreetly mothers him, despite her private reservations about his wilder eccentricities and excesses. And only Doctor Watson may address him by the intimacy of his surname alone. I do hope you approve of my modest attempt at reviving him. I present it in a spirit of humility, as homage to the famous duo. The best I can hope for is that it reads, perhaps, as if a hitherto undiscovered manuscript had somehow surfaced.

Even as I check the final draft of this small offering, I flatter myself, perhaps, that in my head at least, I hear the strains of Patrick Gowers' wonderfully haunting theme music, and the dialogue delivered in those oh so memorable voices of Jeremy Brett and Edward Hardwicke...

It is important to bear in mind the very rigid strictures that constrain the author in any serious attempt at true pastiche; much of the writer's rule-book – through the existing canon's predetermined style and format – is largely prescriptive as to syntax, plot-construction, social mores of the day and, of course, the much studied, analysed, interpreted and debated characters and foibles of our key players, as anyone who has essayed the task of pastiche will know. One may not simply cry repeatedly "The game's afoot!", make lurid and voyeuristic references to narcotic abuse, or – as I believe never actually occurred in the canononical works, have Holmes sardonically and patronisingly declaiming to a slow-witted but dogged Watson, "Elementary my dear Watson!" (Except once, as I allowed myself, in this tale!) – and hope to achieve any great measure of authenticity.

I frankly confess that writing a pastiche of a Sherlock Holmes yarn is a tough assignment. It seems to me that it should be essentially an early embodiment of the classic 'who-dunnit'. In other words, the writer's task is to present a succession of clues and information from various witnesses, lively events and thrilling or chilling scenes of crime more or less simultaneously to Holmes, to Watson, and to the reader, the latter attempting to stay abreast of – or even beat – Holmes to the final solution, although he always retains something to justify a bravura revelation at the conclusion!

Too many early lead-footed clues and the reader quits in disgust – "I guessed the outcome from the third chapter." Too few and the reader is sceptical as to how even Holmes with his prodigious powers of observation and deduction could possibly have solved the case. And a surfeit of red herrings, irrelevant characters and dead-ends will serve only to irritate.

The aspiring pastiche writer encounters further problems: just as the Devil has taken all the best tunes for his own, so too has Conan Doyle taken almost every exotic form of murder and made them a Holmsian hallmark: Andaman islanders blowing poison darts, trained rope-climbing venomous snakes, giant phosphorescent hounds tearing out noble throats, smouldering tropical roots driving people to insanity and death, lethal giant jellyfish, high-powered air-rifles, bludgeonings (both left and right-handed, from the front and the rear!) shootings, poisonings and stranglings – all these and more are introduced to most entertaining, but today, only too well-known effect.

The author's task is even further complicated: Doyle also explored most of the more *recherché* avenues of forensic detection (some more than once); mis-aligned typewriter characters, obscure tobacco ashes, limps, footprints and peg-legs, perfumes and odours, handwriting – left or right-handed, dogs that remain silent when they should bark, inks and nibs, secret codes and ciphers, type-styles used uniquely by certain newspapers, handwriting that varies as the train conveying the writer travels from straight rails to irregular points and junctions... the list goes on.

And while I have fought valiantly to avoid cheap and easy plagiarism, it is well-nigh inevitable for me that when I invoke Holmes once again to cry "Come Watson, the game's afoot!" I risk straying into well-charted territory.

So...

This first story is entirely of my own invention. However, it does feature a number of fascinating institutions and people who truly existed in the year 1889, in which the supposed events of the narrative are set. Simpson's in The Strand still thrives; Rules Restaurant was, and still is believed to be London's oldest eating-house. Both are favourites of mine.

And founded in 1694, The Bank of England has of course existed continuously for well over three hundred years, weathering booms, busts and battles. At the time the narrative's supposed events occur, Mr Frank May was the Chief Cashier.

Mr Henry Petch was indeed an engraver and partner of Perkins, Bacon & Petch of Fleet Street, who operated in the business of security engraving and printing, among several other company diversifications, and he would have been in his seventies in 1889.

M. Louis Lépine, my putative French ally of Holmes in this first adventure (I may well reintroduce him in a future tale; I think Holmes might have held him in high regard) was, indeed, the Deputy Prefect of police in the district of Fontainebleau at the time of the story. A clever and highly intelligent lawyer, he would later become the Prefect of Police for all of Paris and further afield, and earn the soubriquet of *The little man with the big stick* 'through his adroit handling of tense, mass street protests among other achievements.

Now for the apologia...

In order to make my most imperative and revered characters – Sherlock Holmes and Dr John Watson contemporaries with all these intriguing people, events and organisations, not to mention my manufacture of a fictitious and hugely audacious crime, I have taken a few small liberties with timing and precise historical fact, to which I now readily admit. (After all, I do have a few precedents – there was no King of Bohemia, for example, until he was conjured up by Sir Arthur Conan Doyle!)

So reader, in the interests of honesty: The Bank of England *did* actually use independent engravers and printers for the production of bank notes, *but only until 1855,* when the Bank established its own printing plant and thereafter has continued to retain control of this important high-security banking function.

However, rather inconveniently for my purposes, Sherlock Holmes was surely not yet competent to excel in the realms of criminal detection prior to 1855, when official Bank printing plates and watermarked paper were still routinely held by printers outside of The Bank! Thus I have somewhat telescoped time in the interests of the story.

Hampshire-based Portals Papermill, founded by Henri Portal, a Huguenot immigrant, manufactured the high-security watermarked paper for The Bank then, and still exists to this day.

As to the delightfully creaky and cobwebby-sounding Perkins, Bacon & Petch, they too operated in Fleet Street as previously stated. (Contemporary readers may be more familiar with the much later evolution of Perkins, in the arena of commercial diesel engines). In truth however, the nearest that the firm came to supplying The Bank of England with anything at all was to submit, in 1819, a brilliantly innovative technique devised in the United States by Jacob Perkins for hardening engraved steel printing plates, thus prolonging their life and maintaining the integrity of the complex anti-forgery details incorporated within the engraved design. Unaccountably the idea was not accepted by The Bank, and passed over in favour of a simpler, if less secure technology.

For anyone interested in the history of British currency, forgery and The Bank's continuing battle to this day to outwit the wily counterfeiters, I could recommend no finer short overview than that published by The Bank of England – the splendidly entertaining, fascinating and beautifully printed and illustrated full colour publication entitled *Forgery – The Artful Crime*,' along with another, *The Bank of England £5 note – a brief history*' – both absorbing reading at only two or three pounds each, and well worth the money.

Author's Note & Essay

I am much indebted to The Bank of England for their encouragement and cooperation, invaluable historical data, approving my manuscript and tolerating my making rather free with their early history – their Museum and Public Affairs Department have been most helpful and understanding!

Interspersed with these real-life events, people and places, I have populated the tale with fictitious Victorian characters of my own invention; so if, coincidentally, there ever was a real-life Jeremiah Shadwell or Aloysius Hawes, a Baroness Amanti or even a **Feodor Herzog**, Isaiah Pollitt, Dulcie Hobbs, Solomon Warburg or Otto Dietmar von Huntziger, then I apologise to any descendants of these fictitious characters.

Too, I have referenced the notorious Professor James Moriarty lurking somewhere in the shadowy background of the piece, although I know well that in Conan Doyle's canon, his first appearance is in 1891 in *The Final Problem* – some two years after my story is set. However, I felt it reasonable to suppose that a man with Holmes' exceptional and intimate knowledge of the criminal sphere in which he routinely operated would, at the time of my story, already have been attentive to, and wary of, the evil whispered name of Moriarty. Oh, and readers may spot Holmes quoting a line of poetry which had not yet been written, but was too apposite to leave out! And so, with these small but necessary admissions, (and a clear conscience), I offer

"Sherlock Holmes & The Master Engraver" ~ I trust it will not go ill for me with fellow Sherlockians, that I have taken the liberty of not allowing certain historical and temporal facts to get in the way of the story. I sincerely hope you find, as Sherlock Holmes might drily have commented, that *The Master Engraver* is a case "not entirely devoid of interest."

I am well aware that Sir Arthur Conan Doyle's boots are sizeable ones to fill, and while I do not seek to achieve that hubristic ambition, perhaps with my readers' permission I may just briefly borrow them and walk them up and down Baker Street a few times?

(*Explanatory note:* This tale is set in 1889, some two years before Colonel Sebastian Moran makes his first canonical appearance in 'The Adventure of The Empty House,' in which he is arrested after murdering Ronald Adair. However, it would be presumptuous in the extreme for my story to pre-empt this, and thus I may not have Moran captured or hanged, but rather, I have elected to allow him to escape almost empty-handed, that he may make his due reappearance at the correct time of Conan Doyle's choosing, doubly-filled with hatred for Holmes...

Ross Husband;
*Norfolk,
England, and
San Agustin,
Gran Canaria.*

Grateful acknowledgements to the following

SIR ARTHUR CONAN DOYLE – THE CANON

THE BANK OF ENGLAND MUSEUM

THREADNEEDLE STREET, LONDON

'ENGLISH PAPER MONEY' – VINCENT DUGGLEBY

CONAN DOYLE ESTATE LTD

JONATHAN CLOWES

DAVID YAPP BANKNOTES

THE ROYAL BOTANIC GARDENS – KEW

RULES RESTAURANT – MAIDEN LANE LONDON, COVENT GARDEN

WIKIPEDIA & WIKIMEDIA COMMONS

About the author

Ross Husband is a retired film director, marketing and PR consultant, scholar of the English language and etymology, member of The Society of Authors, The Sherlock Holmes Society of London and The Sherlock Holmes Social Network; he lives with Glenys, his partner, in Norfolk East Anglia and San Agustin, Gran Canaria. With some forty years' experience of writing for technical and professional journals, newspapers and documentary films, this is his first work of fiction.

Based on a deep affection from childhood for the legendary characters of Sherlock Holmes and his loyal colleague Doctor John Watson, this debut novel is the first of six stories comprising an officially authorised continuation series – *The Revival of Sherlock Holmes* – offered as a tribute to Sir Arthur Conan Doyle and the immortal characters he created.

About the author

"These stories do not attempt to update, alter, or lampoon the original genre, which in my view requires no improvement. Conan Doyle's format is sound."

Unlike many other Sherlock Holmes pastiches, these stories are authorised and approved under contract in the USA by Conan Doyle Estate Ltd, www.conandoyleestate.co.uk and by Jonathan Clowes in the UK and European Union countries. They are respectfully offered to those many devotees of Conan Doyle's original canon of work who perhaps yearn for some more in the same vein – unadorned, unmodernised, vintage Sherlock Holmes. I do hope you enjoy them.

Ross Husband – you can find me – Ross Martin Husband – on Facebook, or on The Sherlock Holmes Social Network.

Printed in Great Britain
by Amazon.co.uk, Ltd.,
Marston Gate.